Laurie Y. Elrod

The Veihl Coast
BOOK TWO OF THE SO'LADIUN

A LEXOGAN PUBLICATION

The Veihl Coast
A Lexogan Book

Published By
Lexogan Publishing

Copyright © 2016 Laurie Y. Elrod

Cover Art and Design
Laurie Y. Elrod

For more information: www.laurieyelrod.com

ISBN: 978-0998445601

I lift up my eyes to you, My Lord, and give thanks for Your many blessings.

This book is dedicated to my parents, Ray and Rachel Youngblood. You are my heroes.

A N D E R A N

Dragon Isle

Barren Flats

North Province

Trapper's Way
Lakeshore Glen

Salidair Lake Wilderness

Laurel Grove

• Salidair

Veihl Ocean

Bald Mountain Quarry

• Abideen

Fort Denmar •

Greystone •

Isle of Boathen

Boathen • ■ Agadar

Glimmerdale •

• Kit

Midland Province

West Province

Chance's Heath •

Green River Hollow

• Tuhnichi

Jungepointe Hills

Il Kaffa •

Strathe Wood

• *Rheine*

Southern Province

Herronstead •

Marmuht •

Marmuht Bay

Murango •

Desert Stone •

Brackenwood Cove

Traphyt •

Chyrzah

Village of Xyphra

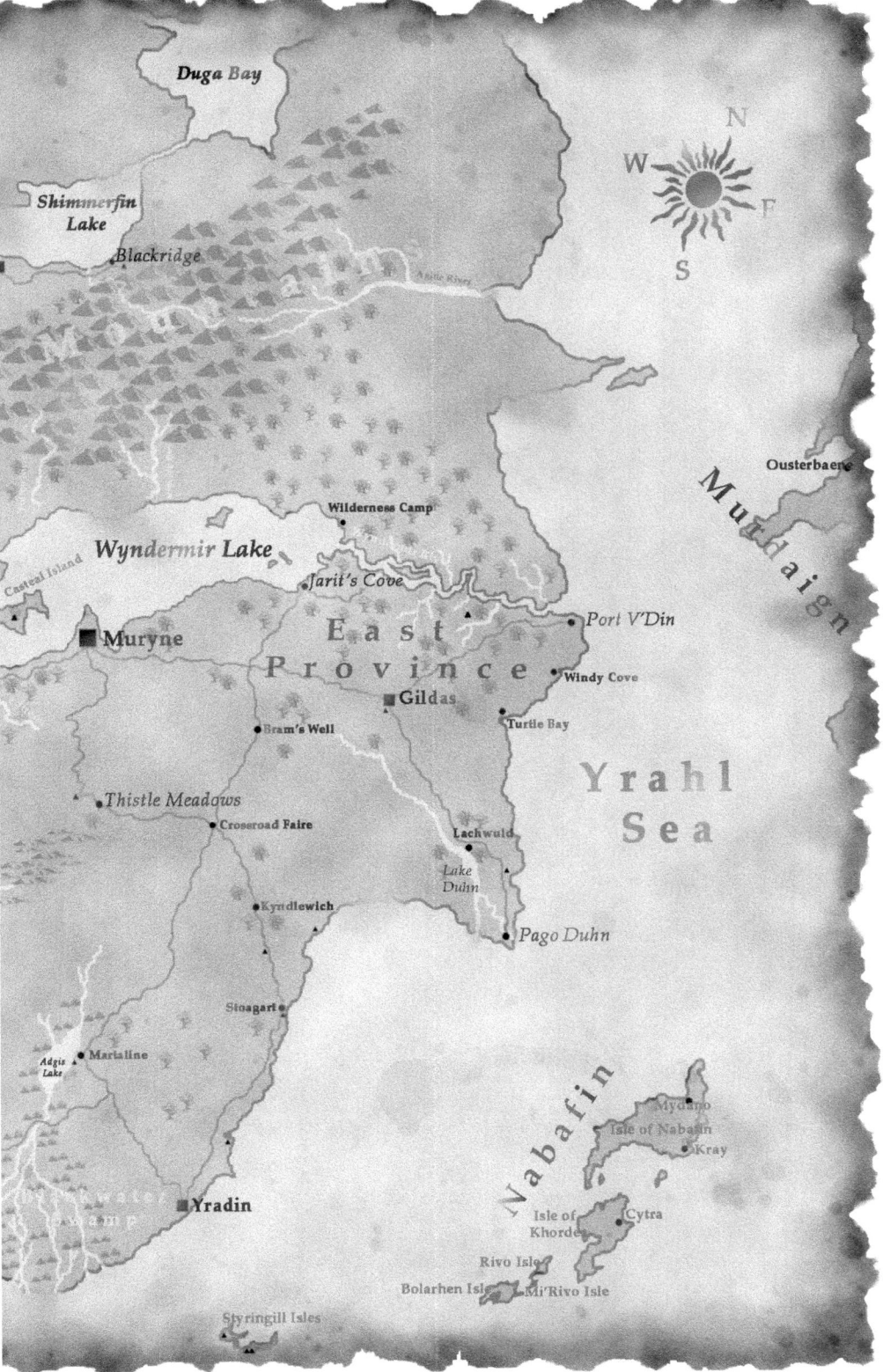

Chapter One

The woman was going to be the death of him someday. He was certain of it.

"Marissa, wait," Clay shouted, trying to catch up to the fiery redhead weaving through the crowd of pedestrians choking the boardwalk of Jarit's Cove. Frustrated, he squeezed through a narrow opening between two of the town's elders which earned him dual looks of annoyance.

"My apologies, ladies," he said, reaching up to tip his hat as he passed, forgetting that Marissa had swiped it from his head in her fit of anger. He tugged on the mist-dampened locks of hair plastered to his forehead instead.

"Marissa got you on a chase again, Clay?" one of the ladies asked.

"Yes, Madam Valiance," he said over his shoulder, hearing the expected giggles from the women. Marissa's temper was no secret to anyone within fifty leagues of the town. "Marissa!" he called out again.

The object of his pursuit glanced over her shoulder with a wicked smile. "You better take back what you said, Clay, or the hat gets it," she said, raising her voice so he could hear her over the noise of the crowd around them. She held up a floppy-brimmed hat. It was his favorite hat, and she knew it.

"Marissa, stop this nonsense . . . ."

Marissa studied him for a moment, then stepped off the boardwalk and into the street without concern for the riders and wagons trying to make their way through thick, slippery mud that rain for an entire week had created. She stopped next to a puddle and dangled his hat threateningly close to its murky surface.

"You wouldn't dare," he said.

"Wouldn't I?" she asked, and he had no doubt she would soak it thoroughly without remorse if he didn't do something fast.

"Please, my beautiful darling," he pleaded, knowing flattery traveled a long mile when trying to squash her anger. "I was only teasing about Freda. You know I love you." He held out a hand for her. "Get out of the street before you get trampled."

"I don't believe you, Clay. Saying breasts the size of Freda's could keep a man's face warm on a cold night isn't exactly the words a man betrothed to someone else should say, do you think?" she growled as she stepped backwards to put distance between them. Her boots sank ankle deep into the soft mud.

He bit back a laugh, trying with a gargantuan effort to keep his face serious. He hadn't known she was behind him when he, Kole, and Anri were discussing the nicer parts of

Freda's female anatomy. "I promise I was not serious. You are the love of my life. I only want your breasts to keep my face warm at night," he said, earning some heartfelt laughs from those listening nearby.

Marissa's face flushed blood red, and he wished on the grave of his departed mother that he could have said something a little less crass. Marissa was never going to forgive him.

Several horses trotted by dangerously close to her, their riders not caring in the least if she was in their way or not. Growling under his breath in frustration, Clay stepped off the boardwalk and tried to grab her arm. "Please, let's discuss this elsewhere, my love."

She jerked back out of his reach. "Don't call me your love," she snarled, and turned to dash across the street unheeding of the conditions of the earth under her feet.

And that was her first mistake of the morning.

Reminding Clay of a scene in a humorous skit he had once seen by a traveling actor's troupe, Marissa slipped and slid in the mud and lost her balance. She then veered headlong into the flank of a large ginger horse standing nearby, bounced backwards and landed on her butt with a splat in the soggy street. An unladylike oath of frustration spewed from her mouth as she pounded her fists into the mud, adding additional splatters of muck onto her ruined clothes.

His hat didn't stand a chance. She pummeled it into a sodden, muddy lump, then tried to stand, but her hands and feet slipped out from under her once again. She landed on her back, limbs sprawled wide in the mire.

"Son of a mangy dog with worms," she yelled in frustration at the dreary sky above as a ripple of laughter swept up and down the street from those who had witnessed her comical fiasco.

"Well, I certainly didn't expect that," the rider of the ginger horse said with a small laugh.

Clay flashed a quick look of apology at the rider who seemed no bigger than a child on her horse as he hurried to Marissa's side. "Marissa, are you all right?" he asked, trying to stifle a grin and knew he wasn't succeeding.

"Do I look all right?" she spat. She rolled over on her side and held up mud soaked hands. "Help me up, you oaf!"

A small laugh from above drew Marissa's attention and Clay winced, knowing that the muddy spitfire was about to explode . . . which was her second mistake of the morning.

"Do you find this funny?" Marissa demanded, glaring at the rider.

"I've seen pigs wallow in the mud less than you, my dear," said a second rider, a captain of the King's Army who sat atop a mahogany bay that was not happy with being still. Agitated, the horse slung his head and pawed at the soft muck, creating deep ruts in the mud.

"Are you calling me a pig?" Marissa sputtered.

"Well, . . . ," said the captain, but was interrupted by the first rider.

"Captain, enough. My lady, he meant no disrespect . . . ," she started to say, but Marissa was inflamed and launched into telling both riders just what she thought of strangers coming into her town and insulting her, and then proceeded to be very specific where they could stick their opinions and observations.

Clay studied the soldier as he listened helplessly to Marissa accuse the two riders of running her over on purpose, wondering what brought the captain to Jarit's Cove. Soldiers were a rare sight in the small fishing village unless it was one of their own returning home. He shifted his gaze back to the first rider who, despite her small stature, seemed to be in charge and scrutinized her closely. His eyes went wide when he saw the pin of a golden eagle on her cloak. This was no ordinary citizen. She was an official in the military or the government—he didn't know which, and Marissa had no idea she was slinging insult after insult at someone who could possibly throw her in jail on a whim.

"Marissa," he said, trying to interrupt her but with no luck. He sent a quick prayer to Solisius, the God of Light, that the two riders were forgiving people because the love of his life was on a downhill roll with her tirade, and he knew that it could only end in disaster. He tried again. "Marissa!"

"What, Clay?"

She whirled on him ready to fight, but at the expense of his own welfare, he trudged forward.

"I think we should let these good people go about their business. It was just an accident," he said, not daring to point out it was her own fault since she had collided into the woman's horse. He watched Marissa's face flush red for the second time in just a matter of minutes and knew that she would consider his actions as some sort of heinous betrayal of her welfare and would no doubt blister his ears with what she thought of him all the way back to her parent's inn. With a deep regret that the wildflowers she loved were gone for the season and he couldn't appease her with a large bouquet, he reached for her hand to force her away if necessary before any permanent damage could be done. But the strong-willed fighter in her would have nothing of it and painfully slapped his hand away.

"Marissa, is it?" the female rider asked. She tugged the hood from her head, revealing shoulder length, wispy brown hair that spiraled from the damp air.

Marissa glared back at the rider. "Yes, that's my name, Miss." She spread her arms wide. "Look what you have done. My clothes are ruined."

"Marissa, it was an accident," Clay sighed in resigned exasperation as he massaged the sting out of his hand from where she slapped him.

"Shut up, Clay!" Marissa spat at him, confirming that reasoning with her was a lost cause.

"I would be more than happy to pay for their cleaning or perhaps something new would be in order," the woman said with a friendly smile, creating dimples on both sides of her pale face. To Clay's relief she didn't appear to be offended. "Allow me to introduce myself. I am Elhrin Caddoch, and the shady-looking soldier with me is Captain Kyne Pittwold. Please accept my apologies for causing your fall."

Clay released an inaudible sigh of relief when he saw that Marissa finally realized that this woman was no ordinary citizen, and her fire fizzled out as if it were doused by the fine mist that drifted down from the dark blanket of clouds overhead.

"No, no, I am sorry. Clay is right, it was just an accident," Marissa stammered as her gaze located the eagle's pin on the woman's cloak. "Uh, maybe . . . ."

"We should be going," Clay finished her sentence, finally succeeding to grasp Marissa by the arm. He tugged her back towards the boardwalk.

"Wait," Elhrin called. "Marissa, I would like to talk with you."

"Really, Miss," Clay said nervously, figuring they should make a hasty retreat, "we need to go."

The lady cocked her head to one side and nodded slightly. "If you must, but you forgot your hat."

She pointed at the miserable object lying half buried in the mud and waved her hand. The hat swept up into the air seeming of its own accord, popped back into a somewhat normal shape, and flew over Marissa's head to land with a sodden thump on top of Clay's head. Cold mud oozed down the side of his face.

The slim soldier whooped with laughter as Marissa stared in shock at the hat slumping miserably over Clay's eyes and ears. She then turned in amazement to the woman on the horse.

"Now would you like to talk to me?" Elhrin asked, grinning wide.

Marissa slowly nodded her head. "I most definitely would," she said softly.

Chapter Two

"Look at this ridiculous mess. We can hardly move," Kyne grumbled, gesturing at the throngs of wagons, horses, and carts moving at a snail's pace ahead of them.

"Kyne, be patient for once. You know they are here for the Yrahl Sea Trade Conference set to begin in a few days. They want to take part in the festivities planned to entertain the delegations from Chyrzah, Nabafin, and Murdaign," Elhrin sighed, wishing that they were already at their destination, the Palace of Muryne, so she wouldn't have to listen to anymore of his complaining. The two of them had been on the road for over three weeks, traveling to Port V'Din and Jarit's Cove, and he had done nothing but gripe about one thing or another the entire time. She liked Kyne well enough. She had to since King Goruth had saddled her with him as her bodyguard, but she could only take so much of his doom-and-gloom disposition and had to remind herself that it would be frowned upon if she melted his lips together with her magical powers.

But wouldn't it be nice if I could, she thought. "I knew there would be a mass of people coming here for the event, but I didn't realize there would be an entire town of tents outside the city walls."

"The city is already near to bursting with permanent residents. It won't be long before we'll see neighborhoods springing up outside the walls instead of tents. I am sure this is a nightmare for the City Guard," he growled, standing up in his stirrups to see over the loaded wagons in front of them. "Come on, people. Get moving!" he shouted.

The driver of the wagon loaded down with stacks of tall crates in front of them leaned out and pinned her with a menacing look. "Madam, you will have to be patient like the rest of us," he barked, apparently assuming she had been the one who yelled because he couldn't see Kyne.

Elhrin hissed at her partner, "Would you be quiet? Everyone's tempers are already on edge. I'm lucky he didn't try to jerk me off my horse. Did yelling at them make you feel better?"

Kyne gave her one of his famous smirking smiles. "Immensely."

She sighed again, thinking sealing his lips wouldn't be good enough. He would still find a way to get on her nerves.

What normally would have been a fifteen minute ride from Muryne's city gates to the Palace of Muryne took them over a half hour, and when they finally reached the courtyard of the massive four-story home of the King of Muryne, they found it just as crowded as the city streets.

"Looks like Chyrzah's delegation has arrived," Kyne said, observing several sun-darkened women and children in bright colored clothing coming out of the palace's portico entryway. "They look like they are wearing Centuron's carnival tents."

"Kyne, be nice. I think they look amazing," she said, admiring the light silky textures of the women's dresses as she maneuvered her horse closer to the portico steps.

He snorted. "Yes, the amazing Chyrzinians, they draw you in with their pretty colors, then rip your guts out with one of their wicked saw-bladed swords."

He watched the Chyrzinians cross the courtyard with his black eyes, looking as if the foreign women and children were a disease that needed to be eradicated. Elhrin hoped Kyne would behave around the Chyrzinians. He had a bad habit of saying what was on his mind, and it didn't matter if it was rude or not. If the Chyrzinians became offended, it would take a mountain of calm words and promises to soothe their quick tempers.

"You better not let your uncle hear that kind of talk from you. He has enough on his agenda with this conference without you offending his guests." Kyne's mother was Queen Egeria's sister, making him an extension of the royal family through marriage.

"Do you think he cares anything about what I have to say? Besides, I don't think the Chyrzinians are to be trusted," he scoffed.

"What makes you think we can't trust the Chyrzinians? Peace between our two countries has lasted for over thirty years, and the trade agreements they are hoping to reach should strengthen the ties between all of the countries involved."

"Just because there have been no open confrontations doesn't mean we can trust them. Look at them. Mother always said you can't trust anyone with dark eyes . . . they conceal the soul."

Elhrin stared at him, speechless.

He glanced at her. "What?" he asked innocently.

"Uh, have you ever looked in a mirror?" she asked, staring pointedly into his eyes which were as dark as lumps of coal.

He slowly smiled in understanding. "Exactly my point. Trusting me might be a mistake. You would do well to remember that."

"I'll have to take my chances, since our king has thrown us together. I'll trust his judgment . . . but you know, your mother may be right in your case. I have had my suspicions all along that you have no soul."

Kyne rewarded her quip with an oily smirk. "You may be right," he said, reining his horse in.

"You're a lost cause, my friend. I think you need to go get a bath and a beer, and relax. Aren't you the least bit glad to be home? We've had a long, but productive three weeks, and I can't wait to tell Master Gryph about our newest addition to the academy."

"Is the minister here?" he asked.

"He is," she beamed, dismounting from her horse and retrieving her pack from behind the saddle. "I felt his magical energy source before we reached the city gates."

"I thought you said he wasn't coming." He climbed down from his own horse and handed the reins to a stable boy that had trotted over to gather their mounts.

"No, what I said was that he would try to do everything in his power to not come," she chuckled, truly excited to see her mentor, who was a Master of Magic and the Minister of Specialized State Defense. It was he who had taught her how to control and use her magic and had been the only male role model in her life since her father had been killed when she was just a baby. It had been six months since she had last been home to Glimmerdale where Master Gryph lived, and she had made it just in time to celebrate his and Marguerite's son Marcus' third birthday.

Marcus. The mere thought of their little boy added an extra twinge of excitement. She could not wait to squeeze him, hoping he was here, too. He was growing too fast, and she didn't get to see him as often as she would like.

She shouldered her pack. "Master Gryph can't stand crowds, and absolutely detests sitting in on formal meetings, but King Goruth is insisting because the foreign ambassadors are going to be here, and he wants his senior advisor by his side."

"I don't blame Minister Idwyr for not liking crowds," Kyne said, as they mounted the portico steps and entered the palace. "I've lived all my life in crowded cities, but this is too much."

"I think you can survive. It's only for two weeks."

"Two horrendously long weeks," he said wrinkling his face in distaste, then nodded his head in the direction of the grand hall of the palace. "There's lover boy."

She frowned at him, puzzled by his statement. "Who?"

He jerked his chin again toward the hall and gave her a look like she was a lunatic. She turned in time to see a captain, dressed in the brown and black uniform of the road patrol, make his way down a set of steps. He noticed her in the crowd, and his mouth quickly spread into a lopsided grin.

"Tomas!" she cried and pushed her way through the people in the hall. He gathered her in his arms and picked her up off the floor. She planted a long, hard kiss on his lips, not caring what the crowd thought of their public display.

"Do you really think this is the way the assistant to the Minister of Specialized State Defense should behave in front of the palace's guests?" Kyne sneered.

Elhrin reluctantly broke the kiss to glare at him. "Go away," she ordered.

A brief bit of anger flashed across his face, but then he coolly smoothed it away and bowed with a mocking flourish. "As you wish, my lady," he said, and brushed by them to mount the stairs.

Why does he have to act like an ass all the time? she wondered. Dismissing him from her mind, she turned her attention back to the gorgeous blue eyes staring at her. "He's right though. You better let me down."

"As you wish, my lady," he repeated Kyne's words and allowed her feet to once again touch the marble tiles of the floor.

"I can't believe you are here. I thought with the conference about to begin you would be on the road constantly. How long have you been here?"

"Which time?" he asked.

"What do you mean, which time? Have you been here more than once?"

"I have. Two weeks ago, I was summoned here to discuss strategies the road patrols needed to take with the increase of traffic to Muryne. Since then, I have been back and forth between here and Glimmerdale on a regular basis and have been disappointed until now to find a certain green-eyed lady was not in residence." He kissed the tip of her nose. "But if you are asking me how long I have been in the city this last trip, the answer is that it has been four days since I had the pleasure of escorting a certain grouchy magician from Glimmerdale."

Elhrin laughed. "I guess King Goruth was not going to leave his attending this conference to chance."

Tomas grinned. "Nope, and I don't think King Goruth needs to know all the creative magical things that the minister would like to do to him for forcing him to attend. He kept complaining that there was no need for him to sit in on what he described as boring, tedious haggling over dropping tariffs, or who used certain shipping routes or ports of call when the king knew good and well he had other things needing his attention."

"He's just being stubborn because he doesn't like being confined to a chair for very long." She clasped Tomas' hand and led him through the crowd, up the steps, and into the grand hall. "He knows that he has to be here for this event, but I know he has been extremely busy juggling his time between this position and the running of our academy. He has finally been able to turn over the head instructor position to Grey Leahr and has Landin teaching the younger ones until we have more adults that gain enough experience to help. Master Gryph can now concentrate on other things, like the opposition we are receiving from the councilors of the Western Province. It irritates me that they are trying to gain support from the other provinces to terminate our program."

"Why do they want it stopped?" Tomas asked, stepping out of the stream of people who were traveling up and down the twin staircases on either side of the hall. The upper floors held the guest and resident apartments and rooms, and the late hour of the day suggested it was time for the evening meal in the main dining hall.

"Because they think we are training them all to be killers. They learned about the fighting force that is being trained in addition to the main program. They think we might become dangerous to the general population. What they can't seem to understand is that the fighting force is separate from the academy. Our primary focus there is to teach students how to control their talents and be less of a danger to themselves and others. We want it understood that we are an asset to the community. Not an enemy. Did I tell you about the little boy who accidentally set his family's barn on fire with his powers and came close to dying trying to save the animals inside?" She crossed her arms over her chest and leaned against the wall.

"Yes, you did."

"I don't think the opposition understands that it is events like those we would like to prevent. Master Gryph said that while those with the gift are still hard to find, he has noticed that with Anderan's population on the rise, there has also been an increase in those with the gift. Right now, people are somewhat tolerant of magic mainly because it is rare and because of Anderan's history of the former Ministers of Specialized State Defense who had powers and were always willing to defend Anderan, but especially with Master Gryph. Many think of him as Anderan's hero."

"You too, Elhrin," he said, softly squeezing her arm.

She smiled, knowing he referred to the fact that she was responsible for ending the Do'athrim War a few years back, but the general public was unaware of the fact, and she was happy for it to remain that way. "No, not me. Other than a few wildly blown out of proportion stories in the newspapers, I am virtually unknown, but he has been around a while and has done many things for this country. Anyway, my point is that because of his popularity, and the fact that there has been no real threat from the magical population, we are more of a novelty to most. But that could change if an increase in the magical population causes an outbreak of violence, intentional or not. People are afraid of what they don't understand, and we could see how this could go bad quickly."

"So you think teaching your students control over their powers will prevent condemnation from the average citizen?"

"I don't think it will prevent hostility from everyone, but if we could show that we are not to be feared, maybe we could divert what could potentially boil over into lynch mobs in the future. We can do good things with our magic, not just kill and destroy."

"I'm well aware of just what you can do, my pretty magician," he said with an obvious leer and started to pull her close, but she held him back with a hand to his chest.

"Later, when there aren't so many eyes around," she said, smiling. "Are you free this evening?"

"As a matter of fact, I am nearly free for the next two days before I have to go back on patrol duty. I have a few meetings to attend with my superiors."

"Just two days? Not much time to catch up." She hated that their busy lives kept them apart so often. "I haven't seen you in a month, and I have missed you—considerably."

"Well, we'll just have to make the most of the time we have, now won't we?" He wiggled his eyebrows.

"Yes, we will," she laughed, then noticed the guarded doors at the end of the grand hall were opening. A stream of Anderan's council members started to file out of the council chamber, some of which were unknown to her since the election at the end of last year resulted in several new members, but she did recognize two Senior Councilors, Diehla Veir from the Eastern Province and Corbynne Entiser from the Midland Province, as well as, several Junior Councilors. "Good, the council meeting has adjourned."

"Are you going in?" Tomas asked.

"Yes, Master Gryph is in there. I don't know what his schedule is for the day, so I want to talk to him before he leaves. You coming?"

"Unfortunately, I have to go. I have a few orders that need to be dispatched to

Glimmerdale and the outpost we have set up on the Eastern Road." He gave her a quick peck on the lips. "I will catch up with you later, okay?"

"Okay," she pushed away from the wall as he started to walk away, "but don't be late."

"Me late? Are you kidding? I've been waiting on you. You don't be late."

"Yes, sir, Captain." She saluted him.

He flashed her a lopsided grin as he blended into the crowd leaving the hall.

Elhrin entered the enclosed foyer of the council chamber when she thought all of the councilors were gone. Taking the arched doorway on the right side of the room, she walked out onto the open hall that overlooked the council floor below and placed a hand on the time-worn dark oak railing separating the hall from the seats below. King Goruth and Master Gryph were not done for the day as they were still seated at the horseshoe-shaped council table conversing with two senior councilors. Not wanting to interrupt what appeared to be a major discussion, Elhrin chose the nearest of the twin stairways that led to the main floor below and stepped down to the uppermost bench to sit and wait until they were through.

Nearly three years of living in the palace had done nothing to diminish the awe she felt every time she entered the council chamber. Here was where Anderan's laws were made. The room was half-moon in shape with a row of floor-to-ceiling windows encompassing the curved wall protruding out into the palace's central gardens—the windows allowed the natural light from outside to filter in, making it unnecessary on bright, sunny days to use the massive hanging chandeliers above her. From where she sat, at the topmost level of the amphitheater-style seating that provided extra room when public meetings were in session, she could see over tall hedges to the fountain in the center of the gardens.

She muffled a laugh. Children were playing in the water of the fountain, and a mischievous boy pushed a little girl in without warning. Elhrin had to give the girl credit. Instead of crying, the child jumped up fighting mad, and the boy did not expect the fists she produced. He ran down one of the garden paths with the girl right on his heels.

Elhrin raised her gaze to her favorite part of the room, the ceiling. A detailed mural of an ancient garden reaching into the heavens had been painted between the gold-gilded support beams. Colorful birds were in flight across the sky, and in one section, a magnificent waterfall spilled into a river running through the garden. The waterfall reminded her of their trek through the mountains to Blackridge Keep when they had spent a night by a similar waterfall. It had been a much needed break from the grueling hike, and it was a good memory that stood apart from the horror of the rest of the journey.

The scrape of booted footsteps sounded overhead. She turned around to glance up at the narrow walk built high across the back of the room. Four armed guards stood in position and were always in place when the council was in session. They would not leave until the room was completely empty.

"Your Majesty, you must see reason. This is why the committee turned down his request for the land grant outside of Glimmerdale," one of the councilors said heatedly, surprising Elhrin with his ferocity and bringing her attention back to the four individuals seated at the table on the council floor. He rose to his feet and pointed an accusing finger at Master Gryph. "It seems to me he has talked you into this, Sire."

Sitting at the apex of the table, King Goruth frowned and narrowed his eyes at the outburst from the councilor seated three chairs away from his right. Elhrin fully expected the king to reprimand the man for his lack of reverence to his sovereign, but instead, he directed his attention to the salt and pepper haired man to his left. "That was sneaky, Gryph. When did you plant this idea in my mind?"

Master Gryph sighed heavily and lifted his gaze to the ceiling then lowered his eyes to look directly at Elhrin. While he wasn't smiling, she could tell he was amused at how King Goruth had handled the situation. He winked at her with his left eye.

"Now, if I had that kind of power over you, Your Majesty, I would have you rethink the use of the color purple in your household." He had to pause to draw in a breath, which was something he had to do occasionally. He had sustained damage to his lungs while he was in Do'athra, the Realm of Darkness during the Do'athrim War and it had ended up being permanent. "Seriously, who in their right mind would toss aside a perfectly decent color of blue for dress uniforms and replace it with purple? It makes your Royal Guard look like a bunch of armed grapes."

Elhrin clapped a hand to her mouth to keep from laughing just as Councilor Idora choked on her drink and started to cough.

"I will have to agree, my friend, but your queen insisted the uniforms should match the royal coat of arms," King Goruth snorted with laughter.

Master Gryph reached over and patted Councilor Idora's back. "Swallow the wrong way, Idora?"

"Gryphon Idwyr," she choked, "that was uncalled for, but funny."

"That's just like you, Minister, making a joke whenever you get a chance. Do you consider this matter funny?" the angry councilor asked.

He was the new Senior Councilor for the Western Province, Reginold Whyse. Young by council standards, single, and not lacking in the handsome department with his sun-streaked fair hair and tan skin, he was the focus of the prominent unwed, and if the gossipmongers were right, quite a few married ladies, as well. She didn't see what the fuss was, but that might be because she was partial to a certain brown-haired, blue-eyed captain of the road patrol.

King Goruth frowned at the young councilor. He had enough. "No one thinks this is a joke," he said. King Goruth had a deep voice that rang with power even when he spoke softly. He rose to his feet and placed both palms on the table. "Reginold, this was an idea that entered my mind four years ago when I needed someone within my army who had powers. I had no one. Gryph was unavailable at the time and Elhrin was needed elsewhere." He pointed at her. "It was I who told him to proceed."

Both councilors turned to look at her in surprise. Apparently, they hadn't known she was in the room. Of course, Master Gryph would have known she was in Muryne before she entered the city gates, and more than likely followed her presence until she entered the chambers. Like her, he could detect anyone with magical energy nearby. An attribute that was sometimes annoying for her whenever she didn't want to be found.

Councilor Idora smiled at Elhrin, but Councilor Whyse stared at her coldly for a moment before he turned back to the king. No, he was definitely not her type. That cold stare told her volumes about his character.

"Your Majesty," Councilor Whyse continued, "it is bad enough he wants to train every person he can find with magical abilities, but to have an elite force of fighting magicians is just too dangerous."

"Not having them is far more dangerous."

Elhrin sighed in aggravation, knowing the fight to keep the Eagle program, as Liselle, an elderly student and Marguerite's house manager, had named them after Master Gryph's personal insignia, was going to be a long, hard fight. The small group they presently had were already deep in training and she hoped they wouldn't have to terminate the program. She felt just as deeply as Master Gryph and King Goruth that Anderan would need such a force of fighting warriors to enhance its military structure.

"Ahem, Your Majesty," Councilor Idora intervened, "I know what we faced during the war could have been potentially disastrous, but we persevered . . . ."

"Idora, we were lucky. Elhrin and Gryph were almost lost to us. If they had been killed, none of us would be alive today. That magical beast, Cynder, and the other magician within the enemy's army," he turned to Master Gryph. "What was his name again?"

"Grom," Master Gryph answered.

"Yes, Grom, those two nearly destroyed us. If it wasn't for Colonel Toome's and General Pyrthenius' brilliant tactical strategies keeping them off guard, we wouldn't have survived as long as we did."

"Yes, Sire, I know, and I agree with you. I can see where a force of magicians would benefit us, but I can also see Councilor Whyse's point of view, as well. The people of Anderan are willing to accept one or two magical authorities, but a magical fighting unit may scare them into thinking we may be building something we won't be able to control."

"Idora, we are not invincible," Master Gryph said. "We can die just as easily as any soldier."

"But your powers make you harder to kill," Councilor Whyse said with venomous heat, sounding like he personally wanted those with magical powers executed.

Elhrin was stunned.

"Reginold," Councilor Idora gasped, "what are you insinuating?"

Master Gryph leveled his gaze on the councilor. "Is there something we need to discuss, Councilor?"

"I'm only repeating what His Majesty has already pointed out with his assessment of the Do'athrim War," Councilor Whyse said, glaring with undisguised hate at Master Gryph. "You may be vulnerable in some areas, but you are hard to reach face-to-face. All you have to do is wave your hand and you can destroy men across distances without them knowing anything is coming. Like Idora said, what happens if you train someone who we won't be able to control . . . maybe instead, they build an army of their own to meet their own desires and use their powers against us?"

"That is why Gryph has and will handpick those he thinks will best fit the positions. He puts them through certain tests and training to make sure they can handle it. Reginold, you don't know him well, but I do. Gryph has an amazing intuition that I have witnessed in no other," King Goruth said. "He will know who is right for this project."

"No offense, Your Majesty, but his intuition should not be a basis for legalizing this idea and incorporating them into the military hierarchy," Councilor Whyse growled with disgust, and abruptly sat back down.

"Councilor," Master Gryph sat forward in his chair to lean on the table, "would it help if we created a panel to assess the ones I suggest?"

"What difference would that make?" Councilor Whyse growled.

Elhrin wondered the same thing. They didn't have a large number of people with the gift to choose from, and he had already chosen the ones that were capable—they were already being trained.

"Well, from now on the final decision on who would be allowed into the group would not be mine," Master Gryph said, pinning Councilor Whyse with an intense crystal blue stare of unwavering authority. "Isn't that what you are afraid of? Me putting a group of fighters together with no approval from the council?"

Councilor Whyse dropped his gaze to the papers in front of him on the table, seeming unable to meet Master Gryph's unwavering look of steel which didn't surprise Elhrin in the least. There weren't many who could endure under such intense scrutiny that exuded the amount of power as he did when it suited him.

Councilor Whyse cleared his throat uncomfortably before answering the question. "Minister, the only thing I am afraid of is what this could do to the welfare of our people. But it seems as if this is one argument I am not going to win on my own. I propose that we put this idea to a vote the next time the council reconvenes when the trade convention is over, but out of curiosity, what kind of panel are you suggesting?"

"Oh, you tell me who you think would be capable of assessing the minds and skills of individuals for this kind of program?" Master Gryph asked, seeming to concede to the councilor's point of view. He leaned back in his chair and waited for the councilor to answer.

Ha! Elhrin thought, recognizing the tactic he was using on the councilor. He was leading the man along, making him think he was in control, and Councilor Whyse had no idea he was being manipulated.

"If the council votes this through," Councilor Whyse said, picking a pen up off the table and twirling it between two fingers while he thought about what he wanted to say, "then you are right, Minister, I do think council members should be the ones to chair the panel, and experts within the military and medical fields should be included, as well."

"Such as," King Goruth prompted.

"Such as General Carthin from Agadar, or possibly, Major Fellen from Tuhnichi—Prince Cahail has recommended him for promotion. From what I hear, he has demonstrated an amazing capability concerning offensive and defensive maneuvers with long-range warfare. You would also need someone who knows the workings of the human mind and has studied subjects with your special powers." Councilor Whyse curled his lips as if his last words left a foul taste in his mouth.

Puzzled by this statement, Master Gryph cocked his head to one side. "And who would that be?" he asked.

Like Master Gryph, Elhrin thought this was a strange suggestion because individuals with the magical gift were hard to find. She had been lucky to find the few she had for the academy, and she could detect magical individuals without confronting them.

"There is a doctor who has been conducting a study of subjects at the University in Gildas," Councilor Whyse smirked. "Doctor Lyrin is his name."

What? Elhrin almost shouted, and had to force herself to remain seated. This was news to her.

"Is that so?" Master Gryph's asked evenly. "Your Majesty, were you aware of this study?"

"Gryph, it is not what you think." King Goruth reached for one of the pitchers placed on the table for the council's use, and poured himself something to drink. "He has only been conducting his study for a few months, and I was assured it was not harmful. Doctor Lyrin is only observing what they can do and asking them questions. He wants to know where your magical energy originates and how you can manipulate it at will."

"We are not animals to conduct scientific tests on, Your Majesty." Master Gryph's face became an impenetrable mask of stone. Elhrin knew that look. It was rare for Master Gryph to become truly angry, which he was right now, but he was not going to openly show it unless he was pushed too far. "I hope all he is doing is observing."

Councilor Whyse sat back in his chair, smirking. Elhrin would have liked to smack the obnoxious grin off of his face. The councilor was enjoying the fact his revelation was new and upsetting to Master Gryph.

"Gryph, do you think I would condone anything that would harm my people?"

"You shouldn't be condoning anything like this at all. What does it matter where our magical energy comes from?" Master Gryph pushed back his chair and stood up. He was an overly tall and well built man in his fifties, and he towered over the king. For that matter, Elhrin thought, he towered over most everyone. His wife, Marguerite, lovingly referred to him as a walking tree, and right now, he was an angry tree.

"Gryph, you of all people can relate to the minds of scientists. You can't rest until you know how everything works." King Goruth poured another glass and handed it to Master Gryph—a gesture to help calm the magician down.

Master Gryph grunted. "I think I will need to take a trip to Gildas."

"That would be a good idea, but it will have to wait until the conference is over. I need you here."

Master Gryph gave the king a hard look, but didn't say anything.

"Councilor Whyse," Master Gryph turned back to the councilor, "why don't you put together a list of panel candidates before the next session. If the council votes in favor of incorporating a new branch of military into service, then we can go through your suggestions at that time."

Councilor Whyse tilted his head slightly in agreement, gathered his belongings on the table, and stood up. Councilor Idora followed his lead.

"Until our next meeting, Your Majesty, Minister Idwyr, Councilor," Councilor Whyse said. He turned on his heel and strode quickly to the stairway on the other side of the room. He gave Elhrin a brief cold, hard look as he topped the stairs and disappeared into the foyer.

Idiot, she fumed silently.

"Gryph," Councilor Idora tucked a strand of her coal black hair behind one ear, "I apologize for what has happened. I tried to stop it."

"I promised him that land, Idora," King Goruth growled. "You do what you need to do to change the committee's mind and push the request through. This isn't a personal gain for him. The country needs a training facility for persons with the magical gift far more than you and Whyse realize."

"Yes, Your Majesty." She looked at Master Gryph. "I will do what I can," she said and placed a hand on Master Gryph's arm. It was a little too familiar for Elhrin's comfort. She knew that Idora had at one time been intimate with him before he met his wife, Marguerite. Muryne was rampant with those wanting to gossip, and in the last three years since Elhrin had been in the city, she had learned more about her mentor and self-adopted father than in all the nineteen years she had known him. She had no idea that years ago Idora Shulftar, along with many in Muryne, thought the councilor would eventually be Master Gryph's wife, but he surprised everyone when he broke off their relationship and married Marguerite a little over a year after the break.

"I appreciate your efforts, Idora," Master Gryph said.

"Anything for a dear friend," Councilor Idora smiled, and let her hand slide down his arm before turning to the table to pick up her things from the meeting.

"Get on it right away, Idora," King Goruth said. "We don't have time to waste. I personally want this fighting force at my disposal. Make it happen."

"As you wish, Your Majesty." Councilor Idora bowed, then crossed to the stairs below Elhrin. "Hello, Miss Caddoch. I did not know you were back in the city," she said when she reached Elhrin.

"I just arrived, Councilor," Elhrin said, feeling a little self-conscious of her dirty clothes in front of the elegantly dressed lady. Councilor Idora was the envy of the social elite in Muryne. Middle-age had done nothing to mar her beautiful honey-colored skin, and Elhrin knew that every one of the numerous rings on Idora's fingers had been given to her by men wanting her attention, or maybe they just wanted what was trying to spill out of the front of her low-cut bodice. Elhrin had to make a physical effort to stop her face from breaking into a grin from that last thought. The woman definitely dressed for the men.

"It is good to see you," Councilor Idora said and turned so she could see the two men on the council floor. King Goruth and Master Gryph were in a hushed, heated discussion and were not paying attention to them. The councilor leaned in to whisper to Elhrin. "He won't listen to me, but maybe you will. I guess you can tell how much Councilor Whyse despises Gryph."

Elhrin nodded.

"I don't know the true reason why he bears such a hateful grudge against Gryph, and it worries me that the man has an agenda to undermine everything Gryph is working towards. Gryph says Reginold likes to spew nonsense and dismisses the matter, but I don't think it is wise to dismiss him."

"What has he done?" Elhrin asked in concern. Councilor Idora was not one to become alarmed over nothing.

"He hasn't really done anything as of yet. He is too slick, but I find it unnerving how Reginold finds any opportunity to slide subtle remarks into conversations that puts doubt into people's minds about Gryph's character and trustworthiness." Idora let her eyes wander to the council floor. For a split second, Elhrin could have sworn she saw desire in the woman's stare, but it was smoothed away when she looked back at Elhrin. "Believe me, a man like that is dangerous. Gryph is content to basically ignore him, and that is why I am mentioning this to you. I think if Gryph won't protect himself, then maybe you and I can keep our eyes and ears open . . . just in case."

"Certainly," Elhrin nodded.

"Thank you, dear," Idora patted Elhrin's arm. "I knew I could count on you. I best be off. Take care."

"You too, Councilor," Elhrin said to Idora's back as she watched the lady sweep out of the council chambers.

"Elhrin," Master Gryph called from below. "Come down here, girl."

"Yes, sir," she said, descending to the council floor. She bowed slightly when she reached them. "Your Majesty."

King Goruth acknowledged her bow with a nod of his head. "Elhrin, Gryph said you were on your way." Up close, the king looked tired and old. Elhrin didn't know his exact age, but in the years she had been in Muryne, what was left of his reddish hair had turned a muddy silver. The war almost five years ago and the pressures of being the country's leader had quickly taken their toll on the robust, stocky man. "How did your journey go? Where's Kyne?"

"It was long and wet, Your Majesty. I told Kyne to get some rest. He was a bit . . . tired," she said.

King Goruth chuckled. "What you really mean is that you have had enough of my surly nephew for the time being."

Elhrin smiled. "Yes, sir."

"Excuse me, Goruth, but I haven't seen my girl for six months, do you mind?" Master Gryph held open his arms. Elhrin grinned and stepped into his embrace. He kissed the top of her head and squeezed her so hard she grunted. "How are you, sweetheart?"

"I was fine until you just rearranged my internal organs," she said.

He chuckled and let her go. "So, what did you find?" he asked.

"The reports turned out to be false as far as Kyne and I could tell. We investigated every report of Do'athrim sighting between Port V'Din and Jarit's Cove, but found nothing."

The Do'athrim were half-man, half-beast creatures. Most resembled the wolves that roamed the forests of Anderan, and were the abominable creation of Obsudius, the God of Darkness. They were extremely dangerous and killed anyone in their path with ruthless abandon, often eating their victims if they had time. Any sign of them was a major cause for concern.

"It is strange that most of the supposed sightings happened along the coast or near the Wyndermir River. You don't think the beasts have learned how to sail do you?" she asked.

"It wouldn't surprise me," Master Gryph commented.

"Gryph, I thought you said Obsudius wouldn't be able to open another portal for a while yet," King Goruth said, lowering his voice so that the soldiers above could not hear him.

"No, I said he wouldn't be able to maintain one comparable to that of the one in Blackridge. It takes a tremendous amount of energy to create a portal between the Realm of the Dead and the world of the living, even for a god. He was considerably weakened after Elhrin closed it and the power of its closure turned against him, and the mark of Solisius that I put on him creates a drain on his powers, as well. If he does regain the strength to create one of that size again, it will be well after our lifetime and those of our children. Unfortunately, he can still open small ones for a brief amount of time, and that is something Elhrin and I have to work on preventing if we can ever find the answer on how to do so."

Elhrin grimaced at the prospect. Facing Obsudius again was not something she looked forward to, but to stop the dark god from opening portals on a permanent basis was vital for the security of the human race. "I'm wondering if these rumors were spread with the intentions of causing fear among the local citizens," she said, turning back to the subject of hunting down Do'athrim. "There was only one man who lives between Jarit's Cove and Port V'Din that I think may have actually seen something, but we couldn't find anything to verify it."

"What's his story?" King Goruth asked.

"He had been out setting beaver traps along some of the small streams that connect with the Wyndermir River, and was heading home around dusk when he saw what he thought at first was a bear, only he said the bear appeared to be walking upright like a human and was dragging something heavy. He had heard the tales of the Do'athrim and thought the beast had to be one. He said he wanted to get a closer look, but it was rainy and growing dark, and he didn't have anything more than a hunting knife on him, so he decided to leave before the creature saw him. Kyne and I had him take us back to the spot. We searched the entire area but couldn't find any evidence of a Do'athrim or something heavy being dragged through the woods. The man still insisted he saw something."

"When did he see the beast?" Master Gryph asked.

"About five days before Kyne and I rode out to his farm." She crossed her arms. "We were in Port V'Din when we heard about his story and left immediately to find him. Master Gryph, even if rain hadn't possibly washed away signs of passage, I still don't think we would have found anything other than bear tracks. If something heavy is being pulled through underbrush there has to be some kind of evidence left behind. Even Kyne, who could find a stray rat hair on a wooly sheep, couldn't find anything other than a pile of deer pellets. There wasn't so much as a broken branch or drag marks of any kind on the ground. I think with it being near dark the man may have just seen a bear and thought it was something more."

"Hopefully, you are right," King Goruth said.

"But," Master Gryph interjected, "we will continue to be vigilant. We cannot afford to let these rumors go by without looking into the matter. There may come a time when they are not just rumor."

"Yes, sir," she said.

"Did you have good luck finding new additions for our academy while you were out?" he asked.

"Well, I had luck. The good part remains to be seen," Elhrin laughed. "I found a girl in Jarit's Cove who has a temper to match her fiery red hair. She is a strong one."

"Redheads usually are," King Goruth commented and winked at Elhrin.

Elhrin grinned at the king's reference to himself. "Yes, sir, they certainly are," she said.

"How old is she?" Master Gryph asked.

"About my age, early twenties, I think. There is only one possible drawback. She has a fiancée who is a fisherman . . . ."

"I like him already," Master Gryph commented.

Elhrin sighed with a shake of her head. Master Gryph had an extreme passion for fishing, and if he couldn't get near water to actually fish, he would talk for hours on the subject to anyone who would listen. "You would. Anyway, he may be the only reason she won't come to Glimmerdale. She doesn't think he will leave Jarit's Cove, and she won't leave without him."

"Is she interested?" he asked.

"More than interested. She says she has longed to know more, that she feels frustrated because she doesn't know how to go about doing the things she believes she could do and is afraid to try."

"What can she do?"

"Mostly the basics. Call fire. Move small objects short distances. But, Master Gryph, she can also create water. I have never seen that done before."

He lifted a hand to stroke the neatly trimmed beard lining his face. A habit that Elhrin knew irritated Marguerite for some reason.

"I haven't witnessed it in person, either, but Lucas Vonduran could do it. Do you remember reading about him in the *Book of Tolman*?"

The *Book of Tolman* was a book written by Solisius the God of Light's So'ladiun who lived in Anderan. Each magician had written a chapter detailing pertinent experiences and magical abilities that they thought would be useful for those who succeeded them. Very few in Anderan knew that she and Master Gryph were So'ladiun, Solisius' warriors, and had been chosen by the god himself to defend Anderan against any conflict created by Obsudius, the God of Darkness, and his servants.

"Yes, I actually read his chapter again after I saw her do it. I couldn't remember if he had discussed how it was done. He hadn't, so I guess it is one of those talents that is special to the individual and cannot be learned."

Master Gryph grunted. "Elhrin, the feat may not be adapted by any ordinary magician such as I, but you may be an exception."

"I tried, but I couldn't do it," she said, knowing why he thought maybe she could when he couldn't. She was different from any other magician in the entire world that she knew of . . . Solisius had given her some of his own powers, and she kept stumbling across things she could do that she didn't know she could do before. It was only a few months earlier when she and Kyne had sailed in a small boat to Casteal Island located in the middle of Wyndermir Lake that she realized she could create a magical wind strong enough to topple trees. When the natural breezed blowing across the water suddenly died on their return trip to Muryne, she had used her magic and her strength almost capsized their boat. Kyne furiously vowed never to sail with her again.

"Don't give up," Master Gryph said.

"Gryph, I have to leave," King Goruth said. "I am already late for a meeting with the city council. You and Marguerite are attending the banquet Egeria has planned for our Chyrzinians guests, aren't you?"

"Actually, I think I'm beginning to feel under the weather." Master Gryph coughed suddenly, not trying to make it sound convincingly real.

Elhrin snorted in amusement.

"Gryph," King Goruth frowned at his obvious desire to avoid the banquet, "as my senior advisor and Minister of Specialized State Defense you need . . . ."

"Goruth, don't get your crown bent out of shape. I will join your festivities after tonight. Tonight, however," he draped an arm around Elhrin's shoulders and hugged her to him, "my family is here, and it has been a long time since we have all been together. I want to spend a quiet evening with them, if you don't mind."

King Goruth sighed heavily, frowning at the guards still positioned in the gallery. He gave Master Gryph a strange look, as if he wanted to say something but couldn't. "Very well, if I don't let you do this, you will disappear without a trace anyway."

"You know me so well, my friend," Master Gryph grinned.

Elhrin was surprised. That was too easy. Usually King Goruth put up more of a fight when Master Gryph tried to get out of something.

"Yes, yes, I do. Sometimes, I wonder if I shouldn't go ahead and replace you with Elhrin. She is more reliable and less of a hassle than you are, you old goat."

Elhrin's eyes went wide. The thought of being thrown into Master Gryph's role terrified her more than facing a fight with a thousand members of the hostile Brothers of M'gelidia, a religious faction dedicated to the service of Obsudius. She was not ready to get involved in court politics or make high-level government decisions.

Master Gryph saw her look of horror and boomed with laughter. "I think you have actually scared our girl, Goruth. That is something not easily done."

King Goruth smiled at Elhrin. "So I've noticed."

Chapter Three

Elhrin followed Master Gryph down the long hall of the second floor almost at a jog to keep up with his long stride. "You said all of your family was here?" Elhrin asked, being a little confused as to what he meant and wondered if his son Griffyn was in the city with his family, too.

"I did at that," Master Gryph said, slowing down when they neared a door with one of the King's Guards manning the portal. At their appearance, the soldier reached for the knob and politely opened the door to Master Gryph's apartment for them without a word. The guard was always a sore spot for Master Gryph, but King Goruth insisted one be there at all times when Master Gryph was in residence due to the fact that many people would not give him any privacy and the fact that there were those who would like to see him dead, especially members within the Brothers of M'gelidia who had tried many times to kill him.

Elhrin stepped into the living area of his and Marguerite's apartment. A lanky, young man was sprawled across the hand-woven rug in the middle of the room wrestling with a giggling little boy who would no doubt look like the tall man behind Elhrin when he grew up.

"Bayle!" Elhrin sputtered in surprise. She hadn't seen her brother in almost a year with him stationed in the southern city of Yradin. As a corporal in the King's Army, he only received two weeks of leave time, and she knew he still had a few months before he was eligible to receive it.

Both boys stopped playing to grin at her.

"Elhwin," the little boy squealed. He squirmed out of Bayle's grasp, and ran over to her.

She dropped the pack she was carrying, scooped him up, and gave him a wet, noisy kiss on his pudgy cheek. "Hey there, little man," she said, breathing in his sweet little boy smell.

"Wook, Bay's here," Marcus said, trying to pronounce his words right, but at three years of age he could not quite accomplish the task.

"I see that," she beamed at her brother who was now towering beside them. He wrapped his arms around her and Marcus and squeezed.

"Hello, sister of mine." He kissed her cheek just like she had kissed Marcus', wet and loud. Marcus mimicked him, slobbering all over her other cheek.

"You two are drowning me," Elhrin laughed, making a show of wiping the drool from her face. "When did you get here? I thought you couldn't leave Yradin for another three months."

"I wasn't supposed to, but my superior received a letter from the Minister of Specialized State Defense saying my presence was required in Muryne for the duration of the trade convention," he said with a grin. They both turned to look at Master Gryph.

"What?" he asked innocently as he unbuttoned his fitted long coat and crossed to one of the cushioned chairs arranged in a conversation setting around a low marble topped table. He dropped into the chair with an exaggerated sigh of exhaustion.

"You arranged for Bayle to be here?" Elhrin asked.

"If I am obligated to be here, I think I can have a say as to who I will need while I am here," he paused to take a breath as the door to the bedroom opened behind him. "A man in my position has certain requirements, don't you know?"

"What requirements would that be?" Marguerite asked, as she walked into the room followed by a pretty young chamber maid.

Bayle let out a low whistle of appreciation. Dressed in a deep blue gown of embossed silk, Marguerite was stunning. Usually, she wore her long sun-streaked blond hair braided down her back for convenience, but her hair had been swept elegantly to the top of her head and was held in place with two jeweled hair combs to match her dress. Strategic rivulets of hair draped down from either side of her forehead to frame her face.

"My sentiments exactly, son," Master Gryph said, admiring his wife.

"You two gentlemen certainly know how to make a girl feel good." She bent over to give Master Gryph a peck on the lips. "Didn't Ceirolwyn do an excellent job with my hair?"

"Yes, she did. Maybe we should hire her permanently. What an amazing improvement," he commented with a straight face.

"Minister Idwyr," Marguerite said with a false scowl and slapped him on the arm, "watch it! I know you hate how I normally wear my hair, but I do it because it keeps it out of my face while I work. Do you want me to cut my hair off like Greta Joelsun? I will be happy to, you know."

"For heaven's sake, no," he said with a laugh.

Greta Joelsun was a woman who lived alone deep in the southern woods surrounding Glimmerdale, and it was apparent she did not bathe on a regular basis. She kept her hair almost as short as a man's and it was usually a dirty, wiry mess.

"If that is the style you would choose, I will force myself to endure your normal look . . . not near as haggish as Greta's."

"You are hopeless," she said with a smile, playfully pushing his head to one side with her fingers. "Are you going to change for the banquet?"

"Ah, yes, the banquet," he cleared his throat, looking a little uncomfortable, "we're not going."

"And why not?" she frowned at him. "Do you know how long it took for me to get ready?"

"I know, love, but," he waved a hand at Elhrin and Bayle, "I told Goruth that I was spending tonight with my family."

"And he released you from the obligation after he made such a fuss about you attending affairs yesterday?"

"Mm, reluctantly, I would guess," he said.

"You do know he will make you pay dearly for missing this banquet later? Egeria, too."

He sighed and nodded in agreement. "That, he will. And she better not traipse over here with another hideous uniform for me to wear," he grumbled. "I'll be damned if I'm going to wear a purple anything."

"Then I guess the sash she sent over this afternoon is out of the question?"

He scrunched up his face in disgust.

"That's what I thought," Marguerite chuckled with a shake of her head and crossed the room to hug Elhrin. "Hello, sweetheart, I have missed you. Did you just arrive?"

"About an hour ago. Watch your clothes. I haven't had time to clean the dust and horse smell off."

"I'm not worried," Marguerite said, kissing her cheek.

"You don't smewll wike horses," Marcus said, sniffing her neck. "Papa buyed me a pony."

"He did?" Elhrin asked. "When did he do that?"

"Whast night." Marcus noticed the gold chain around her neck that held her pendant. Drawn to shiny objects, he pulled on it until the pendant slipped from beneath her shirt and started to play with the green oblong gem dangling from the chain. "But papa said we couldn't bwing it here because it wouldn't wike the noisy city."

"It's home in Glimmerdale? I thought you said he bought it last night?" Elhrin asked with a laugh.

Marguerite snickered. "He actually purchased the pony last month. Marcus gets time a bit confused."

Marcus wiggled in Elhrin's arms, and she knew it was time to let him down. Like his father, he couldn't sit in one place for very long. She acted like she was going to drop him, but caught him at the last second. He howled with laughter as she sat him on the floor and ruffled his wavy black hair. He then galloped off into the bedroom neighing like a horse.

"He is certainly your son," Elhrin commented to Master Gryph as she took a seat on the settee beside his chair.

"He sure is," Marguerite agreed. "Elhrin, Bayle, would you two like anything to drink or eat?"

"No, thank you, Marguerite," Elhrin said. "If you all don't mind, I would like to run to my apartment and bathe, then I'll come back. I feel yucky."

"You look yucky, too," Bayle teased, plopping down beside her. "I won't be rude and say no to something, Marguerite."

Elhrin grabbed his knee and squeezed as hard as she could.

"Don't, Elhrin, stop!" he laughed, pushing her hand away. "I always hated when you did that."

"Did you now?" she grinned, trying to do it again, but he grabbed her hands and held them fast.

Elhrin sent a tiny jolt of magical energy into Bayle's hands. He jerked them back as if he had touched fire. "Ow! No fair! You can't use your magic."

"Who says?" she grinned.

"I say," Master Gryph spoke. "Play fair."

Elhrin laughed. It felt like old times when they were growing up in Glimmerdale. Any time she and Bayle got out of hand, he would always tell them to play fair. It didn't matter who was in the wrong. Thinking of old times reminded her of something. "Bayle, have you been to Glimmerdale lately?" she asked.

"No, I haven't had the chance. Why?"

"I didn't know if you had been able to see the monument."

Master Gryph had purchased the piece of land from Elhrin and Bayle where their home had once been. He then turned it into a park dedicated to their mother and the other villagers who had lost their lives during the Do'athrim attack on Glimmerdale before the war. Master Gryph had secretly commissioned a sculptor to do a statue of a seamstress, and it was the focal point of the park. Elhrin had cried as hard the day she first saw the statue as she had the day she lost her mother. Her mother had been a widow, raising Elhrin and Bayle on her own and the only means of income had come from her sewing for others.

"No, I haven't seen it, yet, but I hope to before I return to Yradin. Thank you, Master Gryph, we appreciate you doing that for us."

Master Gryph just lifted a corner of his mouth and winked at him.

The chambermaid, Ceirolwyn, handed Bayle a plate of meats and cheeses and a glass of red wine. Elhrin couldn't help but notice the flush in the young girl's face or the subtle brush of Bayle's hand when he took the plate from the girl. Elhrin withheld a sigh. It was hard to get used to the fact Bayle had turned into a handsome young man with sea-green eyes and dusky blond hair. His looks and fun-loving nature made him irresistible to the young single ladies.

Bayle took a small sip of his wine. "Master Gryph, are you sure you won't break your rule just once and taste the wine I brought? It's good."

"Maybe later," he replied.

"In other words—no," Bayle said, knowing Master Gryph didn't care for anything that would impair his ability to think rationally, and spirits of any kind were something he avoided.

Master Gryph shook his head just as Marcus came barreling out of the bedroom. He ran full speed into Master Gryph's lap.

"Whoa there, young man," Master Gryph said, pulling Marcus into his lap.

"Papa, wook what Bay give me." Marcus produced two tiny metal soldiers.

"I saw them yesterday," Master Gryph said as he took one from his son's tiny hand.

"No, I found those two in the market today," Bayle said. "I thought I would add to his collection. Elhrin, you need to go to the market. Merchants from other countries have set up stalls on the north side and are selling amazing things I have never seen, half of which I couldn't tell you what it is."

"I'll have to go see it." She glanced at Marguerite. "Have you gone yet?"

"Not yet, but Bayle bought me the most beautiful scarf that was made in Nabafin. I would like to go soon, Gryph. I could use a little time away from the palace, you know?"

"We will, I promise," Master Gryph said. "I may be able to sneak away from here the day after tomorrow."

Marguerite wrinkled her nose in displeasure. "I don't see how. Goruth has made sure nearly every minute of your day is filled with meetings or other events."

"I know, dear."

"Why don't you go without him?" Elhrin asked.

"He wants me to wait for him."

"Why should she sit shut away here if you're too busy to go?" Elhrin asked.

"I didn't say she had to stay shut away. I just think it's best for her to wait until I can accompany her. Too many people here right now," Master Gryph said.

Elhrin frowned at him, puzzled. Yes, the city was packed, but it was always full of people, and Marguerite usually came and went as she pleased. Something was off.

He saw her look and cocked one eyebrow, questioningly. "We'll go soon," he said in a tone that the matter was closed for further discussion. He then held up the tiny metal soldier for Marcus to see, used his magic to make the toy rise from his hand and spin in the air then disappear.

Marcus sucked in a surprised breath. "Where did he go?" Marcus asked, worried that his toy was gone forever.

"I think he is on your head," Master Gryph replied.

Marcus raised a tiny hand to feel the top of his head just as the little soldier appeared. He plucked it out of his hair and laughed. "Do it again, Papa."

Master Gryph ended up making the soldier disappear several more times before he finally told Marcus to get in the floor to play.

"I heard you've been transferred to a new position, Elhrin," Bayle said with a mischievous grin. "Are you enjoying it?"

"Well, it has only been a few weeks and I have only worked with my new superior in this position through correspondence," she suppressed a grin and turned on the settee to face Bayle, knowing what he was doing and deciding to play along. "I hear working with him face-to-face will be tedious, demanding, and overrated." Bayle and Marguerite burst out laughing. "I know from my own experiences he can be grouchy and aggravating sometimes, too."

"Ahem," Master Gryph cleared his throat. "Marguerite, did she just say what I thought she said?"

"Did I say that out loud?" Elhrin asked Bayle innocently.

Marguerite laughed, "Now don't take it to heart, Gryph. You aren't tedious and aggravating all the time. Overrated, yes, and the heavens know you can get grouchy."

"Ha, ha, very funny. Elhrin, you know I can still place you with Director Allahaim," he said with a straight face. "I'm sure you would find working for him fascinating, and I think he would find you useful."

"Useful? No, no, that's okay. I'll stay where I am," she laughed.

Director Nygill Allahaim was the head of the local investigative department for Muryne and had a notorious reputation for being one of the coldest, meanest persons to work for, and she had come close to working for him last year.

Since her arrival in Muryne after the war, King Goruth had required her to work for various departments within the government in order to be familiar with them. Muryne's Office of Investigations was next on the list since they were the one department in the city that worked directly with Master Gryph who usually liked to work alone. He said it cut down on the number of individuals who had to be trusted to keep official secrets. But when the rumors of Do'athrim sightings had started to surface on a frequent basis, Master Gryph stepped in and said it was time for her to work as his assistant in the Office of Specialized State Defense. The title Master Gryph held as Minister of Specialized State Defense was bestowed on him by the king himself, and he reported directly to King Goruth and no other. His position was one part of Anderan's Defense Organization which included all branches of the military and local law enforcement divisions, and no one save King Goruth and a select few would ever know the full extent of what Master Gryph actually did or what she would be doing as his assistant. As far as the citizens of Anderan knew, he was a powerful magical figure who protected king and country from enemies of the state—which was true—but what they didn't know was that his job also entailed eliminating threats to Anderan's security that came from the God of Darkness directly. This usually meant secret missions into deadly situations that the public would never know about because of the panic they could create. Obsudius' portal between his spirit world of the dead and that of the living world was one example. Its existence or the fact that her closing it ended the Do'athrim War was never revealed to anyone outside the close circle who already knew about the event and all of them had been sworn to secrecy. Which meant the defeat of the Do'athrim army was never explained to anyone's complete satisfaction, including the soldiers who fought in the war. The most popular but untrue rumor surrounding the instant disappearance of the enemy army the night she closed the Rift was that they were a magical army led by a magical beast, and when Master Gryph killed the beast Cynder the Do'athrim disappeared, as well. No one tried to correct the rumor.

"Let me know if I aggravate you too much and you change your mind. I'll put in a transfer for you," Master Gryph said with a grimace as he massaged his leg above his left knee. He had an old injury he received years ago when she was little. It had not healed properly and the result gave him a slight limp. "Sitting all day in that council meeting has made my leg stiff. I need to walk it out. Marguerite, let's take Marcus to the gardens for a bit."

"Since when are you willing to go to the gardens?" Marguerite asked in surprise. "Whenever I ask you to go with me, you always tell me no because people won't leave you alone when you are out in public."

"Well, they won't, but I have been trapped in the council chambers all day and I need to get outside," he said, standing. "Besides, you went to a lot of trouble to look so stunningly gorgeous. I think it would be a total waste for no one but us to see you. I will sacrifice myself for you, my lady."

"Since you put it that way, I'm not going to turn you down. Let me get my shawl." She disappeared into the bedroom.

"I am going to go wash the dirt off," Elhrin said. "Unless there is something you need for me to do."

"No, you are free for the day," Master Gryph said. "We'll talk more this evening."

"Right, then."

"I'll walk out with you," Bayle said. "I have something in my room that I found in the market today. I want to show it to you and Master Gryph."

"Take your time, children," Marguerite called from the bedroom. "We will have dinner served here in a few hours."

Elhrin and Bayle walked down the long corridor to the nearest staircase and ascended to the third floor where the apartments of council members and other government officials lived while they were in Muryne, but not everyone stayed in the palace. Some officials had homes outside the palace, liking the privacy their own home offered. Then there were those that had both, like Councilor Idora, who stayed in one place or another, depending on her mood. Elhrin had contemplated finding her own home in the city, but since she traveled frequently and was out of the city more than she was in, she felt her apartment in the palace would suffice until she was required to be in Muryne on a more permanent basis.

The upstairs hall was just as crowded as the one below, and Elhrin noticed as soon as they entered the residential halls that guards were posted on almost every corner. The Royal Guard was making sure the visitors were kept safe from those not happy with their presence in Anderan.

"You must be someone special if you were given a room up here with the palace about to be filled with dignitaries and their entourages." Elhrin nudged Bayle teasingly with her elbow. She was so happy he was here and had been so busy with her own life she hadn't realized just how much she had missed him until now.

"It pays to be related to someone within the favor of the royal circle, my dear sister." He nudged back playfully. "Actually, I am truly going to be working for Master Gryph and he wanted me close by."

"I see. What are you going to be doing?"

"Bodyguard." He lost his smile and glanced around at the people passing by, then leaned in and lowered his voice. "Elhrin, he hasn't said anything definite, but I get the feeling he wants me because he doesn't trust anyone else. Do you know what is going on?"

"No." She didn't like the sound of his news. Since when did Master Gryph feel like he needed a bodyguard? "He hasn't explained his motive to you?" she asked, thinking about Councilor Idora's warning earlier.

"He just said that he wants me to be with Marguerite and Marcus whenever he is not around and to keep a watchful eye for anyone suspicious. How do I do that?" he asked furrowing his brow. "Has he seen how crowded the palace is? With all the people coming and going, half of which are from other countries, they all look suspicious to me."

"You mean you are guarding Marguerite and Marcus, not Master Gryph?" she asked in surprise. A small trickle of unease settled in the dark recesses of her abdomen and made a permanent home.

"Yes, but I am not supposed to reveal that to her. I am to behave as if I am only here for the festivities and spending time with them." He placed a hand in the small of her back as they walked. "I don't think Marguerite is fooled, though. One of the reasons I made a quick trip to the market when she and Marcus attended a mother and child luncheon for the visitors was to keep her from becoming too suspicious."

"What was the other reason?" Elhrin asked, turning down the south corridor where her apartment was located.

"Master Gryph wanted me to wander through and listen to people's conversations and talk to the vendors. See if there was anyone talking about the Do'athrim rumors or the Brothers of M'gelidia."

"The Brothers?" she asked. Bayle was full of surprising information. This was the first she had heard anyone speak of them for the last few months. They were apparently keeping a low profile because she always kept her eyes and ears open for any information pertaining to them and had found nothing in her travels recently. "Did you find out anything?"

"No, but I found something strange one of the vendors was selling. I don't know if it is important, but because it was so weird I thought maybe Master Gryph would like to see it."

"What is . . . ?" Elhrin stopped short in the middle of the hallway, not believing what she was seeing. "What is he doing there?" she growled.

"What's wrong?" Bayle asked.

"Look." She flung a hand in the air with frustration, then marched up to a burly guard standing by her apartment door.

"Why are you here, Private?" Elhrin demanded of the guard.

Standing head and shoulders above Elhrin, he looked down at her in surprise. "I beg your pardon, Miss?" he asked in a high voice that reminded her of a child.

She quickly turned her head away from the guard to give Bayle a wide-eyed look of shock. She hadn't been prepared for the way his voice sounded—several octaves higher than what she expected from a hulking man his size. Bayle hid a smile behind a fist, trying not to laugh. Schooling her face into a serious expression, she turned back to the guard.

"I wanted to know why you are at my door."

"My orders are to stand at this door and allow no one in but you and those you specify," the guard answered, ending on an elongated high note almost singing the last word.

Bayle choked off a laugh behind her, and she could have smacked him because he almost made her lose her composure.

"Who issued these orders?" she asked.

"I'm not sure," he answered, shrugging his wide shoulders. "I'm just doing what my sergeant ordered."

Elhrin sighed. "Very well, I'll check on this later. Come on in, Bayle."

"No, I'm going to go and let you do what you need to do. I'll meet you back at Master Gryph's apartment later." He gave her a hug, and whispered in her ear. "Love your door ornament."

"Shut up, you idiot," she whispered back, "he's standing right there."

He chuckled as he let her go. "We'll continue our conversation later, okay?" he asked, becoming serious as he started down the hallway.

"Most definitely," she answered and entered her door—glad to be home.

Her apartment was not as elaborate as Master Gryph's, but was nicer than the simple rooms reserved for servants and lower employees who lived on the top floor of the palace. It was one large room with a cozy sitting area in front of a fireplace and a small dining table nestled in one corner near the door. Her bed, placed near a window overlooking the palace courtyard, was a four-poster canopy draped with heavy, cream-colored curtains. Through a door across from her bed was one luxury that many employees did not have, and that was a private bath.

With a wave of her hand, Elhrin used her magic to light every candle and oil lamp within her apartment, then dropped her pack and cloak on the table. She tugged her nasty boots off, dropped them with a heavy clunk on the floor, and headed for the bath. It was a small room with barely enough space for the lavatory, hand-crafted porcelain washbasin, and matching tub for bathing.

Before coming to the palace, Elhrin had never witnessed hot and cold water spilling from pipes into a tub. It was a luxury usually reserved for the very rich, but in the last year she had seen its popularity grow, and Master Gryph had installed several lavatories for Marguerite when they had torn down their simple cottage in Glimmerdale and built a magnificent manor home in its place. He claimed she constantly wanted to take a bath and was getting too old and feeble to carry buckets of water from the well to fill the portable tub they had used for so long.

She smiled at the memory. Marguerite had given him a good hard slap on the back of his head for calling her old and feeble.

Elhrin opened the faucets to fill the tub, slipped off her riding tunic and trousers, and settled into the tub's warmth with a sigh. Sinking low enough to wet her head, she then lathered lavender-scented soap in her hair and scrubbed away the dirt, wishing she could scrub away her worries along with it. Master Gryph never did anything without reasonable cause, and having Bayle watch over Marguerite and Marcus meant something serious was happening. She sank back down in the tub and rinsed the soap from her hair.

She knew the relative peace the country had enjoyed since the war wouldn't last. Aside from minor pockets of conflict, she had only dealt with one major encounter outside of Martalaine where she and Kyne had been called upon to investigate a series of murders that looked like the sacrificial work of the Brothers of M'gelidia. It was. The Brothers were notorious for making sacrifices of young, innocent men and women, and eating their hearts to honor Obsudius. After nearly three weeks of searching without any leads, she and Kyne made a breakthrough and had been able to find out where a ceremony was to be held. They had been lucky to survive the ordeal. Sneaking into the ceremony, one of the M'gelidia had surprised them from behind and knocked them unconscious. When she awoke, Elhrin found that she and Kyne had been tied to the sacrificial alter and were about to become the faction's next victims. It wasn't funny then, but now she still had to shake her head at the insane comment Kyne had made when she had opened her eyes.

He had said, "Hello, my love, look what's for dinner."

She had taken one look at the cloaked figure about to plunge a knife in her chest and had replied, "Not for long."

She had quickly covered the both of them with a protective magical dome and sent it exploding outward. Every member of the faction within its path was sent hurtling through the air. She then burned through the bindings on her and Kyne's arms and legs with her magic, allowing them to break free and fight. She with her magic and Kyne with a sword he had picked up from one of the fallen members. In the end, the two of them had killed all of the members attending the ceremony except three that she knew of, and they had disappeared without a trace. Elhrin had to admit, even though Kyne got on her nerves, the two of them did make a good team.

I will never admit that to Kyne, she thought as she stepped out of the tub, dried off, and donned a soft evening dress the color of spring moss.

She smiled at the image reflecting in her mirror, smoothing the wrinkles of the dress around her hips. Tomas loved the dress. He said it complimented her beautiful emerald eyes, and he loved her eyes. She knew he was lying. What he loved was the low cut of the dress' neckline, revealing her ample cleavage which, along with her short stature, was something she inherited from her mother. She decided to put a hint of the perfume he gave her in the crevice of her bosom right below the brooch that covered her pendant to hide it from view, and was brushing through her wet hair when someone knocked on her door.

"Miss Caddoch?" a muffled high male voice called.

She chuckled. She had forgotten about the guard. She crossed to the door and opened it.

"Yes?" she asked the man filling her doorway, seeing that Tomas stood behind him clearly amused by her new protector.

"A Captain Colkitte is here to see you," the guard said.

"Thank you, uh . . . I'm sorry, I didn't catch your name," Elhrin said.

"I'm Irdin Teanser," the guard answered.

Tomas laughed out loud, earning a puzzled look from Irdin.

"Good to meet you, Irdin," she said quickly, trying to divert his attention from Tomas who wouldn't stop laughing. "Captain Colkitte, would you like to come in?" She peered around the guard. "Stop!" she mouthed silently.

"Thank you, Miss Caddoch, I would love to," he chuckled, sliding by the large man and shutting the door behind him.

"Why did you have to laugh at him?" she asked.

"Because I just realized this fellow is the one who has a reputation for speaking in a singsong manner, mostly under his breath to himself. Rumor has it he hums while he eats too," he said, then perused her attire with open admiration. "My sweet, pretty magician, you look beautiful," his voice deepened, and he pulled her into his arms. "When will you consent to marry . . . ?"

"Quit talking." She placed her lips on his and kissed him deeply. He tasted sweet, like he had eaten an apple recently. She raked a hand through his hair. With a groan, his lips left hers to trail down her neck.

"Tomas," she whispered as one of his hands slid down her back to cup her buttock, and press her to him. She could feel how much he wanted her. His lips came back to hers with an increase of urgency. It had been too long since they had seen each other— it was always too long. She groaned, knowing they were obligated for the evening, but how she wished she could be alone with him for the night. Reluctantly, she tore her lips from his. "We have to stop," she breathed.

"Why?" he asked, not bothering to slow down, much less adhere to her voicing the need for them to stop.

"We are supposed to dine with Master . . . ," she couldn't finish her sentence. His hands were wandering, and his touch sent all rational thought scattering into oblivion.

"They can wait," he murmured, and abruptly scooped her up in his arms and crossed the room to lay her on the bed. He leaned over to kiss her, consuming her as only a starved lover could while he deftly untied the laces in front of her bodice and slid a hand under the soft fabric. He broke the kiss and gave her a smoky, seductive smile. "Can't they?" he asked, then without waiting for her reply, clamped his mouth firmly onto the breast he held.

Fire exploded throughout her body and she arched her back as she held his head close. "Yes, they can," she tried to answer, but was sure the thought was never expressed aloud coherently.

Elhrin sat her glass of wine on the stone railing of the balcony and looked out over the palace grounds and the rooftops of the city's buildings to Lake Wyndermir. The sun had disappeared below the horizon in the west, and the first stars of the night could be seen twinkling in the cloudless eastern sky. A soft, cool breeze drifted around her, making her shiver and wish she had brought a coat or shawl.

"Cold?" Tomas asked, noticing her rub her bare arms. He peeled off his captain's jacket and draped it around her shoulders.

"The breeze has a bit of ice in it," she said as she snuggled into the warmth of his jacket, smelling the pleasant, masculine aroma of him in its fabric. "It seems like the weather wants to skip fall altogether this year. The nights on the road back to Muryne were much cooler than when Kyne and I left for Port V'Din."

"It does seem so, at that. We can go back inside if you'd like," Master Gryph suggested, propping both hands on the railing and taking the weight off of his damaged leg.

"No, I'm fine," Elhrin said. She glanced back through the window of Master Gryph's apartment to see if Bayle and Marguerite had finished tucking in a very cranky and sleepy three-year-old. "You asked us out here for a reason. Are you ever going to get around to telling me what is going on?"

"Elhrin," he stared out at the darkened waters of the lake and breathed in the night air, "there are many things going on at the moment, and events are gaining momentum far faster than I would like. You and I are about to become very busy."

Elhrin nodded slowly as she lifted her glass to her lips. "That fits the feeling that's been annoyingly intruding in on my thoughts here lately," she said, then took a small sip of her wine. Out of the corner of her eye she saw him give her a strange look. "What?" she asked, glancing at him.

He lifted the edges of his lips. "I don't think I said anything, sweetheart."

"You gave me a strange look."

"Did I now?' he asked in amusement.

"Uh," she grunted in frustration, knowing he wasn't about to tell her what the look meant, "you know you did, Mister Evasive. I hate it when you don't feel the need to explain yourself." She shook her head. "Anyway, does the gaining momentum of the busyness of our lives concern the Do'athrim sightings?"

"Not at the moment, but it may concern the Brothers of M'gelidia. Director Allahaim has evidence they are in the city."

"What kind of evidence?" she asked, as he looked back out over the city.

The soft light shining out onto the balcony from inside the apartment lit one side of his face. She could tell he was exhausted, and she didn't think it was just from the long, tedious activities of the day. No, she thought he was tired of conflict, tired of fighting—ready to settle down to raise his son and run the academy they were building. She didn't blame him. He had been through a lifetime of fighting for Solisius and the Kingdom of Anderan, suffering through wounds that still plagued him, not to mention he had in fact been killed by Do'athrim before the war. He was only alive by the grace of the God of Light who had opened a small portal to allow Master Gryph back into the world of the living from Solisius' domain of Ts'aura, the Realm of Light, in order to carry out Solisius' mission to stop Obsudius from pulling So'ladiun into his realm of Do'athra and sending them to the Void. It was a one-time, necessary act Solisius had said he would never do again for anyone else and a well-kept secret that only a handful of trusted individuals knew about.

Master Gryph reached into his coat to pull something from the inside pocket. He handed her a scrap of dirty, wrinkled paper. "Read this."

She conjured a tiny sphere of soft light and had it hover just above her shoulder as she unfolded the note. The handwriting was a jerky mess, making it difficult to read and giving her the impression that whoever wrote the note was unfamiliar or uncomfortable with writing—almost as if they had copied it from something else onto the scrap of paper.

My Brother, I have been waiting for our meeting. It has been a long time. I regret that I cannot be more specific as to when or where we will meet, and will have to leave it to fate to deem the time and the place, but rest assured, it will be soon.

She let her light wink out and handed the note back to him. "This is vague. It could mean anything. Are you sure this is from the M'gelidia?"

"It was found on one of them." He placed the note back in his coat pocket. "A dead one, that is, the day before I arrived in Muryne. The innkeeper of The Canal Street Inn in the waterfront district found him hanging in her stables. It appears someone was not happy with him."

"Hanging? That sounds like suicide," she said. "I've heard of several members who wanted out and have taken their own lives so they wouldn't suffer through the brutal torture that the M'gelidia would put them through before they were killed."

"No, it definitely wasn't suicide. I don't think even the strongest of souls could rip their own eyes out before they hung themselves if they were so inclined to mutilate themselves," he commented.

"Oh," she breathed in understanding. She shivered again. This time it wasn't from the cold. The Brothers of M'gelidia were a nasty lot. Even to each other. Tomas clasped her shoulders from behind and stepped close. She immediately felt the comforting warmth of his body on her back. "That does sound like something they would do."

"Yes it does, but two things about the murder bother me." He turned and leaned back against the railing. "First of all, it was no secret that I was coming to the city. The Brothers of M'gelidia would not leave the body of one of their members to be found by authorities knowing I would be alerted to the fact and would come looking for them. Add to that, this note about a meeting was found on the victim. I don't think they would want anyone knowing of a meeting, even if it did not tell the location. They are very careful about hiding their actions."

"Mistakes are made all the time," Elhrin pointed out, even though she knew he was right. They wouldn't leave a body behind to be found on purpose. "Maybe they didn't have time to dispose of his body and forgot about the note."

"Possibly, but that would be a critical mistake on their part, and in my experiences with them, they have made very few mistakes."

"It seems to me, in your experiences, they have made many mistakes. You are still alive." She reached out to clasp his arm propped on the rail.

He smiled and covered her hand with his. "I was lucky, my dear girl. In most of those cases, I had no forewarning of their intentions." He squeezed her hand then let his drop. "Elhrin, with the convention about to start, I am obligated to attend most of the functions. I need you and Kyne to meet with Director Allahaim."

Elhrin groaned. "Do I have to?" The last thing she wanted to do was talk with Nygill Allahaim.

"I know his gruff and sometimes vile demeanor will test your level of tolerance," Master Gryph said, giving her a look that said she was being childish and should do better, "but you are going to have to work with him. He may not be the most pleasant of fellows, but he knows what he is doing. Go talk to him. He is expecting you. See if you can track down who is behind the murder. It would also be helpful if you could find out more about this meeting in the note. Can you do that for me?"

"Yes, sir," she said, bringing her glass to her lips and taking a small sip of the slightly dry red wine Bayle had brought from Yradin. Laughter drifted through the open door of the balcony indicating that Bayle and Marguerite had been able to get Marcus to sleep. "Is this subject something you wish to keep from Marguerite?" she asked.

He glanced into the living room where Bayle and Marguerite were gathering the toys Marcus had left in the floor and putting them away. "I've told her most of it," he hesitated, and sucked in a heavy breath. "There is something else you need to know. Last month, I received an anonymous letter. I haven't told her about it, yet."

Elhrin became uneasy. "What did it say?"

"Basically, it was a threat to harm my family if I did not do what they wanted." He followed Marguerite's movements around the room. The love in his eyes was evident in the way he watched her before he turned his gaze on Elhrin. "All of my family."

Now she knew why Bayle was here. Why there was a guard at her door. He wanted to protect them.

"So you feel the threat is real this time. Have you told anyone?" she asked. He received threatening letters on a regular basis, but they usually turned out to be false threats. She wondered why he felt this time was different.

"Goruth is aware I have been threatened, and that is why he let me be here with you tonight so easily. He knew I needed to talk with you. I have asked him to let me handle the situation, and he is following my lead and will not acknowledge that there is anything amiss." He looked from her to Tomas. "The two of you are to talk to no one about this unless I tell you otherwise. Do you understand?"

She shook her head. "No, not really. What were the demands?"

"Elhrin, for the time being I am keeping my own counsel about the letter. It's not that I don't trust you. It's just that I want to make sure of a few things first before I go any further. When I am done, you and I will sit down and go over everything. However, until then I want you to be alert when you are out in public. You must promise—and I am very adamant about this—not to venture anywhere alone. Have Tomas or Kyne with you, or if they are unavailable take a guard," he said firmly, his eyes drifted to the living room. Marguerite and Bayle had finished putting the toys away and were pouring themselves a glass of wine.

Elhrin turned to look out at the lake. Far out in the distance were several pinpricks of lights, like stars floating on water, meaning more ships were coming into port.

"Do you have any idea who sent the letter?" she asked.

"I have my suspicions."

"But you are not going to tell me, are you?" she asked.

"Not at this time."

"Not at this time," she said, mocking his words under her breath. So like him. He tells her everyone's life is in danger and doesn't give her any details. What could that letter have said to scare him like this and who sent it? The Brothers of M'gelidia were definitely a possibility. He received letters from them often. Somehow, though, that didn't feel right. He probably would tell her more details if he thought it was them. Then who? Wait . . . Bayle said he got the feeling he didn't trust anyone. If that was true then could it be someone close? Which reminded her again of Idora's warning.

"Why does Reginold Whyse hate you?" she asked.

With an abrupt chuckle of amusement he glanced down at her. "He hates me? Now my feelings are hurt."

"Stop joking. I'm serious. Why does he hate you?"

"Who hates you?" Marguerite asked as she and Bayle joined them on the balcony.

"Did you know Reginold Whyse hates me?" Master Gryph asked.

"Of course," she said, handing him a glass filled with a red liquid. "That man doesn't try to hide it. You know that."

Master Gryph sniffed his drink. Elhrin knew he was checking to see if it was wine.

"It's only cranberry juice, Gryph," Marguerite said. "As if you needed to check."

"Never know with Bayle around," he said, eyeing the boy suspiciously.

"If I was to want to pull a prank on you, old man, I would think of something far better than handing you a glass of good wine that you would waste," Bayle said, pointing at him. "I do owe you one, though. Don't think I don't know it was you who told my commander that the night is my favorite time of the day and had a habit of staying up from dusk until dawn, then slept the day away. He jumped at the chance to give me a permanent position on the night watch because absolutely no one wants the job. Not once in the last six months have I been allowed a day shift during guard rotation. Made me feel like a vampire, you did."

"Now what would be the point of me doing that to you, son?" Master Gryph asked with a little laugh.

"To irritate me like you always like to do," Bayle said. "And with me being so far away it drove you crazy that you couldn't do it on a regular basis."

"I am a busy man, my boy. I don't have time the time or inclination to irritate you from a distance."

"Liar," Bayle murmured into his wine glass. "Someone told him that story and it came from up here."

"Master Gryph, would you two stop this nonsense and answer my question?" Elhrin asked, exasperated.

"What question?" he asked as if he had no idea what she wanted.

Bayle wasn't the only one he loved to aggravate when he was in the mood. However, aggravated didn't begin to describe how she felt about him at that moment. She knew he was side-stepping her question on purpose. "Will you please tell me why Reginold Whyse hates you?" she asked, patiently.

"I'll tell you why," Marguerite answered, frowning. "Reginold hates him because of what Gryph did with his sister."

"Do what? You didn't sleep . . . ?" Elhrin couldn't bring herself to finish the thought out loud. Both Master Gryph and Marguerite burst out laughing.

"I'm afraid bedding Reginold's sister is the furthest thing from something I ever wish to do. Is that what you think of me?" Master Gryph laughed.

"Well, I didn't know," Elhrin frowned at Tomas and Bayle who were laughing, too. "Since I've been living here, I've heard more rumors about you than I care to know."

"Now when did you start believing everything you hear?"

"I didn't say I believed the rumors, just that I've heard many, many—many tales."

"Is that so?" He chuckled. "Like what?"

"Um." Elhrin glanced at Marguerite, not really wanting to say what she had heard.

Marguerite smiled, knowingly. "Dear, I have heard the rumors, and I probably know more of them than you do. Over the years, you wouldn't believe how many ladies in this city have come to me claiming to have my best interest at heart, then proceed to spew the many atrocities my husband has done behind my back out of their gaudy-colored lips as if delighted they could do me such a favor."

Elhrin burst out laughing. "That is exactly what happened to me. I now have a reputation for rudely walking away in mid-conversation. I have no tolerance for those who thrive on creating conflict."

"I don't blame you," Marguerite replied with a laugh. "I might adopt the same technique."

"Would you two enlighten me as to the contents of these atrocities I have committed?" Master Gryph asked.

"Later," Marguerite said, waving him off, "right now, she wants to know about Reginold."

He grunted as if he did not want to talk about the subject and looked back out over the city.

"Gryph helped Reginold's sister escape from her family. She no longer lives in Anderan, and Reginold is furious at Gryph for it." Marguerite scrubbed her arms against the cold. "It is cool out here. Can we go inside?" Without waiting for a reply she stepped into the apartment.

Elhrin followed Marguerite into the sitting room. "Her family was so horrible she had to escape?" Elhrin asked as she sat on the settee and leaned over to place her wine glass on the white marble-topped tea table.

"Her father was who she was escaping from. Him and the man he was forcing her to marry. Of course we didn't know this until after the fact," she said softly as she peered inside her bedroom to check on Marcus. She then quietly closed the bedroom door. "At the time, Gryph didn't know who she was. She came to him in the village of Kit, begging him to let her travel with him to Marmuht. She gave him a false name and a false tale about needing to reach a sick relative, and he believed her. He learned later the truth of the matter, and that she had boarded a ship bound for Chyrzah. No one has heard from her since."

"When was this?" Elhrin asked as Tomas joined her on the settee. She placed a hand on Tomas' leg, and he clasped it. His hand felt like ice from the night air.

"That would have been nearly six years ago." Marguerite sat down across from her and crossed her legs. "The summer before our lives turned upside down."

Elhrin stared at her fingers intertwined with Tomas'. She wondered why Reginold blamed Master Gryph. All he did was escort a girl to another city. It wasn't his fault she left her family. The blame rested on the councilor's father. "Reginold must have really loved his sister to blame Master Gryph for this."

"Can't slip anything by you, can I? You really weren't too far off with thinking Gryph had an affair with the girl."

"What? I thought you said he didn't."

"He didn't, but Reginold did accuse Gryph of the act, and that his sister had to leave the country in shame. It gives him an excuse to publicly hate Gryph and he got the added satisfaction of throwing Gryph's character into doubt with those who side with his point of view." Marguerite looked down at her lap and smoothed the wrinkles out of her dress. "Truth be told, I think Reginold is jealous of Gryph. He doesn't like persons with magical abilities—that much is obvious—but I think it's Gryph's close relationship with Goruth that infuriates him most."

"Why?"

"Who knows? It could be he wants Gryph's position for himself or maybe he thinks Gryph has too much influence over Goruth."

Elhrin nodded, thinking the influence idea made sense, but Reginold would be waiting an eternity if he thought he could assume Master Gryph's minister position. "Reginold said something to that effect this afternoon in the council chamber. Master Gryph turned it into a joke about the King's Guard's new uniforms. He said they now looked like a bunch of armed grapes."

Marguerite and Tomas laughed.

"What's so funny," Bayle asked, sauntering back into the apartment, pausing at the nearby dining table to select something leftover from their evening meal.

"Something Minister Idwyr said," Tomas answered.

"What did I say?" Master Gryph asked as he stepped inside and closed the balcony door behind him.

"I was just telling them what you said to King Goruth about the new purple uniforms," Elhrin said.

"Ah, yes. I do think it is a horrible color to saddle on a man," he commented. He joined Bayle at the dining table to snag a few grapes out of a bowl and pop them in his mouth.

Marguerite turned in her chair. "Dear, could you do something with the fire? Leaving the door open has made it chilly."

"Certainly, dear," Master Gryph said. He didn't move from the table, or stop eating. Using his magic, he lifted a log from the wood holder and placed it on the low burning fire in the fireplace. With a negligent wave of his hand, the flames blazed high, reaching well up into the flue and sending a scorching heat blasting into the room.

"Better?" he asked.

Elhrin had to laugh at the look Marguerite gave him—like a mother whose patience was wearing thin with an unruly child.

"It's a bit much," Marguerite said evenly.

Master Gryph grinned at her as he casually popped another grape into his mouth. He loved to tease Marguerite, but he knew when to quit, and he let the flames die down to their normal state.

"Thank you," Marguerite said, turning back around in her chair to face Elhrin. "Maybe I should have asked you, instead. He can never resist an opportunity to annoy me."

"Bayle," Master Gryph said.

"Sir?" Bayle answered with a full mouth as he slathered butter on a fluffy pastry.

"I believe you said you had something you wanted to show us," Master Gryph said. He walked with a slight limp to the chair beside Elhrin and lowered his large frame into it with an almost inaudible groan.

"Yes, right," Bayle said. He stuffed the entire pastry in his mouth and hurried to retrieve a large sack he had left by the apartment door. He reached into the bag and pulled out a cylindrical black spike with a white tip that was as long as Elhrin's forearm.

Master Gryph abruptly sat forward in his chair. "Give that to me," he commanded.

Elhrin raised her eyebrows, taken aback by his harsh tone.

"You found this in the market?" he asked as Bayle handed him the spike.

"Yes, sir," Bayle said, looking as if he had done something wrong.

Master Gryph pinned Bayle with a steady gaze. "What did the vendor say about it?"

"Um, he said that he bought it from a man in Tuhnichi on his way here. The man had purchased it from a boy who lived near Marmuht and had found it along the shore," Bayle said.

"What is it?" Elhrin asked.

"This is a Bynduwhin spike," he said, frowning with displeasure as he inspected the object. "It is from a creature native to an uninhabited land far out in the Veihl Sea. A very dangerous creature, and I would like to know how it came to be found on the coast of Anderan." He turned the large end toward them and held it up for them to see. "Do you see how this is hollow?"

"Yes, sir," Bayle answered, cocking his head sideways to see into the spike.

"That is because it usually holds a deadly, incurable poison. These spikes are located on the end of its tail, and it is capable of firing them at you with amazing accuracy like a bow and arrow. If a direct hit with one of these things doesn't kill you, the poison will in a matter of minutes. If you will notice, the very tip is broken. It cracks or breaks off entirely when it hits something, allowing the poison to spill out. This one is damaged. The back end is usually not open like this."

Elhrin stared at the spike in his hand. "How do you know about these creatures?"

"My father had an experience with one as a young man," Master Gryph said.

"May I see it?" Tomas asked.

Master Gryph leaned over to hand it to him. "Do not touch the inside. I don't want to take the chance there is any residual poison left in it."

"What kind of experience did your father have with this creature?" Marguerite asked.

"Before he settled down permanently in Pago Duhn to raise a family, he worked on a merchant ship. They were returning from a trip to the southern tip of Chyrzah when a storm blew in unexpectedly. He said in all his years on the water it was the worst storm he had ever experienced, and they were lucky to have survived. When it cleared, they found they were hundreds of miles off course, and the ship was in bad need of repair. Unable to sail, they drifted for a week before they came upon a land he had only heard of in tales. The sailors name it Scathlamahn."

"The land of mist and shadow," Elhrin commented. She remembered hearing tales about the mysterious land in the sea.

"Yes, the land of mist and shadow." Master Gryph sat back in his chair and stretched his long legs out before him. "Many think it is just a sailor's fairy tale, but it is very much a real place. My father described it as a land that felt evil and frightening even at a distance. That the waters surrounding the coast were unusually calm, and there is a mist lying like a blanket over the land that prevented him and his shipmates from seeing anything but the beginnings of a jungle beyond a stretch of beach. When they drifted closer to shore, he said the sounds of the land's wildlife were strange to their ears, and they would have liked nothing better than to pass it by, but with the state their ship was in they had no choice, and set anchor off the beach. They chose lots to see who would go ashore. The plan was to quickly cut enough timber for repairs so they could sail home. My father was one of the lucky ones allowed to stay onboard the ship. He watched his mates on shore cut timber from the edge of the jungle and drag it back to the rowboats. They almost made it without incident, but then a Bynduwhin burst out of the jungle and attacked. Only one boat made it out of the beast's reach to the safety of the ship." He pointed to the spike in Tomas' hand. "A sailor was pulled aboard with one of those spikes in him, but he died within minutes of being laid on the deck. My father kept the spike and showed it to me." He furrowed his brow in thought. "I wonder whatever happened to it."

"What happened after the attack?" Bayle asked, wanting Master Gryph to finish the tale.

"They realized the creature could not reach them, but they wanted well away from the island as soon as possible, so they hauled the bit of timber that one boat had salvaged on board, hoisted their anchor, and used what little sail they had to drift away until they couldn't see land any longer. Out to sea, they were able to repair damage to the ship enough to make it into Agadar a few weeks later." Master Gryph yawned, and scrubbed a hand over his tired eyes. "Youngsters, it has been a long day. I think we need to call it an evening. Bayle, I will keep the spike if you don't mind."

"No, sir, I was going to give it to you, anyway," Bayle said.

"Did your father tell you what the creature looked like?" Elhrin asked, taking the spike Tomas offered to her. It was heavier than she expected. She thought it would have been as light as an arrow, but it was a little heavier. She frowned as she looked into its interior. Like Master Gryph, she wondered why such an exotic object was lying on the shores of Anderan.

Master Gryph yawned again. "He did. It was nearly as large as the trees of the jungle were tall, and the long hair on its body covered a hide thick enough to repel the weapons the sailors had with them. He was amazed at the speed in which the creature moved . . . the men didn't have a chance. It plowed through them, catching them in its huge maw, or swiping them down with the long talons on its front paws. Everyone on the beach was dead in a blink of an eye, and when it found it couldn't reach the men in the boats rowing back to the ship, it started firing those spikes. My father watched it raise its tail above its head and release them with amazing accuracy and speed. He said it was so fast, the beast probably fired a dozen or more in the amount of time it would take the most experienced bowman to release two arrows. The men within its range fell as if they had been standing still."

"I'm glad something like that doesn't live in Anderan," Bayle commented as he stood to leave.

"Yes, we are fortunate." Master Gryph frowned thoughtfully at the spike in Elhrin's hand.

"Is it possible this one floated to our shores?" she asked as she handed the spike back to him.

"Anything is possible," he answered.

"Do you think it did?" she asked.

"No," he said, staring at her steadily.

Elhrin sat straight up in bed, barely suppressing a scream. Heart pounding with fear, she took in her surroundings, finding she was in her apartment and Tomas was softly snoring in the bed beside her.

Thank the light. It was just a dream, she thought as she raked a shaky hand through her hair, and sent her senses out in search of Master Gryph. She felt his magical energy pulsing in the direction of his apartment. If her dream had been real, he wouldn't be there. Still, what if it was? Sometimes the dreams of a So'ladiun were a warning, and should not be brushed off as a mere dream. She could not ignore the residual feeling of urgency left over by the dream. She had to find out.

Slipping quietly from bed, she conjured a tiny light sphere. It gave off just enough light to allow her to find her clothes. She dressed quickly in a tunic and trousers, and silently slipped out the door. The night guard in the hall gave her a look of astonishment at her sudden appearance.

"Is everything okay, Miss Caddoch," he called after her.

"I hope so," she said without slowing down. She ran down the hall to the stairwell, not caring that the cold marble tiles were freezing her bare feet.

When she reached Master Gryph's apartment on the second floor, she received another astonished look from his guard. "No need to announce me. I am expected," she said, not wanting to go into details why she was there. His eyes dropped to her bare feet, and he appeared to not believe her, but he knew who she was and allowed her to pass unquestioned. She slipped into Master Gryph's apartment, and quietly closed the door behind her. If she was wrong, then she didn't want to waken them.

Please, let me be wrong, she thought.

The sitting room was dark, but the dim light emanating from the coals left in the fireplace allowed her to make out the open bedroom door without conjuring a light. She padded over and silently peered inside. She could hear the even sounds of sleeping, but she couldn't tell if one of them was Marcus. Hoping she wouldn't trip or knock anything over in the dark, she felt her way to where they had placed his bed along the wall near the door. Thankfully, she made it without making any sound and found his small body sprawled outside of his covers. She almost wept with relief. He was safe. Groping blindly in the dark, she found where he had kicked the covers off the side of the bed and tucked them securely around his body.

She straightened, and was about to leave when a hand clamped firmly over her mouth and an arm reached from behind to pin her securely against a rock-solid body. She reached for her energy. Power instantly flooded every fiber of her being.

"Elhrin," Master Gryph whispered in her ear. She almost fainted from relief, and let her magic go. She had been so focused on Marcus she hadn't realized he had left his bed. "What are you doing?"

"Don't scare me like that," she whispered against his palm.

He dropped his hand from her mouth and guided her into the sitting room.

"I could have hurt you," she whispered, as he silently closed the door behind them.

"I wasn't concerned that you would," he said, donning a robe over his night clothes and securing it with a tie at his waist. In the open neck of the robe she could see his pendant glowing softly against his chest. It was a magical talisman from Solisius, almost identical to hers, but where hers was green, his was white. "I was concerned, however, that you would wake Marguerite. I am guessing you would not have wanted to explain your presence in our bedroom in the middle of the night."

"I'm sorry," she said, knowing he must think she had lost her mind. "I had a dream."

He breathed in audibly and nodded, understanding what she meant. "Take a seat," he commanded then limped over to the fireplace to add wood to the fire. She noticed his limp was more pronounced than usual and supposed it was due to being still while he slept. He bent to place the logs on the fire by hand, but used his magic to add enough heat to the coals to allow the new wood to burn on its own. Watching the flames dance along the logs, he leaned tiredly against the mantle of the fireplace. "You had a dream concerning Marcus." It was a statement, not a question.

"I did," she answered. The fact that he had immediately pinpointed the subject of her dream troubled her. "You have had one, too, haven't you?"

He nodded silently. She felt queasy. If they both had the same dream it was not a good sign. It meant that they definitely had to pay attention to its message and not ignore it.

"Tell me about your dream," he said.

"There wasn't much to it—it was more of a feeling," she said, trying to recall the dream's details. "It was dark, but I knew Marcus was there. He was scared and alone. There was something sinister nearby, and I felt a sense of urgency. I knew I had to get to him before it was too late, but then I woke up."

He pushed away from the fireplace, and limped to the chair across from her and sat down. "How old do you think Marcus was in your dream?" he asked.

"I don't know," she said slowly, frowning at the unexpected question. "I didn't stop to think about how old he was. I just assumed he was the age he is now. That is why I came here to check on him. I had to make sure he was okay. What about your dream?"

"It is very similar." His face was a mask of suppressed frustration. "I see nothing, but I know he is in danger and needs me. I asked you about his age because I can't tell, either. I don't know if this is now or in the distant future."

"Master Gryph, this scares me." She slid to the edge of her chair and leaned forward. "I don't know what your letter said specifically, but with a threat to your family, and our dreams—don't you think Marguerite and Marcus should go somewhere secret to keep them safe?"

"I've considered it," he said, crossing his arms over his chest, "many times. Where would you suggest would be the best place to keep them safe?"

She sifted through the ideas flitting through her mind, but honestly could only come up with one good solution. "With you," she answered finally.

"Or with you," he said with a small smile. "However, I'm afraid both solutions are out of the question for the moment."

"Why can't you leave Muryne with them?" she asked.

"I have to be here for the time being."

"Tomas said you made it known how much you did not want to be here." She reflected. "It was all for show. You put up a fuss on purpose, didn't you?"

He looked away and said nothing.

"Master Gryph, please don't shut me out. Please tell me more. Let me help." She saw a quick flash of pain cross his face before he smoothed it away, and she didn't know if it came from something he was thinking or from an actual physical ache.

"Elhrin, I am not shutting you out on purpose. I am . . . ."

"Protecting all of us," she whispered hoarsely. "Don't do this with me. I am So'ladiun, too. Danger will always be a part of my life, just as it has been for you. You can't always be around to protect me."

"No, I can't, but for now, I am, and you will have to accept the fact that I will always do everything in my power to protect the ones I love."

She sat back in her chair. It was no use. He wasn't going to let her help him. She was going to have to try something different.

Solisius, she sent her thoughts out to the God of Light, *can you tell me what is happening? Do you see the danger?*

Even though there was no door or window open, a soft breeze caressed her skin. Smiling, she knew Solisius was with them.

Master Gryph's lips lifted in amusement. "Thought to go over my head, did you?" he asked as a soft laugh not of the earth whispered within the breeze curling around them.

Elhrin, my child, I do see the danger, and yes, I do know what is happening, but he has asked you to wait and to trust him. I will not betray his confidence. Every time she heard Solisius' voice her heart leapt with joy, even when what he had to say did not please her.

"Don't you think he could use my help?" she asked aloud, not taking her eyes from Master Gryph's. He returned her stare and said nothing.

You will be helping him by trusting him. The breeze evaporated. Solisius had left.

She frowned at the sudden loss of contact. "I wasn't through. Why does he leave like that?"

"You are not the only So'ladiun in the world, or one of his children for that matter talking to him, my dear," Master Gryph said.

"I know, but I wanted to ask him about our dreams," she said.

"You have been So'ladiun long enough to know he will not interfere directly with our destinies. Most likely, if he answers your questions at all, it will be ambiguous."

"You must have picked up that trait from him," she muttered under her breath.

"What was that?" he asked.

"I said, have you asked him?"

He smiled, revealing he knew what she had truly said the first time. "I have." He lost his smile. "Solisius did not send the dream to me."

"I thought all of these dreams came from him." She was confused. "We have talked many times while I slept, and he has said he sends me dreams."

"That is true, but I have learned through the years, that it is possible to have these kinds of dreams come from somewhere else." He stroked his beard. "I am wondering if it has something to do with our magical energy. Grey Leahr has had episodes of dreams similar to ours, and he is not So'ladiun. Maybe that is a question I will take up with Doctor Lyrin if I ever get a chance to talk to him."

Elhrin heard the contempt in his voice, and decided to get his mind off the doctor conducting tests in Gildas. "Even if Solisius did not send the dream, he still knows the future. Doesn't he see what happens to Marcus?"

"What he sees will not be revealed to us. Even though we are his So'ladiun, he will not interfere with the course of nature. You know this."

"I do know, but I thought maybe he could make an exception." She frowned at the floor. "We could use the help. I will not have Marcus in danger."

"I will not, either," he said quietly, "not any of you, but we must remember we are humans subject to the rules of this world. Solisius cannot point out our way. We have to find answers on our own. At least, we have the benefit of the dreams. They have given us some warning." He looked toward the windows overlooking the balcony. "Dawn is not far off, and Marcus has a bad habit of waking when the first rays of the sun touch the sky. Unless you want to explain why you are here, I think you might want to go back to your apartment."

She glanced at the bedroom door, wishing she could stay. She loved it when Marcus first awoke in the mornings. Walking around half asleep and rubbing his eyes with his tiny hands—his wavy black hair stuck out in all directions from where he had thrashed about during the night. He was always so sweet, letting her pull him into her embrace and snuggling up against her shoulder. With a sigh, she stood to leave.

"The threat includes you, too. You do realize I'm not letting this go?"

"I didn't think you would." He pushed himself up out of his chair. "Don't forget to meet with Director Allahaim this morning."

She narrowed her eyes at him. So, that was his ploy—to keep her so busy hunting down the Brothers of M'gelidia, she wouldn't have time to meddle in his affairs. That's what he thought. She crooked a finger at him to get him to lean down to her level. Placing a kiss on his cheek she whispered, "I love you, and I will not have you dying on me again. Promise me like you made me promise. You will be careful and have someone watching your back."

He nodded. "I love you, too." He opened the door for her. The guard outside turned to look at them.

"Told you I was expected," she said over her shoulder as she slipped by him and padded silently down the hall in her bare feet. She was almost to her apartment when she realized Master Gryph had not spoken a promise out loud. His nod could have meant anything.

Chapter Five

Elhrin placed a hand against the rough-paneled wall and looked out the window of Muryne's Office of Public Investigation to the busy street below which was even more congested than when she and Kyne entered the building only a few minutes earlier. They had been lucky to reach the building at all. Word had spread that the delegation from Murdaign had arrived, and a curious crowd poured into the streets to try and catch a glimpse of the foreign dignitaries. She saw several people start to point down the street so she moved to the side of the window for a better look.

As she watched, the entourage crept into view and was having a difficult time making their way through the masses, but a short time later, the ambassador's carriage rolled underneath her window. As luck would have it, he was sitting on her side of the street and she could see him through the open windows of the carriage. He was a large elderly man, pale of face with a bushy white beard and a bare head shiny as a polished steel shield. His Murdaignese escort followed directly behind his carriage and was an impressive lot. She had heard the Murdaignese people were notoriously large in size, but she hadn't expected their soldiers to be muscular giants who made Muryne's guards look like starving waifs in comparison. Scowling from underneath their conical helmets of shiny steel, they watched the crowd carefully. The muscles of their huge arms flexed as if they didn't need to have much of a reason to reach for a weapon. When they passed by her window, she saw their weapon of choice—wicked-looking war hammers strapped to their backs which explained the thick muscles that strained the dark leather of their shirts. It had to take considerable strength and stamina to swing the mighty weapon in battle.

Muryne's City Guard yelled for people to move out of the way as they used shields and poles to try and back the crowd off the street in order for the entourage to pass. She wished she could go help them. She would rather deal with a pressing crowd than be where she was—listening to the deafening tirade Director Allahaim was giving one of his investigators. The man obviously didn't care that everyone in the open room heard all of the degrading names he was calling the woman.

Elhrin heaved an angry sigh, struggling to keep her temper in check and stamping down the urge to throw him as far out of the window in front of her as her strength would allow. No one deserved to be called a worthless whore incapable of finding her own female parts. Elhrin glanced at the poor woman standing across the room, stoically taking the man yelling in her face. It must be frightening to have a walking skeleton with a vulture's head crammed on a stick of a neck mere inches from one's face, yelling at the top of its lungs. At least, that is what he looked like to Elhrin. Thin to the point of being gaunt, he leaned closer to the investigator's face almost touching his beak-like nose to hers. His balding head glistened with sweat from his frenzied rage.

"Get your fat ass out of my building," he yelled, pointing to the stairway with a rolled stack of papers in his hand, "and don't come back, you stupid bitch." He turned on his heel and marched across the room, throwing the papers down on his desk. He pinned Kyne with a venomous bloodshot glare. "Who the shit are you?" he snarled at Elhrin's partner who appeared to be bored to the point of dying as he sat calmly in the chair on the other side of the director's desk.

Kyne narrowed his eyes and tilted his head back, not intimidated by the harsh man in the least. "I am Captain Kyne Pittwold," he said calmly, and nodded his head slightly in Elhrin's direction, "and this is Miss Elhrin Caddoch, Assistant to the Minister of Specialized State Defense."

Allahaim turned his hateful gaze to Elhrin. He looked her up and down, assessing her worth, making her feel like she was a piece of horseflesh on auction. Her temper almost got the better of her.

"You're smaller than I expected," Allahaim sneered. "Not much taller than a child."

Apparently, she didn't pass his inspection. "Is that a fact, Director?" she asked, raising her eyebrows as if the statement surprised her, unable to keep the contempt she felt for him out of her voice. She pushed away from the window and walked over to occupy the chair beside Kyne. "I don't think my size has ever been an issue."

"Whatever," he said dismissively as he dragged his chair closer to his desk and sat down. "Let's get this over with. I'm busy, and now I'm short an investigator." He shifted papers on his desk around until he found the one he wanted. He tossed it at Elhrin. "That is what Idwyr sent you here for."

I wonder how much trouble I would be in if I knocked his ass onto the floor? Elhrin thought as she leaned forward and retrieved the document teetering on the edge of the desk. She quickly scanned the sheet in her hand. It was an accounting of the crime scene concerning the hanging victim. She leaned back so Kyne could read it with her.

The location she already knew was the Canal Street Inn in the waterfront district. The victim was described as a male found hanging from the rafters of the inn's stables. He was missing both eyes, had considerable bruising around his head and neck, scraped knuckles, and he had a completed tattoo of a wolf's head on his chest which proved he was a full member of the Brothers of M'gelidia. All members were required to have the tattoo somewhere on their bodies. His feet were bare, which was strange, and he had nothing extra on his person save one scrap of paper. The rest of the document described the note, the details of the stables, the innkeeper's name, and the time she found the body.

Elhrin looked up to find Director Allahaim ignoring them as he busily dipped a pen in an inkwell and scratched something across a piece of paper.

"Director," Elhrin said, "have you uncovered any further evidence or leads since this report?" Director Allahaim did not answer her and continued to write. Elhrin sighed in frustration. She knew he had heard her. "Director!" she said louder than she knew was necessary.

He slammed his pen down and glared at her. "What?"

"I asked if you had any further leads?" she asked far calmer than she felt. She wasn't about to let him know he was getting to her.

"I do not have the time or the manpower to investigate this at the moment. If you haven't noticed, the city is packed wall-to-wall with people from all over creation. Do you know how much crime that creates? The city guard is handling all the frivolous-ass disputes and petty thefts, but we have to handle the heavy stuff. Since yesterday there have been four murders, and I just found out that one of the Chyrzinian sailors has killed someone on the docks. Now everything has to be pushed aside while I deal with the foreigners and soothe their egos so they don't stir up trouble for the kingdom," he spat out and gathered up the paper he had been writing on. "I told Minister Idwyr there were other cases ahead of this, and if he wants to know more, he was more than welcome to find out. The Brothers of M'gelidia are your and his area of expertise, are they not?" He pushed his chair back with a harsh, grinding scrape and stood up. "What you have in your hands is all the information I have at the moment."

Elhrin stared speechless at the director—a bit taken aback over his seeming lack of concern for a case that had the mark of the M'gelidia all over it. The murderous faction could not be ignored and he knew it. It was too dangerous. And the fact he did not offer any help to solve the crime was absurd. It seemed his less than stellar reputation was well-founded.

"Do I need to speak a little more slowly for you to comprehend what I'm telling you, Miss Caddoch," he growled when she didn't respond right away.

"I understood perfectly what you said, Director. However, it was my understanding this was to be a joint effort between our office and yours."

"Well, I guess you misunderstood. Women usually do," he scoffed, and without another word, he stormed across the room. "Jake, get your ass up and come with me," he yelled as he disappeared down the stairway. A startled young man in a somber gray suit jumped up from his desk in the corner of the room, snatched his hat from a hook, and ran after the director.

Kyne inspected his fingernails. "You know . . . I like him."

Elhrin slowly released a long even breath, trying to calm her anger, and glared at Kyne. It didn't surprise her that he would like such an atrocious fool.

He raised his eyebrows. "What?" he asked.

"Nothing," she growled. She folded the document and stuffed it into her pocket.

"What now?" Kyne asked as he stood and straightened his coat.

"Now, we look for the Brothers of M'gelidia." She perused the desks filled with investigators hunched over their work. "I am so glad I did not have to work here. Come on. Let's see if we can push through the crowd and reach the inn."

"I tell you, Miss," Jyrah said as she unlocked a padlock and slid the rickety barn door in sore need of repairs grinding across its rusty mechanism with an agonizing squeal. "In this section of town there are all kinds of strange things going on constantly, but this was a first for me. I nearly lost my insides when I saw him hanging there with no eyes."

"I bet you did," Elhrin answered with a politeness she did not feel as she waited for the squat woman to finish wrestling the door open. Talking with Jyrah, the innkeeper of the Canal Street Inn, had been an endeavor in patience, and Elhrin's was beginning to evaporate. She and Kyne had been at the inn for nearly an hour, sitting in the common room and listening to Jyrah's overly loud voice jump from one complaint to another about how no one cared about the rundown state of the waterfront district, and the city guard did nothing to protect the innocent, hardworking folks from the cutthroats and thieves slinking about the streets. If it hadn't been for Kyne rudely interrupting the woman, they would still be inside, choking on thick tobacco smoke. Elhrin swore every individual who passed through the inn's doors owned a freshly lit pipe and wouldn't have been surprised if the rats she saw scurrying along the baseboards had pipes clamped firmly in their teeth, as well.

"Ugh," Kyne gagged on the horrible stench wafting out of the stable door. "Is he still in here? What is that smell?"

"What smell?" Jyrah frowned, making her wrinkled face almost comical since she didn't possess any bottom teeth. She disappeared inside the shadows of the stables, but her loud voice carried back to them clearly. "There's nothing in here but some curing meat up in the rafters. We don't get much livestock down this way. Outside of the regulars, most of our patrons come off the docks. I couldn't tell you the last time one of those stalls harbored any cattle."

Kyne leaned in to speak quietly in Elhrin's ear. "If that smell is coming from the meat they serve here, remind me not to eat in this place."

"I wouldn't eat here, anyway," Elhrin whispered, as she reluctantly stepped just inside the stable door to wait on Jyrah to light a lamp. She willed herself to not gag out loud and cover her mouth and nose with both hands. The stench was a thick, nearly tangible cloud within the walls.

After several unsuccessful strikes, Jyrah managed to light the wick of a rusty lamp hanging on a nearby hook. She picked it up and turned to point at an exposed rafter over their heads between the front and back wall. The rafter was well away from the loft, which meant suicide was definitely not a possibility. "Right there is where he was hanging. Horrible sight, I tell you, just horrible."

"Do you always keep the stable door locked?" Elhrin asked, trying not to breathe through her nose.

"Of course, I do. There have been too many scoundrels trying to sneak in here and sleep for free or steal my stuff."

Elhrin scanned the dusty and cobweb infested interior, seeing nothing but a few tools and broken furniture. Not much worth stealing. "Was the door locked when you came out here that morning?"

"Yes, it was. That's what's so puzzling. There's not another way in here, but through the door."

"Madam, do you mind if I look in the loft?" Kyne asked, his voice muffled by a handkerchief he had used to cover the lower half of his face, not caring about the possibility of insulting the innkeeper.

Jyrah frowned thoughtfully at the man, but said nothing about the kerchief covering his face. She offered the rusty lamp she held. "You might need this."

Taking the lamp, Kyne climbed nimbly up the ladder to the loft. The light he carried cast his distorted shadow onto the ceiling as he moved around the creaky floor. Elhrin thought she heard him gag again but couldn't be sure because Jyrah was still prattling along in her headlong manner. Elhrin could only imagine what the meat above looked like if it smelled worse than a rotting corpse.

"I told the man from the investigative place I don't see how anyone got in here. I keep the key in my room all the time and nobody needed it that I can recall, and he wasn't here when I locked up right before dinner time." Jyrah crossed her arms over her ample bosoms. "I distinctly remember we needed two roasts to put in the pot that night so they would be ready by morning, and I didn't come out here again until right after dawn the next day to get some potatoes. I keep them in the bin over by the back wall."

"Jyrah, you're needed in here," a voice yelled from outside.

Elhrin and Jyrah turned to look out the stable door. An old man stood at the back door of the inn.

"Vic, can't you handle it?" Jyrah screeched so loud, dogs somewhere down the canal started to bark.

Elhrin winced, resisting the urge to slap both hands over her ears.

"I swear, you old bag of bones, I can't leave you for five minutes before you come hunting me down like a blind fox hound."

The old man waved an impatient hand at her, beckoning her in, then turned his stooped body around to shuffle back inside. He slammed the door firmly shut behind him, leaving no doubt about what he thought of his wife's comments.

"You'll have to excuse me, Miss. That old man can't do anything right. I don't know what I ever saw in him thirty years ago," Jyrah grumbled. "Look around all you like. I'll be back shortly."

"There's no hurry," Elhrin said, grateful for a break from the woman. "I know you're a busy lady. We'll come back inside when we're done out here. I still have a few more questions for you."

"That will be fine. Just lock up when you're through." Jyrah waddled across the stable yard and climbed the shabby steps to the inn, straining the time-worn treads to their limits.

"Kyne," Elhrin called up to the loft as she desperately fumbled in her coat pocket for her own handkerchief, "did you find anything?"

"Maggots—lots and lots of maggots." He walked to the edge of the loft and peered down. "Some of this meat needs to be thrown out. I hope whoever eats here has a strong stomach."

"Stop worrying about the meat and focus on finding anything that might help us figure this out," she said then covered her nose and mouth with the kerchief. It didn't mask the smell completely, but it was better than nothing.

Elhrin scrutinized the ground below the rafter where Jyrah had said she found the man, but didn't see anything out of the ordinary. She then scanned the stables one more time. The sunlight from the open door didn't push the shadows back far enough, so she conjured a small light sphere and sent it away from the door to keep anyone walking into the stable yard from seeing it. She rarely used her powers in public unless it was necessary because some did not trust those with the gift and she didn't want to cause any unnecessary trouble. Then there were those who thought magicians were novelties and wanted to be entertained. Either way, she did not need the interference.

Methodically, she searched the perimeter of the interior wall as Kyne climbed down from the loft.

"Nothing up there," he said, his eyes crinkled at the corners in amusement. "Couldn't take it any longer, could you?" he asked, referring to the fact she now had her face covered as well.

"Nope, I'm not in the mood to gag through this. I had enough of wanting to vomit at the director's office. Look in the stalls and then let's get out of here," she replied, spying something glimmering in the dirt near the back wall. She stooped down to get a closer look, picking up a broken piece of pure silver ornamentation from a harness or a saddle. "Didn't Jyrah say they rarely had livestock in here?"

"Yes, why?" Kyne asked. He leaned out of the stall he had just entered.

She held up the piece of silver. "This looks like it came from someone's saddle or harness, and whoever owned it has money." She walked to a nook where tack was stored and plundered through old harness that looked like they hadn't been used in years. "Nothing in here to match. I wonder why anyone with means would come here? There are plenty of nicer places all over Muryne."

Kyne burst into laughter.

"What is so funny?" she asked.

"My dear, innocent lady," he couldn't stop laughing. "Certain members of the upper class frequent these types of places when they want to be, uh, discreet, and their own homes won't do. Did you not get a good look at the people in the common room?"

"Yes, I did." Now that she thought about it, while a person can disguise their physical identity if they chose, certain mannerisms that came without thought weren't so easy to hide, and she did see a man pull a lacy handkerchief from a sleeve, which would be something someone with money would own. "Ugh! That's disgusting." She looked at the piece of silver in her hand. It had been round and embossed with a flower, but half of it had broken away. "If they rarely come on horseback, how do they get here?"

"For the most part, they ride in their pretty little carriages and are dropped off a discreet distance away or in an obscure alley such as the one behind you."

Elhrin turned to look out the stable door at the alleyway leading off to the street. Someone could easily enter the inn through the rear entrance without being seen from the street.

"Then the driver comes back at a determined hour to pick them up. Or in this case, they also have the option to travel by boat and dock at the canal steps," he said.

Elhrin nodded her head in agreement, then narrowed her eyes at him. "You certainly know a fair amount on the subject."

"I have been around," he said airily and ducked back into the stall to continue the search. She walked over to the stall door. He held the lamp low and was sweeping his boot through the hay on the floor. "I wonder when the last time ole Jyrah had the barn cleaned." A few piles of dried, decomposing manure were sitting in the moldy hay.

"Looks like it's been awhile," Elhrin commented.

"Indeed," he said absently and pushed past her to search the other stalls.

She decided he had the inside covered, so she stepped outside the barn to have a look around. Breathing in fresh air, she pocketed her handkerchief and scanned the alleyway then walked to the canal steps. Below was a stone platform with two small dinghies tied to a rusty pole. She went down for a closer look, but they were empty save for a coil of rope and the long poles used to propel the boats.

She stared blankly down the waterway. Who would want the man dead besides another member of the M'gelidia? As Jyrah pointed out, the area was rife with cutthroats and thugs, any of which could have done it, and there were plenty of thieves good enough to pick locks, so having a key to the stables did not matter. Maybe it was just a gruesome robbery as Director Allahaim suggested, but that nagging feeling in the back of her mind said otherwise. The fact that the man's eyes were removed screamed that it was the work of the M'gelidia or a killer that was just as deranged as the cult. Then there was the question of the man's missing boots. Why were they taken? Jyrah had said that she had not seen a pair of boots missing their owners, but she had plenty of undergarments if Elhrin wanted to take a look in the bin where she kept everything found left in the inn's rooms. She had Kyne to go through it, but it didn't hold anything related to the murder. Did the killer need a pair of boots? She shook her head slowly at the idea. The missing boots made no sense.

"There you are," Kyne said, standing at the top of the steps. "Did you find anything?"

"No," she said with a hefty sigh and turned to climb up the steps. "Did you?"

"No." He dusted a few trails of cobwebs off of his coat and sniffed the fabric. "I hope I don't smell like rotting meat."

"I hope we both don't. Let's go back inside. I want to ask Jyrah a few more questions and then get out of here. The area has the nasty feel of corruption on a grand scale."

Back inside the dimly lit common room, Kyne led the way through the fog of smoke to a pair of open stools at the bar. Elhrin looked over the crowd. Now that she knew what to look for she could just about guess who was here for a clandestine meeting. One woman oddly darted a glance her way then immediately turned her back to Elhrin. She tried to get a better look at the woman's profile as she sat on the bar stool, but the woman kept her head turned away.

"Would you two like something to eat or drink?" Jyrah asked, as she waddled down the bar aisle, wiping her hands on a greasy rag she had tucked into the sash of her dress.

"No," Elhrin and Kyne said in unison.

"We really must be going, but I wanted to ask you a few more questions," Elhrin said. "Do you remember if you heard anything in the alley that night?"

"No, it gets pretty loud around here at night." She pulled the rag out of her sash and wiped away some spills on the bar. "Hyrim and his wife come in to sing and play their flutes and whatnot right before dinner and they don't leave until late."

It was loud in the room at the moment, so Elhrin thought if there was music too, then it would be hard to hear anything outside.

"And you are positive no one, not even your neighbors, mentioned a fight outside or seeing something odd in the alleyway?"

"Miss, odd things and fights happen around here all the time, but not that night. My neighbors didn't hear or see a thing. I asked. And most of my customers that come in here want to remain anonymous. The last thing they are going to do is talk about witnessing a murder and have people question why they were here."

Elhrin sighed. It was going to be next to impossible to find a witness, if there was one. She leaned back to scan the room. The woman she had noticed earlier was looking at her, but quickly turned her head away again when Elhrin glanced in her direction.

"Can you tell me the names of any of the patrons that came in here that night?" she asked.

"No, I'm afraid I can only tell you the names of the local regulars, but they don't know anything. We've already discussed it 'til it has run itself into the ground, and I can tell you right now they didn't have a thing to do with it. As for the rest," she jerked her head at the patrons in the room, "so many people come and go here I don't catch names, and the ones that come here for their little meetings don't use real names. They use code names like Rooster and Willow, and they disguise their looks so that it is hard to recognize who they really are. Anyways, if I did know their names I'm not about to start rattling them off for you. If word spread we couldn't be trusted, it would ruin my business."

Frustrated, Elhrin nodded at the lady who kept watching her. "Can you at least tell me who the lady is in the large feathery hat near the window?"

Jyrah squinted at the lady in question. "No, she is new—haven't seen her before."

"All right," Elhrin slid off her stool, "that's all I have for now. I'll come back if I think of anything else, and if you have anything new, send a message to the Office of Specialized State Defense in the palace."

"Will do," Jyrah said, and waddled down the bar. The old man, Vic, was asleep in a chair leaned against the wall. She kicked him in the leg. "Vic, you don't have time to sleep. These folks are thirsty!"

Elhrin headed for the front door. This time she got a good look at the woman in the feather hat before the woman had a chance to turn her head away. Now she knew who she was even though she had tried to hide her identity with an elaborate blond wig under the hat and put on a massive amount of makeup. She was the wife of Councilor Vido Andrugh, one of the Junior Councilors from the Western Province and one of Reginold's supporters. He had a bad reputation for creating conflict when it suited his purpose, and for following a more personal agenda without regards to the constituents of the Western Province. To make matters worse, he was just as vocal as Reginold about closing the academy.

Elhrin smiled to herself as she walked out of the dim building and into the bright sunshine. While she couldn't find it in her to respect a person who would actively engage in infidelity, she did have to wonder if it was a just punishment for a self-serving, vindictive man who abused his position in the government for his own gain to have a wife who seemed to care nothing for him.

After nearly an hour of fighting the crowded streets to reach the palace, Elhrin and Kyne made their way to the government offices located in the building's east wing. Master Gryph had an office on the councilor's floor and she could feel his energy source resonating like a pulsing storm from that direction. When they entered the office corridor they found that it was much quieter compared to the rest of the palace. They passed a few assistants and palace staff, but with the council adjourned for the duration of the convention, the councilors not on the trade committee took the opportunity to pursue other interests.

She walked to the end of the hall and stopped in front of an obscure door with no name or decoration like the others along the corridor. She had asked Master Gryph once why he did not at least put his title on the door because it looked like the entrance belonged to a storage closet. He had laughed at her description and said he might just put a plaque inscribed with the words storage closet on the outside of his door. When she pressed for a legitimate answer, he said he knew who he was and where his office was, and if anyone else needed to know, they could ask.

She knocked on the door as she opened it and peeked inside. Master Gryph was alone. He had his elbows propped on his desk and held his head in his hands, but raised his head at her knock. She could tell immediately something was wrong.

"Can we come in?" she asked.

"Please do," he responded and sat back wearily in his chair.

She grasped the back of a chair from a seating arrangement on one side of the room and dragged it to his desk and sat down. Kyne decided to stand beside the window that overlooked the exterior lawn of the palace.

"What's wrong?" she asked.

He picked up a folded paper and offered it to her. It was a simple note written in elegant handwriting.

You are predictable. I knew you couldn't resist. So it begins.

"What is this?" she asked.

"That was on my desk when I arrived earlier. It is a follow up to the letter I received."

"Your letter? You mean the one . . . ?"

He nodded before she finished.

"Who put it here?"

"I don't know. I've asked around, but no one has seen anyone out of the ordinary coming and going down this hall and none of them recall seeing anyone enter my office," he said.

She did not like this at all. If it was this easy to get to his office with guards in the halls, how much harder would it be to get into any of their apartments? She read the note again.

"What does it mean, 'It begins?'"

"It means, he or they, have put their plan in motion."

"And what would the plan be?" Kyne asked.

"To destroy Anderan, my family, me." He opened the bottom drawer of his desk and pulled out a folded document. "I have changed my mind and decided to show you the letter that was sent to me."

Finally, he was being sensible. She reached for the letter and opened it.

To the esteemed Minister of Specialized State Defense, Gryphon Idwyr

Minister, for years you have had the luxury of standing in a position of power, placing yourself above the rest, and basking in the adoration of those who call you hero. That is about to change. I wonder if it ever occurred to you that one day it could all come crashing down around you and that because of you, your country would fall into an age of despair from which it would never recover? The time is now. All is set. Anderan's destruction is assured.

In a few days time, the Trade Convention will begin. You are to stay out of Muryne. If you do, I will give you a short reprieve and leave you and your family, including the two you brought into your household, alone for now. If you make the wrong decision and go, I will have no choice but to proceed with my plans to destroy you personally, beginning with your family, and I don't think you want them to be in my hands. You wouldn't like what I have planned for each of them.

What will you do, So'ladiun? The choice is yours, but if you decide to stay away from Muryne I will offer you one other favor, selfishly of course, and delay your death until everything else has been accomplished. I think I would like to see what the face of the most powerful man in Anderan looks like when all he cherishes no longer exists.

The fate of all is certain, Minister of Specialized State Defense, but you have the power to delay the inevitable. Will you sacrifice family for your country or your country for your family?

Until we meet.

"Is this why you sent for Bayle?" she asked.

He nodded solemnly.

She stared at the letter. Now she understood why he was taking this threat more seriously than any of the others he had received over the years.

"Are you going to tell me who you think sent this?" she asked.

"I have been able to rule out who I had in mind. I am in the dark as much as you are now," he said.

She stared at him, waiting for him to reveal whom he had suspected, but he just raised his eyebrows at her, questioning her silence.

"Well, that was quick. You were able to find out who did not send the letter since talking to me about it last night. Are you or are you not going to tell me whom you had suspected?" she asked again.

He waved a hand in the air dismissively. "It doesn't matter who did not send it at this point. What matters is who did send the letter."

"Ugh, sometimes you make me want to smack you good," she muttered under her breath.

"What did you say?" he asked, cupping one ear.

There was nothing wrong with the man's hearing and she knew he had heard what she had said, but she wasn't about to give him the satisfaction of repeating it.

"I said, it sounds like someone from the M'gelidia. It has to be someone that knows you are So'ladiun," she said.

"Yes, but it doesn't mean whoever it is, is associated with them. Secrets do have a way of getting out no matter how hard we try keeping them hidden. That being said, don't forget about the N'gethwyn."

The N'gethwyn were the So'ladiun's magical opposition who were dedicated to Obsudius, and several had been found to lead small factions of the M'gelidia.

"What about Grom?" she asked, thinking the N'gethwyn they had faced on the journey to Blackridge had to be the one. She knew of no other that had more of a grudge against Master Gryph. Obsudius had allowed the N'gethwyn back into the world through his Rift and Master Gryph had defeated him twice.

Master Gryph shook his head. "A good guess, but for the moment it is not relevant."

She frowned. "What do you mean not relevant? He wasn't sent to the Void."

"No, he wasn't that I am aware of, but his body still lies at Blackridge Keep."

"How is that possible? All of Obsudius' men disintegrated when I closed the Rift, even the dead ones." She was confused. The Rift gave the dead life again once they stepped through from the Realm of the Dead, and Master Gryph had said that the reason the bodies disintegrated was because Obsudius had forgotten to put a condition of life on his portal so that the army would remain alive in the living world once it had closed.

"I can't explain why his body was an exception, but the fact remains, he lies in the keep and until it decays and returns to the earth, he cannot reenter the living world."

She sighed then furrowed her brow. "How do you know he is still there? We never went back into the keep."

"Uh, I did," Kyne said. "I went back to retrieve Jag's knife. I didn't have time to remove it from Grom's body after I killed him so I went back into the keep, and he was still lying there."

"Why didn't you tell me?" she asked.

"If you recall, you didn't like talking to me very much then," he said. "I told Minister Idwyr."

That was true. She didn't like him at all then and barely tolerated him now. She turned her gaze on Master Gryph. "Why didn't *you* tell me?"

"I thought I told you," he said, leaning forward to prop on his desk. "I'm sure I did."

"No, you didn't," she stated, resisting the inclination to wad the letter in her hand and fling it at his head. He was forever forgetting to tell her things. "So, he is still there rotting. It has been almost five years. How long does it take for a body to turn to dust?"

"That depends on conditions surrounding the body, but I made sure it would take as long as possible for him."

"How?" she asked.

"I noticed the caves we went through to get into the keep were cool and extremely dry, so when I went back up north with Goruth to inspect the rebuilding of the town of Blackridge later that year, I had a few workers go with me to the keep to build Grom a proper tomb. I also added a magical crystal seal in case Obsudius wanted to send someone to retrieve his body. I checked on him this past spring. He was still there."

She stared at him in silence. He failed to mention this to her, too. Wouldn't sealing an N'gethwyn's body up in a tomb be something she should know? She looked down at the letter in her lap. What could she do? His natural instinct to keep information to himself was ingrained in him, and she couldn't change it no matter how much she wished she could. He was who he was.

"Okay, so it can't be Grom. What now?"

"For the moment, I think we will pursue the Brothers of M'gelidia theory. We know for a fact that at least one was in the city and where you see one there is a strong possibility there are others."

"Sounds like roaches," Kyne commented.

Master Gryph smiled slightly. "An accurate description, Kyne, and what we need to do is become their exterminators. We will have to locate them as quickly and quietly as we can."

"Good luck with that. Have you been in the city lately? The walls are nearly bursting with the number of people inside, and more are piling in by the minute. How do you expect *us* to find them?" he scoffed, emphasizing the word "us."

"I expect *us* to do what we can," Master Gryph said evenly. He may be frustrating at times, but that was one of the things she loved about Master Gryph. He did not tolerate petulance from anyone, not even an extended member of the royal family.

"We need more help," Kyne pointed out.

"I've already taken care of that," he said. "I sent a message to Grey this morning. I asked him to pick a few Eagles he thought had enough training and escort them here. They should arrive in three days at the latest. I don't think any of them know much about the M'gelidia, so I want the two of you to bring them up to date."

"You are bringing some of our students here?" she asked in surprise. "Master Gryph, what about Councilor Whyse? Don't you think it dangerous to parade members of a fighting force he wants terminated in front of him? What if something goes wrong? It would prove his point and no doubt he would get his wish to shut us down."

"Let's not worry about 'what if's' until we need to, and I will handle Whyse if necessary," he said in a tone that said the subject was not to be discussed further.

He says not to worry. How can one not worry? The whole affair was overwhelming, and to bring barely trained magicians into a potentially hostile situation could mean disaster. "What about the City Guard or the army? Can we get some of them to help us?" Elhrin asked, deciding arguing the point further would be about as productive as tossing sand into ocean waves stirred by a storm one shovelful at a time. It wouldn't make a difference.

He shook his head. "They have their hands full with the crowds. I'm thinking we are on our own with this one for the time being." He stared at the papers on his desk, lost in thought for a moment. "However, I think I will ask Goruth if I can send a message to Chathinwood for help."

"Chathinwood?" Elhrin asked.

"Colonel Chathinwood in Thistle Meadows, he is the closest military post we have. He should be able to spare a few men for a short time. Kyne, will you do me a favor?" Master Gryph picked up a pen, dipped it in an ink well, and scratched something across a piece of note paper. "Find Goruth and give him this for me. I will need to see him before we are to leave for Brodie's Theatre tonight." He put down his pen and held his hand over the note, a small glow emanated from his palm, drying the ink instantly. He then folded the note and handed it to Kyne.

"Yes, sir," Kyne said, taking the note.

"Brodie's Theatre?" Elhrin asked as Kyne crossed the room and quietly closed the office door behind him. "What's happening there tonight?"

Master Gryph grimaced in distaste. "Jaxom Brodie is hosting an invitation-only banquet and show for our foreign guests. He has arranged for various musical and acrobat troupes to come and entertain. I told Goruth we needed to curtail entertainment ventures that go outside the palace, but he says everything is already in place and to change plans unexpectedly would raise concerns we would need to avoid."

"So what do we do?" she asked.

"We keep our eyes open. Goruth is moving men around to add more security." He scrubbed a hand across his chin, smoothing the hairs of his mustache and beard.

"What do you want me to do?"

"I would like for you to watch Marcus for me tonight," he smiled briefly.

Elhrin didn't return his smile. It scared her to the core of her soul that in a place as secure as the Palace of Muryne, he did not feel safe for his son to be left alone with only Bayle watching the baby while he was out of the building, even though Bayle was a highly trained fighter. "I can do that. I will take him to my apartment and have Tomas and Bayle join me. Will that be acceptable?"

"Certainly."

She glanced down to the letter in her lap, thinking how hard it must be to live under the strain of protecting your loved ones when peace is threatened. Marcus was not her brother or her son, but the tension she felt for his safety, loving him as much as she did, could come nowhere near what Master Gryph must be experiencing. "Can I ask you something?"

"You may."

"Do you ever regret it?"

His face took on a puzzled expression.

"I mean, if you could go back in time, knowing what you know now, would you still have married Marguerite? Had Marcus?"

Understanding lit his eyes and he shook his head. "Elhrin, I would not change that part of my life if I could. I don't think I would have made it this far if it hadn't been for Marguerite. She is the light in all the darkness that I face each day. There have been times that I have thought I was selfish because I have brought her into a life of constant turmoil, but I guess every marriage has its turmoil," he chuckled, "ours is just a bit extreme."

Elhrin smiled. "I'd say."

"Now Marcus has entered our life, and his presence has filled a hole I had no idea existed." His eyes drifted to the window, and his face relaxed as he spoke. "Marguerite changed the instant he came into this world. I don't know how to describe it . . . she was like . . . like a beautiful flower bud that had been waiting in the shadow for the sunshine in order to bloom to its full potential. Marcus was her sunshine and she bloomed." He drew in a much needed breath and shook his head slowly. "No, I would not change that for any peace of mind."

Elhrin's eyes had filled with moisture as he spoke. He turned his eyes on her, and she quickly looked down to hide her tears.

"Elhrin, the life of a So'ladiun is hard. I have told you before that it will be up to you to choose what path to follow. I know firsthand. I have lived on both sides of the fence of love."

Elhrin snorted at the analogy.

"That wasn't very eloquent, was it? My point is I have denied myself love and lived in its emptiness. Now I am surrounded by love, and it sustains me when nothing else can. Do you understand?"

She nodded silently, and he cocked his head to one side. "Has Tomas asked you to marry him?"

Damn, he was good at guessing her thoughts. She cleared her throat. "Um, he uh, actually, the subject has come up a few times."

"And you have put him off," he stated.

"Master Gryph, there's just so much going on. Both of us have been busy, and we rarely see each other. How could we even begin to live as a couple . . . where would we live? I just don't think it is the right time. Especially now," she threw a hand in the air, exasperated.

"Hold on," he chuckled. "You don't have to run off to the priest right this minute."

"I know," she said. "It's just that it shouldn't be this hard. I do love him, but I understand why you had reservations about marriage and children before you married Marguerite. Worrying about the danger, I just . . . ," she said, stopping what she had meant to say when there was an unexpected pounding on the office door.

"Minister, are you in there?" called an angry voice. He pounded on the door again, rattling the hinges.

Master Gryph frowned deeply at the overly aggressive interruption. "I think he is trying to break my door," he growled in irritation. With a casual wave of his hand, he opened the door with his powers.

In mid-knock, Director Allahaim was momentarily surprised by the door opening by itself but then placed his customary scowl back on his face and lowered his fist. He was not alone. Behind him stood the same young detective he had ordered to leave with him when she and Kyne visited his office that morning and a colonel of the City Guard.

"Is there something I can do for you, Nygill?" Master Gryph asked coolly.

The director stalked across the room with his man in tow who respectfully removed his hat when he entered the room. The colonel trudged in behind them and ended up standing behind Elhrin's chair. He was a portly man, with a slash of thin hair that rode over the top of his scalp and long, bushy sideburns that covered his jowly cheeks and half his neck. Elhrin could hear the man breathing audibly, making her feel like he was breathing down her neck. She had to fight the urge to leap out of her chair and stand next to Master Gryph.

"We have a problem," Director Allahaim said, glancing briefly at Elhrin then dismissing her as if she was of no importance. He flung three tattered scraps of paper onto the desk.

Master Gryph sifted through them. "Where did you get these?" he asked as he held them out for Elhrin to take. They were notes identical to the one he had shown her the night before, and they all had the same message.

My Brother, I have been waiting for our meeting. It has been a long time. I regret that I cannot be more specific as to when or where we will meet, and will have to leave it to fate to deem the time and the place, but rest assured, it will be soon.

"On more hanging bodies with their eyes cut out of their damn heads," Director Allahaim almost shouted. "Do you know what this is going to cause? A damn panic if it gets out, and that's the last thing we need right now."

So it begins, flashed through Elhrin's mind.

"Where were the bodies found?" Master Gryph asked.

"One was in a warehouse in the Mid-Isle District near the City Market. Another was hanging in a wooded area of Lundsbury Park, and one of his guards," he jerked his head at the colonel, "found the last one a half-hour ago swinging from just inside the canal gate in the city wall between the upper and lower city, and I'll be damned if I don't know how the killer did it without someone seeing him hang a body in broad daylight, especially since word that the delegation from Nabafin arrived. That entire area was filled with people."

"That could be your answer. Everyone was so focused on the Nabafinese they didn't pay attention to anything else. The inside of the canal gates aren't that easy to see unless you are on the water," Master Gryph said, crossing his arms across his chest. "Tell me about the victims."

"We found out the man in the warehouse was here for the duration of the convention, sir," the colonel of the City Guard said, his voice sounding as if he was rattling rocks around in a wood cup. "His wife reported him missing to one of my men stationed at the market yesterday evening. They are from the village of Kit and have a stall where they sell jewelry made from seashells and the like. He left her to go get them something to eat and never returned. One of the warehouse workers discovered him hanging behind a stack of crates this morning."

Director Allahaim picked up a pile of three metal rings that were hooked together from Master Gryph's desktop and inspected them. "A kid ran across the second body hidden in a stand of trees next to one of the canals. The body probably wouldn't have been found if he hadn't gone in there to hide from his friends. We don't know who the dead man is yet, and before you ask, no, he didn't have the wolf tattoo on him. None of the bodies did," Director Allahaim said. He held up the metal rings. "What the shit is this?"

"A puzzle," Master Gryph replied, "you are to try and separate the rings."

Director Allahaim pulled on the rings and grunted. "I don't see how. Anyway, the last body is going to cause quite a stir. It's Councilor Andrugh's wife."

"What?" Elhrin said in shock and sat straight up in her chair. Director Allahaim looked at her with distaste, as if her outburst was an unwelcome interruption to a private conversation. She ignored the look. "Did she have on a peacock feather printed dress, and a matching feather hat?"

"The dress fits. Was there a hat, Jake?" he asked the young man standing off to the side.

"No, sir," he answered, thumbing the brim of his bowl-shaped hat. "Besides the note, the only personal effects on her body were a gold necklace with a rose pendant and three rings on her fingers."

Director Allahaim eyed Elhrin suspiciously. "How do you know what she had on, runt?"

Elhrin stiffened. She didn't care for him calling her a runt. "She was at the Canal Street Inn when Captain Pittwold and I went there this morning."

"Was she with anyone?" Master Gryph asked.

"Yes," Elhrin tried to remember, but she had been so focused on seeing the woman's face, she couldn't recall any of the details of who had been with her. "A man, I think."

Allahaim sighed with disgust. "Minister, if this one can't pay attention to simple details you need to find someone who can."

"Nygill, she does just fine." Master Gryph's face immediately smoothed over. He was angry. She hoped it wasn't because she couldn't remember who had been with councilor's wife.

"Was there anything else of interest on the other body besides the note?" Master Gryph asked with a hint of steel in his tone.

"I don't know. Our men haven't finished with him, yet. I'll send you the final reports when they do," Allahaim said.

"Good enough. Has the councilor been informed of his wife's death?"

"We informed him prior to coming here," he shook his head with a frown. "He didn't seem too bothered by the news. Almost as if he was relieved, wouldn't you say, Jake?"

"No, sir, he seemed more concerned by the fact he had to go with Allyn to identify the body than by her murder," Jake said.

"Strange, these politicians," Director Allahaim said. "Anyway, Minister, I need you to take over this entire affair. My men and I are up to our asses in more work than we can keep up with, and right now I've got to quell a hostile situation with the Chyrzinians," he growled, waving the metal rings at Master Gryph and Elhrin. "We'll cover any initial reports that come into my office, but I thought you and mush-for-brains could handle it after that and find the one who is doing this, since you don't have anything better to do than coddle the foreigners."

Master Gryph froze, then slowly unfolded his arms from his chest, and placed both hands on the desk. "Director, let me remind you that part of my job is to protect our foreign guests while they are on our soil, and that doing so will consume a great deal of my time. However, this situation is of utmost importance, and I can assure you that I will do whatever it takes to handle it, as well. I might suggest you do the same. It would be unwise for you to let go of the investigation altogether, do you not think so?"

"Don't tell me how to do my job, Minister," Director Allahaim growled.

"I would never presume to do so." He held out his hand to Elhrin. At first she was puzzled, but then realized he wanted the papers she held and handed them to him. He slipped them into the interior pocket of his coat. "But as you said before, the deaths are going to amplify a bad situation with as many people as we have in the city. Something like this will be hard to keep secret, and I'm sure the news is already spreading throughout the city. It won't take long for the newspapers to be printing the story, so the public needs to see a concerted effort that we will ensure their safety or your prediction of widespread panic will come to pass."

"I agree," the colonel said. "The City Guard will do what we can, Minister, but I am afraid it won't be much."

"Any help is appreciated, Colonel Drurhey. Actually," he sifted through papers on his desk and pulled out a document with the Brothers of M'gelidia's wolf design on it. He handed it to Elhrin. "Give this to Colonel Drurhey for me, Elhrin. Colonel, if you could pass that around to your men and tell them if they see anyone with a tattoo resembling the wolf or this sign anywhere else they are to send word to me or to my assistant. The more eyes we have in the streets, the better off we are."

"Yes, sir," the colonel responded, looking at the page Elhrin handed him.

Master Gryph turned his attention back to the director who seemed to be studying the colonel closely for some reason. "Well, what say you, Nygill?" he asked.

Director Allahaim shifted his gaze to Master Gryph and nodded. "All right, I will put Jake here on it. He'll have the reports to you by morning." He jerked his chin at Elhrin. "Maybe he can teach your tiny lap dog a thing or two about paying attention to detail."

Flushing red, Jake glanced at Elhrin, as if apologizing for his employer's rude behavior.

Director Allahaim tossed the rings on Master Gryph's desk. "It's one of your tricks, isn't it, Minister. They can't be separated," he growled, then turned on his heel and headed for the door. "Jake, let's go."

Master Gryph picked up the rings. "Director, one other thing," he called out, before Director Allahaim and his detective reached the door.

"What is it?" Director Allahaim snapped.

"I know you are under quite a bit of pressure at the moment. However, I will require a little more respect from you. My assistant's name is Elhrin Caddoch, and from now on, you will only refer to her by her given name. Do I make myself clear?" With a quick series of twists Master Gryph separated all three rings and held them up for the director. "It is no trick."

Director Allahaim glared at him for a moment then stalked out the door. Elhrin thought she heard him mumble "damn magician" under his breath before he left the room. Looking uncomfortable, his young detective quietly closed the door behind them.

"Why does he hate me?" Elhrin asked, releasing a breath she hadn't realized she had been holding.

"Don't take it personally. He gets ugly when there is more work than his office can handle and right now they are drowning in it." He placed the rings on his desk and looked over her head at the Colonel. "Was there something else I could help you with, Colonel?"

"Minister, I wanted to ask a favor, if I may. The guard is basically in the same situation as Director Allahaim's office. The city is over capacity and I have received no orders as to regulating the influx of people into the city proper. Also, the size of the population outside the city gates is enormous and growing. I have spoken to the road patrol about possibly stopping any more travelers from coming to the city who do not need to be here, but they say they are unable to do anything unless they receive orders from army headquarters. General Pyrthenius does not have time to see me, so I wanted to know if it would be possible for you to do something about it. The crowds are becoming too large, and even with the army backing us up, we are still hard pressed to remain in control, especially at night when it seems nearly every street is filled with drunken revelers."

Master Gryph shook his head and pulled a blank sheet of paper from a wooden bin on his desk. "You would think no one in this city has ever handled a major event before," he murmured, dipping his pen in the nearby inkwell and scratching something across the paper.

"You're left-handed?" the colonel burst out in surprise.

Master Gryph's pen froze and he looked up at the colonel with a frown.

"It's just unusual, I mean most," the colonel harrumphed uncomfortably, "yes, uh, sorry to interrupt, please continue."

Master Gryph returned his attention back to the paper. Silence filled the room except for the scratching of his pen, and the heavy breathing coming from the colonel. Elhrin thought she felt the back of her hair move with each breath as Master Gryph finished with one sheet and started on another. Seeing he was going to take a while, she decided to go look out the window. She couldn't take the colonel breathing on her anymore.

Master Gryph glanced up at her when she stood. She pointed at the window, letting him know she wasn't leaving. He smiled knowingly and continued writing.

His office overlooked the side lawn of the palace. Gravel paths that skirted next to the palace and the distant canal branched off to meet in the center of the lawn where a circular dais with a statue of a man in flowing robes holding an upraised burning sun stood in the glow of the late afternoon light. The statue was one artist's interpretation of Solisius. Knowing the statue looked nothing like him, she wondered if Solisius ever saw it and what he thought of the piece.

I like it, the voice of her god surprised her, *but he did get my nose too big.*

She grinned at the same time she heard a small grunt of laughter come from behind her.

"Something wrong, Minister?" the colonel asked. Elhrin knew the man hadn't heard Solisius. Only the So'ladiun were capable of hearing their god's voice.

"No," Master Gryph said, smiling. He was sealing three documents with a drop of wax from a burning candle. He then pressed a heavy metal stamp with the seal of his office into the warm blobs and handed the letters to the colonel.

Solisius, are you still here? I want to talk to you about my dream concerning Marcus. She silently called out, but he did not respond. She was not surprised. He flitted in and out of her awareness like a beautiful butterfly seeking the nectar of the next flower.

"One of those is for you, Drurhey," Master Gryph said. "It is an order for the City Guard to enforce a curfew starting at midnight at which time all gates into the city proper will be closed to any non-resident wanting into the city unless it is an emergency. The gates can reopen prior to dawn. As for during the day, there's not much you can do at this point without causing a riot. I know it will be difficult, but you and your men will need to be patient with the crowd. I do not want to hear of any harassment on our part, understood?"

"Yes, sir." The colonel nodded in agreement.

"The other two documents are for General Pyrthenius. Send them to him for me, if you will. I have informed him that I ordered the gates to be closed at night, and I have requested he take actions necessary to regulate the influx of our citizens still making their way here from around the country. I have no authority in the affairs of the King's Army or the Road Patrol unless we are at war, so we will have to be satisfied with whatever he decides to do. If I see the general before those reach him, I will speak of the matter then."

"Thank you, sir, for your help," the colonel said and started for the door, but then hesitated. "Minister, do you think His Majesty will have a problem with the order to close the gates?"

Elhrin had wondered the same thing. To close the gates was a major act, and unless the city was under attack, the order usually had to come directly from King Goruth himself.

"I will inform him of my actions, but as I said before, it is my responsibility to ensure the safety of our guests. I deem this a safety issue. Therefore, this falls into my jurisdiction."

"I understand, sir," Colonel Drurhey acknowledged. He saluted briefly, then turned and trudged out the door.

Master Gryph slapped both palms on the arms of his chair and pushed himself up out of it, scraping it across the marble floor. "Well, I am beginning to think whoever sent me that letter might also have something to do with these murders. We have our work cut out for us, don't we, my girl?" He searched through the papers on his desk, picking up those he wanted to carry with him.

"Yes, we do," she said, pondering the facts she knew so far surrounding the bodies. "So the note on the first body was no accident. Do you think we should rule out the Brothers of M'gelidia now?"

"Well, the way the victims are murdered is reminiscent of their work, but purposely leaving the bodies out in the open with notes on their person does not coincide with the

Brother's secretive, low-profile methods. However, we won't rule them out altogether as of yet."

The words King Goruth spoke to Reginold Whyse the day before flashed like lightning through her mind. "What does your intuition tell you?" she asked.

"It is strangely silent at the moment," he said with a chuckle, as he picked up one last document off his desk and looked it over.

Elhrin wrinkled her nose at his answer. "That's not good, is it?" she laughed.

"It doesn't always show up when I need it."

He straightened the papers in his hand and folded them together.

"Why do you think the killer removes the eyes?" Elhrin asked.

"I really don't know. It could be symbolism of some kind or . . . ," he tapped the stack of papers on top of his desk, thinking. "Nygill said they were swamped with crimes. It could be the killer needed to make sure they stood out from the rest of the crimes in the city. I would say hanging a few bodies with their eyes gone gets one's attention."

"That's an understatement," she observed. "Okay, if it's to draw attention, who for? Us? The director's force?"

"Maybe, or to whomever is supposed to read that note. It spoke of a meeting," he pondered out loud. "I'm wondering if the locations of the bodies are not just random choices."

"You think they might have something to do with where this meeting is supposed to take place?" Elhrin asked.

"Could be." He walked to a bookshelf filled with stacks of books, papers, and rolled-up maps. He rifled through the maps, but didn't find what he was looking for. "Well, what did I do with it?" He scanned the rest of his office then smacked the papers he had in his hand against his thigh. "That's right. I took it to the apartment. Elhrin, I have a map of the city in my bedroom. Remind me to get it before I leave tonight. You and the boys can go over it while I'm gone."

"Okay, but what about the crime scenes? Do you want me to go take a look at them?"

"Let's let Allahaim's men finish their work first. You and Kyne can go after we read the reports his man delivers in the morning. Come to think of it, if I can work it out, I will go with you." He tucked the documents into the interior pocket of his coat and placed an arm around her shoulders to guide her out of his office and into the hallway. "You know, you and Kyne never got around to telling me what you found this morning."

"Oh, I forgot," she said, feeling like a fool. That was her whole purpose for going to his office in the first place. How could she have gotten so sidetracked? "I'm sorry."

He squeezed her shoulder. "Don't apologize. I'm the one who threw you off by showing you my letter. So what did you two find?"

She briefly told him of the inn and that they hadn't found much of anything that would help them. She pulled the piece of broken silver from her pocket and gave it to him. "I found this in the dirt of the stable floor, but I don't think it has anything to do with the murder."

He squinted at it for a moment then stopped to hold it up to a nearby oil sconce hanging on the wall. "It's a piece of bridle ornamentation . . . pure silver. The bridle would have been expensive . . . a bit unusual for an inn frequented by sailors."

"Kyne said the inn was a place where members of the upper class meet to, uh, to uh . . . ." She stammered, feeling her face flush.

"Have a clandestine affair?" he asked.

"Yes, sir," she said, refusing to look at him. She couldn't figure out why she was embarrassed to talk to him about the subject. It wasn't as if she was one of the patrons. "And the Councilor's wife was there with someone other than her husband."

"Yes, that is a bit of a sticky situation. Elhrin, it would be helpful if you could try and figure out who she was with—we need to talk with him."

"I know. I'll try."

"Ask Kyne. He may remember—he is fairly adept at noticing the little things most of us overlook."

"So I've noticed," she commented. Kyne seemed to see everything. She mentally kicked herself for not being more vigilant.

He looked at the bridle piece one last time. "I can't get past the feeling I've seen this design before," he said pocketing the piece. "Maybe it'll come to me later. Come along, dear."

They continued down the long empty hall and passed the office of Councilor Whyse. His door was ajar and she could see him leaning against the front of his desk in a quiet discussion with Councilor Idora. He glanced at them briefly, taking note of their passage. She saw him grimace in distaste, and Councilor Idora turned to see who he was looking at before Elhrin moved out of the two councilor's view.

Elhrin glanced up at Master Gryph and found him scowling fiercely. "What is it?" she asked, thinking he was displeased at seeing the two councilors together, but then a foreign energy source touched her awareness. Someone with magical abilities was nearing the city. "Do you know who it is?"

He shook his head. "No, but I would like to find out," he said as they walked out of the council's office corridor and into the main passageway leading back to the grand hall.

She focused on what the source felt like, cool with edges of fire. Each source was unique to the individual, and she realized with a start that this one was vaguely familiar. It wasn't any of their students. They both would have recognized them immediately if it had been. Then it dawned on her. "Wait, I know who it is. It's the girl I was telling you about, Marissa, from Jarit's Cove. I guess she decided to come after all."

"Ah," he said, visibly relaxing. "She must not have thought too hard on it to be here just a day after you arrive. This is good."

"Elhrin, Minister Idwyr," Kyne called from a stairway they had just passed. They stopped to wait on him. "I delivered your note. His Majesty said for you and Madam Idwyr to join him in the gold sitting room whenever you are ready to leave for the theatre. You are to ride with him and Queen Egeria."

"Since when did he decide that?" Master Gryph frowned. "That was not the original plan."

Kyne looked a little uncomfortable. "He mentioned something about making sure you were right where you were supposed to be for a change. That he had distinctly requested you to be in the meeting he was currently in, and you never showed up." Kyne shrugged.

"He did? Ah," Master Gryph reached into his coat's interior and pulled out a stack of documents. He separated a letter sealed with the royal stamp from the stack. "That must be what this is. I had some things to take care of this afternoon and forgot all about it. No matter, I don't think the terms of the trade documents they are going over require my attention, anyway."

Elhrin smiled, knowing he had conveniently forgotten he had the summons in order to miss the meeting. King Goruth had just wanted him to be there in an advisory role, but if Master Gryph felt like he had something of more importance to attend to, he would skip the meeting. He was the only person in the entire country King Goruth would allow to get away with disobeying a direct summons.

"Is he still in the meeting?"

Kyne nodded. Master Gryph retraced Kyne's steps to the stairway but stopped before he went up. "Elhrin, go find our new student and bring her here. I would prefer her to be in a safe location than trying to find a place to stay somewhere out there. If there is time, I would like to meet her before I leave tonight."

"Yes, sir." She grabbed Kyne's arm and pulled him down the corridor. "Come on. It's back out into the city for us."

"Great," Kyne drawled the word out, "and here I thought there was a nice glass of aged Martaline Red and something to eat in my near future."

Chapter Six

It had taken Elhrin and Kyne over an hour to navigate the city streets and locate Marissa, who had her fiancée Clay with her, and convince the two of them to return to the palace. Then, when Marissa saw the palace, she became overwhelmed and refused to go any further, claiming her clothes were dirty and she didn't have anything to wear inside such an elegant building. Elhrin had stood on the bridge spanning the canal leading to the palace grounds, arguing with the girl for a good quarter of an hour and trying to convince her that she was sufficiently dressed when Kyne took the matter into his own hands. He had grabbed the woman firmly by the arm and propelled her sputtering and cursing all the way to Master Gryph's apartment door. He had then told her to shut her mouth and watch her manners because she was about to meet the most kind-hearted, sophisticated lady in the entire country, and it wouldn't do for Madam Idwyr to hear the foul language that was oozing out of Marissa's mouth. Marissa may have given him a heated look that could have seared the skin right off his body, but she did clamp her lips tight and said not another word.

Now, as they sat talking quietly with Marguerite, Elhrin noticed that Marissa had overcome her anger towards Kyne and the obvious initial awkwardness she felt in Marguerite's presence. Of course, that was because Marguerite had a way of making anyone feel comfortable. When she had first walked out of her bedroom in her formal evening attire, Elhrin thought Marissa was going to bolt for the apartment door, but Marguerite did not give the girl a chance to move and had opened her arms wide and welcomed the two strangers as if she had known them her entire life.

Elhrin smiled to herself. Seeing the blatant shock on Marissa's face when Marguerite hugged both the girl and Clay without concern of soiling her attire from their dusty travel clothes had been worth the hassle of dragging the reluctant girl to the apartment.

"How nice, Marissa. I, too, am an innkeeper's daughter, but my father passed a few years back. Two of my brothers now operate it," Marguerite said, handing Marcus the small carved horse he had just tossed in her lap. He flopped down on the floor to run the horse across the rug, making soft clip-clopping sounds with his tongue as he followed his horse under the marble-top table. "And, Clay, you said you were a fisherman by trade?"

"Yes, Madam Idwyr," he responded, nervously bouncing one knee. Marissa placed a hand on his leg to make him stop. "My father and I supply the locals in both Jarit's Cove and Wilderness Camp on the northeast shore of Wyndermir Lake."

"Minister Idwyr will be extremely happy to have someone new to trade fishing tales with," Marguerite laughed. "There are two rivers in Glimmerdale, and he spends any free time he has standing on their banks with a pole in his hand. I'm sure he will corner you into joining him when he does. Speaking of him, if he doesn't get here soon, he will have no time to change. Elhrin, is he still in King Goruth's office?"

Elhrin scanned the palace for his energy source and found him moving towards the apartment, but then his source froze in one place which most likely meant someone had stopped him in the hallway to speak to him.

"He is still in the east wing, but he is on his way here," she responded. Marissa stared at her with a bewildered expression. The girl did not know how to recognize energy sources which was one of the first things she would need to learn.

"Good. Now, Marissa, I know you are excited about joining the Glimmerdale Academy, and we are all delighted that you are here, but I am afraid the mother in me has to ask you a few questions."

Marissa looked a little apprehensive. "Yes, Madam?"

"You and Clay are how old?"

"I am twenty-one, and Clay is twenty-three," she answered.

"That is good. You are old enough to make your own decisions. What did your parents think about our program? I don't think I recall you saying."

Marissa's face flushed red, making the freckles spattered across her face deepen in color, and Clay suddenly became extremely interested in smoothing out the dents in the hat he held in his lap.

Kyne barked a short laugh. "I know what that means," he said.

Marguerite raised an eyebrow at him, and Kyne had the good sense to quickly wipe the smile off of his face. Claiming he was thirsty, he uncrossed his legs and rose from his chair, walking to the nearby sideboard to pour himself a glass of wine.

"Uh, Madam, they, that is, I left my parents a note saying I was joining the academy. Clay's father is across the lake in the wilderness camp so he left him a note, too." Marissa looked like she might bolt for the door again.

"Marissa, since you are an adult we do not require your parent's permission for you to be a student, but I would like to know that your parents are agreeable with you being here. Did you discuss this with them at all?" Marguerite asked.

Visibly miserable, Marissa looked down at her lap and silently nodded.

A loud whinny came from the floor. Elhrin bent over to look under the table. Marcus was on his back, running his horse along the underside of the table. She tapped the rug with her fingertips to attract his attention. He looked at her and whinnied again. She beckoned him with a finger. He rolled from under the table and climbed into her lap.

"They weren't too happy with you leaving, were they?" Marguerite asked.

"It wasn't because of the academy, Madam Idwyr. My father is not especially fond of Clay, and he knew I wouldn't leave unless Clay was going. He said the only way he would allow me to go to the academy was if Clay stayed in Jarit's Cove."

"Ah, I see," Marguerite pursed her lips. "Is he aware of your betrothal?"

Marissa wouldn't look up from her lap. Finally, she shook her head no.

"I didn't think so. Well, there is nothing we can do about this tonight, but would you mind if I sent your father a letter and let him know you are here and are safe? I am sure both your parents are worried about you."

Marissa shook her head. "No, Madam, I wouldn't mind."

The apartment door opened and Master Gryph ducked inside. He stopped short at the sight of Marguerite. "My, my, my, now that is a sight I could never tire of . . . why, I should tell . . . ."

"Gryph," Marguerite interrupted him, smiling, "we have guests."

He chuckled. "So we have." Clay and Marissa nervously stood. He waved them down. "Sit, sit, we aren't formal here."

He limped over to Marguerite and placed a kiss on her cheek. "I don't know if I will allow you in public, my dear," he said.

She rolled her eyes.

"You must be Marissa and Clay the fisherman." He shook each of their hands. Both of them looked like they wanted to be anywhere but in the room at the moment. "Elhrin has told me you are interested in our academy," he said as he let go of Marissa's hand and started to unbutton his coat.

"Yes, sir," Marissa said so low her answer was almost silently mouthed words.

Elhrin couldn't blame her for being nervous. One of their youngest students had wet his pants when he met Master Gryph for the first time. He was an intimidating figure if one didn't know him. Unusually tall and solid as an oak tree, and the way he held himself screamed power to anyone, but for Marissa his presence was doubly intimidating because his energy source flooded the apartment and the girl's magical senses were being bombarded without her knowledge.

"How long have you been aware of your abilities?" he asked, flashing a small knowing smile towards Elhrin as he purposely put distance between him and Marissa by moving to stand behind Marguerite's chair. The space wouldn't make a difference at all to the girl's magical senses, but visually it would take some of the pressure off her.

"Since I was a girl, sir, maybe about ten or so," she murmured a little louder, but not by much.

"Hmm, I wonder why I haven't met you before now. Have you always lived in Jarit's Cove?"

"No, sir, we moved there about four or five years ago. I was born in a settlement north of Salidair."

"That would explain it. I don't think I have been to a settlement north of Salidair."

"Most people don't know it's there, sir," she said. "There is not much to the place. It's just a few people thrown together looking for gold. My father ran a tap room until he learned that Jarit's Cove was growing rapidly and business owners were making a steady living. So we moved."

"Jarit's Cove is growing," Master Gryph agreed as he moved to sit in the chair beside Marguerite.

"Don't you dare sit down," Marguerite ordered. "You need to change for dinner."

"I know. I know," he answered, patting her on the shoulder. "Marissa, Elhrin tells me you are able to conjure water. Would you mind demonstrating for me before my wife hauls me into the bedroom by my ear?"

Kyne choked loudly on his drink. "Sorry, just had a mental picture of that," he apologized when he saw all eyes had turned his way.

Marissa's face was white as a ghost. She looked as if Master Gryph had suggested she jump off a cliff.

"Gryph, the girl is not ready, and you have to get dressed. Could . . . ?" He held a hand up for her to be quiet. She set her lips in a firm line and furrowed her brow. That was one quick way to make the lady mad. It didn't matter how it was done or who did it—no one told Marguerite to be quiet.

"Marissa, in the academy you will be asked to do a great many things that you won't like or will be afraid to do. One of the things we work on is overcoming fear. Right now, you are safe. There is nothing to be afraid of by demonstrating your natural abilities for me."

She stared open-mouthed at him for a minute until she finally nodded. She rose from her seat and wiped her palms on her dress. Despite his attempt to put the girl at ease, the glance she shot Elhrin was full of fear.

Elhrin assured her with a nod and a small smile. "This part is easy," she said.

Marcus took that moment to put the head of his toy horse in his mouth and make loud swooshing sounds as he jiggled the toy between his teeth. Marissa laughed nervously at the child and Elhrin gently removed the horse from his mouth.

"Shh, little one, let's watch the lady, okay?" she whispered in Marcus' ear.

"She has red hair," he said loudly and pointed at Marissa's head.

"I know, shh, okay?" she asked before his father could reprimand him.

He nodded, and for once, sat still.

"Sir, I will need a container of some kind," Marissa whispered with a slight quiver in her voice, "to hold the water."

"No problem," he snapped his fingers. Kyne's wine glass was jerked from his hand and it flew over Marguerite's head to land with a smack into Master Gryph's palm without spilling a drop of its contents. "Will this do?"

Marissa nodded, wide-eyed.

"I wasn't finished with that," Kyne complained.

"You are now," Master Gryph said. He dumped the wine into a potted plant on the table and handed it to Marissa. Her hand shook as she raised the glass where they could all see. She stared intently at the glass, concentrating. Slowly, a clear liquid mixed with the residual remnants of Kyne's red wine that had pooled in the bottom of the glass, creating a swirl of purple within as the level of water rose to the top of the glass.

"Impressive," Master Gryph commented as Marissa let go of her magic and lowered the glass. "Now, is filling up a container the only way you can do this feat or can you make the water, say, fall through the air like rain?"

"No, sir, I have never tried to do it any other way," she said, still trembling, and had to grasp the shaking glass with both hands to keep from spilling its contents.

"You will," he stared at the glass for a moment, lost in thought, then realized he had other things to do that couldn't wait any longer. "I guess I had better go change. Elhrin, I think you should begin our student's lessons right away, and ask someone if there is a room available in the palace. I would rather she be close by."

"I have already taken care of that, Gryph," Marguerite spoke up. "The palace is overflowing so they will take Bayle's room and he will move in here. I have sent him to look for a cot and retrieve his belongings. I thought you would approve. This way he doesn't have to traipse back and forth to babysit Marcus and me."

"Excuse me?" he asked, cutting his eyes at Elhrin.

She held up a hand. "I didn't say anything."

"Don't look at Elhrin, Gryphon Idwyr. She didn't reveal your secret, as much as I would have loved for her to do so. I know what you have been doing and I have been waiting on you to get around to telling me why you feel we need a bodyguard. How much longer are you going to make me wait?"

"Tonight," he said simply, "when we get back from the theatre."

Focused on the older couple's conversation, Marissa stooped over to put her glass on the table but misjudged where she was placing the glass. It toppled to the floor, spilling the water on the rug.

"Oh, Madam Idwyr, I am so sorry," she cried, quickly picking up the glass.

"Don't worry about it, dear, it is only water," Marguerite said and stood up. The skirt of her form-fitting black and white velvet gown whispered to the floor, covering the soft black boots she wore completely. "Kyne, would you retrieve a cloth out of the sideboard for me?"

"I've got it, Kyne," Master Gryph said as he used his magic to scoop the spill from the floor. It rose into the air as a quivering ball of liquid. Marcus sat up abruptly at the sight of the rising ball of water.

"Papa, can I touch it?" Marcus asked as he squirmed out of Elhrin's lap to the floor.

"You may." He lowered the ball of water so it was level with Marcus' head. "Marissa, Elhrin tells me you know how to move things with your powers."

Marissa nodded. "Yes, sir, but just small things. I tried to move a bed once, but couldn't."

Marcus poked the floating blob with a tiny finger. When he withdrew his finger, it glistened. He squealed with delight and repeatedly jabbed his finger into the shaking mass, causing multiple ripples to cross round the globe of water. Elhrin was impressed that Master Gryph was able to hold its shape without Marcus splattering water all over the floor.

"Manipulating any object can be tricky, and when you add size and weight, you are then subject to the strength of your own abilities . . . much like if you were to try and pick up Clay using your arms and then walking across the room with him. You might be able to pick him up, but he is heavy and cumbersome and unless you are used to carrying him around on a frequent basis, you would be limited as to how far you could go with him before you would either have to let him down or be forced to drop him." He had to stop to take a breath. "Your magical source of energy is limited in the same way. Sometimes we can exceed our strengths, but we have to be careful when we do so. To continually extend our use of power beyond our limits puts us in danger of destroying ourselves. You will be taught how to recognize the point where you must cease use of your powers." He paused, nodding to himself. "You are a strong one, my dear. You will no doubt be able to move things twice your size once you are trained."

"Gryph, I'm sorry to interrupt, but you really must change," Marguerite said. "You can talk to her later when you have more time."

"All right, dear. Marcus, you heard mother," Master Gryph said. "Time to get rid of it."

Marcus poked the floating blob one last time as Master Gryph waved his hand and the door to the balcony flew open. He then lobbed the quivering ball of liquid at the open door. It elongated into an arc and trailed out the doorway and over the balcony rail.

They heard a distant shriek of surprise come from below. "Son of a bitch! My new dress," a woman screamed.

Kyne doubled over with laughter and Elhrin had to join him.

"Gryph, that sounded like Wileena Tamborden." Marguerite tried, but couldn't contain a wide grin. "She is very particular about her attire and will kill you if she finds out it was you who dumped water on her."

"I'll be sure to avoid her. She is one scary woman," he chuckled, starting for his bedroom door, but then stopped suddenly. "Oh, Marguerite, did you have my ring cleaned?" he asked, holding up his right hand. A pale line encircled his fourth finger where he usually wore his signet ring.

"No," she said, raising her eyebrows, "you never gave it to me."

"I most certainly did," he said pointing to where the ring should be on his finger. "Do you see it on my finger?"

"Don't be smart with me, Gryph. You said you were going to give it to me when you finished dressing, but you went off to your meeting without doing so."

He frowned down at the floor in thought. "I must have left it in the bedroom. Marcus, do you want to help papa look for his ring?" he asked striding into his room. Excited, because he knew his papa would turn the search into a game, Marcus was right on his heels.

"You don't have time to look for that ring, get changed," Marguerite called after him just as Marcus turned to place both hands on the backside of the door and slam it shut with a resounding bang.

Marguerite glanced at Elhrin. "Do you think he shut the door well enough?"

"It sure sounded like it," Elhrin laughed.

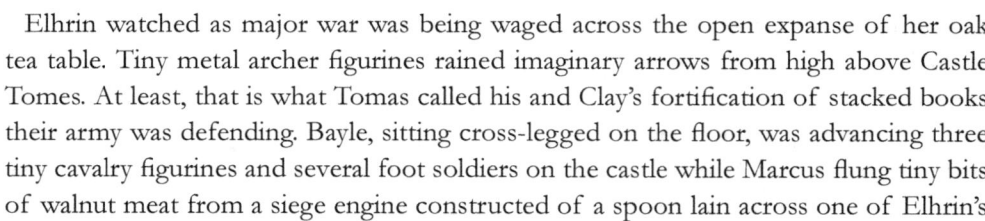

Elhrin watched as major war was being waged across the open expanse of her oak tea table. Tiny metal archer figurines rained imaginary arrows from high above Castle Tomes. At least, that is what Tomas called his and Clay's fortification of stacked books their army was defending. Bayle, sitting cross-legged on the floor, was advancing three tiny cavalry figurines and several foot soldiers on the castle while Marcus flung tiny bits of walnut meat from a siege engine constructed of a spoon lain across one of Elhrin's pens.

"Hey, you're not supposed to take out your own army," Bayle complained after Marcus' latest flight of walnut missiles rained down on Bayle's hand and knocked over several soldiers.

Marcus giggled.

"Are you laughing?" Bayle asked, and Marcus bobbed his head enthusiastically. "That does it. You have admitted to sabotage. I think you are a spy, and I am forced to administer punishment." Bayle held up both hands, flexing his fingers threateningly. "Prepare yourself for your fate, traitor." He grabbed Marcus and began to tickle him. Marcus squealed with laughter and tried to scramble out of Bayle's grasp but couldn't get away.

"Don't make him sick. He just ate," Elhrin laughed as Marcus finally wriggled out of Bayle's grasp and hid under the table.

"He's tough. He can take it." Bayle grabbed Marcus' foot and dragged him from under the table. "Have you learned your lesson, traitor?"

Marcus giggled and kicked his legs wildly at Bayle.

"Not giving up easily, I see." Bayle fended off flying bare feet then grabbed one and began to tickle the underside.

"Stop, Baye, stop!" Marcus yelled with laughter, squirming wildly as he was being tortured.

"I think it's time to rescue my secret spy," Tomas growled. He playfully tackled Bayle and pinned his arms to the floor. "Quick, Marcus, attack before it is too late."

Marcus piled on top of Bayle and began tickling him with his tiny fingers.

Laughing so hard he could barely breathe, Bayle freed himself from Tomas, then lifted Marcus off his chest, and shook him in the air above him. "I give, you little monster."

Marissa laughed. "He is so adorable."

"You have to be talking about Marcus because there is nothing adorable about Bayle," Elhrin laughed.

"Hey, I heard that," Bayle retorted as the boys returned back to the battlefield on the table to continue their war. "I'll have you know, I have been called adorable on numerous occasions."

"By whom?" Tomas asked, climbing back into his chair beside the table. "The Grexler's chambermaid?"

"How did you know about her?" Bayle asked, casting a guilty look Elhrin's way.

"Servants talk," Tomas shrugged with a smile. "I thought you would have learned that by now."

"Ugh, I had forgotten," he grimaced, and then his eyes went wide. "You don't think Marguerite was told, do you?"

"Relax, she wouldn't mention it to you if she had," Elhrin said as she took a small sip of her wine. "Well, at least she won't say anything until she feels there is a need for you to learn a lesson from your indiscretions."

"Yes, that is what I'm thinking, too," Bayle groaned as he righted the fallen figurines on the table. "She certainly knows how to make one feel guilty."

"It works, too. She is not even here and you feel guilty," Elhrin pointed out.

"What are they really like?" Marissa asked. "Madam Idwyr seems nice, but Minister Idwyr scares me."

"You have that backwards," Bayle said, lining up his men. "Marguerite should be the one who scares you, not Master Gryph. Let me give you one piece of advice. Never, ever cross that lady. It doesn't matter if you have powers or not. She can run you over like a rampaging bull, and you won't know that you are in trouble until it is too late to save yourself. Master Gryph is like a kitten compared to her."

"Bayle, stop," Elhrin scolded. "You make Marguerite sound horrible."

"That was not my intention. I was just saying that Marguerite is a fair, but tough lady, and she is the one who keeps everyone in line."

"Well, she has to," Elhrin said as she sat her glass on the table beside her. "Otherwise, certain people tend to get themselves in trouble by drinking until they don't know their own name and ending up in bed with Ulhrin Blincher's daughter."

"Ouch," he winced. "I didn't think you knew about that."

"Master Gryph told me. He thought it was funny Marguerite made you wash your bedclothes every single day for a month and wouldn't let you go anywhere but to Master Toome's for work. What I don't understand is why you would take the girl back home? Did you not realize Marguerite would get upset?"

"I thought they were gone. They had been planning to leave for Muryne that afternoon, and I didn't go back home before I went to the inn to meet everyone. I had no idea the axle on their carriage had cracked, and they decided to delay their trip. I didn't think to check their bedroom before . . . ." He shrugged his shoulders, leaving the obvious unspoken.

"I would have loved to have been there when she caught the two of you," Tomas laughed. "From what I hear Master Gryph had to stop her from pummeling you with her broom, and the poor girl ran out into the night with nothing on but your bed sheet."

"She ran all the way home like that, and it took a lot of talking from Master Gryph to keep Ulhrin from killing me," Bayle chuckled. "Death would have been a blessing compared to the guilt Marguerite put me through."

Elhrin shifted on the settee and faced Marissa. "Don't let Bayle fool you. Like Kyne said earlier today, there is no one kinder in all Anderan than Marguerite. All of our students look on her as a mother figure, especially the younger ones whose family did not move to Glimmerdale when they came to the academy."

"I notice that you call the minister, Master Gryph. How should I address him?" Marissa asked.

"Either title is fine. The students all call him Master Idwyr because to them he is a teacher and the headmaster of our academy. Tomas and Kyne usually address him as Minister Idwyr because of his government position. Bayle and I grew up with him and he insisted we use his given name, but our mother overruled him somewhat and insisted we owed him more respect and made us call him Master Gryph."

Bayle grinned at them. "I, however, have no problem also calling him feeble old man any chance I get."

"Yes, and I remember him throwing you in a pool of freezing water for it, too," Tomas laughed.

"That's his excuse. It was really about the fish I caught. He knows I'm a better fisherman than he is."

"Boys, let's not get started on that," Elhrin said. Bayle was just as passionate about fishing as Master Gryph. "Marissa, you call him whatever makes you comfortable."

Marissa nodded. "I think I will call him Master Idwyr too."

"Wet's pway," Marcus complained with a yawn. He loaded his catapult and smacked a tiny hand on the handle of the spoon. Walnut pieces bounced across the table top.

"It won't be long before he is going to fall asleep," Elhrin commented. "Marcus, do you want a story?"

"No, I want to pway. Come on Baye," he whined and stood up to wrap his arms around Bayle's neck.

"You know what, my little minion? Elhrin is right. It is late, and we have already let you stay up past your bedtime." Bayle pushed himself to his hands and knees, but Marcus wouldn't let go of his neck. Bayle straightened and Marcus was lifted off the floor. "Looks like I have a leech attached to my neck."

Marcus giggled. Wrapping his arms around the little boy, Bayle carried him to a chair and began telling Marcus a story about a girl who had been captured by a monster and had to be rescued by her heroic younger brother. Eventually, Marcus' eyes drifted shut, and Bayle carried him to Elhrin's bed.

"Interesting story," Elhrin said quietly when Bayle returned to his chair.

"I thought so," Bayle grinned. "I didn't get to the end where the heroic brother lavishes in the everlasting adoration of his older sister's beautiful friends."

"Marissa, do you have any brothers?"

"No."

"Consider yourself lucky," she sighed. "Play time is over . . . time to get to work."

"You mentioned we had some things to discuss," Tomas said, collecting Marcus' tiny figures into a pile. Bayle handed him the wooden case they were stored in.

"We do, but I need to talk to Marissa about something else right now." Marissa's eyebrows shot up in surprise. "You boys entertain yourselves for a moment. Marissa, how tired are you?"

"Just a little, I guess. Why?"

"Because we are going to start your first lesson. If you are overly tired, we can wait."

"No, I am fine," she eagerly assured Elhrin.

"Good. What we are going to do is work on disciplining your mind and learning to stay focused on what you are doing no matter what is going on around you. So while you work, I will not ask the boys to be quiet even though they are at the moment. Would you three please talk about something—fishing, fighting, or whatever it is you boys do, and not pay attention to us?"

"Would you like for us to arm wrestle and belch loudly, too?" Tomas asked.

"Maybe, but I am going to have to ask you to restrain yourselves if you feel the need to pass gas," she commented, earning howls of laughter from the boys. She turned to Marissa and shook her head. "Men never change. The mere mention of bodily functions sends them into hysterics. I say we ignore them."

Marissa agreed with a laugh.

"Okay, let's see how to start this off." Elhrin searched her mind for an analogy she could use. "Marissa, have you ever been alone out in the countryside and paid attention to the birds singing?"

"Many times," Marissa said clearly puzzled by the question.

"I know that was a strange thing to ask, but bear with me. When you are alone and are listening to the birds would you say you could determine what types of birds they were and their general locations just by their songs even though you don't see them?"

"I could guess where they are, but I wouldn't know what kinds of birds they were unless someone taught me how to recognize their calls," Marissa said.

"That's similar to what I plan to do. You see, those of us with the gift of magic can detect others who also have the gift. In other words, we can recognize the magical energy source of another magician who is near us or in our area just by feeling them or being aware of them. We don't have to see them or hear them." Elhrin could see Marissa was having a hard time understanding what she was trying to say. "For example, earlier today Marguerite asked me where Master Gryph was and I told her he was on his way to the apartment. I could detect his magical energy source, and our energy source is where we get the ability to do what we do." She waved a hand and the flames in the fireplace roared higher into the flue, then quickly settled back to their original state. Elhrin snapped her fingers and every lamp and candle in the room extinguished, throwing them in complete darkness with the exception of the light from the fire.

"Hey," Bayle complained.

A small glowing sphere popped into the air, casting a soft light over the group. Marissa sucked in a breath of surprise as she stared in wonder at the floating orb of light. Elhrin snapped her fingers again, and all of the candles and lamps blazed back to life. She moved the orb so that Marissa could get a closer look.

"Everything that I have just done comes from my source of energy," Elhrin explained as Marissa reached a hand out to the sphere of light. "Everything you do magically comes from yours."

"Will it hurt me?" Marissa asked, wanting to touch the light.

"No, this is just a light sphere. It will be warm though."

"It is warm." Her fingers disappeared into the light. "So, what you are saying is that our magic uses this energy source you speak of. I wonder how?"

"I don't really know," Elhrin said, thinking of the doctor in Gildas who wanted an answer to the same question. "But what I do know is that our energy supply is not endless. Just like a person gets tired after running for awhile, so do we when we continuously use our energy source. That is why Master Gryph said you will be taught how to recognize your limits. But I am getting sidetracked. I want to teach you how to recognize another energy source."

"And you say Master Gryph gets sidetracked too often," Bayle interjected.

"Hey, I thought I told you three to entertain each other," she scolded with a grin.

He held up his hands. "Sorry to interrupt. It won't happen again."

"Marissa, this is what I want you to do," she said, and methodically explained the procedure that would allow Marissa to recognize Elhrin's energy source.

Marissa tried a few times but couldn't grasp it because the men were distracting her with their conversation and occasional bursts of laughter. It took complete concentration, and the ability to block out one's surroundings, to be able to separate the energy source from what an individual considered to be normal everyday feelings for the first time. Elhrin understood because she had once combined the unknown black and foul energy source of the N'gethwyn Cynder with her fear—not knowing that the two were separate feelings. Elhrin finally asked the boys to be quiet so the girl could concentrate.

The room was dead silent with the exception of occasional pops from the fire.

"Elhrin," Marissa finally whispered with her eyes closed tight. "Is it supposed to feel like—like a sort of burning comfort? I'm not sure that's the correct description, but it feels like when you stare into the sun during a summer day. It is so bright you have to cover your eyes, and its warmth feels good on your skin, but you know if you stay in it too long, you will burn from its intensity. Is that it?"

Elhrin stared at Marissa in shock. Never had anyone described her energy source to her, and to have it compared to the sun was amazing. Not that she had any doubts, but Marissa had confirmed Elhrin was truly one of Solisius' children. What Marissa felt was his gift to her.

"Uh, yes, you are seeing—or I should say feeling—my particular source. You will find each individual has something unique about them that sets them apart from everyone else. Your own source appears to me as a feeling of coolness, like water from a river, yet tinged with a hint of fire. I think it has something to do with our own abilities. Master Gryph's source reminds me of what it must feel like just before one gets struck by lightning. It is like a tingling of white-hot power just waiting to be unleashed."

Tomas snorted. "At one time you thought it was the feeling of passion waiting to be unleashed."

"Shut up!" Elhrin glared at him—her face heated from embarrassment. He was referring to the first time he kissed her. It felt like a lifetime ago when they were on their way to Blackridge Keep. She did not know about this particular ability when Master Gryph had caught her and Tomas kissing for the first time. He had approached the two of them unawares and his energy source had entwined itself with her feelings for Tomas. The both of them were mortified, even though they had done nothing wrong, and Master Gryph had reacted like any father would when seeing a daughter kissed by a boy for the first time. He was not pleased. He didn't get angry with either of them, but the memory of his displeasure was still fresh enough to make her uncomfortable. "Don't pay attention to Tomas. Now that you know what my source feels like, I want you to continue to search for my source when you leave here and return to your room. You should be able to feel it even when you are in your room. If you can't, don't worry. It only means you have gone out of range for your current abilities. Distance will be something you will work on as you train."

"How far can you feel someone?" Clay asked, clearly caught up in the concept.

"Well, it depends on the strength of each individual's source, and their experience level, and the strength of the energy source of the other individual being monitored. But to give you a better idea of distance, I felt Marissa when the two of you neared the area somewhere close to the city gates. Master Gryph felt you before that, but that is because he is more experienced than I am."

Clay's eyebrows shot up. "That is a league if not more from here."

"That sounds about right." Elhrin rose from her seat to retrieve the map Master Gryph had given her before he left for the theatre. "Tomas, will you clear the table?"

He pushed everything to the side to give her room. She unrolled the map and spread it across the table, placing the books from the previous fortress on all four corners to keep it from rolling back up.

"Here we are." She pointed at the palace on the map of the city. Its location was just beyond the city's center hub, and it was surrounded on all sides by a deep water canal. The main city gate was located south of their position in the wall that surrounded the city, several leagues away from the point of the peninsula that Muryne was built on. "And I tracked you until you reached The Gopher Hole where Kyne and I met you."

"Seriously?" Bayle almost spewed the beer he was drinking. "You were going to find a room in The Gopher Hole? You better be glad she found you. You definitely would not have wanted to stay there. They charge by the hour instead of the night, if you know what I mean."

"You sound like you are familiar with the place," Elhrin said with displeasure.

He grinned and raised his glass at her in a mock salute, then drained its contents.

"I really wish I could unlearn things I keep learning about you," Elhrin heaved a sigh, staring at the map. She located the areas where the bodies were found on the map and frowned.

"What's wrong?" Bayle asked, seeing her frown. "I didn't say I frequented the place."

"I'm not thinking about that. Look at this." She picked up some of Marcus' walnut pieces that Tomas had collected into a pile and placed four of them on each of the locations. "Do you see anything?"

"I see four walnuts on a map," Bayle commented. "What are we supposed to be seeing?"

She shook her head. Nothing about the various locations proximity to each other meant anything to her. "I don't know. I just thought maybe where I placed the walnuts might mean something to any of you."

"Are these places holding events this week?" Marissa asked with a yawn.

"No, they are just places of interest to me," Elhrin said, not wanting to reveal the murders to the new arrivals before she cleared it with Master Gryph. "I was just thinking out loud. Marissa, would you like to learn how to create the light sphere? It is fairly simple."

"I would," she said eagerly.

Elhrin spent the next hour teaching Marissa how to construct a small light sphere, impressed with how quickly the girl was able to learn. Marissa would have kept going if Elhrin hadn't pointed out that the girl kept yawning and the hour was growing late. Reluctantly, Marissa agreed to stop.

"Thank you, Elhrin, for everything. Should Clay and I leave for Glimmerdale in the morning?" Marissa asked as the three of them walked to the door.

"No, I think Master Idwyr would prefer for you to remain here for the time being. We'll let you know more tomorrow, but don't worry about sitting in your room waiting for a summons or word from us. We are quite busy at the moment, so it may not be right away. We will find you when we are ready. In the meantime, enjoy the palace. The gardens are beautiful and the Royal Gallery is amazing. There are some interesting artifacts on display and paintings of some of Anderan's most beautiful and popular sites, famous battles, and prominent figures. There is even a portrait of Master Idwyr when he was young and first rose to the position of Minister of Specialized State Defense."

"We are allowed to roam about the palace?" Clay asked.

"Of course," Elhrin opened the door. Irdin, the guard, smiled at her. "Most of the rooms in the west wing on the ground floor are public. The ones you aren't allowed into will be marked or guarded."

"That sounds exciting," Marissa said. "Thank you again, Elhrin, good night."

"Good night," Elhrin said and closed the door. "I like her. I think she is going to be one of our top students."

"I like them both," Tomas said, tilting his glass at Bayle to show him it was empty. "I don't think they will have a hard time fitting in."

"No, they won't." Elhrin sank down in the settee to peruse the map once again.

"It's time to tell us what you held back, sister," Bayle said, refilling his and Tomas' glass. "What's important about those locations?"

"Those are where the murders occurred." She leaned forward to get a closer look.

"Murders, meaning there is more than one now," Tomas said. He leaned over the map. "What were you really looking for?"

"Master Gryph wondered if where the bodies were placed were planned and not random. We thought by mapping them out, we could see something that could help us pinpoint a meeting place. How? I haven't a clue."

Bayle traced the locations with a finger. "The only thing I see is that they are all on the west side of the city. Maybe the killer was traveling in a certain direction and picked victims based on how easy he could make the kill."

"That's as good a guess as any, but still, why the same note on all the victims? Tomas, you read the note he showed me last night, didn't you?"

He nodded.

"They all were identical. Master Gryph thought maybe the killer wanted to draw attention to whoever was supposed to read the note."

"That makes sense," Bayle observed. "If the killer couldn't contact his reader directly for some reason, maybe he needed to do it this way, hoping the reader would stumble upon one of the bodies, and that is why the murders are in these places." He pointed at the map. "Maybe they are areas the writer knows the reader frequents."

"I don't know. It seems there would be a better way to get word of a meeting to someone than a series of dead bodies that would attract attention to the authorities as well as the one who is supposed to read the note," she paused, thinking. "The note says that the meeting place has yet to be determined. What good does that do?" Elhrin threw a hand up in frustration. "Say, 'Hey I'm here, but I can't talk to you right now. I'll let you know later where we will meet. In the meantime, how do you like my work?'"

That drew a laugh from the two men.

"You are right, it doesn't make sense," Tomas agreed, leaning over the map again. "But the note did also say, 'You will know when the time comes.' That suggests a predetermined sign of some kind."

"Which could be anything," Bayle said. "But I bet it would be something more dramatic than hanging bodies with their eyes gone."

"That is what scares me. What does this monster have planned? And what kind of meeting is he talking about? Because it certainly isn't for a cordial evening of dinner and playing cards," Elhrin huffed, and massaged her forehead to relieve a dull throb. A force of energy intruded on her thoughts. "He is almost here."

"Who? Master Gryph?" Bayle asked.

"No, the killer. Of course I'm talking about Master Gryph. They are entering the palace grounds." She forced herself to relax, realizing she had unconsciously been monitoring his location, watching for signs of trouble.

"That must have been some dinner to last this long," Bayle yawned, slumping in his chair and stretching his legs out. "Why didn't you go?"

"Because of Marissa and Clay. I told him I would help you watch Marcus and entertain the two of them since they were new to the city."

"Uh huh," Bayle smiled knowingly, "sure you did."

"Do you two want anything else to eat?" She stood up to clean their dinner off the dining table.

"No," they answered in unison.

"Bayle, do you know Lieutenant Stricklyn Quinne?" Tomas asked.

"You mean Sickling Stricklyn?" Bayle laughed. "The one who pretends sickness so that he can get out of duties on a regular basis?"

"That's the one," Tomas chuckled. "I had the misfortune . . . ."

Elhrin tuned them out as she stacked their dinner plates and placed them on the tray for the chambermaid to retrieve. She had to think. *You will know when the time comes.* Maybe the killer couldn't be specific about the meeting place because he did not know where it was going to be yet, but that didn't sound right either. If he was going to all this trouble to be noticed, he had to have a destination in mind, she was sure of it. Okay, back to the reason for the murders. She had gone through a multitude of different reasons and had finished wiping the crumbs from the table when a knock on the door broke her concentration. The door opened and Marguerite peeked inside.

"We're back," she said softly as she stepped into the apartment. Master Gryph ducked through the door behind her. They were a breathtaking couple in their evening attire. To match the flowing black and white dress of Marguerite, Master Gryph had donned a long black formal coat that fitted tight to his waist and flared down to just above his knees. Dove gray breeches tucked into polished boots and his sword belted at his waist completed his attire.

"Did Marcus behave himself?" Marguerite asked, seeing that her son was sleeping on the bed.

"He was a perfect little gentleman," Elhrin smiled. "Bayle, on the other hand, could use a spanking."

"Hey, I was a good boy, too," Bayle retorted, earning a chuckle from Marguerite and Master Gryph.

"How was the theatre?" Elhrin asked.

"Loud," Master Gryph stated. He noticed the map on the table and limped over to examine it.

"It was wonderful. There were acts that represented the four countries involved in the conference," Marguerite jerked her chin at her husband's back. "He just didn't like the drum corps from Nabafin."

"It wasn't the drums that bothered me. It was that contraption they used to make some kind of screeching noise. Hurt my ears." He lowered himself to the settee, maneuvering his sword so he could lean over the map. "What did you youngsters do?"

"We had dinner then the boys waged war on the table until Marcus grew tired and fell asleep. I did manage to teach Marissa how to recognize energy sources and to construct a light sphere."

"Sounds like a busy night. How did Marissa do?"

"She's a quick learner. I told the boys I thought she would end up being one of our top students."

"Excellent," he said without looking up from the map, "what do you think of her character?"

"Her character?" she asked, unsure of what he wanted.

"Her personality, her mind, would she work well in a team situation, be a good candidate for the Eagle program if she proved worthy in her skills—her character."

"Well, I don't know her yet, but I do know I like her. Like I said before, she is a quick learner so I know she is smart, and she does show initiative. We can both tell her powers are strong, and with training I do think she would be a good candidate for the Eagles, but that would just depend on how willing she would be to fight and possibly die for her country."

He smoothed his mustache and beard with his hand. "Why don't you ask her?"

Elhrin frowned. "Why? The girl hasn't gone through training of any kind, yet. Why would you ask her about becoming an Eagle?"

He furrowed his brow. "Because I want to know, and I won't have time to spend with her tomorrow and ask her myself."

"That didn't answer my question."

He leaned over to pick up some of the walnut pieces on the table. One by one, he placed three more pieces on the map. Elhrin's heart sunk when a pattern became apparent. She bent over for a closer look.

"N'gethwyn," she whispered.

"N'gethwyn," he confirmed.

"How are you getting that from this?" Bayle asked, pointing at the pieces scattered on the map.

"Look," Elhrin started at one of the locations where Master Gryph had placed a piece of walnut meat and traced the trail of body locations for Bayle. "This is Obsudius' constellation sign. The N'gethwyn use it as an emblem indicating their high or celestial status, if you will, much like the Brothers of M'gelidia use the wolf as a symbol of their dedication to Obsudius." She placed a hand on Master Gryph's shoulder and sat down beside him. "He pointed it out to me in the *Book of Tolman*."

There were several instances of So'ladiun fighting against N'gethwyn hidden in the book's histories. Being a magical book, she and Master Gryph could use their pendants to activate its magic and show actual scenes of events that had happened in the past as if they were standing there when it happened. In the scenes they had discovered of N'gethwyn, every one had a patch with that sign on their clothing. Even Cynder, who had been a shape-changer, had one on his robe when he had morphed into his version of a human form.

"So the killer is N'gethwyn?" Tomas asked.

"Not likely," Master Gryph answered.

"I don't follow," Tomas said as Marguerite perched on the arm of the settee beside Master Gryph.

"It couldn't be because we would have felt their energy source in the city," Elhrin answered.

"So, if it is not N'gethwyn, then who?" Tomas asked.

"That is the question we are trying to answer, but I bet whoever it is, is under the direction of an N'gethwyn," Master Gryph said.

"How did you learn about these other murders?" Elhrin asked, knowing no one talked to him before he left.

"Nygill was waiting for me outside the theatre." He propped his elbows on his knees and lowered his head to run both hands through his short cropped salt and pepper hair. "There is more distressing news. While we were in the theatre a messenger was admitted to Goruth's box. It seems there are two confirmed Do'athrim attacks on small farm settlements outside of Yradin. They were burned to the ground. No survivors."

"What?" Elhrin gasped, her mind flashing to the long list of Do'athrim sightings reported from all corners of Anderan. "Then that means the rumors of sightings from other areas are possibly real. What do we do?"

"Goruth is handling it for the moment. The Yradin military is combing the area and they will send a report when they have something new. Goruth has decided to send an alert out to every military post in Anderan. They are to step up security measures in their regions. You and I will continue to work on this current dilemma until we see we are needed elsewhere."

"Okay, but about Marissa," Elhrin tapped his arm so he would look at her, "what are you thinking we should do with her?"

"I think I would like for her to stay close to you and observe what you do. This will also give you a chance to better assess her character. Also, if you could throw in a few lessons along the way it would be helpful. You are right—she is one of the strongest we have found so far, and we may need her assistance. If that is the case, she is going to have to learn in a hurry."

"What if she does not agree?"

"Hopefully, we won't have to ask her to but still, I would like to know if she would consider it should we have need of her."

"And it's okay for her to know about all this?" she asked pointing at the map.

"She will hear about the murders anyway. I will leave it up to you to determine how much of the other information you can entrust her with. For the time being, leave my letter out of it."

"What letter?" Marguerite asked.

"The letter I am going to tell you about when we return to our apartment." He patted her back. "Get Marcus."

Elhrin didn't like the fact he was assuming an untrained, possibly unwilling, magician would be needed. But the letter did refer to the destruction of Anderan. Something major would have to happen for that to come to pass. Lost in thought, she stared at the walnut pieces on the map, slowly realizing something was missing.

"One of the points is missing on the constellation. There should be one going this way." She traced a finger from the last point which was near the coliseum to the central hub of Muryne's main road. Master Gryph clasped her hand and moved it further along the map. He stopped when her finger fell on the palace.

"Son of a . . . ," Bayle whistled.

"Gryph," Marguerite gasped. She had retrieved Marcus and his sleeping face was snuggled up next to her neck with his thumb in his mouth. "Do you think there is a body somewhere on the palace grounds?"

"I don't know, but I believe I will have a quiet search conducted just in case." With a heavy sigh, he stood up. "You and Bayle take Marcus back to our apartment and go on to bed. I'll be back as soon as I can. Elhrin, Tomas, I will need your assistance."

Chapter Seven

After extinguishing all but one oil lamp in her bathroom, Marguerite set her wine glass on the back ledge of the marble tub and sank down into the soft foam of the rose petal bath oil Bayle had brought for her from Yradin. Immediately, the warm water began to relax the tension in her muscles from the stress of the evening.

The theatre had been wonderful, but the long hours trying to communicate with the ambassadors and their wives when Gryph was too busy to translate became tedious. She really did need to find time to learn a rudimentary understanding of their languages if Gryph was going to be forced to attend the yearly conferences they were proposing.

Now she worried about a possible murderer being on the palace grounds. She and Bayle had waited on Gryph for awhile to find out what his search turned up, but the time had lagged on, and she wanted to take a bath before going to bed, so she had bid Bayle a good night.

She massaged her temples, trying to ease a headache. She couldn't wait for the convention to be over and they could go back home—back to the relative peace of over thirty students of all ages coming and going through her house, traipsing mud and dirt everywhere, complaining about this unfairness or that unfairness, creating a laundry load that rivaled the heights of the distant Northreach Mountains, not to mention the chaos that resulted at mealtime. Gryph was right. She needed to give in and hire more help, especially when the dining hall addition to the academic building was complete. It was becoming too much for her, Esmeldra, and Liselle to handle, even though chores were doled out to the students residing under her roof.

She smiled to herself. Yes, she could not wait to get back home to the chaos. Home was where she thrived.

She leaned her head back against the cool surface of the tub and closed her eyes, allowing the warm water and soft aroma of the oil to calm her pounding head. She drifted for awhile, allowing her thoughts to sift through the things she needed to do when she returned to Glimmerdale. Slowly, she became aware that someone was in the bedroom. She thought it had to be Gryph. By now, Bayle was asleep and Marcus rarely woke once he was down for the night. She decided to let Gryph find her. She was not ready to leave the comforting warmth of her bath.

She heard him rifle through the small desk he used when he did not want to go to his office. Then there was silence. She waited a few moments, thinking he would come looking for her when he was through with whatever he was doing. Finally, she heard him approach the door, and reached for a towel draped across a chair next to the tub.

"Gryph?" she called out softly, glancing at the bathroom door.

She had left it ajar in case Marcus needed her, so all she could see was a slim shadow in the opening. She had doused most of the lights in her bedroom.

The bathroom door unexpectedly swung wide and banged hard against the wall, causing the glass globe from an oil sconce to fall from its perch and shatter on the floor. A dark figure rushed at her. She did not have time to scream before he grabbed her throat in a vice-like grip and drove her head under the water. She thrashed about, trying desperately to break his grip. She reached for his face, hoping to dig her nails into his eyes, but he turned his head out of her reach. Her lungs started to burn from the lack of air. She tried to use her legs, but she couldn't wedge them between their bodies or kick him. Her legs fell hard on top of the ledge of the tub, swiping a ceramic pitcher to the floor. She was losing. Her lungs screamed for air. Darkness was coming for her. Horribly, she realized she was going to die, and she would not be able to see her little boy grow to be a man.

Marcus!

Desperately, she tried to beat the man's arms away from her throat. He banged her head repeatedly against the bottom of the tub. She continued to claw at the man's arms, face, anything that her hands came in contact with until she knew it was over. Her arms flopped to the tub's sides, knocking her wine glass to the floor. Her strength was gone.

Gryph . . . Marcus . . . I love you!

His hands jerked violently away from her throat, but it was too late . . . she slipped into oblivion.

Elhrin and Tomas reentered the palace and made their way down a short hall to the west wing's main corridor. They had meticulously combed every inch of the interior gardens with no results save startling a young couple trying to have a private moment in the garden's gazebo. Now they were going to help Master Gryph search the exterior of the palace. He had put a quick team of off duty guards together to help search the grounds and was somewhere on the north side.

"Okay, so the killer wants his victims to be found, but not right away," Tomas reasoned, as they entered the well lit corridor and turned right. "The palace is filled to a near bursting level with people, so he would have to choose a relatively quiet location without . . . ." He paused to let a group of ladies they were approaching to pass by and move out of hearing range before continuing. "Without being concerned with getting caught."

"Apparently, he is well skilled in not getting caught," Elhrin commented. "He has been able to kill at least six people within a few days time."

"Yes, and think about the locations where those bodies were found. They were hidden from direct view, but he knew someone would find the body quickly." He ticked off each location with his fingers. "The innkeeper goes to the barn frequently. The canal is always used. The warehouse opens every morning. There are people in the park daily, so it was a matter of time before someone stumbled across the body. The crane on the loading dock was broken, but people walk by it frequently. The coliseum's stable was empty, but he knew they would be using it tomorrow."

They entered the hall where the north and west wings met and Tomas grabbed the door handle that would take them into the vestibule of the wing's side entrance, but he did not open the door.

"If you were the killer, where in a crowded, heavily guarded building would be the best spot to hide a body and still have it found within hours?" he asked. "The grounds are patrolled constantly, and there are not many trees save along the avenues and that is out in the open. The exterior of the palace, maybe?"

Elhrin thought about the building's features. There were many places where a body could be placed, but it would be difficult. Like he said, guards patrolled the grounds and the rooftops non-stop.

Laughter drifted out of the corridor behind them, and Elhrin saw Councilor Idora and a well-dressed couple emerge from one of the sitting rooms the councilors used for entertaining personal guests. Idora bid her guests a good night and turned to go back into the sitting room, but noticed Elhrin standing at the end of the hall. Her face broke into an elegant smile.

"Miss Caddoch, I am so glad to see you," she called out. "Do you know where Minister Idwyr and his wife would be at the moment? I invited them to join me and a few guests after the theatre, but they haven't arrived."

"Minister Idwyr has a private matter to attend to, and Madam Idwyr felt it necessary for their son to retire for the night, Councilor," Elhrin said.

A quick look of disappointment flashed across Idora's face before she smiled again. "That man never rests, always busy, and I can certainly understand a mother's obligation to her child always comes first. I regret that I never had the opportunity." She sighed dramatically. "Can't go back in time, now can we? Well, I must return to my guests. Have a good evening."

"Thank you, Councilor."

With a tiny wave of her fingers, Idora reentered the sitting room.

"Interesting dress," Tomas commented as he opened the door.

Idora had been wearing a red and gold brocade gown that had a myriad of tiny red gems sewn in a swirling pattern all over its fabric. The neckline was so low-cut that Idora's nipples on her bosoms were close to being revealed.

"It just dazzled you, didn't it?" she muttered, knowing he probably didn't even see the dress.

"Oh, Miss Caddoch," Idora stuck her head back out the doorway. "If you happen to run across Councilor Whyse tell him we are still waiting on him."

"I will, Councilor," Elhrin responded even though Idora had already disappeared back into the room without waiting for her answer. Elhrin walked into the cool air of the stone-encased foyer, bracing herself once again for the chill of the outdoors. "What were we discussing?"

"Where to hide a body," Tomas answered, descending the short stairway to the exterior door and opening it for her.

The cold air of the night hit her in the face like a wall of ice. Shivering, she drew her cloak tight around her. As Marguerite had said the night before, winter did seem to be trying to arrive earlier than usual.

"You know, if our guess is that the killer was trying to create the sign of Obsudius with the location of the bodies and the palace is his final destination, I would think the place he would pick would not be just anywhere. He would want to have a major impact, don't you think?" She looked across the dark lawn as they crunched down the gravel path that eventually led to one of the canals. From there they could clearly see the street lanterns lining both sides of the canal in the distance. Tomas was right. The palace lawns didn't have many trees. She turned around to look up at the building's exterior. Bright light filtered out of many windows. Occasionally, the silhouette of a person would drift by and cast a shadow. Even at such a late hour, the castle was alive with activity.

"If it was me, I would," Tomas stared up at the building with her. "He is going to a lot of trouble to be noticed. I would think his last act would have to be spectacular."

"So where would you put a body in the palace if you could?" she pondered, scanning the rooftop and noticing a guard was looking down at them. A thought struck her and she sucked in a breath. Tomas glanced at her sharply, seeming to come to the same conclusion.

"The council chambers," they said in unison.

They bolted for the door. Tomas slammed the door open and didn't bother to shut it as they ran up the stairs and into the west corridor. They ran down the long corridor, passing several arched openings until they rounded the corner leading into the southern corridor. Being the main public corridor, since it traversed the length of the front of the palace, there were more people walking its hall than the one they had just left. Elhrin didn't slow down and accidentally bumped the arm of one of the Chyrzinian guests. The young girl yelped in surprise.

"Please forgive me," Elhrin yelled over her shoulder as she ran, hoping the girl understood her. The Chyrzinians were known for being offended easily, and King Goruth would not be happy with her if one of his guests felt they had been treated rudely.

"Elhrin, come on," Tomas yelled ahead of her.

She sped up, sidestepping a stream of people leaving the main dining hall.

"Elhrin, where are you two going in such a hurry?" one of the men called, turning out to be Kyne.

She waved a hand at him. "Come on!"

Without question he ran after them. The three reached the main entrance and took the steps to the grand hall two at a time. They skidded to a halt when they reached the council chamber doors. The doors were unguarded since there was no session.

Tomas rattled the door. "Locked!" he said, breathing heavily from their mad dash through the palace.

"Move," she panted.

"Can you tell me what is going on?" Kyne asked.

"Looking," Tomas huffed, "for another body. Elhrin, I hope you aren't going to blow the door to pieces."

"No," she breathed. She sent a trickle of magic into the lock of the door, and tried to maneuver the locking mechanism. Nothing moved. She closed her eyes tight to try and concentrate, but then she was jostled out of the way.

"Let me do it," Kyne said.

He pulled some kind of tool from a pouch on his belt and stuck it into the keyhole. After a few twists they heard an audible click.

"Nothing to it," he said.

"I always thought you would make a good thief," she commented and pushed the door open.

The council chamber was pitch black. Elhrin conjured a light sphere, and they hurried out onto the right side balcony that overlooked the chamber floor. Elhrin increased the intensity of the light and sent it high over the room fully expecting a body to be dangling from one of the large chandeliers. Nothing was there. They turned around to search the guard's walkway. It too was empty.

"I'll search the other side," Tomas disappeared through the foyer to go to the left side balcony and then came right back. "Nothing there either."

"There is nowhere else in here to hang a body," Elhrin said.

"What makes you think there is a body here somewhere?" Kyne asked. Elhrin quickly gave him a condensed version of what had transpired over the evening.

"What makes you so sure that the killer has already killed?" he asked.

Elhrin hadn't given that thought any consideration. "We aren't sure. We are just going by what has happened today and Master Gryph wanted to check to make sure. Maybe we are looking too soon. Maybe he is waiting for a specific time."

"Or he couldn't get in here," Tomas said. "That is if he wanted to put a body here."

A guard with a drawn sword rushed into the foyer of the council chambers.

"Who's here?" he demanded. "The council chambers are off limits."

Kyne stepped where the guard could see him. "We are just leaving, Sergeant."

"Captain Kyne," the guard stammered. "I didn't realize it was you. It's just that I saw the open door, and with all the action happening upstairs, I thought you were an intruder."

"What action upstairs?" Elhrin asked.

"Someone broke into the Idwyr's apartment and . . . ."

Elhrin didn't hear what the rest of the man said. Heart pounding wildly with fear, she ran out of the chambers and vaulted up the stairway of the grand hall. Guards were everywhere. She sprinted to Master Gryph's apartment where the door stood wide open.

"Move," she ordered the guards blocking her way. Recognizing her, they let her pass.

King Goruth stood in the middle of the sitting room with several men from the Palace Guard.

"Elhrin," he said, the sadness in his eyes made her blood turn to ice.

She dashed for the open bedroom door. Bayle was leaned against one of the posts of the canopy bed, sobbing uncontrollably. The king's personal doctor was straddled over Marguerite lying on the bed, furiously pressing her chest. Marguerite's face was an unearthly blue.

"Oh, god, no!" Elhrin screamed. Bayle whirled around. Blood oozed from a long gash on the side of his head.

"Marcus," he choked, helplessly.

Marcus' bed was empty. His bed sheets were spilled onto the floor. A blanket lay in a heap across the room next to an open window.

Elhrin shook her head, trying to bring it all together. "What?" she asked hoarsely.

Firm hands grasped her arms from behind. She turned to look into the sympathetic eyes of the king. "Elhrin, Marcus has been taken."

"No," she wailed. Her knees failed her. She started to drop to the floor, but he held her steady.

"Elhrin, I can't find Gryph," King Goruth said calmly. "Can you tell me where he is?"

Oh, Solisius, why? This is so unfair, she screamed in her mind.

Stay strong, my child, dark days are ahead, whispered the voice of her god.

"Elhrin, did you hear me? Can you tell me where Gryph is?" King Goruth's voice broke through her haze of grief.

She sucked in a tremulous breathe, trying to focus on locating Master Gryph. "Service courtyard entrance. He's coming inside the palace," she said with difficulty.

"Captain, go get him," he ordered Tomas who was standing just inside the doorway with Kyne.

She glanced at the bed. The doctor continued to pump Marguerite's chest.

"Come on, Madam, don't let go, come on," the doctor muttered as he pushed repeatedly on Marguerite's chest. He then jumped off of her and rolled her to her side. Elhrin saw Marguerite's back spasm. "That's it." The doctor pounded her on the back. Marguerite coughed and vomited. "She has cleared her lungs," Doctor Dryke said in relief.

Sobbing, Bayle sunk to the floor and put his head in his hands. Elhrin thought she was going to faint with relief, but King Goruth held her fast.

The doctor wiped Marguerite's face with a corner of the bed sheet then rolled her onto her back.

"I thought she was awake," Elhrin cried, seeing that Marguerite's eyes were closed.

"She has undergone a traumatic experience and is not out of danger. I do not know if or when she will awaken," the doctor replied. "At least, she is now breathing." He pulled a blanket from the foot of the bed and covered her body.

Elhrin felt Master Gryph's energy source near at a rapid pace, thankful that he had been nearby and Tomas was able to locate him quickly. A moment later he rushed into the bedroom.

"Marguerite!" he cried as he rushed for the bed. He pushed the doctor out of the way and scooped up Marguerite's limp form in his arms. "Dear god, what has happened?" He smoothed strands of her wet hair out of her face. "Marguerite, can you hear me?"

She didn't respond.

Master Gryph glanced at the doctor, terrified. "What happened?" he asked, his eyes darted from one individual to the next, waiting for an answer. "What happened?" he roared, when no one answered him fast enough.

"An intruder tried to drown your wife, Minister," the doctor said, then pointed at Bayle. "If it hadn't been for this young man, she would not be alive. I was able to revive her, but I'm afraid she is still in danger."

Master Gryph's eyes fell on Bayle's form hunched in the floor. He hugged Marguerite to him. "Where is Marcus?" he asked, his gaze rose from the floor to bore into the king.

"He has been abducted, Gryph," King Goruth answered.

Master Gryph's features fell into a grim mask of cold fury as looked back down at his wife. He then leaned over to kiss her. "You are so cold," he whispered against her lips. He tugged at the blanket and pulled it further up over her chest. He then hovered his palm above her. A faint glow emanated from his palm and slowly spread over her body, creating a soft blanket of warmth with his powers.

"I have never seen that done before," the doctor whispered in awe. The blue hue in Marguerite's skin faded slightly.

Master Gryph let the glow disappear. He kissed her briefly once again. "I love you," he said, then lowered her gently to the bed. He slid off the mattress and walked around the bed, but stopped when he came to Bayle's sobbing form on the floor. He bent over to place a hand on Bayle's shoulder.

"Protect her, son," he said roughly, then straightened. The look he turned on King Goruth was fierce. "What is being done to find my son?"

"Gryph, I have every able body looking for him. The palace is on high alert and no one will be allowed to enter or exit the grounds," King Goruth said. "It just happened. There is no way anyone could have carried a small boy anywhere without being seen."

"How did someone get out of this room with my son in the first place?" Master Gryph raised his voice, but caught himself in time to keep from shouting.

"Over here," Kyne said. He was leaning out the open window. "It looks like they were going to come in through your balcony door, but for some reason they chose the window instead." He leaned further out the window for a moment then ducked back inside hauling a rope with him. "They used this." He looked at the rope. "I wonder what changed. The balcony would have been easier."

"Bayle," Elhrin said. Bayle raised his head to look at her. His face was flushed a deep red from crying. "They weren't expecting him to be in the apartment."

"Son, what happened?" King Goruth asked Bayle.

"I failed you, Master Gryph," he croaked, miserably.

"No, you didn't." Master Gryph snapped, impatiently. "What happened?"

"I was asleep, but awoke when something crashed and realized it came from the bedroom . . . ," his voice broke. "When I opened the door to check on Marguerite, I heard the struggle in the bathroom . . . There was a man holding her under the water . . . I jerked him away from her . . . slashed his throat." His face turned into a mask of pure hatred. "I pulled her out and she wasn't breathing." He looked at Master Gryph helplessly. "I put her on the bed and yelled for the guard to come help. He finally heard me and ran to find the doctor while I pounded on her back. I didn't know what to do."

"The guard must have known I was in His Majesty's apartment. Otherwise, I wouldn't have been here quickly," the doctor added.

"Master Gryph, I didn't know Marcus was gone until he took over," he pushed the heels of his hand into his eyes and rocked back and forth. "I didn't protect them like you asked."

Master Gryph turned on his heels and stalked into the lavatory. A blaze of light filled the darkened bathroom as he lit every single lamp and candle inside with a snap of his fingers. Elhrin reached the door in time to see him bend over, grab the collar of the dead man's tunic and rip the fabric of the shirt to expose the man's chest. Part of a wolf tattoo was visible underneath the blood that had spilled from his mutilated neck. Master Gryph angrily flipped the loose fabric back over the man's chest. He then brushed past her back into the bedroom.

"Have him searched," Master Gryph barked.

Elhrin surveyed the lavatory. It was ransacked from the struggle, and the man lay in a dark pool of his own blood. When Elhrin turned back to the bedroom Master Gryph and King Goruth were gone.

"Where are they going?" she asked.

"Down to search below," Tomas answered, standing just inside the doorway.

She nodded and went to Marguerite's side. She leaned over to kiss the lady's cool forehead. "Don't worry, Marguerite, we will find him. Let's go, boys," she growled as she headed for the door.

"Wait, this is faster," Kyne said. He slipped through the window and disappeared. Elhrin and Tomas leaned out the window to see him slide down the rope until he reached the top of the hedges growing against the building. He pushed away from the wall with his feet and dropped soundlessly on the grass of the lawn. Elhrin conjured a light sphere and sent it zooming down to hover above the area. From her view point she could see where someone had broken through the hedges near where the rope dangled.

"Think you can do that?" Tomas asked.

"I'm going to try." She scooted out the window and reached for the rail. Like Kyne, she slid down the rope until she reached the top of the hedges. She pushed away from the wall and let go of the rope. Her feet hit the ground harder than she expected causing her knees to buckle under her. She rolled across the grass, ending up on her back, staring at the dark cloud-covered sky.

Kyne held out a hand to help her up. "How about conjuring up another light, will you? The last one fizzled when you hit the ground."

She zapped one into existence as Tomas landed on the lawn. The three of them scrutinized the area around the hedges.

"Definitely two sets of prints. Both male," Tomas said, squatting to examine the area under the broken hedge.

Elhrin enlarged her light sphere so that the entire area from the wall to a gravel path across the grass was well lit. The light drew the attention of late night revelers.

"Tomas, go see if anyone in that party saw something," she said as a group of young adults wandered over to the boundary of her light.

"Right," Tomas said, dusting his hands off on his breeches.

Elhrin watched him jog over to the group as bobbing torches carried by guards could be seen all across the palace grounds, searching the area. She noticed that several were heading their way in a hurry.

"It's weird," Kyne remarked as he methodically walked the area.

"What is?" She fell in step with him and scrutinized the ground herself.

"There are no other footprints in the wet grass but our own."

He was right. Moisture from the cool air had collected on the short grass, and in the light, she could clearly see where the three of them had walked, and she had fallen, but no other tracks led off in any direction. She walked back to the broken hedge. The footprints were in the dirt, but the shadows of the hedge made it hard to see. She conjured a second light and maneuvered it next to the ground, chasing the shadows away. Something on the ground next to the wall caught her attention. She pushed her way deep into the hedge, ignoring the branches scratching at her face and crouched to pick up the object.

"Damn it," she hissed in frustration. It was Marcus' favorite toy horse.

"Did you find something?" Master Gryph's gruff voice called, surprising her. She had not been monitoring his energy source and did not know he had arrived.

"Yes, sir," she called out. She was about to retreat back to the lawn, but then noticed footprints disappearing into the darkness along the line of the wall. She realized that the branches of the hedges had created a tiny tunnel along the wall. "There are footprints leading through the hedge. I'm going to follow them through."

As she moved through the narrow tunnel of foliage, Master Gryph and whoever was with him followed her progress on the other side of the hedge. She rounded a corner in the building and let the large light sphere wink out behind her. She sent her smaller light on ahead. Several paces further down was a small archway cut into the bottom of the wall. It turned out to be a drainage well for storm water, and the iron grate that had covered the opening was missing.

"Master Gryph, it looks like they went down a drainage well. The footprints stop here." She sent her light in the opening. The narrow well dropped straight down into darkness.

The hedges behind her snapped and popped. Kyne crawled through with an unlit torch and wedged himself beside her to look down the hole.

"These things run into the sewer and then back out to the canal. I'm going down. Minister Idwyr said for you to meet him at the canal. They are searching the perimeter for a boat."

"If they had a boat, why not run across the lawn. It's faster?"

"Too much of a risk being seen." He went in feet first, dropping the torch to the ground.

"How are you going to see?"

"I'm hoping you will light my way until I get to the bottom then throw me that torch." He glanced at her before climbing down. "Will you light it for me?"

"I can do that, but I'm going down with you."

"No, you're not. At least, not this way, you'll break your neck."

"Look, I know you're an expert when it comes to climbing up and down the sheer faces of rock, but I can do this," she said, seeing the uneven texture of the hole and felt she could make it down safely.

"Do not argue with me, Elhrin. We don't have the time. There are stairs inside," he snapped. "Use them if you must come down, but you will not follow me here. Besides, I told you, Minister Idwyr wanted you to meet him at the canal."

Elhrin growled in frustration as she watched him disappear down into the hole. She was amazed at how quickly he climbed down, finding obscure hand and footholds in the stone wall of the drain. When he neared the bottom, he dropped to a ledge on the sewer floor, narrowly missing the trench of flowing waste.

"Not pleasant. Not pleasant at all," his voice echoed up the hole. "Elhrin, they definitely came this way. There is a rope lying in the sewage canal and some kind of sack is on the ledge across from where I'm standing. Can you throw down the torch?"

"Here it comes," she said as she dropped the torch down the hole.

"Almost missed it," he grunted as he snatched it out of the air before it landed in the watery trench. He held it up over his head and waited for her to light it for him. He then waved the fiery brand low over the ground, searching. "There are no definite footprints down here. I will check the direction straight from here first. It runs to the east."

"Right, I'll let them know," she said letting the light orb near him fade away. She then pushed her way through the thick tangle of branches. Tomas was waiting for her on the other side and practically jerked her out of the hedges.

"This way," he said, leading her at a dead run across the lawn towards the canal. Master Gryph had already reached the water and produced a large light sphere. He and King Goruth leaned over the rail that lined the waterway. Guards were combing the area, searching for any boats or signs of passage, or . . . she refused to complete the thought of what else might be found. She slowed to a halt beside Master Gryph.

"Kyne said he did not see any clear prints in the sewers, but he would check the outlet coming this way first," she panted.

"Which one?" he asked.

"It should be directly below us." She leaned over the rail. Four outlets poured out of the retaining wall of the canal. Every one of them had a rusty metal grate firmly in place.

"What is that?" a guard shouted. He pointed to the sky.

The clouds directly above the palace had turned a sickly red. As she watched, a bright light descended through the red haze and sped for the earth. It disappeared behind the silhouette of the palace to boom far off in the city. Several more bright lights fell out of the sky—one right after the other—to slam with a massive boom somewhere in the city.

"Are those meteors?" King Goruth asked.

"No, definitely not. And I can't hit them from here," Master Gryph growled as he grabbed Elhrin painfully by the arm and dragged her with him, running back towards the palace. Another light descended and hit the city with a resounding explosion. They were getting closer. Bells started to toll over the city. It was the city's way of warning the population that there was danger. Bells from atop the palace joined in, clanging loudly at a desperate pace.

"What is happening?" Elhrin yelled, thankful he had let her go and was half-running, half-limping ahead of her.

"Obsudius, Elhrin. There is a rift above those clouds," he yelled. A sixth light fell from the sky. It exploded in the southwestern part of the city. "Get yourself ready. We are next."

Fear lanced through her body. All the people inside—Bayle—Marguerite! A bright spot lit the red sky. The fiery light zoomed through the clouds towards them.

"Elhrin, make it count." He slid to a halt in the wet grass. He raised both hands over his head and smacked them together. She followed his lead. In succession, they both fired a blazing sphere of deadly energy into the air. Both missiles flew above the palace at a rapid rate. His collided into the falling light, hers detonated inside the resulting explosion, creating a tremendous second explosion that rocked the ground beneath her feet and spraying a massive amount of sparks over the palace grounds and the nearby streets of the city.

"Your pendant, girl!" he yelled. He jerked his from under his collar and pulled it over his head. The pendant flared to life as he raised it above his head. A beam of pure white shot up into the red haze. She jerked her pendant over her head and matched his white beam with one of green. Both forces slammed into the façade of the hidden rift. The sky flared an angry red, and then the light winked out with a deafening boom that was so powerful that it shattered several windows in the upper floors of the palace. The dark of night descended once again over the city, cold and seemingly heartless within its deep, colorless shadows.

Breathing heavily, the both of them lowered their raised hands. Master Gryph let his head fall back to allow the frosty air of the night cool his sweat-drenched face.

"That didn't make sense," Elhrin panted. "We didn't close it. Why did he?"

"One—Obsudius didn't need it open any longer. The point had been made," he answered hoarsely, trying to catch his breath. "Two—we touched his power with that of Solisius'." He looked at her knowingly. "While he is not afraid of us, I'm sure he didn't want to chance a repeat of events that occurred inside Blackridge."

"Right," she said in understanding. "Yet, he didn't finish the pattern. He didn't destroy the palace."

"No, he didn't," he hauled in a huge breath. "It would have been a plus for him, but like I said, he already accomplished what he wanted—for the people of Muryne to suffer and to be terrified."

"If those weren't meteors then explain what happened here?" King Goruth growled ferociously, striding up with Tomas and an entourage of guards.

"You men move the crowd off," Master Gryph ordered the guards. The bells ringing throughout the city had brought many from inside the building out onto the grounds. They stood nearby watching curiously. Once the guards moved off to do Master Gryph's bidding, he lowered his voice to answer King Goruth so that no one could hear what he had to say. "Goruth, Obsudius opened a portal and allowed an N'gethwyn to attack us from above."

"You mean to tell me he and his N'gethwyn will be able to attack us like this anytime they want?" King Goruth asked in anger.

"He could if he dared to drain his powers on a grand scale. I have told you before that it takes a tremendous amount of energy to rip through the planes of existence between the spirit realm and that of the realm of the living, even for a god such as he," Master Gryph growled. "Obsudius is not like his father, The Creator, who is infinite in his powers. Obsudius is a limited god, and has to plan carefully. He thinks on a large scale. The destruction of one city will not be enough. He is seeking the demise of the human population of the entire country."

"So as we speak he could be doing this over another city?"

"It is possible. Only time will tell, but I have my doubts that he would deplete his energy on opening portals on a frequent basis. I would think it would benefit him more to use those he has on the ground to do his work for him," Master Gryph said.

"Damn it! I don't like the odds that he won't," King Goruth hissed and stormed away. "Gryph, use who you need to find your son. I now have a city in chaos to attend to. You men, with me," he yelled to several of his personal guards who were moving the crowd away.

"Sir, before I left the canal, Kyne had made it to the drain opening. He could not budge the grate. He said they must have used another route and retreated to search the other paths," Tomas said.

"Tomas, round up whoever you can find and go help Kyne. I want every corner of the sewers searched," Master Gryph said then yelled at one of the guards that was nearing them. "Major, have your men fan out across the entire perimeter of the canals. I want all openings into the sewers monitored. There are to be no boats allowed to enter or exit the waterways next to the palace."

"Yes, sir," the guard replied.

Master Gryph started back towards the palace. Elhrin had to jog to keep up with his long stride. Something in the pocket of her breeches poked her leg, reminding her that she had Marcus' horse.

"Master Gryph," she said, reaching into her pocket as she trotted beside him.

"Yes," he growled.

"I found this in the hedges." She produced Marcus' toy horse.

He took it from her without breaking stride, looked at it briefly, and then clasped it tight in his fist. They mounted the steps of the palace's east terrace where a crowd of onlookers had gathered to watch their defense against the attack. Seeing the deep anger on Master Gryph's face, the crowd parted without a word to let him pass unhindered to the entranceway. Master Gryph flung out a hand. The double doors of the entrance were ripped from their frame with his powers and crashed to the stone pavements of the terrace. Several women screamed from the unexpected violence. Elhrin was just as startled, but couldn't blame him. She wanted to destroy something, too.

The two of them crunched over broken glass and into total chaos within the building. It seemed as if every person within the palace was out in the halls and on the edge of falling into a state of panic. Master Gryph plowed his way through the mass of hysteria, ordering those who blocked his way to move aside.

"Gryph," a familiar voice called out, but Elhrin could see that he was intent on reaching a circular tower stairway and did not heed the call.

Councilor Idora pushed her way through the crowd and grabbed onto his arm before he entered the stairwell. "Gryph, what is happening?" she cried, her chest heaving as if she was trying to hold herself back from crying.

"Idora, I don't have time to talk right now," he growled and tried to leave, but the woman would not let go.

"Is it true? Is Marguerite dead?" The councilor's eyes filled with moisture.

Elhrin's heart slammed against her chest in fear. Had Marguerite died while they were outside?

Master Gryph glared at Idora then shook her hand from his arm. He rushed to the stair and mounted the steps two at a time.

Idora looked her way. "Elhrin?" she implored.

But Elhrin ignored the woman as she ran up the stairs after Master Gryph, following him as they rushed back to his apartment.

Two guards were now posted on either side of the door. One reached for the knob and opened it for them without hesitation. Inside, Marissa and Clay were sitting quietly in the living area, but they immediately stood when she and Master Gryph entered the apartment. He did not spare them a glance and disappeared into the bedroom.

"Elhrin?" Marissa called out to her.

"I'm sorry, Marissa, I can't talk right now," she said, rushing past the girl into the bedroom.

Master Gryph stood next to Marguerite's side, holding one of her pale hands to his lips. With relief, Elhrin leaned over to rest her hands on her legs, trying to stem the emotional wave that was threatening to drown her. Marguerite lived.

"Master Gryph," Bayle said softly, "I think you will want to see what is lying on your desk."

Master Gryph gently lowered Marguerite's hand to the bed and crossed over to a small desk in the corner of the room. He sighed heavily in anger at what he saw. He picked up a long coiled rope from the desk's top and stared at it for a moment. He then walked to a nearby window, opened it wide, and heaved the rope far out into the night, setting it on fire with his powers as it sailed far out across the palace lawn. The rope unraveled in midair and looked like a fiery serpent as it slithered to the earth. He turned and stalked back to his desk and scooped up a scrap of paper. It suffered the same fate as the rope. Out of things to fling through the window, he propped both hands on each side of the window pane and lowered his head.

Elhrin longed to go wrap her arms around him . . . to offer some sense of comfort, but knew he wouldn't want to be touched at the moment.

"She was to be the next victim, wasn't she?" she whispered to Bayle.

"Yes," he said miserably.

An unwanted mental picture of Marguerite hanging with her eyes cut out of her head flashed through Elhrin's mind.

"So that means the man in the bathroom was the killer we sought," she said.

"Yes," Master Gryph answered as he pushed away from the window. He turned a fierce gaze her way. "But he was not the one issuing the orders. That person is still out there." He stalked across the room and grabbed a long black cloak from his personal wardrobe. He whipped it around his back and settled it on his shoulders.

"Right," she growled in anger. "Unless you have something else you wish for me to do, I'm going down to help Tomas and Kyne search the sewers."

"No, I will do that myself. I want you to go back outside and check with the guards around the canals again. Dispense any orders you deem are necessary." He glanced to the open doorway where Marissa stood looking in. "Marissa, I want you and Clay to help her."

"Yes, sir," the girl said timidly.

"I have no authority to dispense orders to the guard," Elhrin said, watching him cross back to his desk and go through one of its drawers.

"You do now. Come here," he said as he pulled out a small black box and opened it. "Put this on and no one will question your command." He handed her the insignia pin of a high-ranking officer.

She was stunned by what he proposed she do. "I'm afraid I don't understand why you are giving me this. It is against the law to impersonate an officer of the army."

"You are not going to be impersonating one. I have just promoted you to the rank of Major in the King's Army." He swept by her to the bed and bent to kiss Marguerite.

"You have the authority to do this?"

"I do," he stated, smoothing Marguerite's hair. "Bayle, watch over Marguerite for me." He started for the door.

"With my life, sir," Bayle stated angrily. "I'll not fail you or her again . . . ever."

Master Gryph stopped in mid-stride and turned to look at Bayle. "Son," he said evenly, "don't you let me hear you say that again. You have not failed either of us." He then stalked out of the bedroom.

Elhrin followed right behind him. "I thought you told Colonel Drurhey that you have no authority in the military," she said.

"I normally don't, but in times of war there is an edict in place where my title changes from Minister to General. Elhrin, our city was attacked. We are now at war." He opened the apartment door and stepped into the hallway. "Which means your status as my assistant puts you under my command. You are now an officer in the King's Army."

"Why haven't you ever explained this to me before?" she asked, hustling after him.

"Elhrin, damn it!" Unexpectedly, he rounded on her. "You place me too high up on a pedestal. I am far from perfect, and things do tend to slip my mind. If it is not necessary at the moment, why does it matter when I tell you something or if I fail to tell you something?" Without waiting for her to reply, he stormed away.

Elhrin watched him go as she pinned the officer's insignia on her cloak. "Because sometimes I feel as if you shut me out on purpose," she said, angrily.

Surprisingly, he heard what she said and stopped in his tracks far down the hall. "No, Elhrin, I do not shut you out on purpose," he said, piercing her with a fierce scowl. "You must come to an understanding within yourself about this matter. You may not understand what I mean now, but one day you will." He turned away once again and wove his way through the people milling about in the corridor who had witnessed their exchange. Perplexed by his obscure statement, she watched him until he disappeared into the stairwell of the southeast tower.

"Marissa," she called to the girl still inside the apartment, "if you are going with me, let's go."

Chapter Eight

—◦◦❋◦◦—

Elhrin strode down the gravel path lining the north perimeter of the palace grounds. Marissa and Clay tailed her just steps behind. So far, they had traversed three sides of the palace, talking with each guard they came across to see if they had any news. Nothing had turned up. Now she was going to check the palace's boat landing that was situated on the north side of the grounds. Two guards stood in place at the top of the stairs that led into the canal, watching her approach.

"Corporal," she acknowledged the higher ranking guard.

"Major," the guard answered.

It is amazing, she thought. Just like that, a piece of metal on her shirt could demand this kind of respect, and being unused to a position of high authority, it made her extremely uncomfortable. It didn't feel right to her. She had not earned the position like the soldiers had, working their way up through the ranks with hard work and dedication. She wanted to take the pin off, but she had to admit it did save time to bypass questions as to who she was for those that did not know her.

"Have you anything new to report on the whereabouts of Minister Idwyr's son?"

"No, Major. Captain Fieldcrest just came by asking the same question."

"How long have you been here?"

"We arrived right after the meteor shower fell from the sky. We were ordered to stay at this post until notified."

They thought the attack on the city was fiery rocks falling out of the sky like King Goruth had at first. That was good. If the public knew the truth . . . she couldn't fathom what would happen if the general public knew a god was working towards eradicating the human race.

"Has anyone come here wanting to leave?" she asked.

"Just a few who were here at the invitation of the councilors, but we told them the palace was on lockdown and no one was allowed to leave until further notice."

She peered down at the line of boats tied to the boat landing and decided to have a closer look. Oil lanterns on the stone pillars of the landing cast a dim glow on the platform and the still, black waters of the canal. Not much light to see by. The guard followed her down while Marissa and Clay watched from the railing above.

"Has anyone tried to use the canal to pass through?"

It and the southern canal in front of the palace were major waterways for boat traffic, but the north one was used on a more frequent basis since it connected two major city features—the palace on the east side and the City Market on the west side.

"No, we have sealed off all entries into the canals surrounding the palace."

She looked up and down the waterway. To her left, the palace's north bridge spanned the canal, and she could see that it was well guarded. To the right, the canal turned a sharp right corner to continue down the east side of the grounds, but there was also another waterway branching off to the left, going under another bridge of one of the city's roads.

"Where is the blockade for that branch?" she asked pointing to the darkened hole of the connecting canal.

"The next block over has a boat access. They are stationed there."

Behind her there was the unexpected sound of metal scraping against stone then something heavy dropped into the water by the boat landing with a huge splash. Both guards drew their swords. Elhrin grabbed her magic. A light sphere popped overhead, but it wasn't hers. She was impressed with Marissa's instincts.

A sewer drain missing its rusty grate yawned black and empty in the canal wall. Below, the black water of the canal writhed with violent ripples across its normally calm surface. Elhrin stepped closer to the edge of the landing just as someone broke the surface of the water with a gasp. She started to render him immobile with her magic, but then realized who he was.

"Tomas?" she cried in surprise.

"Elhrin," he gasped, swimming to the boat landing. She and the guard helped him out of the water. "Water . . . is . . . freezing," he chattered, his body shivering violently.

"Then why did you dive in?" she asked. She hovered a hand in front of his chest. "Stand still." She used the same magical technique on him that Master Gryph had used on Marguerite to warm him up.

"That feels good," he chattered, as the warmth spread across him and started to dry his clothes. "I didn't mean to fall in. All the grates I have checked so far have been stuck in place. As soon as I pushed on that one, it gave way. I wasn't expecting it and couldn't stop my fall."

"Elhrin, look," Clay called out from above. "A boat." He pointed to the connecting canal. The prow of a boat was visible from inside the other waterway. In the shadows, it had been completely hidden.

She let go of her magic, and she and Tomas clambered into a flat-bottomed punt tied at the dock. The guard untied its rope and pushed them off. Tomas grabbed the boat's long pole and shoved it into the water until it hit bottom. Then he propelled them down the canal. He shifted to the other side to turn the bow of their boat so that they came alongside the empty one. Elhrin reached out to grab the rough edge of the other boat's side as she zapped a light sphere into existence. The entire underside of the nearby bridge lit up, and something small and furry squeaked and disappeared into a tiny black hole on a narrow ledge above them.

"Dear god, we found it," she choked. Lying in a crumpled pile in the bottom of the boat were Marcus' night clothes. She leaned over and snatched the tiny shirt and breeches out of the boat and held them up for Tomas to see. "Why did they take off his clothes?"

"Probably to put something else on to make him look less suspicious." He pointed to the bridge. "Especially, if they needed to be out in the open and didn't want to draw attention to themselves."

"Why would they take the time to do that if they were in a hurry to get away?" she said. "And I'm sure he would be scared and crying. Wouldn't it be too risky out here?"

"Maybe they changed him before leaving the sewer and just dropped them in the boat when they jumped in."

"Okay, but how did they get from there to here without being seen or heard?" She pointed a finger at the sewer drain, trying not to think about what they had done to Marcus to keep him from crying out. "And where did they go from here?"

The top of the canal wall was high out of reach and there was a protective iron fence cemented into the stone as well. It would be difficult for anyone to get out and almost impossible if one was carrying a child.

"You there! Don't move!" a stern voice ordered.

Two of the City Guard were rowing towards them from the blockade positioned on the other side of the next bridge. Behind their boat she could see the dark figures of three more guards standing in the hazy, dim glow from the landing's flickering lanterns.

"Steady, Private. I'm Captain Colkitte from the Glimmerdale Road Patrol and this is Elhrin Caddoch, assistant to the Minister of Specialized State Defense. We are searching for his son," Tomas called out and pointed at the empty boat they found. "Did you men not see this boat?"

"Sir, that was not there earlier," one of the guards answered as their boat neared.

Elhrin held up Marcus' clothes. "They were here. How did you not see them?"

"Major," the guard said, Tomas visibly started at the title and looked at her in surprise then he noticed the pin on her cloak, "I assure you that no one was on or near this section of the waterway before the meteors fell from the sky because we had just patrolled the entire area from this intersection to the next landing five blocks in the other direction."

"And where were you during the . . . meteor shower?" Elhrin asked.

"We were a few blocks up on the other side of our blockade . . . watching the sky," the guard admitted.

"Where were they?" she asked, pointing to the men on the boat landing.

"Up on the road," the guard said hesitantly, "also watching the sky."

Elhrin grunted in frustrated anger. "Your failure to stay vigilant as ordered will not sit well with the minister, you do know that don't you, Private?"

"Yes, Major," he said, seemingly remorseful for his failure.

Furious that the men's negligence cost them the opportunity to save Marcus, she couldn't look at the soldier any longer. She turned to Tomas. "They used the meteor shower on the city as a diversion to get away from the palace."

She scanned the underside of the bridge. "At least, we know they didn't escape the canal by boat landing, but they had to get out somehow." She was sure Marcus' abductors had not slipped by the blockade because even if the guards were on the street above, they would have noticed a boat going past the landing.

"Corporal," she called out to the guard still standing on the palace's boat landing, "locate Minister Idwyr and let him know his son is no longer on the palace grounds, and I want every available breathing body on the streets above me looking for that boy right now! Marissa, you two get over here. Tomas, push us to the other side of the bridge. They had to climb out somehow."

Tomas grunted as he heaved the boat into motion. Elhrin sent her sphere higher to light the canal walls on both sides.

The guards in the other boat turned around and followed them. "Stinger, you and Jaxom go up and question anyone you see in the area," the private yelled to his companions at the blockade. "If anyone has a child, don't let them go until someone verifies it is not Minister Idwyr's son." Both men quickly vaulted up the stairs to the street above.

As she and Tomas drifted out from under the other side of the bridge, she scanned the moss and algae covered wall above her. On both sides of the canal were three-story brick row houses built back to back with a narrow alleyway running between them.

"The bridges would have been too risky if they wanted to climb up without being seen. Do you think the alley drain is big enough for a grown man to slide through?" Elhrin asked.

Tomas glanced at the rectangular hole at the bottom of a tall brick wall hiding the alleyway between the row houses. "No, and going over would be dangerous with those ornamental spikes at the top," he answered.

"Then the only other option are the houses, but which one?" she asked, studying the flat exteriors of the buildings. There were no ledges or balconies, only firmly shut windows. She looked back to the bridge when she saw movement. Marissa and Clay stopped briefly to look down at her then ran across, following a group of guards. Elhrin started to examine the houses above her again, but her brain registered something amiss about the buildings to her right. What was it? She retraced the line of sight her eyes had taken and stopped on a darkened window that was not firmly shut as she had first thought. It was slightly ajar, as if someone had closed it, but had forgotten to fasten the latch and it had popped slightly back open. She would have never noticed it if she hadn't been looking for something out of place.

"Tomas, look at the window on that house." She pointed. "It's open. Do you think it might be something?"

"Let's find out. Private, we are going topside to investigate the house with the open window. Let us know if you find anything else," Tomas ordered as he navigated their boat to the blockade landing.

The guard still manning the blockade reached out a hand to help them out when they collided with the landing. They rushed up to the street and over the bridge to the house they suspected was being used for an escape route. A group of guards from the palace rounded the corner of the next block, saw them, and ran their way. Elhrin vaulted up the two steps to the door landing and pounded on the door.

"Hello, is anyone home?" she called out. She pounded on the door again.

Someone noisily flipped several locks in the door of the next house and opened it a mere crack.

"What in the name of the God of Light is going on out here?" the gruff voice of a man asked angrily.

"Sir, who lives in this house?" Elhrin asked.

"Who wants to know?" he barked.

"I am the assistant of Minister Idwyr. We have official business with whoever owns this house," she barked back, losing patience with the man.

"His assistant? I don't know," he answered, opening the door wide enough to reveal a portly man dressed in a long night robe. Behind him stood an elderly woman holding a stubby candle whose flame was promptly snuffed out by the drafts wafting inside from the open door

"Sir," Tomas said sternly, "if you don't tell us who owns the house, I'll have one of these guards drag your ass to the palace for a conversation with King Goruth himself. Who owns the house?"

The man sputtered in outrage, but when he saw the guards fanning out on the street below them, he decided to cooperate. "That's Kahlin Marteen's house. He owns Marteen's Precious Gem Emporium in the Mid-Isle District, but you won't find him at home tonight. He's been living in the apartment above his shop because of the trade conference. Says he doesn't feel his shop should be left unguarded with all the people in the city. Why?" The man stepped out into the night, wrapping his robe tighter around him.

Elhrin tried the door, but it was locked.

"Sir, there has been a child abducted from the palace. Have you seen or heard anything unusual tonight?" Tomas asked.

"My mother and I heard several booms that shook the city and then the warning bells started ringing . . . I'm still wondering what caused that commotion. Do you know?"

Tomas waved a hand impatiently. "Other than the booms, did you hear or see anything out of the ordinary?" Tomas asked, skipping over the question.

"No, we were sleeping before then . . . ."

Elhrin didn't wait to hear anything else and blasted the door off its hinges. It fell with a tremendous crash against the home's interior stairway. With a wave of her hand she lit every candle and lamp throughout the entire house.

"Hey, you just can't tear a man's house apart." Elhrin heard the old man yell as she ran into the house. Beside the stair was a hall leading to the rear of the house. A sitting room was located to her right, but it only took a quick glance to see it was empty. The open window was in the rear. She ran down the hall, slamming open each door she passed with her magic and quickly looking in to make sure no one was inside. Behind her, Tomas and the guards entered the home.

"Search the house," she yelled, entering the last doorway on the right side of the hall as footsteps pounded up the stairs and in the hall behind her. The room was a storage pantry filled with clutter all across the floor and on the many shelves lining the walls and it was colder than the rest of the house from the night air spilling through the open window. Elhrin and Tomas made their way along a narrow path amidst the junk on the floor. Lying in a heap below the window was a bundle of rope and a lump of coarse fabric.

"There has to be more than two men in all of this," Tomas said, pushing the window open and calling to the men on the water below. "We have found the escape route." He bent to pick up the rope. It had a sling large enough to hold a child safely on one end.

Elhrin started back to the hall but tripped over something on the floor. A small object skittered across the wooden floor with a tiny clink and slid underneath a pile of old blankets. She glanced down at what she had tripped over, and stopped in her tracks.

"Tomas, look," she said, retracing her steps. She picked up a worn brown boot covered with scratches and dark, splotchy stains. She handed him the boot and searched under the blankets for the object that she had kicked. It was a tiny brass key.

"Why do you want me to look at a boot?" Tomas asked.

"Isn't that dried blood on it?" she asked.

"It appears to be," he said. "So?"

"The first body that was found was missing his boots." She held up the key. "This came out of it. Do you think they belong to the man?"

Tomas turned the boot over in his hand. "I don't know, but look here," he said, showing her the interior of the boot. A hidden pocket was sewn into its side. "I wouldn't think the common man would need something like this, do you? It is a relatively safe place to keep something small and valuable."

"Like a key? Have someone find the owner of this house and bring him back here. I want him watched until we can talk to him," she said, pocketing the key.

She hurried across the hall and pushed on a partially open door while Tomas located one of the guards to issue her orders. The room was a small kitchen and was just as cold as the storage pantry. A door leading into the alley was standing open. Quickly conjuring a light sphere, she darted outside and was immediately hit with a nasty stench, smelling strongly of rotting vegetables and spoiled milk. She covered her mouth and nose and sent her light down the narrow alley, scaring the vermin amongst the rotting garbage in its shallow drainage trench. It was empty, but the wooden gate at the far end was ajar.

"Tomas," she yelled, "out here!"

She jumped down into the alley and ran through the far gate, nearly colliding with Clay on the other side.

"Elhrin," he yelled, grabbing her to keep them both from falling on the pavestones of the sidewalk.

"Clay, they came this way."

She ran into the middle of the street, searching for any clue that would tell her the direction Marcus' abductors went after leaving the alley. She knew it couldn't have been back towards the palace or the road where she and Tomas had entered the house—if they wanted to go that way they could have left via the front door, but she knew that would have been too risky with the guards nearby on the boat landing. That left the two remaining roads at the intersection.

She ran to the intersection, but the only thing she saw down their empty lengths was the flickering of the street lamps on the corners, a few lit windows casting a dim glow on the sidewalks, and a light fog that was beginning to form with the approaching dawn. She wondered where the people were who lived in the surrounding neighborhoods. Had no one but the man they had spoken to and his mother been bothered by the warning bells that had rung incessantly over the city and the intense explosions that rocked the city's foundations? Did they think the noise had something to do with festivities surrounding the arrival of the foreign dignitaries? It didn't make sense, and the silence and lack of life felt eerie and unnatural.

"Which way?" she hissed under her breath at the empty street, taking a few steps towards it then turning to step towards the other. She felt like she was going to explode. She did not know what to do. The abductors could have headed for the waterfront district or taken the direction to the eastern perimeter road which would eventually lead to the southern gate if they wanted out, but the gates would be closed . . . per Master Gryph's orders. So where would they go then?

"Elhrin," Marissa called out, jerking her from her thoughts.

"What?" Elhrin snapped, whirling on the girl.

Marissa stood in the middle of the street with Clay, Tomas, and a few guards that had joined them. She pointed to the dark silhouette of a tall figure advancing with purpose in his hindered gait. With him was a group of men carrying lanterns and torches.

Elhrin took a deep breath to steady her nerves and prepare herself for the news she had to share with him. She found it a bit difficult, not because she was afraid of him or any reaction he would have to her news, but because his energy force felt like a tremendous storm rolling in, and like she had told Marissa, she felt like she was about to be hit by lightning.

"What have you found?" Master Gryph asked when he strode into the circle of light cast by the street lamp. Kyne and Director Allahaim were with him. The rest were a mixture of palace and city guards.

"Whoever took Marcus escaped through a sewer drain near the boat landing then rowed to a house owned by a jewel smith named Kahlin Marteen and climbed through a window. Then they came through the alleyway behind the house and had to go down one of these two streets, but I don't know which one." She flung a hand in frustration at the two streets, realizing when she did so that she still held Marcus' clothes.

He stared at her hand with an expression of stone. He held out his hand and she gave them to him. "Where were these?" he asked as he examined them.

"In the boat they used to cross the canal."

Satisfied that the clothes held no blood or signs of harm to Marcus, he rolled them up and stuffed them under his sword belt. He then scrutinized both roadways. "What did Master Marteen have to say?"

"He wasn't there. His neighbor said he was staying above his shop in the Mid-Isle District. Tomas sent someone to find him and bring him back to the house to wait until we could question him."

"I hope he is still alive. That area was hit," he said then turned to the group of guards. "Captain, I want every door to every house in this entire vicinity knocked on and their inhabitants questioned thoroughly. If anyone saw so much as a roach crawl through a crack or heard a neighbor sneeze I want to know about it."

"Yes, sir," the captain of the city guard responded, waving for his group to follow him.

"Nygill, can I trust you to take care of the questioning of Master Marteen?" Master Gryph asked.

"You're damn right. I look forward to it," he growled. He pinned Elhrin with his beady eyes. "Which house is it, shit, ahem, . . . Miss Caddoch?"

Elhrin was a little surprised. He was almost cordial. She pointed up the road. "The last house on the left before the bridge."

"You will recognize it by the lack of a front door," Tomas added.

Director Allahaim grunted. "Let's go, Jake."

The short, dark-haired fellow dressed entirely in gray separated from the crowd behind them.

"Director, wait," Elhrin called out. She produced the key from her pocket. "We found this hidden in a pair of boots in the back of the house. There is a slim possibility it could belong to the dead man found hanging in the inn's stables."

"Elhrin, let me see it," Master Gryph said as he reached for the key. His scowl deepened. A tiny light sphere popped into the air above his head to give more light. He held it up and turned it to look at both sides of the key. He let his light wink out and handed the key to the director. "See what he knows about this."

"I intend to," Director Allahaim said, waving for Jake to follow him.

"You didn't want us to question him?" Elhrin asked her mentor when Director Allahaim was out of earshot.

"We will when we get time. I do want to meet the man, but for now, Nygill is good at what he does. We may learn more through his questioning than if we did it ourselves." He stared back down the empty streets. "Tomas, take these men with you to the neighborhood stables two blocks over. I require horses for all of us. If the stable owner balks at our request, tell him I will come see him personally, and if I am forced to do so, he will not enjoy my visit."

"Yes, sir." Tomas saluted and the men sprinted off into the night.

Elhrin noticed Kyne methodically walking down one of the streets with his head down and realized the night wasn't as dark as before. She glanced up at the cloud-covered sky. Dawn was ushering in a new day.

She groaned in frustration, realizing what that fact meant. "The gates are open, aren't they?" she asked.

"They should be," Master Gryph said.

"That is not good," she hissed under her breath.

"No, it isn't," he agreed. "Marissa?"

"Yes, sir," she answered quietly.

He waited for a moment then looked around for her. She stood frozen beside Clay a short distance away. "Would you please come here?"

"Yes, sir." She clasped Clay's hand and hauled him with her. The two of them stared at him with open expressions of apprehension.

"Elhrin taught you how to recognize energy sources. Are you comfortable with the technique?"

Marissa silently nodded.

"Do you recognize mine?" he asked.

"No, sir, I don't, really. There is so much overwhelming power jangling my senses that I am almost inclined to run as far from the two of you as fast as I can," she stammered fearfully. "I'm sorry, sir."

"You will need to know how to separate sources when they are entangled," he said without compassion for her plight, glancing back at Kyne who was coming back towards them. "You already know what Elhrin's feels like, do you not?"

"Yes, sir," she said, seemingly on the verge of crying.

"Look for that. What is left is mine. Quickly work on it because I don't have time for us to move far enough apart for you to distinguish our differences."

"Now?" she asked.

"Now," he ordered harshly.

Marissa sucked in a tremulous breath and closed her eyes to concentrate.

Instead of joining them, Kyne walked around the corner and moved to investigate the other street.

"Elhrin," Master Gryph said.

"Yes, sir?"

"Where were the guards who were ordered to watch the canals when Marcus' abductors left the sewers, secured a boat, rowed him several hundred yards down a canal, and then hauled him up the side of a wall in plain view of anyone passing to the inside of a row house?"

She pointed up. "Watching the sky."

Unhappy with her answer, his lips thinned into a straight line. "Our enemy is clever, isn't he?" he asked.

"Yes, sir," she said.

"Marissa, hurry, girl," he said impatiently.

"I . . . I'm sorry, I'm trying," the girl whimpered.

"You're not making it easy for her," Elhrin said.

"I wasn't trying to," he snapped. "Kyne, did you find something?" he called out when the man stooped over to pick up something off the ground.

"I don't think it's anything, sir," Kyne replied holding something aloft, but he was too far away for them to see anything beyond a small dark shape the size of his hand. "Looks like a broken piece off of a wagon or carriage. I can't tell in the dark."

"Sir, I'm not sure, but I may have it," Marissa said. "Elhrin told me your source felt like one is about to be hit by lightning, and when I started to concentrate on that trait, it seemed to come from you. It is so strong, it almost hurts."

"You are correct, Marissa," Elhrin said.

"Good, now what I am going to need you to do is stay here and be our liaison between myself, Elhrin, and anyone who has information for us. I realize you do not know the city, but you can point out the direction where you feel our energy. If you no longer feel us, then that means one of two things has happened. We have either gone too far for your abilities or we are dead."

Marissa's face fell.

"Which is not going to happen," Elhrin said then glanced up at him. "Don't scare her."

"I don't have time to be tactful," he said with a deep frown. "They didn't take Marcus for the fun of it. They wanted me out here. Marissa, are you willing to help us with this?"

"Yes, sir," she whispered.

"Master Gryph, do you think Marguerite is still in danger?" Elhrin asked. In the turmoil of the evening she had not considered all the possible implications of Marcus' abduction. If they were out of the building then Marguerite was vulnerable despite Bayle being there to watch over her.

"Possibly," he answered. "I placed guards in and around the apartment before I left. No one will get to her without a fight. My concern right now is you."

"Well, don't worry about me. I can handle myself." She frowned, knowing the letter had been aimed at all of them. *Please, Solisius, don't let them hurt Marcus.*

Solisius' voice curled around her like the morning fog that was rising from the damp streets. *For now, he is safe.*

"But where is he?" Elhrin whispered looking up at the lightening sky, wishing she could see his face. Solisius did not answer. "Where is he?" she asked again.

Master Gryph clasped her shoulder and squeezed. "He cannot interfere with the course of destiny, Elhrin," he said so softly she had a hard time hearing his words.

"How can you be so calm?" she hissed in anger. "He knows! Damn it! He knows where Marcus is! Why can't he tell us?"

The group around them stared at her, puzzled by her outburst. Master Gryph gripped her shoulder painfully and forced her to walk with him towards Kyne who was at the next corner of the street he had been searching.

He bent to her ear. "Do I have to remind you that claiming you are So'ladiun in the midst of a crowd is not a good thing? Just because those around us are on our side does not mean they won't speak of what happens here to someone who is not on our side. You do not need to make yourself more of a target than you already are."

"But he knows," she whispered hoarsely.

"Yes, he knows." He ground to a halt. She winced when his fingers dug into her shoulder. "I am just as frustrated as you are about the fact, but I understand why he does not tell us. At the expense of my own son, I have to follow the course of events laid out for us and pray that he will give me the strength to see this through because there is something bigger at stake here than just the welfare of my family."

"I still don't understand why he can't tell us," she cried softly.

"Elhrin, we touched on this last night. Sometimes you have to push your personal feelings aside." He clasped both her shoulders so she would face him and bent down to her eye level. "I know that sounds out of place since you saw me lose control of my own personal feelings earlier. I do not apologize for doing so, nor will I if it happens again. But laying all that aside, what I am trying to explain to you in a hurry is that there is a time and a place for certain events to happen during the course of fate. To change these events before their time could create a catastrophe that you, me, the nation, or the world would not be able to recover from. Do you know that Obsudius would love nothing more than for Solisius to tell me exactly where to find Marcus?"

"No," she whispered, looking past him to where Kyne was working his way back to them.

"Well, he would, because if we were to find Marcus before it was time, that might very well be the one thing that could change fate enough to shift Obsudius' hold on this world to his favor. I know that seems unlikely and absurd, but it is what it is, and Solisius will not take that chance."

She shifted her eyes back to his with a glare. "I guess I have no choice other than have faith that what you say is true, but you will have to forgive me when I say that I have a hard time agreeing that finding one little boy can change the balance between the two gods."

"There is nothing to forgive. You are entitled to your thoughts," he said.

Elhrin blew out a long, frustrated breath. "The time for finding Marcus had better damn well happen soon."

"Yes, it had," he agreed. "Elhrin, Solisius won't point our way, but that doesn't mean he has abandoned us. Think about what he has given us that allow us to accomplish our trials. We have our unique abilities that not many in the world have. He sometimes gives us dreams that allow us to see something we need to see. And what about the tools he has given us," he touched his chest where his pendant lay, "and the people he puts in our path to help us? Do you think Kyne is here because he has nothing better to do with his life? Can you think of someone more qualified to be your partner or your protector than he?"

"Yes," she said.

"Is that so? Who?" he asked.

"You."

"Ah, but that is not my place. For now, it is his."

"But this is so hard."

"It is hard," he shook his head, "very hard, but I have to trust Solisius is doing what he can to make sure we do not fail. In the meantime, he did give us a bit of good news."

"What is that?" she asked.

"Marcus is safe for the moment." He gave her a brief, sad smile.

Tears flooded her eyes, but she refused to allow herself to give in to despair. Marcus was safe, as in not dead, but what kind of terror were they putting him through. He was just a baby. He needed to be home with his mother, and his mother needed him as much as he needed her.

Far off across the city, the sound of bells tolled at a frantic pace. They were not marking the hour. Master Gryph straightened with a jerk and dropped his hands from her shoulders . . . listening . . . waiting. Another set of bells, a little closer, picked up the call then the bells from atop the palace started to ring as did others all across the city.

"Oh no," she whispered.

Master Gryph ran back towards the intersection. She was right on his heels. He stopped at the corner, seeing Tomas and the guards had been able to procure horses and were clattering down the street.

"What is happening?" Marissa called out, as she moved out of the middle of the intersection where Tomas and the men brought their horses to a sliding halt.

"The city is under attack," Elhrin yelled then froze. An N'gethwyn had stepped into her range of awareness somewhere outside the city gates where thousands of Anderan's citizens would be unprotected. Feeling as if she had dove head first into a vat of pure evil, his energy source washed over her—poisonous with an edge to it sharp as a freshly honed blade.

A distant boom rolled over the city. The N'gethwyn was attacking.

"Elhrin, I have to go," Master Gryph growled in frustration, grabbing the reins of a riderless horse from one of the guards. "It will be up to you to find Marcus for me."

Elhrin went numb. *No, don't do this,* she thought selfishly. "Let me go instead. Marcus needs you more."

He hauled himself up into the saddle and looked down at her fiercely. "No matter how much my heart cries for me to do just that, I cannot. I made a commitment to my king and the people of this country. I have to honor it." Another boom rolled over the city. "I would entrust my son's life in no other hands, but yours. You are in charge." He kicked his horse and pounded down the street.

The N'gethwyn had better prepare himself, she thought, *because he is about to be struck by lightning.*

"Kyne," she yelled, whirling around to find him right behind her.

"I am right here. You don't have to yell," he frowned.

"I didn't know that," she retorted. "Did you find anything to help us?"

"Only this," he said, showing her a piece of polished black wood with a portion of a formal motif painted in gold on one end. "This had to come off a wealthy citizen's carriage or hackney, but there is not enough of the crest to tell which house it belongs to."

"How does that help us?" she asked.

"It may not be related at all," he said with a shrug, "but it could be a part of the vehicle used to take Marcus away from here."

"Which part?"

"The part that had a painted crest on it," he said.

She took a menacing step towards him. "You are wasting time, Kyne," she growled.

"Elhrin, I don't know where on a damn carriage this came from . . . the door? The front? The lid to the storage compartment that some have built on the back? I don't know and it doesn't matter. What matters is that most likely, Marcus was placed in a carriage and transported somewhere, and if I was to make a random guess as to where they were going, I would say it would be to the docks." He angrily jerked a thumb back over his shoulder.

"No," she whispered, thinking he was probably right. The one who wrote the letter wanted Master Gryph out of the city, and since he was here, what better way to get him back out than to take his son out. She grabbed the reins of the horse Tomas held and hauled herself into the saddle.

Kyne mounted, as well.

"Marissa, you and Clay mount up. We are changing the plan." Her mount started to prance in a circle, picking up on her highly agitated state and wishing to be off. She turned his head with the reins so that she faced Tomas. "Tomas, let's split up. Kyne and I will take the direct route to the docks. You take Marissa with you down the other road and parallel us, just in case we are wrong. If you find anything and need us, send Marissa, she will be able to find me. Otherwise, we'll meet at the waterfront." She pointed at the waiting guards. "You three come with me."

She whirled her mount around. He was more than willing to run, so she let him have his head to speed through a city that was finally coming alive. This time the city's citizens were heeding the bell's call. Lights bloomed in darkened windows and people stood in open doors, trying to figure out what was happening. The streets were starting to fill, and Elhrin had to keep alert for those brave enough to cross the street in front of a pack of running horses. She tried to take in all that she passed just in case something stood out that would tell her they were right or not.

"Kyne, let me know if you see anything," she yelled. He was riding neck-and-neck beside her.

"I don't know why you felt the need to tell me that, Major Caddoch," he yelled back, emphasizing her new title. "You know I would, anyway."

Always a smart ass, she fumed, briefly shooting him an I'm-going-to-kill-you-when-I-get-a-chance look.

He saluted her. Then his eyes widened and he lunged for her reins and hauled back on hers and his at the same time. A carriage had entered the road in front of them and they had nowhere to go. Both their horses reared back on their hindquarters, sliding on the paving stones of the road. Elhrin grabbed her mount's mane and the edge of the saddle to keep from falling. Startled whinnies from the guard's horses surrounded her as they, too, struggled to keep from colliding into her and Kyne.

"Elhrin," Kyne huffed in a huge breath when they finally came to a standstill, "I see a carriage."

"Thank heavens you did," she breathed. The carriage clattered past at a rapid pace, speeding towards the palace. It had the crest of the Eastern Province on its side. "I think we need to be more careful at intersections," she said, watching the carriage disappear down the road but did not feel the need to pursue it. Her instinct told her they needed to move on. She kicked her horse into motion, and they made it through the east gate into the waterfront district without further incident.

"No," she shouted when they could see the lake clearly. She pulled her mount to an abrupt halt. "No! No! No!"

The lake was teeming with departing ships of all sizes. Meteors falling from the sky and now bells issuing the warning for an attack had been enough for the captains to seek safety away from the city.

"It doesn't mean we are too late, Elhrin." Kyne kicked his horse and led the way to the docks. "It will take time for all of them to get away," he yelled back to her.

There were several docking stations in the Waterfront District, but only two sites allowed the large tall ships access to the stone wharfs, and they were on either side of the peninsula's tip. The east side, where they were, was the older of the two docking sites, and was used by the smaller and less prominent shipping companies. The west side was reserved for the major shipping companies because of its closer proximity to the business and market districts on the west side of the city. The west side was also where the foreign visitors had berthed their ships.

Elhrin scanned the busy wharves as she followed Kyne through the throngs of seamen, dock hands, and shady-looking characters, searching desperately for a small body with unruly black hair. She almost panicked. Unlike the virtually quiet streets of the neighborhoods they had passed through, there were hundreds of people scurrying around, trying to load and launch the ships still docked. Distantly, she heard a series of booms, rapidly reporting one after the other. Master Gryph was engaging the enemy—lightning was striking.

Solisius, keep him safe, too, she prayed silently, feeling torn between her duty to help him defend the city, and her desperate desire to save Marcus.

"Kyne, we need to start asking people if they have seen Marcus. There is no way we will be able to find him in all of this," she said. "Guards, spread out, take this area, and work your way down. Kyne, I'll take the middle, you go on ahead."

They spread out, asking anyone they came in contact with if they had seen someone with a small dark-headed boy. Finding it hard to maneuver her skittish mount through the sea of humans, she dismounted and weaved through the crowd on foot. Most of those she asked just scowled at her with an angry shake of their head and pushed past her. Some didn't even bother to look at her and she was rapidly becoming frustrated. She pushed through a crowd of dock workers rolling crates to one of the few remaining ships tied to the wharf, and spied two men off to one side overseeing the loading of the ship. One was a burly, older man dressed in the black attire many sea captains wore and had a seaman's cap crammed over his wiry, gray-shot hair. His face was wrinkled and weather-worn from his time spent on the water and he had a bushy beard that hung to his chest. The young man beside him was tall and lanky, and bore the arm badge of a dockmaster. Both men were deep in conversation over a leather-bound ledger in the dockmaster's hands.

"Excuse me," she said, interrupting their conversation. The dockmaster looked at her questionably while the other man was clearly irritated at the intrusion. "I am looking for a three-year-old boy with black, wavy hair. Have you seen him?"

"Miss, do we look like we have time to people watch? I'm trying to get my ship on the water," the older man growled.

"I understand that," she said evenly, bracing for a fight. She was tired of men judging her and brushing her aside because of her age and small size, thinking she was no more than a child. "The boy I'm searching for is the son of the Minister of Specialized State Defense and has been kidnapped. If you have any information that can help me, you better damn well tell me." She ended up shouting.

Both men were clearly shocked by her outburst.

The big seaman recovered first and narrowed his dark eyes. "Gryph's boy?" he asked.

It was her turn to be shocked. She wasn't expecting the man to be familiar with Master Gryph enough to use his given name without a formal title.

"Yes," she answered. "You know him?"

"Know him? Of course I do. We grew up together in Pago Duhn." The man's bushy eyebrows deepened. "I have not seen the boy, Miss, but I can promise you if I come across those who have him, I will be more than happy to send them to the Realm of the Dead for you. I have yet to meet Gryph's boy. What does he look like?"

"He is three with black hair and blue eyes. He looks like his father," she said. "There would be no mistaking him if you saw him."

He reached up to scratch under his chin. His hand disappeared completely under his bushy beard. "You haven't seen a boy have you, Hix?" the captain growled.

"No, Captain Ostied," the dockmaster replied.

"Elhrin." She heard her name called. Tomas, Clay, and Marissa, were plowing through the crowd. In their wake, the guards that had accompanied him were helping an elderly lady navigate the rushing sea of humanity.

"Elhrin," Tomas said when he finally broke through the masses, "we have news."

Her heart leapt. "What is it?" she asked.

"We had to stop at the city gate because I almost ran over this lady," he helped the lady forward. "This is Madam Karolyn. She may have seen a carriage with Marcus inside."

"I was watching the ships this morning," the elderly lady spoke up. She was a frail lady with bright blue eyes to match her cloak and the lacy bonnet on her head. "I love to watch the ships, but can't make it to the docks like I used to. Just get as far as the gates on the hill."

"She's been there since before daybreak," Tomas added, incredulously.

"Well, I can't sleep and most ships like to leave with the rising sun, so I get out early. Won't be able to much longer, though," she said wistfully. "These old bones can't take the cold much."

"She saw a carriage come through the gates not long after the, uh, meteor shower," he pointed to the sky.

"I haven't seen anything like it in all my eighty-four years. Now I have seen one or two stars shoot across the sky, and there was this one time that a star with a long tail rode across the sky all night—I was young enough to be able to stay up and watch it—but I never witnessed them hitting the ground," she pursed her lips. "It was pretty, but frightening."

"Madam Karolyn, about the carriage, was there anything you can tell us about who was in it or driving it?" Elhrin asked. She didn't have time to hear the lady's tales.

"Dear, you sure are pretty with those curls framing your face. Not many women can pull off such a look, but it looks fabulous on you." She reached out to tug at a wisp of hair near Elhrin's cheek.

"Thank you, Madam," Elhrin tucked the lady's bony hand between both of hers, feeling like she was holding onto a satin chunk of ice, "but could you tell me anything about the carriage you saw?"

"Oh, yes," her face saddened. "it was terrible. I don't know what kind of parent yells at a child like that man was. Telling him to shut up or he would smack him again. The poor thing was crying his heart out."

"Did you see them?" Elhrin choked against a lump in her throat. She had said "him" which meant she had to have heard the man say him. It had to be Marcus and the man had hit him. Her anger started to grow again.

"No, dear, it was too dark and they only stopped briefly at the gates. Then they took off like Obsudius himself was after them."

"Elhrin, Madam Karolyn said they came down this way," Tomas said.

"Miss," the dockmaster called. "I didn't see a boy this morning, but I did see a little girl and she was crying pretty hard."

"Where?" Elhrin and Tomas asked simultaneously.

"They boarded the *Shifting Winds* right before it pushed off," the dockmaster said.

"Come to think of it, the captain was in a hurry to get underway. He had yelled over the side at the men with the baby to hurry aboard."

"How long ago was that?" Captain Ostied asked.

"I would think about an hour ago."

"What did the girl look like?" Elhrin asked.

"Well, they had her wrapped tight in a blanket, and her head was covered by a bonnet." He squinted, trying to recall what he saw. "I was standing at the gang plank directing the dock hands when the three men with the child rushed by me. I remember the child looked in my direction and was crying. She might've had dark hair under that bonnet but I couldn't tell you if it was or not. I'm sorry, that's all I know, except I do remember thinking it strange that three grown men were alone with a baby and no mother was with them, but I've seen stranger things around here so . . . ." He shrugged his shoulders.

It had to be Marcus. Elhrin's instincts screamed it was him. She balled her fists tight, wanting to blow apart something in frustration. She looked out over the lake, listening to the far off steady booms of the fight raging on the other side of the city. What should she do now? Duty dictated that she join the fight, but her heart said otherwise.

"Where were they headed, Hix?" the captain asked.

"Uh, let's see." Hix thumbed back through his ledger. "Here it is. They reported their final destination was Chyrzah, but first they are to port in Marmuht and drop off part of their load."

"Who owns the ship?" Captain Ostied asked.

"Agadar Shipping Enterprises," Hix answered.

"I'll be damn," the captain growled. "That's Roarke Whyse's company, the old son of a bitch. If that boy is on one of his ships, I'll be more than happy to send it to the bottom of the lake."

Elhrin jumped when the captain yelled in her ear.

"Get those boxes on board, you dog turds," the Captain roared at the dock hands attaching the crates to a rope. "Hix, you store the rest of my load for me. I'm shoving off. I'll get Gryph's boy for you, Missy."

"Captain," she grabbed his sleeve. Right or wrong, she made a decision. "I am responsible for his son. I am coming with you."

"I can't allow a little thing like you go. You might get hurt." He patted her hand on his sleeve.

A loud snort of laughter sounded from behind her. "No, Captain, you have that all wrong. If you don't let her go, you might get hurt." Kyne ducked under one of the tie lines attached to the wharf. "She may be small, but she is feisty and extremely stubborn. As a matter of fact, mules come to her for lessons."

"Shut up, Kyne," Elhrin spat. She was in no mood for his smart mouth. "Captain, I am Minister Idwyr's assistant. He entrusted me to find his son because he had no choice but to defend the city. If you refuse me passage, I will have to take possession of your ship for obstructing official business of the Office of Specialized State Defense and order your crew to do my bidding."

The captain's eyes glimmered with laughter instead of the anger she expected. He smiled wide to reveal a row of chipped and yellowed teeth. "Gryph was right. You are a force not to take lightly. I don't get to see Gryph often, but when I do, that old fart talks of only two things—fishing with a boy named Bayle and spending time with the loves of his life, his two girls." He clapped her on the back. "Come, come, welcome aboard my ship, *Storm's Defiance*."

Chapter Nine

"Marguerite, this is not good. You should be in bed. You are too weak," Bayle panted. He held her trembling body firmly by the waist and waited for her to be able to continue up the stairs.

Marguerite wanted desperately to reach the top of the palace's south watch tower. She had to see for herself the fighting outside the city walls. Bayle had told her that Gryph was fighting a magical adversary and a host of Do'athrim.

"Bayle," she said with a wince. Her throat was extremely sore from where the man tried to—no, not tried to—from where he choked her. She had been told how close she had come to leaving this world, and when she found out about Marcus, she wished they had let her die. "If you say that one more time . . . I will find the strength to kick you in the shins."

"If Master Gryph finds out I let you talk me into this I am a dead man," he frowned at her. "You have only been awake for an hour."

"I will deal with him if it comes to it. Just help me get to the top," she ordered.

A boom rattled the window pane beside them. The booms had been steady since she had regained consciousness earlier. That was why she had decided to make the nearly impossible journey to the watch tower. Bayle wouldn't let her leave the palace, and she couldn't take being shut away in the apartment any longer, even though her body screamed for her to remain in bed and sleep.

She took another step. Bayle tightened his grip and allowed her to lean on him as they slowly made their way to the top and out into the crisp wind that whipped her loose hair into her eyes. She ran an unsteady hand through the long strands and pushed them away.

"You shouldn't be up here," a guard said. He was one of three that were on duty in the tower.

"This is Minister Idwyr's wife, Private," Bayle answered. He guided her to the wall of the tower. "She wishes to see what is happening."

All three guards stared at her curiously. She supposed they had been made aware of her situation or could see the substantial bruising around her neck, but they said not a word to her. She turned to look out over the city. Smoke dominated the western sky where fires blazed out of control from the N'gethwyn's aerial attack the night before. To the east, she glimpsed ships of all sizes out on the lake, taking flight like a flock of startled seabirds seeking safety. Her gaze fell to the neighborhoods surrounding the palace. The streets were clogged with people in a state of panic, and somewhere out there her son was with the bastards who might harm him and she could do nothing about it. She shut her eyes, sending a trail of tears down her cheeks, the cold wind making them feel like rivers of ice on her skin. Elhrin had not been spotted with Gryph. Marguerite hoped she was still looking for Marcus.

Bayle wrapped an arm around her shoulders and pulled her close to keep her warm. She tried to muster a smile to show him she was grateful that he was with her but failed. He rubbed her arm against the cold and looked to the city walls where the battle raged.

An explosion unexpectedly shattered the top of the wall near the main gates. Stones crashed into the facades of nearby buildings, and soldiers caught up in the attack were flung in all directions. A brief flash of light blossomed from the other side of the wall and a resounding boom followed. Marguerite could not see what was happening on the other side of the city walls like she had hoped. The watchtower was not tall enough.

She scanned the masses of foot soldiers and archers on the ramparts. Near a guard tower east of the main gate, she thought she caught a glimpse of Goruth in the midst of Palace Guards, distinctive from the rest of the army being attired in purple uniforms.

"Why do the archers not shoot?" she asked, her throat was so raw she sounded hoarse.

One of the guards moved beside her. "They fire if they think they have a clear shot, Madam Idwyr, but there are hundreds of our people out there making it difficult." He shook his head. "And I'm afraid they are being slaughtered without much opposition. The gates are blocked with those trying to get in, so our soldiers cannot get out. Only the small force that had been assigned to keep order in the tent city, a few others, and now Minister Idwyr are outside."

"How did my husband get out?" Another flash of light came from the other side of the city walls followed by a streaming comet of green fire that soared high into the air and disappeared into the cloudy sky. A retaliatory boom resulted.

"He went over the walls." He pointed to a section of wall where soldiers were disappearing over its side at a steady rate, repelling down numerous ropes that had been anchored to the top of the wall.

Three orbs of green energy rose above the wall in sizzling arcs from different directions. Two balls of fiery white rose from near the gates and sped towards the green light which told her exactly where Gryph stood. A third missile from him sped high into the air after the others. Four orbs collided in mid-air with a thunderous detonation and sent sprays of white hot sparks raining down on the ground below. His third missile missed his target and arced high across the wide expanse of the meadows in front of the city to land somewhere in the forests on the other side. A silent flash of light lit the horizon from where it exploded. The enemy's luminous green missile zoomed below the line of the wall to hit something out of her sight with a tremendous explosion.

"Bayle," Marguerite gasped, "he is up against more than one N'gethwyn."

"He will be fine," he said, but his voice belied his optimism.

A volley of enemy arrows soared high into the air towards the wall followed by a flaming blaze of red magical energy. At the same time, a second N'gethwyn launched a crackling luminescent orb of green towards the area where Gryph had to be standing.

The arrows rained over those on the rampart while the blaze of red energy ricocheted off something invisible, spiraled over the wall, and blasted through the roof of a nearby building. The green orb disappeared from her view behind the gate's watchtower and exploded, making the stones under her feet tremble from the resulting concussion.

The soldiers trying to get down to the meadow froze momentarily where they stood, but then started going over the side at a dangerously rapid pace. Archers near the gates leaned over the wall and fired directly below their position. The rest launched a wave of arrows far out over the meadow, seemingly no longer concerned for the innocents on the field.

Without warning, two unimpeded N'gethwyn attacks blasted through the walls, killing dozens of soldiers and leaving large gaping holes in the fortifications. A blaze of red energy then soared over the wall and into the city unhindered. It exploded into the central spire of the Cathedral of Light, a house of worship dedicated to Solisius. The spire ripped from its foundation and slowly tipped to the side. It toppled into a screaming crowd on the street below.

Tears flowed steadily down Marguerite's face. What was left of her resolve to be strong despite her weakened condition evaporated. Her knees buckled.

"Marguerite?" Bayle cried out, startled when she lost her balance. He tightened his grip on her.

She looked into his fear-filled eyes. "He's not fighting back," she whispered hoarsely. Her emotional dam burst, and she couldn't stop the onslaught of tears that had been threatening to overcome her since she found out about Marcus. She crumpled against him, sobbing hard into his shirt. Marcus was gone! Her baby was gone! Now Gryph had to be gone, too. He wasn't fighting back so he had to be gone. She couldn't take this again. She had to endure living without him once. There was no way she could endure living without him and Marcus.

"Marguerite, it doesn't mean he is dead," Bayle tried to reason with her, but she wasn't listening. All rational thought left her.

"Not again!" she wailed into Bayle's chest. "Damn it! Not again!"

"Here, man, help me get her down," Bayle said to the guard.

On the edge of her awareness she felt gentle arms guide her back into the stairway. After that, she remembered nothing.

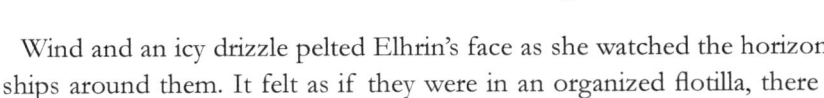

Wind and an icy drizzle pelted Elhrin's face as she watched the horizon, scanning the ships around them. It felt as if they were in an organized flotilla, there were so many ships heading east for the Wyndermir River wishing to reach the Yrahl Sea, but none of them was the one they were seeking. The *Shifting Winds* had over a two hour head start on them, and from what she understood, the ship was fast. Catching up to her would not be easy.

"I bet it won't be long before the north sees snow," Marissa commented as she tugged her hood low over her face against the weather.

"No doubt," Elhrin murmured. Her mind was in turmoil. Before the ship had left the range of Muryne, she had felt the strong energy sources of two more N'gethwyn enter the area near the city. Master Gryph was outnumbered, and she was consumed with guilt for leaving him to face them alone, knowing the last time he was outnumbered had resulted in his untimely death. If he died again, Solisius would not allow him to return a second time.

She rubbed a hand over her tired eyes.

She had to think that attempting to rescue Marcus was the right choice to make instead of staying to fight. He was just a baby. He was in danger. And Master Gryph had told her to carry on the search for him. But what if Muryne were to fall? The leaders of the country would see her absence as a betrayal.

Dear god, had she made the right choice? She slapped the rail of the ship in frustration, causing Marissa and Clay to give her a questioning look, but Elhrin ignored them. She would not feel guilty for following her heart. She would face the consequences of her actions if she had to . . . Marcus needed her!

She pushed away from the rail and joined Tomas, Kyne, and Captain Ostied who stood behind the helmsman steering the ship.

"How long does it take to reach the river?" she asked.

The captain squinted down at her. His beard was covered in droplets of water and they dripped at a steady pace down the front of his heavy coat. "If the wind stays steady like this, we should make it there by morn."

"Will we catch up to them, do you think?" she asked.

"I would like to say yes, but I would be pushing it. I don't think we'll see them before the river. What I am hoping for is to catch up to them before they reach the open sea." He wiped the moisture from his face with a scarred and callused hand. "Most likely, they will reach the river before daybreak tomorrow, so the night should slow them down at that point with all the cloud cover and no moon. If they are already in the river by the time we get there, hopefully, we will be able to catch up to them with a few tricks I have learned navigating it to gain us more time." His gaze roamed the ship to make sure everything was in order. "Hopefully," he said again after a moment.

Elhrin studied the billowing sails. Sailors scampered through the rigging, and a lookout was posted in the ship's crow's nest on the main mast. "Would more wind help right now?"

"NO!" Kyne protested rather loudly. "Elhrin, I told you to never, ever to do that again with me onboard."

"Kyne, I don't have time for you," she turned on him and smacked him in the chest with the palm of her hand and pushed him back a few steps. "I will do whatever it takes to get to Marcus. If you have a problem with that you can leave."

"How so?" he asked.

She angrily pointed to a dinghy tied to the ship's wall.

"Calm down," he growled, holding up both hands. "I am on your side. I just think we could reach Marcus sooner if the ship stays on top of the water instead of under it."

"I know what I'm doing," she fumed, and turned her back on him. "Captain, would more wind help speed us up?"

"It could as long as the waters are not too rough. What do you have in mind?" he asked.

"I have the ability to create a force of wind and make it as strong as you wish and any direction you wish. You just tell me what you need."

His eyebrow arched in surprise. "Can you now?"

"I can."

He looked back over the ship, thinking. "I don't know, young lady. This lot," he nodded at the sailors working hard at their various tasks on deck, "is a bit superstitious. I don't know what they would think if a mysterious wind were to suddenly blow up out of nowhere and affect only our sails and not the ones around us." He glanced out at the nearby ships that were sailing at the same speed.

"Marcus is more important than coddling your men's superstitions, Captain." She stood firm. She was not going to allow anything to stand in her way of reaching Marcus as quickly as possible.

"Miss, I agree the boy is more important, but you must be careful when you trod on a man's superstition. I don't need an entire crew decide to quit on me," he glanced up into the rigging then back to her. "I tell you what. You nudge the wind a bit and let's take it a little at a time. See how it goes. If the men get antsy, we'll have to rely on my skills to get us ahead."

"Fair enough, Captain," she said. "Tell me which way to send it."

"Right now, the direction is good if you can follow it."

"I can."

"Just a little now. Anything too heavy might cause more of a hindrance than help like your friend said."

"See," Kyne said.

"I will take it slow and keep it streamlined for the sails, Captain. I will follow your guidance as to the amount of force you need." She shot Kyne a hateful glare and retreated to the stern of the ship. She leaned against the rail for support and sent her energy aloft, gathering it above her and then forcing it to ride the natural currents into the sails.

Seeing that her suggestion was going to work, the captain issued orders for his crew to adjust the sails to compensate for the increase. Steadily, the two worked together under the curious stares of the sailors until the captain called out that what she had was fine. The sailors, for the most part, appeared untroubled by her using her magical powers, but she did catch a glimpse of one sailor in the rigging making some kind of sign with his hands. She couldn't tell if it was a gesture to ward off evil spirits or if he had put a hex on her.

"If you ever find yourself in need of a job, young lady, come look me up." The captain grinned. "You would make my life so much easier."

"I don't think so, Captain," she said. "I'm afraid I wouldn't last long as a sailor. I prefer the ground beneath my feet to stand still."

"How long can you keep this up?" he asked.

"I really don't know. I guess we'll both find out."

He nodded, turning back to the ship to check on their progress. Slowly, the ship pulled ahead of those who had been running alongside them. It wasn't much, but any extra speed brought her that much closer to Marcus.

"What is a merchant vessel doing with heavy assault ballistae on board?" Kyne asked. "Do you have that much trouble with piracy?"

"I've had an occurrence or two with a few scoundrels thinking they wanted my cargo more than I did." He glanced at the mounted weapon on a platform behind them, one of two onboard, the other being situated in the bow of the ship. They looked like oversized crossbows mounted onto a locked swivel contraption. The captain clasped his hands behind his back. "They found out the hard way I wasn't willing to let them have my load, though."

"I've seen a few of these on warships," Tomas said as he inspected the weapon. "I've heard they are fairly effective."

"They are in the right situation," the captain agreed.

"What do they use?" Clay asked. He joined Tomas to get a closer look at its mechanics.

"We use different types of bolts, depending on what we need done—the basics that I'm sure you are all familiar with," he rocked on his heels, "but I also have a special creation that I reserve for the vessels that I think would make a good home for the fishes."

"What would that be?" Kyne asked.

The captain grinned and walked to the rail of the sterncastle. "Mister Rindleson, would you please retrieve an Ostied's Specialty for me?" He looked up as the sudden flapping of the sails caught his attention. "Miss Caddoch, the wind has shifted somewhat."

Elhrin took note of the new direction and adjusted her flows. The sails snapped back in place. The captain winked at her, giving her his approval.

"It took me some time to work out an idea that was inspired by Gryph himself," he said as a sailor mounted the stair to the ship's sterncastle holding a long, sturdy-looking bolt four times the size of any ordinary crossbow bolt. On its tip was a strange narrow glass and metallic cylinder. The captain took the bolt from the sailor and held it up for them all to see. "You see, when he and I were lads, I watched him blow a few things up a time or two and I always wondered what it would feel like to have that kind of power."

"That's not crazy thinking at all," Kyne muttered.

The captain chuckled, "Oh, but it is a crazy thought, no? And my crazy thought has produced a spectacular invention. The tip of this beauty is powerful enough to blow a hole the size of a plow horse in a ship's hull, and when I finally work out all of its quirks, I will present it to our military officials and see if they would like to buy my insane idea."

Kyne whistled in appreciation. "If it works, you will be a rich man."

"If it is successful, I will be a comfortably retired man," he said with a satisfied tilt of his head.

"How does the tip work?" Clay asked.

"Ah, ah, ah," the captain shook his head, "that is a secret I have only shared with a trusted few who are invested in the idea, and it will remain that way for now." He handed the bolt back to the sailor.

"Captain, can I speak with you for a moment?" the helmsman asked.

"Excuse me, if you will," he said and turned to join the sailor at the wheel.

Tomas crossed the deck and lowered himself to the planks beside Elhrin. He yawned loudly. "How are you holding up?" he asked, huddling down into his coat.

"I'm fine," she responded, thinking she was so tired that if she sat down or did nothing for one second, she would lapse into unconsciousness.

Tomas yawned again, this time with an audible crack of his jaw. "Do you realize we have been up since before dawn yesterday?"

"Yes," she responded. Of course, she had not revealed to him she had been up longer with her adventure into Master Gryph's apartment to check on Marcus. The thought made her want to scream. Why didn't she pay more attention to her dream? She had allowed herself to feel secure with the guards in the halls and at the doors, and with Bayle and Marguerite watching over him, but it hadn't been enough . . . she should have done something—anything to keep him safe. She bit back a grunt of disgust, knowing that she was being too hard on herself. Like Master Gryph had said, there was no indication that the dream was to happen right away or the distant future.

"I don't see how you do it?" Tomas said, nodding at the sails. "Aren't you tired?"

"I am too worried about Marcus." She shifted her feet to keep her balance against the rolling of the ship. "Tomas, they hit him. What if they do worse?"

"Don't think about it, Elhrin. You said he was safe, and I think if they were going to do anything more, they would have done it where they could be sure Master Gryph saw their results like they did with those bodies."

Elhrin swallowed hard. "I guess you are right." She ran through the events of the previous night. They now knew there were, at the very least, four men involved directly with the murders and Marcus' abduction and one, if not all, were a member of the Brothers of M'gelidia, and she didn't need to forget the jewel smith. He had allowed them to use his home for their escape. Then there was Reginold Whyse.

"Do you think Reginold Whyse's hatred of Master Gryph is strong enough to devise a plan to kidnap Marcus?" she mused out loud.

"With the ship belonging to his father, it does look suspicious," Tomas said. "But then again, he could have no knowledge, whatsoever, as to what is going on. Even the captain of the *Shifting Winds* could be oblivious if the men who have Marcus booked passage on the vessel as ordinary travelers."

"That is highly unlikely, Captain Colkitte," Captain Ostied said, balancing himself against an unexpected series of rolling waves with the experience of a man who had been on the water for a long time. Elhrin had to grab the rail and Tomas reached over to grip her leg and keep her from stumbling across the deck. "The *Shifting Winds* takes no passengers. She is not outfitted for it. My guess on the whole affair is that the captain had prior knowledge of his responsibilities. They timed it well from what Hix said. The ship was ready to depart the second those men and the boy stepped on board."

"I wonder how close the councilor and his father are," Elhrin pondered.

"Oh, they are close," Kyne answered. "Roarke Whyse makes sure they are. Who better than one's own son to do your bidding at the nation's highest law-making level? And Reginold has not disappointed him. He pushed a new tax cut through recently that was very beneficial for large shipping companies which includes Agadar Enterprises, and if Roarke has his way, his company will be handed an exclusive contract with the government to ship timber from the northwest to Traphyt where they will be building a new naval shipyard next year. Oh yes, the two are very close."

"He better not," the captain grumbled low under his breath.

"How do you know this, Kyne?" Elhrin asked, wondering why the captain didn't want Agadar Enterprises to receive that contract.

"A few months ago, I had a very uncomfortable, but fortunate meeting with Roarke Whyse when he was in Muryne visiting his son."

"Fortunate?" Tomas asked.

"Fortunate," Kyne confirmed. "He may not be the most honest or pleasant character one will run across, but he does know the shipping business inside and out, and he knows that I am interested in the industry. During the course of our conversation, not only did he offer me a job, but he also let it slip about the contract and how grateful he was to have a son who looked out for his father on the council floor."

"I find it hard to believe that Roarke shared that kind of information to you. The man does not usually reveal his company's business with outsiders," the captain commented.

"Well, he has the strangest of notions that I am a family friend," he said, curling his lip in distaste, "and that he is doing my mother—the dearest of his friends, a favor. I don't think he would have spoken to me at all if he knew that my mother would rather run through the city naked in humiliation than have me go into the shipping business. She is hoping I will take Reginold's place on the council one day."

"If that is true, then what benefit could he possibly gain from helping someone kidnap a child?" Elhrin asked.

"Money speaks volumes to a man like Whyse," Kyne said.

"But wouldn't being involved in the kidnapping of the son of the man closest to the king be too risky," Marissa chimed in.

All eyes glanced her way.

"I mean, isn't Master Idwyr close to King Goruth?"

"He is," Elhrin said. "Master Gryph is his friend first before all the titles come into play."

"And you are right, Miss, it would be too risky a venture for Roarke," the captain said, and then roared a command to the sailors working the deck to retie a loose crate that had been placed mid-ship. He didn't miss a beat and continued his conversation with them. "Roarke does many things that fall into a shady area, but I don't think he would put himself into such a high profile situation unless there was something very high at stake to outweigh the risk of falling under royal scrutiny and the hangman's noose."

Elhrin could think of only one thing that would compel a man to take a high risk. An N'gethwyn threatening to obliterate him off the face of the earth. She decided to keep that thought to herself.

"Maybe he didn't set it up. Maybe Councilor Whyse arranged all of this without his father's knowledge," Marissa said.

"Could have," the captain stated.

"Could have," Elhrin agreed softly.

No one had anything else to add, and one by one they all drifted back to the rails, watching the distant shoreline slide by, and at one point Elhrin overheard Clay tell Marissa that they should pass Jarit's Cove after nightfall. This reminded Elhrin that Marguerite never got the chance to send a letter off to Marissa's parents.

A wave of heartbreaking emotion washed over her. Marguerite was like a second mother to her, and to see such a strong, beautiful lady brought to near death . . . could very well still die if her body failed to recover . . . was almost more than she could bear. She banished the thought immediately, vowing to believe Marguerite was strong enough to live and turned her attention to her flows of energy.

She felt Tomas' hand slide down her leg to the deck and glanced down to find him sound asleep. He had his legs pulled close to his chest and his head had fallen onto his knees. She reached down to smooth his damp, windswept hair. He needed something to cover him. His officer's coat didn't provide enough warmth or a hood to cover his head. Every once in a while she would see him shiver and wished she could spare the energy to warm him. She moved closer and wrapped part of her cloak around him to cover his head. It wasn't much, but at least it would help shield him from the drizzle.

Nearly three hours later, Elhrin finally had to stop and let her magical energy go. The ship slowed noticeably back to its normal state. She watched the sailors hastily adjust the rigging, hating that she was exhausted and no longer had the energy to continue, but she did feel a little better that they had made up some time. Earlier, Captain Ostied had pointed out a ship they were passing and said that it had left port approximately a half hour before they had. She slid down beside Tomas and put her head in her hands. She was so tired.

"Miss Caddoch, I am impressed," the captain said, climbing the stair up to the stern's deck. He had been below deck, checking on something, and she guessed he had noticed the drop in the ship's speed and had come back to see why.

"I'm sorry I couldn't keep going," she said, wishing there was a quick way to recharge her energy. She didn't want to stop. "We have had a long night."

"I'm sure you have." He took note of her and her companions trying to stay warm from the icy wind. Marissa and Clay were on the other side of the stern, huddled together, and Kyne had situated himself on the foredeck where he could watch their progress. "You all are welcome to go below deck where it's a bit warmer. I had my quarters cleaned out for you and the other young lady to use. The men can claim whatever hammock they find empty for themselves."

"Thank you, Captain, that is kind, but I prefer to stay out here," she shrugged.

"I understand, but I can tell you there will be nothing to see until tomorrow at the earliest. I suggest you get some sleep if you can. I will let you know if we come across the *Shifting Winds.*"

She knew he was right. She would need to be more rested if it came to a fight, and she definitely wanted to be as strong as she could possibly be when she met up with Marcus' abductors. They were going to pay for hurting her little man and Marguerite. Oh, how they were going to pay.

"Elhrin, will I be the oldest student at the academy?" Marissa asked softly. She and Elhrin were squashed into the captain's narrow bunk, and Elhrin, being on the outside, hoped they didn't hit any hard waves because she was sure she would be flung to the deck if they did.

"No, it's different from the primary schools of Anderan that only teach the young until the age of seventeen. We have students of all ages. I think our youngest is maybe ten and our oldest is a lady named Liselle who might be somewhere in her seventies." Elhrin glanced over her shoulder at Marissa and smiled. "But don't you dare tell her I said that because she won't tell anyone her actual age. I'm just guessing."

Marissa grinned. "Are there any our age?"

"There are several close to our age, some older, some younger," Elhrin replied with a yawn.

"What are they like?"

"Well, let's see, there's Eowhyn. You will like her. She is very easy to get along with and loves to help out wherever she can, so if you find yourself struggling with something, and Landin or Grey are too busy, she would be the one to go to." Elhrin shifted so she didn't have to strain to see Marissa behind her. "Then there is Kory who is originally from Chyrzah. He is a little older and an interesting character. He claims to have the ability to communicate with certain creatures of the sea, but we have yet to see him do it." Elhrin chuckled, remembering the initial interview with Kory. "Master Gryph asked him if he could talk with the fish in the river because he thought it would be nice if more fish would make their home closer to his in Harper's Stream so he wouldn't have to make his rounds to his other fishing spots on the Green River and could stay home, fishing until he was content."

Marissa laughed. "What did . . . what was his name? Kory? What did he say?"

"He said no. For some reason he can't hear them," Elhrin yawned. "He says he can only hear the creatures that are in the whale or porpoise family."

"That is interesting. Do you think he really can?"

"I don't know, but I don't have any reason to doubt him."

"Are there any others?"

"There is Kull who used to be on the Martaline Road Patrol until Bayle met him one day and convinced him to contact the academy, and Barron who is our scholar. We have trouble when he and Master Gryph get together."

"Why? Do they not get along?"

"No, just the opposite, they get along too well. They like to debate and spend hours on one subject or another. Drives Marguerite crazy when she is trying to get them to the dinner table and they won't stop talking long enough to eat. Barron hopes to enter the university and become a physician when he is done with our academy next year if he can save enough to pay for it." Elhrin smiled to herself, thinking Barron wasn't going to have to worry because she knew Master Gryph planned to pay his tuition. He just wasn't going to tell him yet, and said the boy needed to save his money for living expenses, anyway. Then, like someone had thrown cold water on her, she remembered the three N'gethwyn in Muryne he had to face by himself and hoped he was safe.

Her arm started to cramp from where she was trying to keep it away from Marissa to give the girl room and decided she wasn't going to be able to sleep while trying to hold herself in place. She crawled out of the narrow bunk and padded over to the tiny metal stove in the corner of the captain's cramped quarters. The temperature in the cabin wasn't as cold as the outside, but it wasn't toasty either. She sat cross-legged on the floor beside the little stove and warmed her hands, thinking how much she missed Glimmerdale and the students in the academy. She hadn't been able to spend too much time at home to really get to know them all, but she was able to hear more about each of them when she corresponded with Master Gryph and Marguerite.

"There is a man named Tover whom I think is older than me, but I don't know him that well, and Ashlyn who I know is close to our age. Now she is tough and is quick to let you know what she thinks, so if she ever comes across to you as rough, don't take it personally. She grew up lost somewhere in the middle of a large brood of siblings and learned at an early age that the only way to get ahead was to take control of things herself." Elhrin opened the stove's tiny door and added a few lumps of coal from a wooden storage bin. "The last student that is closest to us in age would be Leesha. She is younger, seventeen I think, and comes from a wealthy family. I usually wouldn't say anything about any of our students, but I will have to say that while Leesha is harmless, she is used to getting her way, so don't let her push you around. She likes to do that with

Eowhyn, and Eowhyn lets her."

"Why does Eowhyn let her?" Marissa had turned over on her stomach and was looking at Elhrin with her chin propped in her hands.

"Because Eowhyn has a big heart, and she doesn't like to stir up controversy, so she just takes whatever Leesha sends her way."

"Doesn't anyone try to help her?"

"Oh, Marguerite has spoken to Leesha about it, but Leesha just denies she has done anything wrong, and Liselle," Elhrin snorted, "Liselle will gripe all day long about how the girl could use an old fashioned tail-tanning even if she is as big as she is which, truthfully, Leesha isn't that big, but compared to Liselle's tiny frame, I'm tall."

"I think I will like Liselle," Marissa grinned, "she reminds me of my grandmother."

"You will. Everyone calls her granny, and she acts like everyone's grandmother. Even Master Gryph calls her granny from time to time which earned him a good smack on the hand with a wooden spoon the first time he called her that," Elhrin laughed. How she missed the early days of their academy when they all were putting things together and blindly feeling their way through the ins and outs of what they wanted to accomplish. It was difficult, but it was fun. "Liselle told him she wasn't old enough to be his granny and to keep his hand out of her cake batter before she used the spoon on his backside."

Marissa laughed out loud. "I just can't imagine anyone talking to Master Idwyr like that and getting away with it."

"Marissa, I know with his high profile position and the fact that he is very powerful makes him intimidating, but he is not the harsh, unapproachable figure you are expecting him to be. Don't ever be scared to talk to him. That is the one thing he tells all of us. He says he is never too busy if we need to seek him out, and he has proven it time and again."

"Do you think he is okay?" Marissa asked.

"I hope so," Elhrin whispered, staring at the tiny coals through the door in the stove. "I certainly hope so."

Chapter Ten

Marguerite was startled awake by the tiny clink of dishes being moved and had to take a moment to figure out she was in the living area of her apartment. Bayle had laid her on the chaise lounge near the fire and tucked her handmade quilt around her. She glanced up at the mirror on the far wall. In its reflection she could see him talking quietly with Ceirolwyn as they unloaded covered serving dishes from a tray onto the dining table behind her. The window overlooking the balcony also reflected their movements and the light of the apartment, and did not allow the blackness beyond to intrude on the inside. Night had fallen.

Marguerite waited, straining to hear the sound of fighting, but nothing came. She turned her head to stare at the dancing flames in the fireplace. She was terrified. She longed to call out to Bayle and ask him if there had been any news, but she couldn't, not yet. She needed a moment to gather her wits, to gather her resolve, to fortify herself before she had to face the horrible truth. Marcus was not in the apartment. Gryph was not in the apartment. She could sense it. That meant they were out there in the darkness somewhere . . . in the darkness. She raised a trembling hand to cover her tired eyes. She was so weak, and it infuriated her. She wanted to be running through the streets with Elhrin, looking for her baby.

"Marguerite," Bayle called her name gently, as he placed a tea tray on the table in the middle of the sitting area, "would you care for something to eat or drink?"

"Not right now," she croaked. She let her hand fall lifelessly to her lap. She rolled her head to look his way and saw a folded sheet of paper lying on the table where he had placed the tray. "What is that?"

He hesitantly picked up the paper. "Marguerite," he said with a slight pause, giving away the fact he was not happy with whatever news was inside, "Elhrin sent this."

Marguerite started to shake. It was going to be bad news. She just knew it. "Let me see it," she whispered.

"Marguerite, please," he pleaded.

"Let me see it," she ordered, holding out a trembling hand for the paper.

Reluctantly, he handed it to her.

On the outside, it looked like a page that had been ripped from some kind of ledger. She saw names of ships and cargo lists, along with port destinations. She unfolded the page and read what Elhrin had written on the backside.

Bayle,

Give this to Master Gryph when you see him next. Tell him and Marguerite that I, along with Tomas, Kyne, Marissa, and Clay are on a ship by the name of Storm's Defiance. He will know the ship and its commander, a Captain Ostied, who has been kind enough to offer his services in pursuit of a ship by the name of Shifting Winds. Marcus' abductors have taken him onboard and it is our hope to overtake them as quickly as possible. If we are successful, we will return to Muryne. If circumstance prevents us from catching up to the ship soon, we will continue to give chase, even if we end up following the Shifting Winds to its proposed final destination. On the other side of this paper, I have encircled the information pertaining to its travel plans that were given to Muryne's dockmaster.

Tell them both I will not give up! I will return Marcus to them safe and sound, this I promise.

I love you all,

Elhrin

Marguerite turned the page over. She saw where the ship's final destination was Chyrzah. She felt the blood drain out of her face. Did they plan to take him to another country?

She swallowed hard, feeling the raw pain as the muscles in her throat contracted around her injuries. "When did this come?" she asked.

"One of the guards that had been with Elhrin delivered it sometime around midday," he answered as Ceirolwyn offered Marguerite a cup of water.

"What time is it now?" she asked, realizing her throat was dry and took the offered cup. It was all she could do to keep from spilling it when she brought it to her lips for a painful sip, she was shaking so badly.

"It is late, close to midnight, I would guess."

She had been sleeping for over half a day. She handed the cup back to the maid before her trembling hands dropped it in her lap. "Did the guard say anything else when he brought the letter?"

"He said that Elhrin's ship departed approximately two hours after the *Shifting Winds*, and that an elderly lady had seen a carriage containing a crying child head to the waterfront in a hurry. The dockmaster confirmed that he also saw three men with a child board the ship and that Elhrin was sure the child had to be Marcus." Bayle lowered his tall frame in a chair close to Marguerite.

Marguerite wanted to scream at the ceiling in frustration. She wanted more than anything to be on that ship. Her baby was scared.

Marguerite drew in a shaky breath. "How long would you think it would take to sail to Marmuht?" her voice broke, and a trail of moisture escaped from the corner of one eye.

"I really don't know, but I can find out for you," he said as the maid disappeared into the bedroom. "But let's hope they don't get that far. Surely Elhrin will find a way to catch up to them."

She desperately hoped so. She stared at the tea tray. She felt so numb, like all of the feeling had seeped out of her body and she was just an empty space inside her own skin. Tears continued to steal quietly down her cheeks. She had to know. She couldn't put it off any longer.

"Bayle," she whispered, "have you heard anything about Gryph?"

"No, there has been no news yet," he said, sadly. "I stopped hearing the attacks from the N'gethwyn over an hour ago. I asked the guards, but none of them have heard anything concerning what has happened outside the city . . . the news so far about what has happened inside the city is not good."

Marguerite swallowed hard. No news of Gryph. *Gryph, are you safe? I need you.* "Tell me," she whispered.

"The N'gethwyn were able to destroy a good portion of the city near the gates with their attacks flying over the walls. The crowds in the streets were in such a state of panic no one knows how many deaths have occurred just from people being trampled and crushed. It is reported that the streets are lined with the dead. There were even reports of drowning when people were shoved off into the canals. Fires are a problem, especially in the waterfront district from the attacks that came from the sky last night. No one has been able to put them out and the winds off the lake are causing them to spread. I guess the only good news is that the Do'athrim and the N'gethwyn have been kept out of the city so far."

She smoothed Elhrin's letter on her lap. She should feel guilty that because of her family the only other person capable of magically stopping an N'gethwyn was out on the lake pursuing her little boy and not in the city doing the job that was required of her. All those people . . . why didn't she feel guilty?

"Marguerite, you really should eat something. Ceirolwyn had the kitchens to make you a mild chicken soup. It shouldn't hurt your throat too much when you swallow." He started to rise from his chair.

"I can't, Bayle," she said. The mere thought of eating made her nauseous. "Maybe later. You go ahead and eat if you wish."

"No, I just thought you could use something to help get your strength back. The doctor said it would be important for you to sustain yourself. He doesn't want you to put yourself at risk for an illness to set in. Your body is weak right now."

"I'm fine, Bayle," she snapped and turned her head towards the heat of the fire, "let me be."

He sat silent for a moment. "Yes, ma'am, rest then. Just let me know when you are ready."

He rose from his chair and returned to the dining table. She could see him covering dishes in the mirror. She hadn't meant to snap at him, he was only concerned about her. She closed her eyes. She was so tired.

"Corporal Caddoch," Ceirolwyn whispered. Marguerite opened her eyes a slit to see the maid held an armful of bed linens. "The bed is ready if Madam Idwyr wishes to use it. I also checked the bathroom to make sure Heralina didn't miss anything when she cleaned it, and I put fresh logs in the fireplace. I am going to take these to the laundry. Is there anything else you wish for me to do before I go?"

"I can't think of anything, Ceirolwyn, thank you," he replied.

"I will be back soon. Do you need anything while I am out?"

"Actually, there is something I wish for you to do," Marguerite responded.

"Yes, Madam?" Ceirolwyn moved around the settee towards the door.

"Find someone who has accurate information concerning the whereabouts of my husband."

"Yes, Madam, I will," Ceirolwyn answered and shifted her load into the crook of one arm to open the apartment door. "OH!" she squealed when she opened the door, surprised by someone standing on the other side.

"I beg your pardon," a deep voice said. "I didn't mean to startle you."

Marguerite's heart nearly burst out of her chest at the sound. She slapped a trembling hand over her mouth, trying to stem the wail that threatened to escape from her lips.

Ceirolwyn backed into the room, pulling the door open wide. Gryph leaned heavily on the shoulders of a burly soldier, his face screwed up in a fierce scowl of pain. He was covered from head to toe in blood and dirt, and his clothing was ripped and shredded as if the Do'athrim had tried to disrobe him in their attempt to kill him.

Marguerite burst into tears.

His eyes met hers, and a look of desperate relief crossed his face. He disengaged himself from the soldier and limped into the room, barely able to walk, having to hold onto the furniture for support in order to make it to her chair. He dropped heavily onto the chaise by her legs and pulled her into a hard embrace. She sobbed into his shoulder, letting go of all the emotion she had been holding inside. He held her close, saying nothing, allowing her to release her grief into his care. He was her rock, and she clung to him desperately.

Finally, he pulled back and cupped her face with both hands. "My love, are you well?" his deep voice rumbled. She could hardly see him through her tears. She nodded. He leaned in and kissed her hard, almost angrily, pressing into her as if he could not get close enough to her. He tasted of earth and iron, a steadfast combination that personified who he was.

With a low moan of anguish, he broke the kiss. "I'm sorry," he whispered.

"Don't," she bunched the fabric of his shirt into her fists, seeing the pain in his eyes, knowing he was placing the blame for Marcus' abduction squarely on his shoulders. "Don't you dare apologize. This isn't your fault. This is none of our fault. It is the fault of the monster who schemed all of this."

He smiled at her sadly. "I love you." He kissed her again. This time he was gentle, using his thumbs to wipe away the river of tears flowing into his palms. "Marguerite," he whispered, "we will get him back safely. Elhrin is chasing them down and has left the city."

"I know," she said.

He leaned back, puzzled. "You know?"

She picked up Elhrin's letter in her lap and gave it to him. He tilted it towards the fire for more light.

"Huh, if that isn't something," he said, turning the sheet over to read the ship's entry on ledger side. "I told Elhrin Solisius would manipulate events to help us."

"What are you talking about?" she asked, rubbing a hand over his chest, grateful to be able to touch him.

"She is with Ostied. It is rare for him to be in Muryne. He usually runs the ports in the southern waters. I find it hard to believe it is just happenstance that Elhrin ran into the one captain I would have chosen above all others to help us." He squinted and pushed the paper further away from him. "What is the name of the shipping company? I can't make it out."

"Agadar Shipping Enterprises," she answered, remembering the entry.

He lowered the paper. "Agadar Shipping Enterprises," he repeated stonily.

"What does that mean?" she asked.

"It means I need to have a discussion with Reginold Whyse. That is his father's company." He glanced at the window across the room. "Did Bayle go outside?" He used his magic to open the balcony door. "Bayle, get in here, boy."

"Yes, sir?" Bayle appeared in the doorway.

"You don't have to leave the room."

"I just thought to give you some privacy," Bayle said with a sheepish half smile. He stepped inside the apartment and closed the door behind him. "What happened out there?" he asked as he crossed the room and sat in a chair facing them.

"A total disaster is what happened," Gryph frowned. "The folks outside the walls panicked when they realized they were being attacked and hundreds were massacred before anyone was able to get into the fight. There is no telling how many more have died trying to squeeze through the gates. The smart ones ran off into the countryside away from the Do'athrim. By the time I made it to the wall, one of the N'gethwyn was already inside the perimeter of the tent city."

"We saw that there was more than one," Bayle said.

"Did you now?"

"I forced Bayle to take me to the watchtower . . . shhh," she said, and placed her fingers to his lips when his scowl deepened, and she knew he was about to reprimand her for being foolish. "I was fine." He grasped her hand and kissed her fingers. "We stayed until we saw an attack hit in your area, and you no longer fought back. What happened?"

He lowered her hand to his lap. "That must have been when one of their attacks hit a cart near me. It flipped and knocked me down. There were Do'athrim in the area who saw me fall and took the opportunity to try and take my head off."

"Looks like they were almost successful," Bayle commented. "Your head is covered in blood."

Gryph reached up to touch the top of his head and winced. "I didn't realize I had been hit." He wiped his bloody fingers on his ragged cloak, then unclasped it, and tossed it aside to the floor.

A sharp, forceful knock rattled the door. Bayle rose from his chair to answer it, and seeing who was on the other side, opened the door wide with a slight bow. King Goruth stood in the hall administering orders to a group of guards and his personal entourage.

"I told you what to do. Why are you still standing here?" he bellowed. A group of men broke away and dashed down the hall. "The rest of you stay here until I return. Dryke, you are with me." Furious, he stalked into the room with his personal physician in tow. "Gryph, what in damnation did you think you were doing? I told you to wait and I meant it. Didn't you realize the danger you were in?" He motioned for his physician to get busy. "Don't you ever put yourself in such a position again. We didn't have enough men on the ground, yet."

"Goruth, I had to get off the walls or the N'gethwyn would have torn them to pieces trying to get me which put you and everyone else on the wall in danger. Being in the meadow allowed me to draw their attention away from the city and those trying to escape." Gryph eyed the doctor, warily following the man's progress as he skirted around the backside of the seating arrangement. "What is he doing?"

"He is going to take care of your wounds, you ass," King Goruth growled. "Pardon my language, Marguerite, I'm glad to see you are doing well."

"Thank you, Goruth," she murmured, thinking she was not doing well. As a matter of fact, despite Gryph's presence giving her some sense of comfort, she was on the verge of an attack of anxiety. Her baby was with madmen who might do him unspeakable harm and she knew he was terrified, and the thought of her baby being terrified was pushing her resolve beyond her limits to be calm and rational.

Gryph waved the doctor away. "I'm fine."

"Please let him check you over." Marguerite touched his arm. Now was not the time to be stubborn about his health. *Guess I need to take a little of my own advice*, she thought.

"Oh, all right," he growled. "But I tell you I'm fine."

"Minister, could you move to the chair, sir?" the doctor asked, indicating the seat beside Marguerite. He sat a leather satchel he had been carrying on the floor beside it.

Gryph tried to get up, but couldn't manage to put weight on his leg. It was too painful. He leaned over and used his arms to hoist himself into the chair with a groan.

"I can see you are fine," King Goruth commented sarcastically, as he seated himself in a nearby chair and crossed his legs comfortably. "Could you please tell me where Elhrin is? No one seems to know."

"She is chasing after Marcus' abductors." Gryph grimaced when the doctor started to probe the wound on his head. "They have taken him aboard a ship bound for Marmuht."

Displeased with his answer, Goruth's lips drew south in a deep frown. "Gryph, Marguerite, what I am about to say is going to sound callous, but as the ruler of this country I have to say it, anyway. My duty is to defend and protect this country's citizens, and those sworn into my service are expected to do the same. Your little boy is important, I do not deny that, but you saw what happened today. It was Elhrin's duty to be here. How many lives could we have possibly saved had she been here?"

"Goruth, Elhrin realizes where her duty lies," Gryph said evenly, his tone less than cordial. He was gearing up for a fight.

"And you are saying that it is with you," Goruth growled, "not the crown."

"No, Goruth, her duty is to Solisius first," Gryph responded with steel in his voice. "All of this," Gryph waved his hand in the air, talking about the entire attack on the city, her, and Marcus, "is tied together. Where do you think the Do'athrim and the N'gethwyn come from? This is ultimately Obsudius' plan and is his indirect way of getting back at Solisius. Marcus' abduction is a part of the plan as well. I don't think they were expecting me to be here for this attack. I am sure I am the one who is supposed to be on that boat giving chase. Not Elhrin."

The doctor motioned for Bayle to help him. "I require clean cloths and water to clean the area."

Goruth glared at Gryph. "Still, from what I understand, there were others who could have given chase. When the country is at stake, Gryph, personal matters have to be pushed aside."

"Don't talk to me about pushing personal matters aside. Have I ever failed you in that matter? Do you not see me here, Goruth?" Gryph barely restrained himself from shouting. "Marcus is MY son! MY son! And I AM HERE!" He leaned forward and angrily pointed at the floor between them. He stared hard at the king—a man on the edge of violence. "I have possibly sacrificed him to be right here!" he then said low and deadly.

Marguerite was shaking again, feeling like she wanted to come out of her skin. How could Goruth do this to them? The last thing they needed was for him to attack them about duty.

Gryph's deadly gaze drifted to her. Seeing her, the fire went out of his eyes. He breathed hard, seeming to let his anger go. "Besides, I told her to go," he said finally. He flipped his hand in the air negligently and leaned back in his chair, allowing the hesitant doctor behind him to continue tending to his head wound. "If you have a problem with it, then I am the one to blame. Not her."

"Gryph, I'm not going to lie to you, there will be questions raised about her absence. Whyse for one will be at the lead," Goruth growled.

"Well, let him. I for one have a need to talk to Councilor Whyse concerning the abduction of my son," Gryph responded. "Ow," he growled, and grabbed the doctor's arm when the man started to dab a wet cloth onto the top of his head. "Easy there, man."

"I apologize, Minister, there is a shallow gash and some bruising. I am just clearing debris out of the area."

"What do you mean you need to talk to Whyse about your son?" Goruth asked.

"Bayle, hand Elhrin's letter to His Majesty, please."

Bayle did as he was asked and Goruth frowned over the letter. Meanwhile, the doctor moved in front of Gryph.

"I will look at your leg now, sir." Opening his satchel, the doctor pulled a pair of shears out of its contents.

"What are you going to do with those?" Gryph asked.

"Unless you wish to drop your trousers, I was going to cut them so I can examine your leg."

"Cut away," Gryph responded. "There is nothing there to fix."

"We shall see," the doctor murmured as he ripped into Gryph's pants.

"Does this say Agadar Shipping Enterprises?" Goruth asked.

"It does," Gryph answered.

Goruth rose and stalked across the room to jerk open the apartment door. Those outside immediately stood at attention. "Osgar, find Reginold Whyse and bring him here immediately." He slammed the door without waiting for a reply. "All right, Gryph, let me hear just how all of this is connected." He returned to his chair.

"You know about the letter," Gryph started.

The letter, Marguerite thought, *he didn't tell me about the letter*. "I want to see this letter," she said interrupting him.

Gryph glanced at her sideways, and she could tell he was hesitant, but then he nodded. "I did promise to show it to you, didn't I?" He turned to look at Bayle. "Son, the coat I wore yesterday is in my wardrobe. There are some documents in its interior pocket. Would you retrieve them for me?"

"Yes, sir," Bayle said and hastened into the bedroom.

The doctor probed at Gryph's leg. "Damn!" Gryph roared. He grabbed his chair's armrests and nearly launched himself out of it.

The doctor backed away a bit to get out of his way. "It appears you have deep bruising in the area of your old wound, sir," he said, "as well as, damaged your knee. You are right, other than wrapping it and the hopes that you will stay off of it for awhile, there is nothing I can do."

Gryph settled back in his chair with an unsurprised grunt at the doctor's diagnosis. Marguerite looked for herself. His knee was incredibly swollen and ugly bruising covered most of the outside of his thigh down past the knee to mid-calf. If that was the result of the cart knocking him down, he was lucky it didn't break his leg.

"Gryph, the letter," Goruth reminded him to continue.

Gryph related all of the information he, Elhrin, and Director Nygill Allahaim had gathered so far. "There is an N'gethwyn at the helm of all of this and he is who I will need to find." He glanced at Marguerite. "I am almost certain that those who abducted Marcus are taking our son to him."

Her lips trembled, but she held herself in check. Now was the time to push aside her fears and get well. Now was the time to go after who was responsible, and it wouldn't do for her to remain weak any longer.

"So, you don't think the N'gethwyn responsible for all of this is any of those lying dead out in the meadow?" Goruth asked.

"It is possible, but it doesn't feel right," Gryph said with a wince as the doctor started to wrap his knee with a roll of bandaging he had pulled from his satchel. "Those on the field were strong, but they were not too terribly smart in their battle tactics. They allowed your men on the ground to get the upper hand despite the odds against them, plus, one of the N'gethwyn was brought down easily by a mere boy wielding a pike. Not the highly trained or skilled leaders I would put in charge if it were up to me."

"This is absurd. Why would anyone send men unable to issue intelligent orders to their forces against a fortified and heavily armed city if they had no chance of succeeding in taking it over, especially with you here?"

"They may not have taken the city, Goruth, but they did succeed at massacring hundreds of Anderan's citizens, destroying a good portion of Muryne's infrastructure—and most importantly to Obsudius—creating chaos and overwhelming fear among the rest of the city's population. When word spreads of this attack, what do you think will consume the minds of those living across Anderan?"

Goruth expelled a long, anger-filled breath.

"But you are right. They may have had a better chance of taking the city if I had not been here, which brings me back to the question as to why I was sent the letter in the first place warning me to stay away. Anyone who knows me understands the last thing I would ever do is respond to a direct threat and it was possible that I would not come to the conference in the first place because I was busy with the academy. Why make sure I would leave Glimmerdale by threatening me and yet, turn around and try to get me right back out of Muryne before they attacked?" Falling silent, Gryph frowned at the far wall, thinking.

Bayle came back into the room and handed Gryph a small stack of folded documents.

"It sounds like you are being manipulated for a reason," Marguerite whispered.

He glanced at her briefly then frowned down at the documents in his hand, nodding silently. With a knowing sigh, he sorted through the documents in his hand and pulled one from the stack. He handed it to her. "Like I said before, they did go through a great deal of trouble and considerable risk of getting caught to try and kill you and take Marcus which is a part of what is in that letter." He nodded at the document in her hand. "And then, when they succeeded in taking Marcus, they provided just enough clues for me to follow their direction, but how could they expect me to know my son was on board a ship, or for that matter, that particular ship if it had already left port?" He touched the belt at his waist and ran a hand along its length, releasing a low exasperated sigh when he didn't find whatever he had been looking for.

"What if they had someone in place looking out for you?" Bayle asked.

Gryph leaned back in his chair, waiting for Bayle to continue.

"I mean, someone you wouldn't suspect was a part of the plan but would direct you if you were unsure where to go next."

"Do you have anyone in mind?"

"I don't know—maybe. The guard who brought the message from Elhrin said there was an old lady who told them a carriage with a crying baby inside passed by her near the east waterfront gate shortly before dawn. She said she likes to watch the ships depart each morning and sits by the gates nearly every day. Maybe her story was true," he wrinkled his face in doubt, "but I find it strange that an old lady would want to brave the cold and then stay through a firestorm of magical orbs from the sky to watch the ships leave port."

Gryph breathed in deeply. "You may be right. We will need to find this lady again and talk with her, and I would also like to speak with the dockmaster who handled the affairs of the *Shifting Winds*." He glanced at Goruth. "If Elhrin does not return in a few days then I am going to Marmuht."

"Gryph, we have a city in a state of disaster. As we speak, half of the western waterfront district may be lost to fire. I need you here," Goruth said.

"Goruth, my three-year-old son is in the hands of murderers. I stayed to defend Muryne. Now I'm going after them. If they are taking Marcus to Marmuht . . . ."

"How can you be sure that they are?" Goruth interrupted. "There are hundreds of leagues of coastline between here and Marmuht. They may not be planning to come into port at all. What if they intend to hide out in any of the inlets or river basins or perhaps sail to another country?"

Please don't let that happen, Marguerite cried silently. "The ledger did say the ship's final destination is Chyrzah," she said, unable to keep the worry out of her voice.

Gryph reached for her hand and gripped it hard. "It doesn't matter where they go. If Elhrin does not catch up to it before me, I will find this ship, Marguerite, whether it anchors somewhere in Anderan or on the other side of the world. I will find it."

She squeezed his hand and brought it to her lips, knowing no earthly or supernatural force would stop him from keeping his word to her.

An urgent knock rapped loudly on the door.

"Corporal, see who it is," Goruth ordered.

"Is Idwyr in there?" a voice growled when Bayle opened the door.

"Yes," Bayle answered and looked over his shoulder at Gryph. "It is Director . . . ."

Director Allahaim pushed Bayle aside and stalked into the room, towing Idora Shulftar firmly by her arm.

"Let go of me, you bastard," Idora hissed and jerked her arm out of his grasp. She took in the room's occupants. An almost imperceptible flash of hatred crossed her face when her eyes swept past Marguerite then a short flicker of fear when she saw Goruth. Coolly, she smoothed her features of all emotion.

"What is all of this?" King Goruth barked.

"This man is out of his mind, Your Majesty," Idora said as she rubbed her arm where the director had painfully held her. "He rampaged into my house, tore it apart, and hauled me here without my consent, and has yet to tell me why he thinks he can manhandle me the way he has. I am a councilor. I deserve respect."

"Here is your respect, Councilor," Director Allahaim snarled. He held up a small key. "Minister, this little object fits nicely into the servant's door of Councilor Shulftar's home. I thought it best to wait to question her with you."

"What is the meaning of all of this? So what if that fits a door on my home? You could ask any of my staff for one."

"This key was retrieved from the boot of a dead man. A dead man found hanging in the stables behind the Canal Street Inn in the waterfront district. A dead man who has been confirmed as a lover of yours truly, Madam Councilor," the director growled.

"That is preposterous! I have never stepped foot inside that establishment." She glared at the director. "I don't even know where it is. And I certainly don't know who you could be talking about. I am not seeing anyone presently."

"Madam, lying will get you nowhere. I have had men run all over this city despite blazing out-of-control fires and its extreme state of chaos and have come up with three persons who will confirm everything I am about to reveal to Minister Idwyr and His Majesty." He grabbed Idora by the arm and forced her to sit on the settee. "You will be here for a bit, so sit down!"

Marguerite removed the blanket draped over her lap and put her feet on the floor. From the man's tone, there was something important about to be said concerning this woman, and she was not about to show her own weaknesses. She sat up straight, holding tightly to Gryph's hand.

Director Allahaim glared at Gryph. "We tracked down the little rat of a jeweler. He was cuddled up with his merchandise in the attic of his shop, hiding from the looters who have ransacked that section of town. Are you aware of the looters rampaging through the business district, Your Majesty?"

"I am. Now that we have eliminated the enemy outside the city, we are focusing on the ones inside. Continue," he ordered.

Director Allahaim briefly nodded his head in reverence. "As I was saying, the jeweler confirmed all my questions with hardly any urging at all."

Marguerite wondered what type of urging the director was talking about. Gryph had once mentioned the director was ruthless sometimes, and did not approve of some of his methods which tended to be on the hostile side.

"It seems that the councilor has, indeed, been to the Canal Street Inn on more than one occasion. As a matter of fact, she goes so often she has a room preference that will be cleared for her use even if it is already occupied."

"You are lying," Idora yelled. She clasped her hands together tightly. "You . . . ."

"Let him finish," Goruth ordered.

"He's lying, Your Majesty. Are you going to let him talk about me in this fashion?"

"Let him finish," Goruth repeated. His eyes flashed a look of steel. "You will have your chance to defend yourself."

"It seems the esteemed councilor has been enjoying the company of the jeweler and the dead man hanging in the stables. What did the jeweler say their pet names were? Let's see, his is The Trader, the other man's was The Wolf, and yours, Madam Councilor, you are The Tigress."

Idora paled. "Who is this jeweler?"

"Kahlin Marteen, the one who gave you the diamond ring on your pretty little finger."

She glanced at her hand. "I bought this ring."

Director Allahaim waved her answer off, negligently. "It doesn't matter. When you are to have your rendezvous with your companions, he picks you up at the Dwyer Street boat landing and you travel to the inn together where, on at least three occasions, you met with The Wolf together." He screwed up his face in distaste. "Sick lot, you are."

"That is not true," Idora denied. She turned in her seat to implore her case to Goruth. "I do know Kahlin, but it is only because I have purchased a few pieces from him. He is lying about the rest. He must be trying to ruin me because I haven't had time to pay the balance for my last purchase."

"Lying again, Councilor? You have never paid for anything from this man. He keeps extensive accounts on his entire inventory and everything that has your name on it says it was given as a gift and written off his ledgers as an expense. This has been going on for years. You must be something else, lady, for him to spew out such extravagance because the man is tighter than a bowstring with his finances."

"Nygill, do you have proof other than the word of Master Marteen?" Gryph asked quietly.

"I'm getting to it. Let me finish this first. You see, the jeweler was with her the night they found their partner hanging in the stables."

Marguerite noticed Idora clasped her hands together tightly and started to rub her thumbs together nervously. Director Allahaim must be hitting on the truth despite Idora's vehement denials.

"The councilor immediately panicked. He said she was almost hysterical. She had the jeweler help her remove the man's boots, stating that they held something linked to her and they wouldn't have time to search for it. Apparently, the man is in love with her, and did not think twice about following her orders without question." He held up the key again. "Anyone finding the key would be able to pinpoint it to her house. It has her house number etched on it. I tested it and it fits."

Gryph held out his hand and the director tossed it to him. Holding the key away from him, Gryph squinted at it. "I didn't see those numbers last night."

"It looks like you aren't seeing much of anything the way you are squinting and holding it as far away from you as you can," Goruth commented.

"I can see just fine, Goruth," Gryph shot back. "Continue, Nygill."

"After they retrieved his boots, they locked the stable door, and departed in his boat to go back home. In her haste to get back, she had forgotten about the boots and he put them in his storage closet until he saw her next. He claims he does not know anything about the abduction of your son or the use of his house during their flight. He did say that the councilor has a similar key to the back of his home, which is how I am guessing the abductors were able to gain entry without force. She also was aware he would be staying at his shop during the duration of the conference."

Idora looked as if she wanted to run. She slid to the edge of her seat. "You just have the word of Kahlin. You could have procured that key anywhere," she said hoarsely.

"Elhrin found the key, Idora. In Kahlin's house last night," Gryph said, fingering the key in his hand.

Idora looked at him imploringly. "You don't believe him, do you, Gryph?"

He stared at the women without reply. "Nygill, what else do you have?" he asked, instead.

"Two of the councilor's servants confirm that she went out late that night and returned home earlier than expected quite upset. They remembered it well because the councilor is not very nice to her help when she is in a foul mood." He reached into a coat pocket and pulled out a scrap of paper. "I also found this in her desk at her home. I think you will find it interesting." He handed it to Gryph.

Marguerite leaned in to read it with him.

Shulley, it is most distressing that you have chosen to be unfaithful during our separation, and with one of my own men at that. I suppose with the distance between us, you thought I wouldn't find out, but you would be most astonished at what I can accomplish. I have eyes everywhere. I am everywhere.

Ah well, I suppose I should not be the jealous lover, knowing your nature. I choose to forgive you this time. However, I am certain you now know what happens to those I do not forgive. No matter, he proved to be useful as a good start to my plan in the end, but I warn you to remember his fate if you feel the need to continue with any future indiscretions.

Oh, and do not worry. Our agreement is still in place. Just follow through with what has been set and all will be well.

As he read over the note, Gryph's hand tightened onto hers. "Idora, I think the time has come for you to tell the truth," he said clearly furious. He held up the note. "Bayle, please give this to His Majesty."

"Gryph, I . . . ," Idora cleared her throat, as she nervously watched Bayle hand off the note to Goruth. "I don't know what that is."

"NO MORE," he shouted unexpectedly, gripping Marguerite's hand painfully. She slipped her hand from his grasp before he broke it. "No more denying that you don't know what is going on. The note proves it. Who is it from?"

"Gryph, I swear, I don't know what that note is. Director Allahaim could have written it himself for all I know."

"No, Idora, the writer addresses you as Shulley. The name I called you privately years ago when we were alone. I never spoke that name in the presence of anyone else, so I highly doubt Nygill would know it. Who else did you ask to use it?" he raged. "WHO is the letter from?"

Idora started to visibly shake and tears formed in her eyes. "Gryph, I . . . ." She broke under the pressure of his glare. "It was supposed to be you and me. YOU AND ME!" she screamed, pointing an accusing finger at Marguerite. "Until that bitch came along and ruined us. She ruined all my plans. Derrick said he could make things better. That he understood what it was like to . . . ."

"Who did you say?" he shouted, interrupting Idora's tirade.

Idora's eyes widened, realizing her mistake.

"Who did you say, Idora?" Gryph repeated, pushing himself to the edge of his seat. His face screwed up in pain, but he continued to glare at Idora.

"Derrick," she whispered hoarsely, dropping her gaze to her lap.

"Son of a bitch," he barked, shaking his head in knowing disbelief. "SON—OF—A—BITCH!" He emphasized each word by pounding a fist on the arm of his chair. He tried to stand, but fell back into the chair when his leg wouldn't hold him.

"Gryph?" Marguerite grabbed his arm to keep him from launching out of his chair and ruining his knee permanently, if he hadn't already. In all the years she had known him, she had never seen him so upset.

Expelling a disgusted grunt, he raked a hand across his face in exasperation. "I should have known, Marguerite. I should have known. I suspected, but then dismissed it because he was seen in Chyrzah as recent as a month ago. Those notes on those bodies were for me." He pounded his chest. "Not anyone else. Me."

"Gryph, what in damnation are you raving about?" Goruth asked. "Who is this Derrick?"

"My brother, Goruth," Gryph turned his heated gaze on the king. "He is my brother. He is the one responsible. He is the N'gethwyn."

Marguerite's body went numb, knowing just how dangerous Derrick could be. "And you helped him take my son," she said to Idora.

"He was supposed to be my son, you bitch," Idora hissed through her tears.

Marguerite forgot about being weak. She forgot about being tired. She launched herself out of her seat and dove over the marble-topped table, slamming into Idora. The settee toppled over backwards carrying them both with it. Idora screamed as they landed with a crash to the floor. Marguerite reared up and punched her in the face. Idora's nose snapped and blood burst from her nostrils. She screamed again.

"You bitch! You took my son!" Marguerite started to hit her again, but rough hands clamped onto her arms and held her fast before she could take another swing. "Let me go, damn it! Director, let me go." She tried to wrench free, but the man was stronger than a bull and jerked her up off the writhing harlot underneath her.

"Madam, as much as I would love to see you pound the councilor into the floor, I don't think your husband would want you to hurt yourself any further than you already are," the director growled.

Marguerite glanced at her husband, seeing that he had managed to stand, yet leaned heavily to one side. As long as she lived, she would never forget the raw anguish on his face as he motioned for her to come to him.

Sobbing, she broke free from Director Allahaim and stumbled into the love of her life's embrace.

Chapter Eleven

————✦————

Elhrin laid her head on the rail of the ship with a profound sense of relief. Sweat poured from her forehead and down the center of her back, and she thought she was going to be sick despite the fact they had made it through safely. For the last few hours, she hadn't been so sure. Captain Ostied had taken them through an offshoot section of the Wyndermir River system no sane captain would ever dream of navigating. Huge boulders dominated the waterway—some were hidden below the surface of the water just waiting for one mistake to rip the hull right out from under the ship—and sharp bends in the narrow channel made for interesting, stomach-sickening maneuvers to avoid collisions with the rocky banks on either side of the ship. She didn't know how he did it, getting them through with only one minor scrape against a rock jutting out over the water when he rounded one of those sharp bends, but they were now in the main—and delightfully wide—channel, back on course.

A hand patted her shoulder. "Are you all right, little lady?" Captain Ostied asked.

She raised her head, finding a huge grin on his leathery face. "Captain, I have faced many terrifying things in the last few years that I cannot speak of, yet I have to say, the last few hours ranks right up there with the top five."

He boomed with laughter. "It's not for the weak. That is a given."

She straightened. The wide river ahead was empty of boat traffic. Behind the ship, the two waterways converged and a small sloop trailed them in the regular shipping route, but it was not the *Shifting Winds*. According to Captain Ostied, they were looking for a boat similar to the one they were on, only it was a lean ship with more sail. That was why it was fast, he said. It made use of its sleek line and extra sail to speed across the water. If they made it to the open sea, he would be hard pressed to catch them.

"Do you think they are behind us?" she asked.

"No, we didn't gain that much time." He took note of the proximity of the sun peeking in and out of clouds that were trying to break apart. "It is after midday. I think we may have gained around a half hour's extra time than if we had taken the regular shipping route. The *Shifting Winds* probably passed this point not long ago."

"How can you be sure?" She scanned the forested banks on either side of the wide expanse of the river. Up ahead, a lazy bend curved off to the left.

"A captain knows these things," he assured her. He nodded to Tomas climbing in the rigging, heading for the crow's nest. "Your friend there told me about Gryph's wife. What a shame. Whoever has it out for Gryph, has it bad."

"Yes, they do, and they had better hope that neither he nor I catch up to them," she growled.

"I wouldn't want to be on the receiving end of a fight with Gryph or you either, if you are anything like him."

"I'm not like him, but I can hold my own," she grinned.

His eyes crinkled around the edges, producing a map of crevices as he smiled. "I'm sure you can." He patted her back and headed for the bow where his crew was readying a sling for someone to be lowered over the side to inspect the hull for damage.

She noticed Marissa sitting alone atop the crates in the middle of the ship and decided to join her.

"Not exactly what you had expected when you left Jarit's Cove, is it?" Elhrin asked as she climbed atop the crates and perched beside the girl. Marissa looked a little pale from their trip dodging rocks. Elhrin wondered if her own face looked the same.

"Not really," she chuckled nervously.

"I told you this was going to be dangerous. You should have listened to me when I asked you and Clay to stay behind."

"Maybe I should have," Marissa agreed, "but what would have been the fun in that? I would have missed the opportunity to be involved in a narrow escape from a possible shipwreck."

Elhrin grinned at her. "I have to admit it did get my blood pumping."

"Mine, too."

"Do you feel up to a little lesson time?" Elhrin asked, needing to get her mind off her frustration of not seeing the *Shifting Winds*.

Marissa sucked in a breath of surprise. "Yes, I do."

Elhrin thought a few minutes about what to teach her and decided it would be best to start with some defensive techniques. The girl might need them in the near future.

"Come on," she slapped the girl's knee, "let's go back to the rear of the ship where there is more room."

When they reached the stern, Elhrin spied a boat hook with a long wooden pole hanging near one of the ballistae. She unlatched the clasp holding it in place and slipped it out of its nook, then turned to face Marissa.

"Marissa, I don't want to scare you, but I do want to remind you that when we catch up to this ship, there will be a fight." Elhrin leaned on the tall pole that reached several feet over her head. "A very violent fight, and death is a possibility."

"I know," Marissa replied. Her eyes wandered to the river behind Elhrin. "And the thought does frighten me. Other than some out-of-hand bar fights back home, I have never had to face danger before but the fact is, despite my fear, it just feels like this is where I am supposed to be."

Her statement surprised Elhrin. "What do you mean?"

Marissa shrugged her shoulders. "When you asked me and Clay to leave on the docks, I almost did, but then that little boy's face flashed in my head, and I felt leaving wasn't the right answer. I just couldn't see myself turning my back on you. Elhrin, I don't know what I can do, I might even just be getting in your way, but if there is any way I can help, I want to."

"Good, because you will be a help, I'm sure of it." Elhrin was reminded of what Master Gryph said about Solisius putting people in her life to help her, and wondered if that was why Marissa was here. If so, she was not going to question it, and would make full use of the help. "Okay, what I am going to show you now is how to build a shield. It will involve creating a weave of energy flows all at once, so I'm going to demonstrate first and then we will work together to build yours. Hold this." She handed the boat hook to Marissa.

Elhrin placed both hands in front of her and reached for her energy source. "I will infuse the weaves with light so you can see them. Usually, they are invisible." She started to build her shield slowly, allowing Marissa to see how the energy flowed out of the palms of her hands, looking like soft ethereal rivers of light that fused together to create a wall-like barrier from the deck to as high as Elhrin's head. "Do you see how they meld together? When this is done right, it will be stronger than a stone wall." Elhrin completed the barrier. "Okay, that's big enough."

"Big enough?" Marissa asked, surprised. "You can make one bigger?"

"I can, but there are limits. If I make it too big for my abilities, it will weaken the shield. A weak shield will shatter if something stronger hits it, much like a glass window would if you threw a rock at it." Elhrin noticed she had the attention of several sailors. If they had a problem with what she was doing, she couldn't help it. Marissa needed to learn how to protect herself, and the idle time waiting to catch up to the *Shifting Winds* was perfect for teaching her. "Use the pole to see what I'm talking about."

Marissa slowly tapped the pole against the shield.

"Hit it harder," Elhrin instructed.

Marissa jabbed the pole so hard it jarred out of her hands and clattered to the deck. "Ouch," she grinned, shaking her hands. "I didn't mean to do that."

Elhrin let the shield disappear. "Well, you get the idea," she said. She used her magic to pick the hook up from the deck. The pole slapped into her palm. She handed it back to Marissa. "Now, I did the shield slowly so you could see how it was done, but in reality, if you need a shield, you will need it instantly." Elhrin popped a shield into place. Marissa jumped back in surprise. "And you will need to do it without thought. It will need to happen so naturally." She let the shield go then popped another one in place in a different location. "It would be like you were breathing shields into existence." She let that shield go then popped one into place behind her on the outside of the ship above the river. "Do you see what I mean?"

Marissa stared at the shield in wonder. "I do," she breathed.

"You asked about size," Elhrin increased the size of her shield to encompass a large portion of the width of the river before she let it wink out. "Like I said before, you can build one as large as you think you are capable of holding safely against whatever harm you are against, but bigger doesn't always mean better."

"Have you ever had a shield to fail?"

"I have been fortunate," she said, "so far."

"Meaning, you have come up against something where you needed these shields."

"You could say that," Elhrin grunted. "Okay, let me show you what happens with a weak shield." Elhrin created a small, very weak barrier. "Hit it with the pole."

Marissa jabbed the pole at the shield. It exploded with a pop and Elhrin had to jump back to keep Marissa from impaling her with the pole's tip.

Horrified, Marissa sputtered an apology, "Elhrin, I'm sorry. I wasn't expecting it to be that easy to break."

"Don't worry," Elhrin grinned. "I was ready. Now I am going to show you what the shield will look like in its natural state." She produced one without it being infused with light. Marissa waited patiently, looking for the shield to appear. Elhrin wondered how long it would take for the girl to realize the shield was already in place.

Marissa stared at the space between them for a moment then raised her eyes to Elhrin's. Elhrin slowly smiled at her.

"I take it, it is already there." Marissa raised the pole and tentatively poked at the space between them. It tapped against the invisible barrier. "Unbelievable."

Elhrin let the shield go. "Now it's your turn."

Elhrin worked with Marissa for the rest of the afternoon, helping her to create a tiny shield. The girl was quick to grasp the concept, but Elhrin had to help her with technique. For some reason, Marissa wanted to turn the flows in the wrong direction which left holes in her barrier.

Meanwhile, she kept an eye on the river whenever they came around a bend, hoping that they would catch a glimpse of a sail on the other side, but no such luck. They did pass a fisherman in a small skiff near dusk who told the captain that the last ship that had passed him had done so about an hour ahead of them, but he hadn't paid attention to the ship's name and they couldn't be positive if it was the *Shifting Winds*.

Later that night, Elhrin found Kyne in the prow of the ship leaning on the rail, eating the meal that had been provided from the ship's cook.

"What do you think?" she asked as she mimicked him by leaning on the rail and picking up a slab of bread from her bowl. The meal was some kind of stew and she guessed they were supposed to eat it with the bread since she was given no utensil.

"It's not roast chicken in a thick, cream sauce, but it will do," Kyne said eyeing her sideways. He ran his piece of bread through the stew and took a bite.

"I'm not talking about the food. I mean about all of this." She gestured to the moonlit river ahead of them. They had been lucky that the cloud cover had broken away, and the waning three-quarters moon shone bright onto the water. "Everything we are up against."

Kyne snorted. "Elhrin, we might as well be chasing the wind. I know you are prone to be your usual sunshiny optimistic self, but I don't think we will catch up to them before

Marmuht. That is, if they actually go to Marmuht."

Well, she asked for it, true Kyne, ever the pessimist. "What makes you think they won't?"

"Elhrin, if I were stealing a little boy, would I announce where I was going with him?" He swabbed his bread around the rim of his bowl. "Especially, if the child's father could blow me up? No, I would think not."

"I'm going to have to disagree with you on this," she said, tasting her own stew. It was salty, but not bad.

"That is nothing new," he commented. "Agreeing with me on anything is against your nature."

"I'm serious, Kyne. I think whoever is behind this wanted to lead Master Gryph on a chase after his son. I'm almost sure of it." She thought a moment. "Maybe he expected Master Gryph to be on this ship in pursuit, not me."

"Well, the Minister being out of Muryne would have certainly been a plus for the N'gethwyn attacking the city." He tipped the bowl to his lips and drained the stew's juices.

"So you don't think I could have handled them by myself?" She narrowed her eyes at him.

"I didn't say that," he wiped his mouth with the back of his hand. "Maybe you weren't supposed to be there, either."

She sat her bowl on the rail. "Where was I supposed to be?"

"You have a short memory, I see," he said. "Do you not remember we cut our trip short? We were supposed to stop by Bram's Well on our way back, but you said it would take too long and it could wait until next week. If we had continued with the original plan, we would not be here right now."

He was right. The original plan had been to go to Bram's Well, but they had wasted so much time in the Port V'Din area in foul weather and she was just ready to go home for a short break. The reports they were supposed to investigate in Bram's Well had not sounded realistic but more like the ravings of a hysterical old lady. Now with confirmed reports of attacks, Elhrin felt hugely guilty. The woman could have seen Do'athrim near her home. She tossed her stew into the water below. She was no longer hungry. She was going to pay dearly for shirking her duties.

"Why did you throw it out?" Kyne asked, frowning at her. "I would have taken it."

"Sorry, I assumed you wouldn't have wanted to eat after me."

He just shook his head. "You assume far too much with me sometimes."

She ignored his comment. "I suppose you could be right about being in the city." She scanned the shadows of the deep forest on the river banks. "Maybe neither of us were supposed to be in the city in the end. I wonder how the city fares now?"

"Sail!" came a shout from the crow's nest.

Elhrin jerked up straight, knocking her bowl over the side into the river. They had rounded a bend, and far down river was the rear of a ship, disappearing behind the next bend that veered off to the right.

"Miss Caddoch, if you will," the captain shouted from the stern. He was gesturing for her to hurry aft. She ran down the deck and vaulted the short stair to the rear deck. "You want to give us a little nudge, young lady?" he asked. "We have a straight way here and the curve ahead is easy. We should be able to take on more sail for a bit."

"Do you think it's the *Shifting Winds*, Captain?" she asked as she grabbed her energy and pulled a gust of wind into the sails, making sure she did it gradually. The ship steadily increased its speed.

"We will find out," he replied, then began issuing commands to both the sailors and her until the ship's state was all set to his satisfaction.

Tomas came up from below deck where he had been napping. The cool, damp weather and his swim in the canal had given him a runny nose, and he wanted to take advantage of any rest he could get while he had the opportunity.

"Did I hear a sail was spotted?" he asked. His nose was clearly congested.

"Yes, the ship just rounded the next bend," she said. "How do you feel?"

"I'm all right," he said, "just a little stuffy."

"Don't get sick on me, soldier," she said, her heart was nearly pounding out of her chest, hoping that this was the ship. "We have work to do."

He sidled up beside her and gave her a brief peck on her cheek. "I won't, Major."

"Ha! Funny," she said with a brief smile.

The bend in the river couldn't get to them soon enough. When they eased out of the curve, they caught a quick glimpse of the ship before it slid behind the line of trees on the next bend, but they were a little closer.

"Looks like she isn't in any hurry," the captain commented. "They should have more sail. There is enough light for it tonight."

Elhrin became concerned. "Would that mean it is the wrong ship?"

"It might be." The captain blew out a breath. "We'll keep chase, anyway. This section of river is fairly easy to navigate. The sand bars stay to the sides and the outer edges of the bends. Continue sending a steady breeze into our sails until I say otherwise."

Each round of a bend made Elhrin's heart beat faster. They were easing closer by the minute, and when they reached a straight, narrowing stretch of the river, the ship was clearly in their sights.

"It's her," the sailor in the crow's nest yelled. He held a spyglass on the ship. "They're flying the Agadar Shipping flag. It's the *Shifting Winds*."

Elhrin felt weak in the knees. Finally! Finally! *Hold on, baby, I'm coming*, she cried silently.

Storm's Defiance inched closer. Marissa and Clay rushed up the stair to the castle and watched their progress from the ship's rail.

"They're raising sail, Cap'n," the sailor yelled.

"What did he say?" Elhrin asked.

The captain rumbled a low growl of displeasure. "She's raising sail. They don't seem to want company."

"How would they know we are looking for them?"

"They may not know, but they can see we are closing in on their position, and if I were her captain, I would take that as a sign to move along."

"Can I increase our speed?" she asked.

He shook his head. "We are pushing it as it is for the river. Don't worry. We should still be faster even with them at top sail."

The *Shifting Winds* was heading down river at a noticeably faster pace as each additional sail was unfurled. Elhrin couldn't tell if they were gaining anymore. It looked to her as if they were running about the same speed. Up ahead, the river veered sharply to the right.

"Miss Caddoch, this bend is going to be tight, but don't ease off," the captain said and took over the wheel.

A force of power slipped into her awareness. Black and cold, with an edge of pure hate, a viper coiled to strike. Then the lonely cry of a wolf echoed over the water, coming from the thick tangle of wood on the river's edge.

"NO!" she yelled at the top of her lungs, grabbing everyone's attention. She let go of her energy flows. The ship slowed.

"What's wrong?" Tomas asked as the sailors flew through the rigging to adjust for the drop in speed.

"We are about to be attacked." She scanned the riverbanks with her senses. "Up ahead—in the bend of the river on the right."

"Are you sure?" the captain asked.

"Trust me, Captain, you need to prepare for an attack. Kyne, N'gethwyn to the right." She yelled to the foredeck.

"Son of a bitch," the captain growled. "Sailors, snap to, mates! We are heading for a fight!"

The deck became a flurry of activity, someone issued a whistle warning, and sailors who were off duty came swarming from below deck. All of the ballistae were readied for use. A hatch was opened and chests holding weaponry were hoisted to the deck. Bows were sent up into the rigging for the sailors up high to use. Clay and Tomas jumped from the sterncastle to the deck and grabbed a bow and a quiver of arrows then positioned themselves at the rails on the side of the ship.

"What can I do," Marissa asked fearfully.

"Use your light when I tell you. The moon exposes us out here on the water, but they are hidden in the shadows of the trees. If you can place it as far as the riverbanks it will not only help us see them better, but it might also blind them a little." She yelled over her shoulder as she jumped to the deck below and pushed her way to the bow, "Make it as bright as you can."

Kyne was helping the sailors set out the narrow crates of bolts for the ballistae. "Just one N'gethwyn?" he asked.

"One is enough, isn't it?" she replied as she perched herself on a ledge in the bow. They were nearing the bend in the river. The *Shifting Winds* had already disappeared around it unscathed. "I guess that proves it."

"What?" Kyne grunted as he stacked a crate beside the ballistae.

"The ship has gone past the N'gethwyn without trouble. We have been set up for ambush." She scanned the forests as they drifted closer. The N'gethwyn stood somewhere near the rim of the bend. *Show yourself, you bastard.*

The ship drifted towards the shore the closer they came to the bend.

"What is the captain doing?" she wondered out loud, thinking the ship was coming too close to the riverbank. "It's going to put us right on them."

"He has no choice," Kyne said and positioned himself beside her. "It's where the channel is. If he edges to the other side we will go aground and a still ship is a dead ship."

"Nothing is going to die but an N'gethwyn and his friends tonight," she growled. They were close enough. She slapped both her palms together over her head and pushed outward. A fiery orb of hot white energy shot across the water into the trees of the river's bend. Briefly, pricks of reflected light could be seen among the foliage before her orb exploded with a deafening boom into the trees, splintering them into pieces. Short canine yips of pain echoed over the water.

A flash of light erupted from the bank a little further down from where her attack exploded and a green comet of sizzling energy sped towards the ship. Elhrin conjured a shield within its path. The comet slammed into her barrier, causing her to clench her jaw from the force, the orb ricocheted into the water, sending up a huge geyser of water into the air.

The boat drifted under the falling spray, drawing closer to the N'gethwyn. Twangs from bow strings on the riverbank broke through the insect and frog calls of the night. Thuds pounded into wood planks and the sound of ripping fabric came from above as arrows flew into the rigging. A deep scream shattered the night from somewhere above followed by a huge splash on the other side of the boat.

"Marissa, now!" Elhrin yelled as she sent a blaze of energy at the N'gethwyn. It exploded in a dazzling array of red and yellow plumes of fire when it hit the N'gethwyn's shield.

Marissa created a light orb near the riverbank. Snarling wolven Do'athrim stood among the trees readying bows. Marissa screamed and her light went out, having never witnessed the horrid beasts who looked half-man, half-wolf. The men on the ship fired their arrows at the banks, hoping to hit something even though the Do'athrim were lost in the black shadows of the forest.

"Marissa," Elhrin yelled, "focus!" She flung a series of fiery orbs along the bank, briefly illuminating the area before they exploded into the trees. The men on the ship fired at will.

The N'gethwyn sent a series of green missiles of energy at the ship. Elhrin deflected the first two, but the movement of the ship caused her to miss the last two and one zoomed over the heads of the men at the rail and exploded behind them, ripping a gaping hole out of the ship's wall on the other side. The other orb exploded into the rigging of the foremast. The top gave way. Kyne grabbed Elhrin and threw her away from the prow onto the deck and landed on top of her. The top sail crashed onto the railing next to where Elhrin had been standing and flipped into the river. Ropes, block and tackle slammed into the deck before it all was jerked over the side by the sinking mast.

Kyne shouted in pain.

"Use the Ostied Specialty, lads," the captain roared.

"Kyne, get up," Elhrin grunted. She was pinned face down to the deck. "Kyne, I can't move. Get up!"

He rolled to the side with a groan.

"Where are you hurt?" Elhrin grabbed his arm.

"My back," he croaked. "Go fight."

"Stay right there." She pushed herself to her feet.

"Where would I go?" she heard him answer as she launched an attack at the N'gethwyn. It exploded into the trees near him, but she couldn't tell if he had been hit.

Marissa overcame her fear and positioned her light in the line of sight for the Do'athrim. They snarled in anger at the blinding light, but launched their arrows at the ship. Elhrin created as big a shield as she could to protect them. The middle was spared as the arrows bounced off of it and splashed into the river, but Marissa's light winked out and Elhrin was afraid she had been hit. She searched the stern and was relieved that the girl had just ducked behind the wall of the ship. If they escaped the battle unscathed, she was going to have to talk to the girl about indirect magic usage.

The sailors working the ballistae beside Elhrin released a bolt. It flew over the short water span into a line of Do'athrim with a small explosion. A second bolt exploded a little further down river. The sailors quickly cranked the bolt string back into firing position and adjusted its aim to compensate for the ship's forward movement which had rounded the sharp curve of the bend and was heading back into the middle of the river. Elhrin could hear the Do'athrim crashing through the brush, following their progress. She launched a series of fire orbs into their midst while Marissa created another light, revealing the beasts among the trees. Arrows from the ship zoomed into the area and the ballistae's strings slammed forward sending two more of Ostied's Specialties over the water. Successive, blinding explosions ripped into the trees, and pockets of fire blossomed from the forest floor as dry tinder caught ablaze from the searing offshoots of sparks.

The N'gethwyn recovered from the attack and ran through the brush to catch up, stepping into Marissa's circle of light.

"Didn't expect that," Elhrin murmured to herself. The N'gethwyn was female. Energy sources did not reveal gender and she had assumed she faced a male because all the N'gethwyn throughout history have been male. Obsudius usually considered females to be too weak for his purposes.

She glanced at Kyne who had managed to crawl next to her. "Are you all right?"

"Yes, get down," he hissed.

Elhrin quickly ducked low as Do'athrim arrows flew into the ship.

"Pay attention," he said angrily, his face contorted in obvious pain.

"I was. I blocked some of those, but couldn't keep the shield in place or I would cut off our own arrows. Don't move," she said, then pushed her way towards the stern of the ship.

"Keep your head down," he yelled after her.

The N'gethwyn paused long enough to fire comets of red flames at the ship. Marissa's light winked out when she saw the attack was aimed at her. Elhrin started to create a shield, but then a huge wall of water shot up from the river. The N'gethwyn's missiles burst into the wall and died with a cluster of dull thumps of light within the shimmering aquatic shield.

"Where did that come from?" Elhrin barked a laugh at the unexpected defense.

Tomas answered. "Who cares? It worked."

"Yes, it did," she agreed and raced up the stern's castle stair. "Did you do that, Marissa?" She slapped her palms together and sent another fiery orb of white at the N'gethwyn. It increased in size as it sped across the water. The N'gethwyn deflected the brunt of the attack, disappearing behind her shield within the explosion.

"I did, but I couldn't tell you how. All I know was that I needed to defend myself, and that was the result."

"Amazing," Elhrin commented.

The N'gethwyn slid down an embankment and stumbled after the ship on a sand bar along the river bank. Elhrin smiled. The bitch was hurting.

"Let's go fishing," she growled. She sent an invisible stream of her powers out over the water, wrapped it around the N'gethwyn, and squeezed her body tight. The N'gethwyn screamed in angry surprise. Elhrin sent a wave of intense heat into her flow before the N'gethwyn could break her hold. The invisible flow of energy turned a fiery yellow, reminding her of the rope Master Gryph had flung out of his apartment window and set on fire.

Elhrin's anger went white hot. The reminder of the death that had been planned for Marguerite sent her over the edge of reason. The N'gethwyn screamed again, this time in pain. She tried to retaliate, but Elhrin wrapped more flows around the woman and sent scorching heat through them all. The resulting ear piercing cries of intense agony were not for the faint of heart.

"Not feeling well, are you?" Elhrin growled under her breath. "Let's cool you down." She braced her feet wide on the deck for balance then used her fiery ropes of magic to jerk the woman into the air and slam her into the middle of the river, forcing her under its surface. The fiery ropes glowed beneath the water like lit trawler lines as Elhrin held the woman under until she felt the N'gethwyn's energy source fade from her awareness which told her the N'gethwyn was dead.

She let her magic go and turned to find Marissa right behind her, obviously protecting them both from the constant barrage of arrows with an invisible shield as Elhrin fought the N'gethwyn. The girl stared at Elhrin with a horrified expression on her face. Elhrin wasn't about to apologize for being ruthless. Marissa needed to understand that dealing with N'gethwyn was serious business, and they all had to be eradicated by whatever means necessary. Without a word, Elhrin pushed past Marissa to help the men finish off the Do'athrim.

The broken shadows of the forest hid the beasts as arrows flew over the water from both the ship and the riverbank. She shot two orbs of red light into the air. They sizzled high, revealing for a moment where the beasts were located. She then fired an intense comet of energy into a group of trees where she had seen more than one beast. It exploded with a tremendous boom and a blast of light. Howls of pain resulted as Do'athrim arrows thudded into the ship. A cry rang out from above, but no one fell from the rigging.

Marissa conjured an orb of light near the water's edge just as arrows zipped to the riverbank, making sporadic contact with the enemy. A pack of Do'athrim crashed through the brush and dove into the water. Elhrin immediately sent a crackling wave of power into their midst. Tendrils of deadly light crawled across the surface of the water as if her magic had a mind of its own and was seeking prey to feed upon. One by one, the Do'athrim were hit with the deadly light, blasting into their bodies with magnificent force. One by one, each died a horrific death. None were spared. None survived.

The remaining Do'athrim on the riverbank seemed to hesitate. Their yips and growls echoed over the water, sounding not as confident as they were before. Without hesitation, Elhrin fired into the woods repeatedly, not bothering to aim. She wanted them scared. She wanted them to tuck their tails and run. Run back to their master. Tell him that they couldn't handle the fight. Tell him she was here and she wasn't going away. One boom after the other echoed over the water. Hers combined with those of the ballistae. She saw a shadow move. Boom! She saw glowing pinpricks of eyes reflecting the light of Marissa's light sphere. Boom! She heard a bark. Boom! The bastards were going to die.

"Elhrin," she heard someone call her.

She did not heed the call and sent another orb of energy into the forest. It exploded in a flash of brilliant light.

Someone grabbed her arm and violently jerked her around.

"Elhrin!" Tomas shouted, scowling at her in concern.

"What?" she yelled back, breathing heavily from exertion.

"They are gone," he said. "The ones that were left ran back into the forest."

She scanned the trees, but didn't see anything but pockets of fire and a line of pure destruction back up the river. She had made them pay, but they weren't the right ones. They weren't the ones holding Marcus.

She looked at Tomas helplessly. "Where is the ship?" she asked.

He shrugged his shoulders.

"Captain, where is the ship?" she yelled.

"It is well ahead by now, young lady," he called out.

"Can we catch them?"

The captain's face was a mixture of menacing shadows and moonlight. "Miss Caddoch, we will do well to reach Port V'Din this night. Our chase for now is at an end."

"Damn it," Elhrin breathed in angry frustration. She leaned heavily against the ship's railing staring at the empty moonlit waterway ahead of them, not believing that they had failed to reach Marcus. "We were so close."

Elhrin and Tomas walked back to the shipyard in Port V'Din, hoping the repairs to the ship were nearing completion. Luckily, the yard had everything that would be needed for repairs, so all that had to be done was the work on the ship itself, and it was taking all day. Already, the sun was starting to slide below the horizon, and Elhrin's hopes of catching up to the *Shifting Winds* were going down with it.

"Do you think we can trust him to do what he said he would do?" Elhrin asked.

"I don't know. Kyne said we could trust him as long as the money was good and it's no secret Minister Idwyr is a wealthy man," Tomas replied.

Elhrin hated that it had to be done this way, but she had no choice. She needed her letter to reach Master Gryph and Marguerite in a hurry, and going through the regular mail routes could take weeks for it to make it into their hands. Kyne had suggested a fellow who would do any job, of any kind for the right price, but they were all low on funds, having left Muryne without their belongings. The only other option was to promise the man Master Gryph would pay him handsomely when the letter was received. He had not wanted to do the job at first, not trusting them until she showed him her signet ring which proved she was employed by the minister's office. But she also had to offer him her solid gold Eagle's pin from her cloak as partial payment up front because they had very little coin to pay. When he still hesitated, she then had to add an incentive to the offer and had agreed that they would double the amount if the man could deliver the letter to Master Gryph within the week.

The man was no fool. He could see she was desperate. The ending agreement had come to triple the amount if he delivered her letter within a week and she had to sign an agreement on Master Gryph's and the Ministry's behalf that if he failed to pay, the man could take it up with the crown. She hoped it wouldn't come to that because she wasn't sure of her good standing with King Goruth at the moment.

"Still, I don't like it," she halted on the side of the muddy street to let a wagon pass before crossing to the other side, "trusting something so important to a greedy character like him."

"Sometimes, you just have to let things go and hope it will work out. Like me, for instance. I am hoping Minister Idwyr was able to vouch for me and tell my superiors that I am not a deserter." He smiled down at her.

She couldn't help it and grinned back. "I think you are safe in that area." She reached for his hand, but he brushed it away. Instead, he put his arms around her shoulders and pulled her in close. She wrapped an arm about his narrow waist.

"I love you, Elhrin Caddoch," he said, kissing the waves of brown hair on top of her head.

She squeezed his waist. "I love you too, Tomas Colkitte."

"Then quit running away from me and marry me." He pulled her into the shadowy entrance alcove of a vacant building.

"Tomas, I . . . ," she stopped midsentence, surprised by what she had been about to say. She couldn't look him in the eye and frowned down at the weather worn planks underneath her boots. She wished he wouldn't start this now. They had too much to think about, too much to worry about, and this was not the right time.

"Don't push me aside again, Elhrin," he said, "and don't talk to me of the dangers. I know about them. I know who you are, and what you will face for the rest of your life, and none of it makes any difference to me. Why does it make a difference to you? I have stood by you in the past, I am standing by you now, and I want to stand by you for the rest of my life." He cupped her face with his hands. "Please, Elhrin, let me." He kissed her softly on the lips. "Please, marry me," he whispered.

"Tomas, don't do this now," she begged. How could she make him understand it wasn't the danger to her she was concerned with, but the danger that would involve him? Like the danger that Marcus was in right now. "Why do we have to get married? I mean, it's like we are already married. We just don't live together."

He dropped his hands and stepped away from her. "It is not enough," he said with a spark of heat, leaning back on the wall behind him and crossing his arms over his chest. "It is not enough to say you are my girl. I want you as my wife, Elhrin. I want to live together. I want a home wherever you say you want to live. I will quit the road patrol. I will do whatever it takes to have a lifetime with you, whether it is one night or eighty years. That is what I want."

"Tomas, do you see what is happening now? Once again Master Gryph has become a target, and this time his son has been taken and he almost lost Marguerite. This isn't the first time he has been targeted, and won't be the last. This is my future. You say you know what I face, but do you, really? What if we marry, and aside from having to watch my back constantly, what if you or I are killed or any child we have is killed or taken? What then? Is that the kind of life you want for us—for yourself?"

"YES, damn it!" Tomas shouted, earning curious glances from two men passing the doorway. "That is exactly what I want because that is your life, and I want to share YOUR life!"

She lowered her head to hide the tears filling her eyes. She loved Tomas, she did, and she had hurt him so many times in months past. She didn't want to hurt him anymore.

"Yes," she whispered, as drops fell like a light rain from her eyes, creating dark blotches in the layer of dirt on the wooden planks.

"What did you say?" he asked.

She raised her head. "I said, yes, Tomas. I will marry you."

He pushed away from the wall, propelled her backwards, and pinned her against the wall behind her, melding his lips hard against hers. His beard stubble scratched harshly against her cold skin as he kissed her, but she didn't care. In the midst of all the dark distress of the last few days he was a glimmer of complete happiness. She clung to that thought desperately, trying to justify a decision that she felt in her heart to be wrong.

Chapter Twelve

Gryph limped down the empty hallway, leaning heavily on the crutch Doctor Dryke had given him to help keep pressure off his injured leg and feeling far older than he was. He should be resting, but he wasn't about to lie in bed waiting to heal. He couldn't waste the time, wouldn't waste it. He had spent the days since the attack on Muryne coming to terms with everything that had happened, putting all the pieces together, and he had to admit, trying not to lose control of his emotions. He needed to be strong for Marguerite's sake. This was his fault, no matter what she wanted to believe. This was his fault, and he had to make it right, but he was at a frustrating standstill for the moment because he was waiting to hear something, anything, from Elhrin. By now, she could be as far as Port V'Din which meant the ship Marcus was on had made it to the sea, and possibly out of Elhrin's reach.

A searing pain shot through his leg, and he had to pause a moment to let it subside back to its more manageable throbbing state. Goruth had been right. He had put himself in an extremely dangerous position and maybe should have waited until more soldiers had made it to the ground with him before he had moved further away from the wall, but all three N'gethwyn had targeted him the moment he came into their range and that meant whoever was around him was a target, too. He remembered the unusual look the N'gethwyn closest to him had shot his way before he and his cohorts coordinated what had to be a previously planned attack that took him down. The N'gethwyn had known Gryph's weaknesses when he aimed. It was not a lucky shot to hit Gryph directly in the one spot sure to make him fall. Oh, no, they knew. His brother had made sure of it.

He rounded the corner of the palace's westernmost wing. The corridor was empty, as well, save for the two guards stationed at a door near the hall's end. Most halls within the palace were now empty. The conference and all festivities surrounding it had understandably been cancelled, and those who were not needed in the city were asked to go back to their homes so that the recovery efforts could be handled without the extra burden. The foreign entourages were also on their way home, leaving behind only their condolences and a sincere desire to send any aid if King Goruth should require it.

The hall was empty like most in the palace, but for a different reason. It had been placed off limits for everyone save for Goruth, a few hand-picked servants, and the guards. He had been asked to stay away due to the delicate nature of the situation with her being a prominent member of the High Council . . . and the fear that he would become irrationally volatile, but there was no way they were going to keep him out, could keep him out if they tried, so King Goruth had finally conceded that he could have one brief interview with the woman as long as the guards bore witness to the meeting. He knew that if anyone could, Gryph would be the one to get the answers that still remained unanswered.

After Marguerite's attack on Idora, Nygill and Goruth had hustled the councilwoman out and continued to question her elsewhere. Nygill had reported her answers back to Gryph later when everything had calmed down. Gryph now knew Idora had given the key to Kahlin Marteen's house to one of the men who were responsible for Marcus' abduction. She confirmed the man was to wait inside the house for the boat and help the others climb through the window with Marcus. She had also provided the carriage that carried them to the docks. Allahaim had said the questioning of the neighbors had turned up one man who had been awakened by the aerial attack on the city and had looked out his window. He had seen the carriage and had confirmed it had the crest of the House of Shulftar on its side. Gryph also now knew that the captain of the *Shifting Winds* had been paid handsomely to take Marcus to Marmuht safely and that the Whyse family had no prior knowledge of any of this, which puzzled him given that no one had seen Reginold Whyse since the night they all attended the affair at Brodie's Theatre. Idora had also told them Marcus was to be taken to a rented home and kept there until she could get to Marmuht, and that the dockmaster named Hix and the elderly woman were planted cohorts in Marcus' abduction and they were the ones who were to direct him after the *Shifting Winds*. Hix was now in custody, but the elderly lady had seemed to disappear and could not be found. All of those questions had been answered. Now he wanted the answers to the questions that had not been asked.

He approached the door and one of the guards opened it for him without hesitation.

"Minister Idwyr is here, Madam Shulftar," the guard announced.

Gryph ducked his head instinctively under the doorframe, even though leaning on the crutch kept his head low enough to clear the doorway, and limped into a well-lit, very red room. It had been over twenty years since he last stepped foot into the sitting room of Idora's palace apartment and yet he found it virtually unchanged. He detested the room. It made him feel like he was drowning in a sea of blood and flowers.

Idora rose from one of the numerous red and gold upholstered chairs situated on a plush circular rug depicting oversized roses. She wore one of her best gowns—one that, in another age, in another time, would have interested Gryph very much, but not now, not ever again. He was immune to Idora's tricks and had been since the day he first laid eyes on Marguerite in her father's inn.

In fact, the woman looked horrible—not the elegant lady everyone was accustomed to seeing. Her face was overly pale and puffy with substantial bruising around her nose and eyes from where Marguerite had hit her. She clasped her hands together and held them tightly against her stomach. "Gryph, I am . . . ," her voice quavered.

"Do not speak unless I require an answer," he ordered harshly, stumping over to the chair closest to the door, far away from Idora. He had to sit down. His battered leg demanded it. He pointed at Idora's personal maid who stood silently near a serving table behind Idora's chair. "You, get out!"

The maid ran like a startled deer, disappearing through the glass double-doors of the apartment's dining area and into the next room which Gryph knew to be Idora's bedchamber. He heard the latch on a door snick shut.

He lowered his tall frame into the chair and laid his crutch on the floor beside him, then leaned back and glared at the woman. "Sit down," he snapped.

Idora dropped into her chair like a rock, moving to its edge as if she would take flight at the first sign of danger. That suited him. She needed to be afraid, like Marcus was at the moment, he was sure.

"This interview will be brief and to the point," he said. He knew he sounded cold, which was just as well—he felt dead inside. "I will not tolerate hysterics or dramatizations. I know you, Idora. You are a callous bitch, and it is to that person I am going to speak to right now."

Despite her fear, Idora's eyes sparked fire, but she remained silent.

"Good, I see you understand me." Resting his elbows on the arms of the chair, he brought his hands together and steepled his fingers in front of his chest. "When and where did you meet Derrick?"

"Gryph, please let me apologize," she begged.

"Answer the damn question," he snapped. "I have no use for your apologies."

She swallowed hard. "I met him several years ago in Yradin. It was during the war when I went back to gather the southern troops for King Goruth. Derrick was in the street when my carriage passed. I . . . I thought he was you, which I knew was insane at the time because you were supposed to be dead. I had my driver halt and I called to him. When he looked my way—Gryph, he resembled you so much."

He waved an impatient hand. He didn't care that Derrick looked like him. The image of their father ran strong in both of them. "Just how long did it take for you to become intimate?"

She shrugged her shoulders. He could tell she did not want to answer the question, and she did not offer any more information. The room was dead quiet. He expected an answer and she knew it.

"Don't make me repeat myself, Idora," he said evenly, breaking the silence. She jumped as if he had shouted. She knew he was furious.

"That same week," she whispered.

He wasn't surprised. She was a feral creature. "And how often have you seen him since then?"

"We meet in Yradin when the council breaks sessions each quarter. That is the only time he will see me."

He sat clenching his jaw. "Do you know what he is, Idora?"

"All I know is that he reminded me of you," she said, staring miserably at the fall floral arrangement on the squat mahogany tea table in front of her. She couldn't look at him.

"I did not know he was an N'gethwyn until you said so the other night."

"Did you know his plans?"

Idora shook her head. "Gryph, he was just helping me with . . . ," she rubbed her palms on her thighs nervously.

"Helping you abduct my son," he finished for her. "Were you aware that your lover found dead at the inn and the men who took Marcus were members of the Brothers of M'gelidia?"

"No," she denied. "You know I would never knowingly deal with the M'gelidia. I know how ruthless they are—what they did to you. Derrick sent those men to me. He said I could trust them."

"How could you not know? You are aware of the tattoos they are required to have on their bodies. How could you not see one on your lover's chest?"

"I never saw him unclothed. He . . . ," she hesitated, obviously uncomfortable with discussing details of her affairs with him, "he made sure it was always dark before we . . . ." She trailed off, unable to finish her sentence.

"Why did he have a key to your home?"

"Sometimes . . . I wanted to be home," she shrugged her shoulders.

Gryph's mind churned furiously. His blood boiled. How could he ever have cared for this woman? She was disgusting.

"Aside from the fact that I know Derrick's true reasons for helping you abduct my son, enlighten me as to what he told you he sought to gain from all of this, and while you are at it, tell me what you wanted to gain?"

"He wouldn't tell me why, but said he just wanted you to hurt like he had been hurt," she raised her eyes as far as his hands in front of his chest. "I just wanted you."

He slapped the arms of his chair. "And just how did you think to accomplish that by taking my son?"

She started to rise.

"DON'T MOVE," he roared.

She settled in her chair, wrapping her arms tight about herself. Tears slid down her face.

"ANSWER ME!"

She flinched. "Marguerite was supposed to die, and I was going to be Marcus' rescuer. I swear, Gryph, I was never going to hurt him. I thought maybe with her out of the way, I might have a chance."

His jaw clenched furiously, and he had to grip the armrests hard because he had never wanted to hurt a woman in his entire life as badly as he wanted to hurt her at that moment.

The guards standing post in the hall listening to the interview must have thought so as well, because out of the corner of his eye, he could see one step just inside the open door. He couldn't care less. They were the least of his concerns at the moment.

"I am having a hard time understanding your motivation. Our relationship ended over twenty-five years ago, Idora. Twenty-five years!" he snarled. "Why now? Why do this now?"

"You had Marcus," she whispered. "You told me you would never marry, yet you did. You told me you would never have children, then there was Marcus. All I have ever wanted was for you and me to be together, to have a family together. Gryph, I have never stopped loving you."

"You went to all of this trouble for nothing, Idora, nothing!" he fumed. "For as long as I live, there will never be another woman for me but Marguerite, and if fate deems she does die before me, I can assure you I will be one lonely old man until I pass."

Idora swiped at the tears trailing down her face with trembling hands. "She is a lucky woman to have you," she whispered.

"You have that wrong," he growled. "I am a lucky man to have her."

He shifted in his seat, trying to give his leg any relief from the tremendous pain he was in, and to give himself a moment to calm down because he was not done.

Idora sat silently crying, slumping as if the life was slowly being sucked out of her.

"Derrick's letter to you mentioned the start of his plans which turned out to be an attack on Muryne. He told you this, yet you say you know nothing," he grimaced when an unexpected jolt of pain shot through his leg.

Her head snapped up in anger. "I didn't know his plans, Gryph," she hissed. "I am not a traitor to Anderan. I have had no contact with him in four weeks with the exception of that letter. If he is behind the attack on the city, I promise you, I did not know."

"Never, in all of your meetings, did you suspect or discuss anything that seemed out of the ordinary to you?" he asked.

"No. I knew he could be cold and distant . . . sometimes . . . violent, which gave me pause about seeing him, but I couldn't help it, he was as close to you as I could manage," she croaked. "He never spoke about anything concerning himself. He just seemed to be interested in talking about you and your family and what went on in Muryne."

"And you provided him with this information." *What in the name of light happened to the woman I once knew?* Idora was an intelligent, conniving woman who had risen above the powerful men from the Southern Province to gain and hold her position as a Senior Councilor far longer than any other councilor, and was as slick and cautious as a mountain lion on the council floor. The woman before him now resembled nothing like her.

"I didn't provide him with any information that would betray this country or you. I only spoke of things that were common knowledge to anyone on the street. Please, believe me."

"Do you know where he is now?"

She shook her head. "When we parted last, he said something about leaving the country, but I'm not so sure because his letter arrived right before I left for the theatre the other night. He has to be close."

"Yet, you say it has been four weeks since you last saw him?"

She nodded.

"In Yradin?"

She nodded again.

"And he said he was leaving the country?"

"Yes."

"My brother gets around," he muttered, rubbing a hand across his chin. The ambassador's wife from Chyrzah had commented that she had seen a man who looked exactly like Gryph on the docks the day they sailed from their country for Anderan and had described him accurately, leaving no doubt that the man she saw was in fact Derrick. That was why he dismissed his suspicion of Derrick in the beginning. He, too, thought Derrick was out of the country.

Solisius, is Obsudius capable of opening portals in different locations frequently? He sent his thoughts to the heavens.

A faint stir of the air let Gryph know his god was with him. *He can open small ones,* Solisius responded, *but ripping through the planes is vastly draining, so he would not want to maintain it for a long period of time if he wishes to conserve his energy for a larger one later.*

Will you answer my question now? He was going to give it another go. *Can he be permanently prevented from opening rifts?*

I cannot answer that, Solisius responded.

Which leads me to believe he can, Gryph thought. Solisius did not respond.

Idora fidgeted in her chair, uncomfortable with the silence. Gryph ignored her.

Can Obsudius move a living N'gethwyn around instantaneously in Do'athra as you did for my spirit in Ts'aura? Gryph asked silently, fairly certain the answer would be yes, but he wanted to make sure. The Realms of the Dead were exact replicas of the living world. Solisius' realm being full of spiritual life and healthy abundance—eternal happiness. Obsudius' realm, on the other hand, being the exact opposite, desolate, dark, gray, nothing but dirt and rock—full of despair and eternal fear. If Derrick was inside the Realm of Darkness, using it as a stepping stone to move about the world, he would still have to get to the location where the rift was to be opened.

Yes, Solisius answered.

Gryph mentally kicked himself for not thinking about the concept sooner. He scrubbed a hand across his weary eyes. He was so tired, so beat up, and feeling far too old to actively fight on a continuous basis. Now he needed to know where Derrick was at the moment, and he needed to find him quickly.

"Idora, where exactly are they taking my son?"

She cleared her throat. "I already told King Goruth."

"Good, now tell me," he snapped.

"Derrick rented a house south of Marmuht called Brackenwood Manor. He said it was perfect for our plan because it is isolated and overlooked a sheltered cove. They are to drop Marcus off there for me."

"Was Derrick supposed to meet you there?"

"No, he said he would step to the side after Marcus' abduction so that I could . . . ," she shrugged her shoulders, keeping her eyes anywhere but on his.

Gryph snorted in contempt, "You are, or I should say were, one of the smartest, most cunning lawmakers for Anderan, Councilor, and I am stunned by your lack of intelligence, or for that matter, simple common sense in all of this. What lover steps aside for another man? Look at me, Idora!" he commanded, leaning forward in his chair when she glanced his way. "You have handed my son to my deadliest enemy."

She raised trembling hands to cover her mouth, the horror of her actions finally sinking in. "Oh, Gryph, no! I never meant any harm to come to Marcus. Derrick promised me he would be safe."

Gryph picked up his crutch. "Derrick has no intentions of keeping my son safe." He hoisted himself out of the chair and left the room without a backward glance, leaving Idora behind sobbing uncontrollably.

Gryph needed time to cool down, to think, and he needed to do it alone. If Elhrin didn't return to Muryne by midday the next day, he was going to assume the ship she was after was still on its way to Marmuht. He planned to be in Marmuht before it reached the docks or the cove Idora spoke of—if it reached the area. If it wasn't there, then he would commandeer a ship and track it down. And once he had his son safely in his possession, he would then hunt for Derrick and finish the fight his brother had started long ago.

He painfully made his way down the back stairs to avoid the more occupied halls on the ground floor and was able to reach the corridor leading to his office before his luck ran out.

"Minister Idwyr," a young court page called out. Dressed in the purple and gold livery of the crown, he ran down the hall to catch up with Gryph.

Damn, he fumed silently, Goruth had found him. "Yes?"

"Sir," the lad panted, "His Majesty has requested your presence in his office."

"Does he now?" Gryph grunted. "Tell His Majesty, I am presently busy and I will see him as soon as I am through."

The young page looked uncomfortable with his answer. "His Majesty said I was not to leave your side until you walked through his office door."

"Is that so?"

"Yes, sir, he said you were known to avoid him sometimes. And if that was the case on this occasion, I was to follow you, even if you had to go to the lavatory to take a shit." Embarrassed, the lad dropped his eyes to study the marble tiles under his feet. "His words, sir, not mine."

Gryph couldn't help himself and laughed a much needed laugh. The boy looked up in surprise. "Well, son, I wouldn't wish that unpleasant task on anyone. I suppose I had best follow you then. Lead away."

Goruth's offices were on the second floor above the council office wing, which meant Gryph had to clamber back up the stairs with his injured leg. By the time they made it to

Goruth's office door, Gryph was in so much pain his mood was beyond black.

"Open the door," he ordered the guards posted on either side.

One guard tapped on the door then stuck his head inside to announce Gryph. Gryph reached over the guard's shoulder and pushed the door out of his hand. It slammed loudly against the wall making something fall to the floor with a crash.

"I'm here," Gryph announced. He brushed past the guard.

Goruth's head shot up from the intrusion. He was sitting at the head of a conference table surrounded by Osgar, his steward, and several top military officials and advisors, including General Pyrthenius and Colonel Drurhey of the city guard.

"We can all see that," King Goruth growled. "You already owe me two doors. Are you trying for a third?"

"If it is damaged, take it out of this month's salary," Gryph shot back. He saw they were hovering over a map, and if Goruth summoned him here only to discuss recovery efforts, he was not staying. "Whatever you require of me needs to be quick. I plan to leave for Marmuht tomorrow, and I don't have much time to spare. I have pertinent matters that require my attention, and I am to meet with Director Allahaim within the hour."

Goruth leaned back in his chair at the head of the table, eyeing Gryph steadily. "Gryph, I fully understand what you need to do. However, I think you will want to hear what I have to say," he said without anger at Gryph's less than congenial behavior.

Gryph glanced at the map again. "What is it?"

"I'm afraid the news is not good. Sit. You look as if you are about to fall."

Gryph lowered himself in the vacant seat beside Major Riffkin, Goruth's cavalry tactician.

"Gentleman, we can continue with the details of the recovery efforts a bit later. Since Gryph has now joined us, I want to make you all aware of a major threat to our country. This afternoon I received two missives—one from Thistle Meadows and one from Abideen. Both have been attacked by Do'athrim. The beasts were repelled, and Abideen is fortifying itself against another possible attack. Troops from Fort Denmar are on their way to help. Thistle Meadows' attack was minor, and I think those beasts were a part of the group that was involved in our own attack. A third messenger from my son Cahail arrived right before our meeting and delivered even more distressing news." Goruth picked up a pair of spectacles and perched them low on his nose. He unfolded a multi-page letter. "He says that we are to expect a major invasion on Anderan sometime before the beginning of next month. General Shifwood of Marmuht has received information from—let's see," Goruth slid a finger down the page of his letter, "ah, here it is, a Captain Prajheet of the *Daybreaker*, a Chyrzinian merchant ship who reported that a large fleet of unknown ships are anchored off the northwest coast of Scathlamahn."

Gryph furrowed his brow at the news.

"What would a merchant ship be doing that far out in the middle of nowhere?" General Pyrthenius asked.

Goruth glanced up briefly from his page. "I don't know, but he was seen by those on the island and was chased by one of their ships. He managed to outrun them, and they discontinued their pursuit before he neared the Chyrzinian coast. He reported the fleet, and King Tryzzanine sent two naval vessels out to investigate. They ran across the foreign patrol ship well before they reached Scathlamahn and overtook it. The ship was filled with Do'athrim creatures who fought to the death. None of them were willing to be captured alive. The Chyrzinian vessels lost a fair amount of their own crew and had no choice but to turn around and sail home without confirming the fleet off of Scathlamahn. That is the last word from the Chyrzinians as of the date of this missive. However, we have further information to add to this." King Goruth pulled a sheet of paper from behind the ones he held and passed it to General Pyrthenius to his left. "Here is the original missive from Tryzzanine." Goruth turned to the next page of his letter. "As soon as he received that letter, Mayor Nambacus had Admiral Zoscalese send out our own scouts from Marmuht, and a bit of luck was on our side. The naval warship *Intruder* ran across another foreign ship off the Veihl Coast near Brackenwood Cove on its way out to sea and pursued it to investigate."

Gryph exhaled grimly. Derrick had devised a well thought out plan and another piece of his plan slammed into place like the stone doors of a mausoleum.

My Brother, I have been waiting for our meeting. It has been a long time. I regret that I cannot be more specific as to when or where we will meet, and will have to leave it to fate to deem the time and the place, but rest assured, it will be soon.

Brackenwood Cove was the site of the mausoleum, he had no doubt, and he was the one Derrick intended to inter inside its cold walls for eternity.

"The ship allowed the *Intruder* to draw alongside and all seemed to be well—they claimed to be merchants from Goltivias on their way to Agadar—until a crewmember screamed he was a prisoner and the ship's crew were enemies of Anderan. The man was murdered by one of his mates on the spot, and the foreign crew knowing their true identities had been compromised, attacked the crew of the *Intruder*." Goruth's gaze found Gryph. "Do'athrim poured up from below deck to join the fight. Again, all fought to their deaths, but six human sailors were spared, two of which were from Anderan who had been forced to work as slaves."

"Were they interrogated?" Gryph asked.

"I was getting to that. Turns out, the ship was on a scouting mission of its own," Goruth turned to the next page in his stack, making sure of the facts he was about to present. "The two Anderan men confirmed the mysterious flotilla is destined for Anderan, and their ship was sent to assess Marmuht's defenses. They had anchored in Brackenwood Cove and sent men inland. They were on their return trip to Scathlamahn when they were overtaken by our ship."

Major Riffkin slid the missive from the King of Chyrzah to Gryph. Gryph glanced down at it briefly. He didn't need to read it. Goruth was giving him all the information he needed. He couldn't read it, anyway. The man's handwriting was too small and as much as Gryph would like to deny it, his eyesight wasn't like it used to be.

"You said they are to land the first of next month. There is nothing more specific?" General Pyrthenius asked.

"The landing is planned to coincide with the next full moon," Goruth answered. He paused for a moment, frowning at the map on the table, then his gaze pinned Gryph. "Gryph, those men also said that the fleet would have one or more men with magical powers on nearly every ship, and there was a cargo ship being readied to carry deadly beasts with terrifying capabilities."

Gryph could only guess those beasts would be bynduwhin unless the island held more secrets, which was a high probability.

"How many ships?" he asked.

"There was not a specific count, but it is estimated at no less than forty," Goruth answered.

Gryph looked down at the paper on the table, thinking. He had known this invasion would possibly occur—that the dream he had years ago was going to pass while he was still in the realm of the living—the clues were obvious, even though he had not seen himself in the dream. And he had been working hard the last three years to be prepared, but the sad truth was, they were not. Fate was hurtling them down this deadly path far sooner than he would like.

"We will need the Eagles," Goruth said.

Gryph glanced up sharply. "You realize that only eight or nine out of thirteen candidates are old enough or ready enough for this."

"What choice do we have?" Goruth asked.

"Your Majesty," Major Riffkin spoke up, "what is the naval force doing about the threat?"

"According to Nambacus, Admiral Zoscalese has his entire fleet patrolling the coast. He has sent word to Yradin, Pago Duhn, and Agadar for help. Hopefully, they will be able to hinder the attack. But the fact is, gentlemen, we do not have a naval force with the capabilities to defend against magical attacks such as we saw on Muryne the other day. A landing on our soil is imminent, and we will have to plan accordingly."

"Your Majesty, how do we plan if we do not know the landing site?" Colonel Hascomb asked. He was Muryne's infantry commander.

"That is why I have sent word to Cahail to send scouts out to comb the coastline around Marmuht for the best possible landing sites. There can't be many because the entire coast is nothing but cliffs with only a few coves and beaches large enough to hold a landing of this size."

"It will be in or near Brackenwood Cove," Gryph said.

All eyes turned his way.

"How can you be sure?" Goruth asked.

"Derrick named it specifically when he told Idora that he would take Marcus there for her, remember?" he asked with a grimace. The pain in his leg had become unbearable.

He had to leave soon. "I now believe Derrick wanted me to follow Marcus out of Muryne to ensure I would be where he needed me to be on his timetable. The ship Marcus is on registered its destination as Marmuht. These clues are not by chance. I have been led across this city by the nose on purpose. Derrick wanted me in the south, far too late to save Marmuht from attack, I'm sure," he gazed steadily at Goruth, "but he wants me there all the same."

Goruth's lips thinned in a grim line. He nodded in understanding.

"Derrick? Who is Derrick?" General Pyrthenius asked.

"Derrick Idwyr, gentlemen . . . my brother," Gryph said grimly.

His revelation earned a few murmurs of surprise from them. He had kept his brother's existence relatively secret. He was not one to speak openly about his personal affairs or his past. It was no one's business, but his own.

"He is the enemy, and this fleet we are speaking of will be under his direction. The Do'athrim attacks are a part of his plan. My brother is like me . . . ," Gryph took a deep breath, "except he is N'gethwyn."

"N'gethwyn?" General Pyrthenius leaned over the table so he could see Gryph. He knew that the N'gethwyn were dangerous individuals with magical capabilities and that they were usually associated with the Brothers of M'gelidia. He also knew that Gryph had spent most of his lifetime hunting down and eliminating members of the group. "Your own brother?"

Gryph tilted his head back and didn't bother to answer.

Pyrthenius grunted, "That must hurt."

You have no idea, Gryph thought silently.

"Your Majesty, what is it you wish for us to do?" Lieutenant Colonel Albrennan asked. He was in charge of Muryne's Artillery Defense. "We are going to be spread thin if we have to defend against random attacks throughout the country, as well as a major invasion in the Southern Province."

"Yes, we are. As soon as I received the reports, I sent runners out to the governors of all provinces. I have ordered them to declare a state of wartime emergency. Every city, town, village, or settlement will know that an attack is possible and they are to prepare accordingly. I will also send a message to the Governor of the Western Province that we will need as many men as can be spared from all his cities and have them march to Marmuht as soon as possible. Governor Blythsedell in the south will send what he can from Murango. Cahail is readying his men as we speak." Goruth removed his spectacles and dropped them with a tiny clink on the table. He rubbed his eyes with both hands. "We will have to do the best we can. Pyrthenius, it will be up to you to determine how many we can take to the Veihl Coast from here without leaving Muryne undefended. Osgar, did you set up a meeting with the councilors for me?"

"Yes, Your Majesty," the steward answered.

"Good, I will also need you to send for Movlin in Gildas. I want him here with Egeria while I'm away," Goruth said, wanting to ensure his youngest son, who was currently attending the University of Gildas, was where he needed to be in case something went wrong in the south.

"Speaking of the council, where is Councilor Whyse?" Lieutenant Colonel Albrennan asked.

"If someone could tell me that, I would appreciate it," Goruth answered.

So would I, Gryph thought.

"What do you have planned for Councilor Shulftar, Your Majesty?" Colonel Hascomb asked.

"I have executed a formal royal order to proceed with a private judicial hearing," Goruth said. "I did not want to take the chance that Gryph would vanish from the city before he and his wife had a chance to issue an official testimony against Idora."

Gryph reached for the crutch he had propped against the table and stood up. He couldn't sit still any longer.

"The High Court Justices will be accepting our official statements tonight." Goruth frowned at him. "Where are you going?"

"Out." He limped to the door.

"We aren't done," Goruth growled.

Gryph halted at the doorway. "Your Majesty, I will see you tonight. If there is anything else I need to know you can tell me then. In the meantime, I need to talk to Director Allahaim and go over the things I need for him to do while I am gone." He jerked open the door and ducked into the hall, hearing Goruth direct a few expletives his way in disgust for coming and going as he pleased, but he couldn't stay and indulge Goruth's dependence on him. He needed answers to questions like where was Reginold Whyse? If the man had nothing to do with any of Derrick's plans, then why did his missing status bother Gryph so much? Gryph hated to do it, but he was going to have to force himself to climb another set of stairs.

When he reached the third floor he had to lean against the wall for support. He couldn't catch his breath and a cold sweat covered his forehead. Obsudius and his realm of Do'athra had done an excellent job of damaging his lungs. Even in the best of health Gryph found he needed to take occasional conscious deep breaths.

Wiping sweat from his brow, he pushed away from the wall and made his way down several corridors until he reached the western residential wing. He needed to stop by Elhrin's apartment while he was in the vicinity, but first he wanted to check Reginold's.

"Good evening, Minister," a maid said as she passed him in the hall.

"Evening," he responded.

The corridor was relatively quiet. The maid and a few other members of the staff were traveling its path, hurrying about their various tasks of the evening. One young lady had a dinner tray and knocked on the door he knew belonged to a junior councilor from the Eastern Province. She saw him coming and dropped a simple curtsy. "Good evening, Minister."

"Evening, young lady," he said as he crossed over to the other side of the hall and stopped at the next door. He knocked even though he was sure it was empty.

"Sir," the maid at the junior councilor's door said, "Councilor Whyse is not in."

"Have you seen him?" he asked.

"Not since the night before the city was attacked, sir," she said as the door to the junior councilor's door opened.

"About what time did you see him that evening?" he asked.

One of the councilor's personal staff took the tray from the maid and shut the door. She turned to face him.

"It was late," she squinted at the ceiling, trying to remember. "I'm sure it was when the unusual meteor shower began. He ran out of his apartment and nearly knocked me flat to the floor."

"Where was he running to?" Gryph asked.

"He ran that way to the southern corridor," she said, pointing back the way he had come. "I don't know where he went after that."

"Thank you, miss," he said. He tried the doorknob and found it was locked. He used a miniscule tendril of his energy, flipped the lock, and opened the door. The maid stared at him curiously. He raised an eyebrow at her, and she took the hint to hurry off to her next destination.

Reginold's apartment was dark and silent. Gryph snapped his fingers. Every lamp and candle blazed into life. He limped into the room. It reminded him of his own apartment before Marguerite came into his life—not very orderly and definitely male. Deep leather chairs faced a darkened fireplace. A portrait of Whyse hung over its cherry wood mantelpiece. Bookshelves lined the wall on his left, and in one corner was a desk filled with a scattering of books, papers, and a pen and ink station. On the far back wall, situated next to curtained windows, was a small table with two chairs that Reginold used for private dining.

He limped to the desk and searched through the papers finding nothing but documents relating to the last council meeting and the rough draft of a speech Reginold had planned to give at the next council meeting concerning why he thought Gryph's academy needed to be shut down.

Good luck with that, Whyse, Gryph thought darkly. The academy was needed more than any of them knew, and if they tried to shut it down, they were in for a fight they didn't want.

He pulled open the two desks drawers, finding nothing of interest in their cavities. He then ran a hand along the interior and bent over to look underneath the desk, searching for a secret compartment. Unlike his own desk, Reginold's didn't appear to have one.

He slowly perused the room one more time, but nothing caught his eye out of the ordinary or spoke to his heightened So'ladiun instinctual abilities.

He made his way to a darkened doorway on the right side of the room and used his magic to light the lamps inside. It was Reginold's bedchamber. A large canopy bed draped with heavy, deep blue velvet drapes centered the far wall. Its bed linens were in a serious state of disarray, and the feather pillows were indented as if it had been last occupied by more than one person. He peeked into the nearby lavatory door just to make sure it was empty, then scanned the bedroom again. What he was looking for, he had no idea. His eyes fell on one of the two bedside tables. It was cluttered with books, papers, and an empty wine glass. Reginold obviously slept on the left side. He limped over for a closer look and picked up one of the books that turned out to be a history of Anderan's clans and their territories. Gryph flipped through the pages, finding nothing of interest then tossed the book on the bed. He sifted through the papers on the table but found nothing. He turned to look at Reginold's dark mahogany wardrobe. The right door was slightly ajar and a white shirtsleeve dangled limply through the bottom crack. He crossed over and opened the door. The inside was in disarray as if Reginold had jerked clothing off the hangers and shelves without thought. He noticed a crumpled wad of parchment lying on top of the shirt at the bottom, and used his magic to retrieve the paper.

It turned out to be a note—a note in a very familiar handwriting. He limped back to the bedside and tilted the page next to a lamp for a better look, wishing now he had brought the spectacles Doctor Dryke had given him to try, but he was able to make out the blurry words without them.

Councilor, I have acquired the serum for the disposal of the minister's assistant. I will deliver it to you soon. All is well.

Gryph stared at the note. Derrick was actively engaged with more than one councilor which meant that the one he had been seeking for a long time could very well be Councilor Reginold Whyse. He exhaled heavily. His innate instinctual abilities said no, so what did that mean? Was Reginold being coerced into doing something against his will?

He nodded to himself. That scenario seemed more likely. Reginold Whyse, while an intelligent lawmaker, did not seem to be the type to achieve a high-level position within the dangerous society that was the Brotherhood of M'gelidia. No, he wasn't the Alpha . . . the one who led the entire organization within the country of Anderan, but someone in Muryne was, and that was what Gryph needed to discuss with Nygill Allahaim. Events were spiraling out of control, and Gryph was not going to be able to continue to pursue the matter. He was going to have to trust Nygill to do it for him. The Alpha had to be found, and he needed to be found as quickly as possible.

Gryph read over the note one more time, his gaze returning to the word serum—a word that made his blood boil. He had resigned himself to the dangers Elhrin would face as So'ladiun long before Gryph even knew her. Still, it didn't change the feelings that washed through him knowing that there were plans to poison her. Elhrin was his daughter, maybe not legally or by blood, but he had played a vital role in her upbringing, and to him she would always be his little girl.

He folded the note and slipped it into the pocket of his coat. With an angry sigh, he stumped out of the apartment, throwing the entire interior into darkness with a negligent wave of his hand as he doused the lights and slammed the door of Reginold's apartment with his magic. A sharp feminine cry of surprise came from behind him, but he did not bother to see who he had startled. He was furious and in no mood to soothe someone's feelings.

A few corridors away brought him to Elhrin's door. He used his key to unlock the door, lighting the room with his magic as he stepped inside. It was exactly the same as it had been the night Marcus was taken. The map of Muryne lay open on the table, and the walnut pieces were still positioned in the spots where they had mapped out the locations of the dead bodies. He sat down wearily in one of the chairs and stared blindly at the map. This event was going to test him. Facing Obsudius had been nothing compared to this. Then, it had been only him and the dark god, a vile celestial being he had spent his entire life trying to thwart at every series of events the dark god sent Anderan's way.

But this time—this time was different. This time he had to face Derrick, his own flesh and blood—someone he once loved, and this time he had to finish a fight that had started long, long ago.

The memory of a black-haired, blue-eyed boy of sixteen emerged, standing in the middle of the road outside of Pago Duhn, yelling angrily at him to come back or else. And when Gryph didn't stop, Derrick had attacked him with a weak force of energy that Gryph easily deflected. Derrick hadn't understood that Gryph had to go—it was his destiny. All Derrick knew was that Gryph was leaving for the grand opportunity to train with the famous Minister of Specialized State Defense, Odrun Jorme, and that he had to stay in Pago Duhn with a father who seemed to hate him.

Gryph shook his head. That was the one thing he never understood. His father was a good man, a good husband, and for the most part, a good father, but for some reason he never seemed to get along with Derrick. Derrick could never do anything right by his father, and his father would always compare Derrick to Gryph . . . wanted Derrick to be like him.

Gryph leaned forward and put his head in his hands.

What would his mother think if she were alive? She had loved Derrick with her entire being, even when Derrick was at his worst . . . which was remarkably horrid. Would she tell Gryph that what he had to do was understandable—that Derrick had committed unforgivable acts and had to be held accountable, or would she be disappointed that he had not tried harder to find Derrick all of these years and bring him home like she had asked him to do—to try and change him to be the good man she had always believed Derrick could be?

He hoped she would understand. He could not change Derrick any more than he could change the past. He had to face the future, his own destiny.

With resigned frustration, he scrubbed his face hard and glanced up at the landscape painting on Elhrin's wall—a façade for a safe he had built for her to hide the *Book of Tolman*. It depicted a row of cottages on the lane where Elhrin and her family had lived in Glimmerdale. He had it commissioned last year and had given it to her for her birthday. She had hugged him so hard it felt like his bones cracked.

He smiled briefly at the memory, then let it fade. Two of his children were on the sea in harm's way. He prayed they were safe.

He pushed himself to his feet, and made the mistake of crossing to the wall without the aid of his crutch. Pain seared through his leg when he put any pressure on it which was not good. He was going to have to fight, and he needed to be mobile.

He gripped the frame of the painting and pulled hard, but it did not budge. Immediately, four blue crystals embedded in the corners of the frame turned a deep red. Red beams of energy shot from one crystal to the next. A glow spread across the entire façade of the painting creating a pulsing shield of deadly energy.

Good, the magical crystal seals he had put in place worked as they should, and if he proceeded with trying to remove the painting, he would likely end up dead.

He unbuttoned the top of his coat and pulled his pendant from the neck of his shirt. He directed his magic through the stone and back out at the painting. This time, the façade of the painting turned a deep blue, recognizing Solisius' power within the flow, and he heard an audible click.

He swung the painting out of the way to reveal the exterior of a solid steel surface embedded in the stone wall. This was another layer of safety he devised to protect the book. There was no handle or lock on the outside of the safe's door. He placed a hand on the right side of its surface and used magic to slide two steel bars inside the door to the left. The door popped open and he swung it wide. Inside, the book lay safely on top of a few other items Elhrin thought needed safe-keeping. He grunted with a smile, and picked up a tiny doll made out of sticks, vine, and old corn husks. He had made it for her one late summer's day when he had taken her into the countryside around Glimmerdale for training. She would have been only ten or eleven at the time and she had kept it all this time. He wondered how she had managed to save it since her home had burned during the Do'athrim attack years ago. He started to place the doll back, and noticed a sheaf of papers under the *Book of Tolman*. He picked the book up, glanced at the paper on top and smiled. She had finally become serious about her art, and was talented. He slid the sketch out for a better look. It was a drawing of the four horse fountain in the palace's courtyard. He glanced back into the safe and saw there were others, but he didn't want to invade her privacy any further. He would ask her about it later.

He turned his head towards the door—concentrating. Four forces of magical energy intruded upon his awareness. They were coming from the direction of Glimmerdale and were nearing the city at a rapid pace. He separated the forces. It was Grey, Kull, Tover, and Barron. Grey made excellent choices, but he was too late for what Gryph needed him for in Muryne. He would, however, need all four and the others back in Glimmerdale soon, and he was going to be forced into making a difficult decision concerning the younger ones. He grimaced at the thought. Sometimes the dreams that came to him revealing important events were more of a hassle than a help.

He replaced the doll and closed the safe, reassured that no one would be able to move the painting unless they had one of Solisius' pendants.

Chapter Thirteen

"How is your back?" Elhrin asked, placing both hands on the ship's railing.

Kyne lowered the spyglass he had borrowed from the helmsman. "Better," he said.

One of the ropes from the falling mast had slapped him in the back like a whip when it hit the deck. The result was an ugly red welt the entire length of Kyne's back from his hips to his right shoulder. The ship's cook, who also happened to be the ship's surgeon, had slathered some kind of smelly salve on the welt which Kyne said seemed to help, but it made him stink like rotting fish.

"Have you noticed all of the warships on the water the last few days?" he asked, offering her the spyglass. "Since Pago Duhn, I have counted twelve."

That would have been four days ago. They were now past Yradin and had been on the water over two weeks since leaving Port V'Din. She pointed the glass at a sail farther out to sea. The ocean waves were rolling the ship, making it hard to hold the glass steady on the vessel out on the horizon, but she did catch a quick glimpse of an Anderan Naval flag flying atop one of the masts.

She gave the glass back to him. "Is it unusual for them to be out?" she asked.

"No, but it is unusual for them to all be heading west at the same time." He lifted the glass to his eye again. "Patrols usually run up and down the coastline around their ports. These are all running ahead of us and none have turned around to head back to port."

"I wonder if they know about Marcus?"

"There hasn't been enough time," he said, lowering the glass. "If Mayor Whitpyle sent a messenger like he said he would, the fastest runner to Pago Duhn from Port V'Din would have been at least a day or two behind us and if one from Muryne had been sent, he wouldn't have made it there in time, either."

"What does the captain say?" she asked.

A loud splash and a burst of laughter from the stern of the ship made her look over her shoulder. Clay was watching Marissa practice her water techniques she had been working on the past week. Elhrin had sped up Marissa's magical instruction. She wanted her more prepared in case of another fight, and they had accomplished more than she expected. Marissa had mastered launching orbs of fire without trouble, and now she was experimenting with her unique abilities. There was only one other student they had who was just as capable at catching on as quickly, and that was Phalen. He picked up on the magical procedures faster than the other students, but even he took a little while longer than what she was experiencing with Marissa. Probably due to the fact he was just sixteen and easily distracted and Marissa was more focused.

"He is just as puzzled, and is going to hail the next ship we come close enough to and see if he can get any information," Kyne answered.

"I wish the next ship we see would be the *Shifting Winds*," she muttered.

"Give it up. It is not going to happen," he said, tucking the glass under his arm. He perused the ship. "Where is your betrothed?"

She didn't like the way he said it . . . as if Tomas was something nasty, and wondered for the millionth time why Kyne did not like Tomas. She pointed up.

Tomas had found he liked crawling around in the rigging and was currently learning how to work the sails from one of the sailors. She shielded her eyes against the sun to find him. He was high in the foremast straddling the uppermost spar with a sailor.

"Dear god," she breathed, not liking his precarious perch. "I wish he would come down."

"With the way the waves are tossing us around, he may come down faster than you think," Kyne snorted.

"That's what I'm afraid of," she said. She couldn't look anymore and decided to go check on Marissa's progress.

Elhrin mounted the stair to the stern and stood off to the side to watch what Marissa was working on. The girl was still trying to work out how to conjure water in a pattern resembling rain. So far, the best she had been able to accomplish was large blobs of water that popped into the air and fell with a huge splash into the ocean.

"You know that would be a nice trick to use on Camlyn. You could dump it on his head like he did you with the water bucket over the barn door," Clay commented.

Marissa turned to grin at him, noticing Elhrin had joined them. "I think I will remember that the next time we are in Jarit's Cove. He deserves it after all the jokes he has played on everyone over the years."

Clay chuckled. "I think my favorite was the one he played on mean old man Hoovenstyer."

"Which one was that?" Marissa laughed. "He played several on Mister Hoovenstyer."

"The one where he doused the man's doorstep with water on a freezing night then let all of Mister Hoovenstyer's livestock loose in his yard early the next morning. Mister Hoovenstyer ran out in his stocking feet and slipped on the ice that had formed and landed face first into a pile of dung one of the cows had left behind," Clay laughed. "Camlyn told me he hadn't planned for the dung to be there. He said Mister Hoovenstyer was so mean even the cows hated him and had helped him out with the joke."

"That's funny," Marissa agreed with a laugh then her face took on a thoughtful expression. "Elhrin, is it possible for us to form ice?"

"Good question," Elhrin said, trying to remember if any of her predecessors in the *Book of Tolman* had mentioned it, but couldn't think of one, and wished she had the book with her. She joined Marissa at the rail of the ship. "Everything I have ever done, involves heat and the intensifying of energy. I wonder what it would take to freeze something. Let me think about it a moment. Why don't you continue to work on what you are doing."

She watched Marissa go back to practicing, as she mulled over the concept of freezing something. The girl started to form various sizes of water balls and dropped them into the ocean. At one point, she managed to form more than one at the same time which meant she was on her way to accomplishing her goal.

Elhrin decided to experiment. She saw a bucket on the lower deck and used her magic to retrieve it much to the surprise of the surrounding sailors who were startled by the sudden appearance of a flying bucket. She grinned at them when the bucket hit her hands. They returned her grin. The fight against the Do'athrim had overturned any suspicions or superstitions they had towards her, and they had come to accept her and her abilities.

"Marissa, fill this for me," Elhrin said, holding the bucket out for her.

After Marissa filled the bucket, Elhrin sat cross-legged on the deck with the bucket in front of her and stared at the sloshing water inside blindly, thinking about what she knew of how water froze in winter, and what she wanted to do.

"You see, I know I can heat this up like so." She placed the tips of her fingers into the water and used her energy to heat it up. As the temperature rose to boiling, she removed her fingers from the water yet continued to pour her energy into the bucket. The water bubbled.

Marissa plopped to the deck across from her. "You are sending energy into the water," she observed. "Is it possible to draw energy from something?"

Elhrin let her magic go. The boiling water subsided. "That is another excellent question." *This girl is good*, she thought, glad that Marissa had not left the ship when they docked in Port V'Din, but it had been close. Marissa had avoided Elhrin after the fight on the river, unable to come to terms with what she thought was a cold-blooded murder of the N'gethwyn despite the fact the woman had tried to kill them all on the ship. Elhrin didn't know what had been said to change Marissa's mind, but the change had come after Kyne had a talk with her. The next thing Elhrin knew, Marissa was not only willing to stay with them, but she wanted to learn how to fight, as well.

Elhrin stuck her fingers in the warm water of the bucket. How would she go about drawing energy from something? Is it possible? She closed her eyes and shut out everything around her. She felt the sun on her face, and the rise and fall of the ship as well as the warmth of the water on her fingers. Everything else washed away from her. She focused on her energy within herself. She knew how to push it out . . . could she pull it in? Could she reverse the flows inside? She thought about how she used her pendant . . . or could you . . . ? She decided to try something. Placing both hands on either side of the bucket, she pushed a tiny flow out of one hand sent it through the water and back into her other hand, creating a circle of energy. It felt strange, but remarkably exhilarating. She smiled when she realized she had started to pull energy through the water instead of push it through and could feel the heat she was taking from the water.

"Elhrin, look at the water," Marissa's voice intruded in on her concentration.

Elhrin opened her eyes. She had cooled the water down so much that a thin film of ice had formed across the surface of the water. Elhrin grinned at Marissa. "I guess it can be done."

"I think you are right," Marissa laughed. "Tell me what you did."

The rest of the afternoon was spent working with their new found technique. Marissa started to try it with her ability to form water in air. She wondered if she could ever get the rain technique down, maybe she could eventually make it snow.

But Elhrin began thinking along a different line. If energy could be taken from something and diverted or converted into different usages, how could she harness the technique in other instances and utilize the concept to her advantage?

"Masstersun," hailed a sailor in the crow's nest, breaking her concentration. "Starboard side."

"Mister Lindley, change course to take us alongside," the captain called from the foredeck, and started to make his way back to the stern. "Mister Sneid, flag him down. I want to talk to him."

"Yes, sir," the sailor in the crow's nest answered. He waved two bright red flags in a strange pattern.

Elhrin moved to the side of the ship for a better look at the approaching sail. It was a smaller vessel, sporting only two masts, and was moving east towards them. She hoped they had information concerning the *Shifting Winds*.

The captain leaned on the rail beside her. "Have you met him?"

Elhrin was puzzled by the question. "I'm sorry. Met who?"

The captain grinned and pointed at the approaching ship. "Griffyn Masstersun, Gryph's eldest son."

"That's him?" She wasn't expecting this to happen. How strange that they were on the hunt for one of his sons only to run across the other. "I did when I was little, but I don't really remember him."

"Then you are in for a treat," he said, then moved off to give orders to his crew.

The other ship changed course and veered towards them. When they drew near, both ships started lowering sail, slowing them down to a near standstill. A tall figure moved toward the bow of the other ship.

When she could see him clearly, she had to shake her head at his appearance. Master Gryph certainly reproduced replicas of himself. Griffyn was tall if not taller than his father with the same dark features and suntanned skin that those raised in the south seemed to have, even though his was noticeably darker from being on the sea.

"Oh my word," Marissa breathed as she and Clay edged in beside Elhrin at the rail. "Who is he?"

"That is Master Idwyr's oldest son," Elhrin said and had to grin when she saw the open admiration on Marissa's face.

"He is not hard to look at," Marissa commented. "And those muscles . . . I wouldn't mind touching those at all."

Elhrin laughed.

"Excuse me?" Clay said, raising his eyebrows at Marissa. "You do know I'm right here, don't you?"

Marissa patted Clay's arm absently. "You are handsome, too, sweetheart."

"Thank you for noticing," he grumbled with a smile.

Elhrin thought Clay had to be the most easy-going man she had ever met. Nothing seemed to anger him.

"Hoy there, Ostied," Griffyn hailed across the short expanse of water between the two ships. "It didn't take you long to get out of Muryne. Did you find the lake waters too calm for your taste?"

"There's been some trouble, Masstersun," Captain Ostied replied. "The city has been attacked, and I'm afraid your father's young son has been abducted. We are giving chase."

Griffyn face fell into a deep scowl. "What do you mean abducted? By whom?"

"I don't know who is responsible, but I do know he is aboard one of Roarke Whyse's ships the *Shifting Winds*. You haven't seen it by chance, have you?"

"No," Griffyn growled, "I've just come from Traphyt. How far ahead is he?"

"He is a day ahead of us. You should have passed him," the captain said.

"Not necessarily. If he has seen all the naval ships on the water heading for Marmuht, he may be trying to avoid them," Griffyn said.

"That is something else I wanted to ask you. Why are all the naval ships heading west?" the captain asked.

"Rumor has it there is an impending invasion on Anderan somewhere near Marmuht."

"What?" Elhrin asked, stunned. "By who?"

Griffyn's deep blue gaze landed on her, reminding her so much of Master Gryph it made her wish more than anything to be able to speak with her mentor at that moment. "No one knows who the invaders are, Miss, but I have to assume the rumors are true with all the boat traffic heading west."

"Masstersun, this young lady is Elhrin, your father's assistant," the captain said.

"Well, well, we meet at last, Elhrin." Griffyn's face transformed into a smile, revealing a row of healthy white teeth.

"I think my legs just melted," Marissa said low under her breath, earning a growl from Clay.

"My father has written extensively about you to me over the years. I had hoped you were going to be with him when he, Marguerite, and Marcus visited Pago Duhn this past spring, but he said you were being forced to work with Prince Cahail and had to leave for Tuhnichi the first of summer," Griffyn said. "How did that go?"

"It was different," she responded. King Goruth had asked her to spend a month with his eldest son because eventually they would have to work together as a team when he rose to the throne. It had been a tedious and difficult month. Prince Cahail was arrogant and made no effort to hide how much he detested her presence. He was nothing like his father.

"I'm sure it was," he said, then his scowl returned. "Tell me more about what happened to Marcus."

Elhrin related the entire tale, including the attempted murder of Marguerite, the attack on the city and how Master Gryph had to fight against three N'gethwyn, and ending with how they had been waylaid by the Do'athrim and N'gethwyn on the river. He grew more furious the further she got into the tale and did not have his father's ability to control his face when he was angry.

"It seems our country is in a bit of trouble. I wish I knew more to tell you about the rumored invasion, but I don't. Ostied, if the *Shifting Winds* wanted to avoid the naval fleet, she is probably out there," he jerked his head toward the darkening horizon. "The winds and the current will work against her and slow her down. How about I head farther out and parallel you? That way we can cover more water. If I see anything, I'll signal."

"I appreciate the help," the captain answered. He roared to his sailors to raise sail.

Captain Masstersun's voice echoed over the water as he issued his own commands. The two ships parted ways, but Masstersun's came about and headed out for the horizon.

"Elhrin, you say he is Master Idwyr's son?" Marissa asked.

"Yes," Elhrin replied.

"I didn't feel an energy source," Marissa commented.

"He doesn't have the gift," Elhrin said, watching his ship grow smaller.

Before night fell, his sail was just a distant speck on the horizon, paralleling their course.

The next day dawned foggy with a relatively calm sea. Elhrin peered out of one of the cabin's tiny windows and saw nothing but an impenetrable wall of white.

Wonderful, she thought as she padded over to the tiny stove. *If the Shifting Winds was right next to us, we wouldn't be able to see it.*

She tested her shirt and found that it had dried. She and Marissa had cleaned their clothes the night before and draped them close to the little stove to dry. It had been a bit comical trying to get breeches and shirts scrubbed clean with only a small bucket of water and a scrub stone, but they had managed. She pulled on her shirt, and picked up her breeches. Finding they were still damp, she used her magic to finish drying them then tugged them over her hips, liking how their warmth felt on her skin. She then pulled on her boots and quietly moved to the door of the cabin, trying not to awaken Marissa who was still curled up in the narrow bunk.

She opened the door and let out a soft squeal of surprise. Tomas was on the other side.

"You scared me," she whispered.

He grinned wide, thinking it funny that he had been able to startle her.

"Everything okay, Elhrin?" Marissa mumbled sleepily.

"Fine, Marissa, go back to sleep," she said, pushing Tomas backwards into the narrow, dark passage outside of the captain's cabin. She quietly closed the door.

"Does my beard make me look so ugly I scare your?" he asked.

"No, I just wasn't expecting to see anyone when I opened the door," she said quietly, peering past him down the short passageway and into the sleeping quarters of the sailors. Soft snores from those off duty drifted down the hall, but no one moved about in the open room.

He followed her gaze then grinned wickedly, seeing they were as alone as they could be on the crowded ship. He plastered her to the wall with his body and planted his lips on hers. The beard he was growing scratched at her skin and she wished he would shave, but he said being on the ocean made him want to grow one, and he liked the break from having to shave constantly.

"Why are you so warm? Feels good," he murmured against her lips.

"I cleaned my clothes last night and had to dry my pants with magic," she nipped at his bottom lip and slid her hands around his waist. It was nice to touch him without the fear of others watching, if only for a moment.

He groaned and leaned into her. His hand moved from her shoulder to cup her breast. It was her turn to groan. "Tomas, stop," she implored, sure one of the sailors in the common area would wake at any moment.

"No," he objected as he explored her lips, and she felt him grin. He had used his thumb to caress her nipple, and had felt it betray her runaway feelings as it harden noticeably from his touch. "Feel good?" he asked, and pressed his hips into her. She had no doubt as to what was on his mind.

"Yes, but . . . ," she closed her eyes as he squeezed her. What she had wanted to say, she couldn't remember.

His lips found her earlobe and then he trailed down the line of her neck. She wanted him, she needed him, but they were not in the right place.

"Tomas, we really have to stop." She placed her hands on his shoulders. He wasn't listening to her. He moved lower to briefly kiss the bare skin of her chest between the opening in the top of her shirt then dropped his head to firmly clamp his mouth onto the breast he held.

"Oh," she gasped as a fiery jolt of pleasure shot through her body.

"Elhrin," he groaned, returning to her lips and dropping his hands to cup her buttocks. He pressed her to him as he plundered her lips with an intensity that was quickly running out of control.

It was one of the hardest things she had ever had to do, but they had to stop. She pushed hard on his chest, making him stumble back into the wall behind him.

"We can't do this, you maniac," she breathed, leaning back against the wall for support.

"You are no fun," he said, then grinned wickedly. "Can I interest you in a quick stroll through the hold of the ship?"

"As lovely as that sounds," she grinned, "I am going to have to pass. The fine aroma of chicken dung and the prospect of rats running over me first thing in the morning is something I would rather leave for another time."

"How about this evening?" he asked with an obvious leer.

"You are hopeless," she laughed.

He crossed back to her and pulled her into his arms. "I can't help it. You are too beautiful." He kissed the top of her head.

A flicker of a foreign energy source touched on her awareness briefly then disappeared. She stiffened in his arms.

"What's wrong?" he asked.

"I'm not sure," she said, sending out her senses. "I thought I felt an energy source, and it wasn't Marissa." She pulled away from him. "Let's go up."

When they stepped out onto the deck, the fog was so thick she could barely see the prow of the ship from the rear of the ship. She and Tomas joined the captain and the helmsman on the deck of the sterncastle. It was eerily quiet aside from the creaking of the ship's rigging and the soft voices of the sailors echoing out over the water.

"I didn't think the southern waters had too much of a problem with fog, Captain," Tomas said.

"Occasionally, a fog will arise close to shore," Captain Ostied replied. "We are moving out a bit to see if we can get out of it and we'll run that way until the fog clears out. Ones like this are usually gone by midday."

The foreign energy source touched her again. She frowned. It had come from behind them. She moved to the stern's rail.

"Did you feel it again?" Tomas asked, placing his hands on the rail beside her.

"Yes," she said, "it is strange. It is such a brief feeling, I wonder if I am imagining it."

"How far from Marmuht do you estimate we are, Captain?" Kyne asked as he mounted the stair from the lower deck.

"We are nearing Traphyt. I'd say if we were to run straight through, it would take us a little over a week to get there."

"Can I ask your honest opinion?" Kyne leaned against the rail in front of the helm to talk to the captain.

"You may," the captain replied.

"Would you take an abducted boy directly into the port of Marmuht or would you go somewhere less likely to have authorities waiting on your arrival?"

Elhrin turned to stare at Kyne. He was looking straight at her with his black eyes.

"What is your reasoning, Kyne?" she asked before the captain gave an answer.

"I'm thinking that if it takes a ship somewhere around four weeks to travel from Muryne to Marmuht, yet it takes a little less over land, wouldn't that give someone time to get to the city before the ship . . . like, I don't know . . . say, a messenger or worse yet, the boy's father?"

"You are correct, young man," the captain said. "I think we do have to consider the possibility of an alternate landing site, and with the naval forces being increased in the area, I'm not sure what the captain of the *Shifting Winds* will be able to do to avoid them."

"You don't think they will go ahead and take him to Chyrzah, do you?" Tomas asked. "The dockmaster said that was the ship's proposed final destination."

"I would if I wanted to avoid getting tangled up with Anderan's Navy," Kyne commented.

Elhrin put her hands on her hips and frowned at the deck in frustration. *He is right. What do we do now—Marmuht or Chyrzah?*

"But," Kyne emphasized the word so that she would look at him. "I don't think that is what they want to do."

"Why?" she asked.

"There is a purpose to Marcus being abducted as opposed to being killed," he pointed out.

"I told Elhrin basically the same thing," Tomas said. "If they had wanted him dead, I think they would have done it in the palace where Minister Idwyr could have witnessed it."

A slight flicker of annoyance crossed Kyne's face. "Yes, thank you for that bit of obvious information, lover boy."

Tomas stiffened at Kyne's sarcasm and Elhrin placed a calming hand on his arm. It wouldn't do for them to start fighting.

"Let me throw out an idea and see what you think," Kyne smirked at Tomas. "Whoever is behind all of this sent Minister Idwyr a letter warning him to stay away from Muryne. The result of him not heeding the warning is the loss of his son. Elhrin and I have already established Marcus' abduction was designed, in all probability, to get him back out of the city. Possibly so he would not be there to be able to defend Muryne against the attack it suffered, or is still suffering." He shrugged his shoulders. "We don't know for sure, but here is another question. Why does this person want the Minister to remain alive? If I were plotting the demise of Anderan, I think the first to go would be the biggest obstacles that would prevent me from achieving that goal."

"Which means the Minister and Elhrin would be a good starting place," Tomas said.

"Exactly," Kyne replied. "But he or they did not want that in his case, at least, not at that point in time. We don't know what they had planned for Elhrin. So what I'm thinking is that Marcus was to lead the Minister somewhere, and what good would leading him to Chyrzah do?"

"It would get him out of the way for a major invasion on the country," Tomas pointed out.

"Yes, it would," Kyne smiled mischievously. "But why lead him out of the country just to get him out of the way when killing him would seem to be the easier route. I go back to the question—why does this person want Minister Idwyr alive?"

"The letter said Master Gryph would be the last thing he would take care of," Elhrin said as she glanced past him out into the fog bank. It felt like her mind was just as clouded and she couldn't break through to the answer she sought. "He wanted to see Master Gryph suffer. This is personal. Damn, Kyne, I was right, this is personal. The M'gelidia, in general, just want him dead. They don't care about his suffering, and we ruled out Grom. Who else would want to do this to him besides Obsudius himself?"

"I can think of someone," Captain Ostied growled.

"You can?" Elhrin asked. "Who?"

"His brother," he said.

"His what?" Elhrin barely kept herself from shouting. She didn't think she heard him right. "Did you just say his brother?"

"I did," the captain said. "Did he not tell you he had a brother?"

Elhrin thought this had to be some kind of joke. "No, he didn't."

"Well, I'm not surprised. After the boy ran away from home, he never spoke of his brother even to me, and believe me, I brought the subject up on several occasions. Tight-lipped, that man, when he wants to be." Captain Ostied raised his hat and scratched at his head.

"That is an understatement," Elhrin huffed in disbelief. Why wouldn't he tell her something like this? Her mind flashed to his angry face when they were in the palace, telling her to quit placing him on a pedestal and that he was far from perfect, that things slipped his mind. This wasn't something that just slipped his mind. This was something he purposely did not want her to know.

"Captain, can you tell me about his brother?" she asked as a sleepy Marissa and Clay trudged up the stairs to join them on deck.

"Well, I can tell you a bit about the boy. I have no idea what the man is like," the captain said. "Derrick is his name, and he was a rowdy youth. Always finding trouble to get into or trouble seemed to always find him. Gryph spent the better years of his youth defending his younger brother either from bullies, the local authorities, or from their own father."

"Why their father?" Elhrin asked. "Master Gryph said his father was a good man."

"Oh, he was for the most part," the captain squinted out at the fog enshrouded water, "but Derrick tried his patience, they couldn't get along, and he had a strong dislike for the boy. I was told he beat him nearly every day after Gryph left, but I don't know how true that is."

"How can a father dislike his own son?" Marissa asked.

"It happens more often than you think," Kyne said with contempt. Elhrin knew that Kyne was speaking from experience. He didn't have the best relationship with his own parents.

"So if Minister Idwyr spent his time defending his brother, that sounds like he should look up to him instead of hating him." Tomas said. "It's their father he should hate."

"You are right, but then there was this girl," the captain said.

"There is always a girl," Kyne snorted. "Females are nothing but trouble. Every time we men . . . ."

"Kyne, shut up," Elhrin growled. "I want to hear this."

He saluted her mockingly. She narrowed her eyes at him. Since she had told him about her betrothal to Tomas, he had been more obnoxious than usual to them both. She didn't know what was wrong with him, but she had enough of his smartass antics. She used her magic and smacked him hard in the back of his head.

"Ow, damn it, Elhrin," he yelled, clapping a hand to the back of his head. "What did you do that for?"

Tomas started to laugh.

"Don't mess with me anymore, Captain Pittwold," she fumed, realizing that she was truly angry, not just with Kyne, but with the frustration of the whole situation. Being behind Marcus' ship by a day, the fog, and now information she should have known years ago. She turned her angry gaze on Tomas. "Enough, Tomas."

He raised his eyebrows at her tone, and quit laughing.

"Captain Ostied, please continue," she said.

The captain looked puzzled by what had just taken place, but he overlooked it without question. "Like I said, there was a girl, and it really should not have been a problem, but Derrick made it one." He clasped his hands behind his back and started to relate the tale. "Gryph and I grew up with a young girl named Lynh Masstersun, and yes, she is Captain Masstersun's mother," he added before anyone would interrupt him one more time with questions. "We were all friends, the three of us and a few other boys in Pago Duhn, including Derrick, until we reached our teenage years. That was when things began to change. For the first time, we looked on Lynh as a girl. Before, she just seemed to be one of the boys. Lynh was a pretty little lass, and I suppose we all might have had fond thoughts toward her at one point, but Derrick was extremely infatuated with her. He paid special attention to her, did things for her, but she only had eyes for Gryph, and looking back on it now, I guess it had always been that way for her. Now, Gryph's feelings were a bit different. He loved her in his own fashion, but not as much as she did him. Even so, they eventually became a couple until he decided it was time to leave Pago Duhn. Derrick didn't take their relationship well and Lynh's obvious lack of affection for him, so he became more hostile as time went by. I told Gryph the boy was jealous, but he denied it, thinking Derrick's troubled nature came more from the new boys around the docks he had started spending time with instead of our old group. I think there was a culmination of things that combined to make Derrick fall over the edge into hating Gryph, but one event stands out in my mind that showed me beyond doubt the boy hated his brother."

"What was that?" Marissa asked.

"Gryph is going to kill me for this," the captain said. "Derrick saw Gryph and Lynh together—intimately."

Kyne whistled. "The boy didn't want his woman tarnished."

"No, he didn't," the captain agreed.

"How did you know he saw them?" Elhrin asked.

"Because I saw Derrick run out of the woods they were in. You see, when we were kids we built a small fort in those woods and when we grew older, we would go back from time to time to visit the place or camp overnight. Gryph and I had planned to meet there that evening to spend one last night for old time's sake before he left for Muryne. He hadn't told Lynh he was leaving, and I found out later he had taken her with him to break the news to her. When I arrived at our camp, it was a bit obvious as to what they had been up to, and Lynh was crying because Gryph was leaving her . . . it was a difficult situation . . . she ended up running back home." He trailed into silence. "Later, when Gryph and I were sleeping, a portion of our fort collapsed and would have fallen on top of Gryph had he not happened to sit up because he thought he heard a sound. He was able to roll out of the way. The rocks of our fort were heavy and if they had hit him, it wouldn't have been good. I'm certain Derrick had something to do with it. Those rocks were solidly in place in that fort and there was no way they would fall on their own."

"Did you tell Master Idwyr about Derrick?" Elhrin asked.

"I did, but once again he denied it, saying that Derrick had been nowhere near the fort at any time that day or he would have known it," the captain said.

"He would have known it?" Elhrin's eyes widened with realization. "Does Derrick have a magical gift?"

"Yes, he does. Didn't I mention that?" the captain said.

"Oh, no!" Elhrin paced off to the rear of the boat. "Oh, no!"

"What is wrong?" Tomas asked.

She whirled around. "Tomas, his brother has to be the N'gethwyn we had suspected was behind the deaths in Muryne." She shook her head, thinking. Something was out of place with his story. "Captain, Master Gryph said he did not know Derrick was in the woods, but you definitely saw him run out?"

"I did," the captain replied.

"It doesn't make sense," she said.

"I'm afraid I don't follow, Miss Caddoch."

"Captain, persons with the magical gift can detect when others with powers are nearby. If Derrick has the gift, then Master Gryph would have known Derrick was in those woods." She raked a hand through her fog dampened hair. "I don't know how he managed to avoid being detected."

"Is it possible to mask an energy source from others like one would shield a candle flame from view?" Marissa asked.

Elhrin stared at Marissa wide-eyed, astounded by a simple question that had never occurred to her. "I don't know," she stammered. "I do know it is possible to hide one's self from view if you are born with that skill—Master Gryph can do it—but he never spoke of being able to mask an energy source. Whenever he demonstrated his ability to hide himself, his source was still very much detectable even though I couldn't see him physically."

"Then masking an energy source would be a useful tool if your enemy was another person with power and didn't want to be detected by you, wouldn't it?" Kyne asked.

Elhrin's heart plummeted. "Yes, it would, and it would also explain how an N'gethwyn could roam about a city without me or Master Gryph knowing about it."

And no sooner had she uttered those words when a powerful black and violent foreign energy source slammed into her awareness. This time, it was right behind them.

"Dear God," she said as she whirled to face the rear of the boat, seeing nothing but a wall of white mist, "he's here."

Chapter Fourteen

Marguerite shook herself out of her thoughts and studied her husband's back. Usually he sat tall in the saddle, but at the moment he leaned a little to the left. He was hurting and she knew he wouldn't admit it if she asked. Shifting his weight to his right, he slung his long black cloak out of his way over the rear of his equally black horse and propped his right hand comfortably on the hilt of his sword, trying to find a way to relieve the pressure on his left knee.

She sighed. She didn't see how he was going to make it all the way to Marmuht on the back of his horse, Tyton, a fiery steed only he could handle, but he insisted on riding. He said he needed to be mobile. Riding in the supply wagon was out of the question and the suggestion of their enclosed carriage just earned her a silent frown. He didn't have to say what was on his mind. She knew him. He had endured being in it on the way home to Glimmerdale, but he wasn't about to be stuck inside an enclosed space all the way to Marmuht. He needed to be able to see his surroundings without obstructions.

She looked beyond him to see if she recognized any landmarks that would tell her where they were exactly, but all she saw was the flat countryside of the midlands and six of the twelve armed men who had been ordered to escort them on their journey to Marmuht by King Goruth. The other six brought up the rear.

Gryph tried to turn around to look behind him, but couldn't manage to get around far enough to see her.

"Marguerite, are you behind me, love?" he asked.

"Yes," she said. "I have been for the last hour. I thought you knew I was here."

He shook his head, hauling back on his reins to stop and wait on her. "No, I guess I've been lost in my own thoughts. Why didn't you join me?"

She shrugged. "I suppose I've been thinking, too, and not really paying attention to the road." She noticed he was sweating profusely, yet the weather was cool, and with the sun sliding down in the sky, it was getting cooler. "Gryph, please let me give you something for pain."

She had been begging him since leaving Muryne, but he refused her every time. He did not want to relinquish any control over his senses. He would not take any medicines, and he would not drink any type of alcohol. He said he couldn't afford it, but he paid a high price, anyway. The effort it took him to manage the pain cost him in bodily fatigue and energy.

"I'm fine," he said, smiling to ease her worry, but she wasn't fooled. "Did you straighten the girls out?"

"Yes," she grimaced.

Not long after midday, Ashlyn and Leesha had begun an argument that escalated into near blows. He or Grey would have taken care of it, especially if the girls had started using magic on each other, but she said she would handle it, and being the men that they were, they let her. Girl fights were not something they wanted to be actively involved in. "It was over nothing, really. Something about taking up too much space in the tent last night and using things that weren't theirs without asking—I think they are exhausted with the pace we are taking and being unused to sleeping on the hard ground." She thought for a moment about the three girls that were allowed to accompany them. Ashlyn and Eowhyn were highly skilled with their magical talents, but Leesha, while talented, was young and spoiled. "Gryph, are you sure bringing Leesha was a good idea? I'm not sure she is ready for this." She grunted at the thought. "They are all so young. I don't think any of them are ready for this."

"No one is ever ready for war, my love," he said. "But when it happens, those of us destined to fight have to face it, ready or not. I gave them a choice."

"I know you did." She checked her horse when it stumbled over something in the road. "I admire you for giving them that choice even though they have already committed to the program."

"It is one thing to think about fighting for one's country. It is another to actually do it, and all of them followed through. I fully did not expect Leesha or Tover to come." He wiped sweat from his forehead. "I had reservations with those two being in the program in the first place."

"You never mentioned that to me," she said.

"I didn't? I thought I did," he frowned.

"No, you mentioned that Emyngre wanted in, but you didn't think he would be a good candidate," she said.

"I was right on that call, wasn't I?"

"Yes, you were," she agreed, remembering the man who wanted to join the program and had been a good student, but then he had been caught stealing from Triva's shop in Glimmerdale. After Gryph looked into the matter further, it turned out Emyngre had been stealing from others the entire time he had been in Glimmerdale and Gryph had dismissed him from the school.

"What made you have doubts about those two?" she asked, even though she thought she already knew the answer. He did not put up with those who were petulant and self-serving which basically described both Tover and Leesha.

"I need people who are dependable without question. Those two are questionable." He reached down to adjust a beautifully carved staff under his right leg. He had complained only once about his crutch being uncomfortable but it was in front of Landin, one of their instructors of the magical arts. The man had immediately gone to his room to retrieve a staff he had carved himself, and presented it to Gryph. That was all that was needed for Gryph to give up the crutch and toss it on a burn pile behind their stables.

"Then why allow them to come?" she asked, sidling her horse closer to his to help him. The carved eagle's head on the top of the staff was caught on the breast strap of the saddle, and he couldn't get it to move.

Not liking his space being invaded by her horse, Tyton turned his head with the intent to bite.

Gryph pulled the steed's head away from her mount. "Not today, old man," he ordered. Displeased, Tyton snorted noisily and tossed his head up and down.

"I had to let them come. I didn't have a choice," he said as she reached over and unhooked the staff from the breast strap and adjusted it so it was not sticking into his leg. "Thank you, love," he said. "If the reports are accurate, we will be outnumbered as it is."

She didn't like the look on his face. He was struggling with the fact he had to bring them at all. He cared for his students, and the last thing he wanted to do was lead them to their deaths.

"Gryph, have I told you I love you today?" she asked with a tiny smile, and was rewarded when he returned her smile with his own.

"I think you may have mentioned it this morning," he chuckled as he reached for her hand and brought it to his lips. "I love you, too."

"The sun is getting low," she noted. "When are you planning to stop?"

"Are you tired?" he asked, resting their clasped hands on top of his leg. He was still concerned with her health, even though she was fine. Her stamina was not back to normal, but unlike him, she had been able to get plenty of rest while they were in Glimmerdale for the few days it took them to prepare for their journey to Marmuht. Her house manager Liselle made sure she did.

"No, I'm fine. I honestly wish we could just travel straight through," she said.

"That would be nice," he murmured distractedly and grinned.

"What's the smile for?" she asked.

"We are being followed," he chuckled.

She twisted in her saddle for a look. The road behind their caravan dipped out of sight over a hill and on the left side was a small patch of trees, but they were sparse and she saw no one within its shadows.

"Who is it?" she asked. "I don't see anyone."

"It is three boys who were told to stay home and didn't listen," he said.

"Oh no, don't tell me it's Jayce, Jayme, and Zeike," she groaned.

The three boys stuck together like a band of brigands, and were always into something. Zeike was the eldest of their little group at fourteen years of age, but Jayce was their leader and had a bad habit of dragging his younger brother Jayme into trouble right behind him.

"Gryph, you have to send them home before we get too far away. There might be Do'athrim out here."

"I know, which is exactly why I won't be sending them home," he said, squinting into the late afternoon sun.

"Well, where are they? Go get them."

"Not yet, I think," he said. "I have been monitoring them, and I want to see how they handle themselves on their own."

"Just how long have you known that they have been following us?" she asked.

"Since yesterday evening." He grinned at her sideways like a little boy who had been able to get away with some kind of mischief.

She squeezed his hand as hard as she could. "Gryphon Idwyr, how could you leave those boys out in the country alone with all the danger surrounding us?"

"Easy now, woman, don't break my hand. I'll need it," he chuckled. "They are not as far away as you think. They are tracking me with their senses. When they brush upon their awareness of me they back off until they no longer feel me. What they don't realize is that they are well within my range of awareness for them and have been since yesterday evening."

"Do the others feel the boys?" she asked.

"Grey does," he said, "and the others may have felt them when they come closer, but they have not mentioned it, which is something I will have to talk to them all about when I finally bring the boys in."

Marguerite shook her head, wishing she understood their magical inner workings a little better. "Why hasn't Grey said anything about them following us?"

"I asked him to keep it to himself."

She jerked her hand from his and slapped him on the arm. He instinctively jerked away and grimaced in pain from the sudden movement.

"I'm sorry," she apologized, feeling remorse for making him move unexpectedly. "I didn't mean for you to hurt your leg."

"Who said my leg was hurting?" he grinned through the obvious pain he was experiencing. "You have muscles in those arms of yours, woman."

"Excuse me," Bayle said as he trotted up beside Gryph. "Do I need to break up a fight here?"

"Yes, do something about this old lady. She's mean," Gryph said, massaging his injured leg.

Marguerite rolled her eyes. "Seriously, Gryph, if you don't get those boys. I will. I don't like them being alone."

"Very well," he surrendered. He turned his mount and halted so that he could see the road behind them. "Bayle, do me a favor and go get Jayce, Jayme, and Zeike. They are just over the hill, probably in that copse of trees we passed down in the meadow below."

Marguerite was surprised. He wasn't joking when he said they were close.

"What are they doing there?" Bayle asked, studying the countryside behind them.

"Not minding me," Gryph said.

"Ah, I see," Bayle said, grinning at Gryph. He knew first-hand what happened when someone disobeyed Gryph—being quite headstrong and rambunctious in his childhood—he'd had plenty of experience on the receiving end of the man's just punishment. "This should be good." He spurred his horse and galloped off down the road.

Gryph turned his horse back around and Marguerite fell in beside him again.

"What are you going to do?" she asked. "Don't you think taking them to Marmuht will be dangerous?"

"Right now, being with me is probably safer for them," he exhaled a long heavy breath. "I don't want to put them in harm's way, my love, but they are in the Eagle program."

"For heaven's sake," Marguerite smacked her own leg. This man of hers was so frustrating. "Do you mean you have been training them for combat? Since when did you start putting thirteen and fourteen-year-olds in a fighting program?" She huffed in exasperation, "Jayme is only twelve and hasn't had his powers for long."

"Marguerite, I have to do what is necessary to ensure the safety of this country. We cannot afford to wait on the boys to grow into manhood to train them for battle. Obsudius threatened to eradicate the entire population dedicated to Solisius when I faced him in his realm. He told me Solisius does not see everything he does. He did not reveal what he meant by that, but I have a feeling that what we are about to face is a part of what he was referring to." He cut his eyes at her. There was no humor in them now. "Marguerite, I have known for quite some time that there would be a day when one or two So'ladiun would not be enough to fight him."

A long forgotten memory entered her mind. Being married to him for so long and knowing what to look for, she knew immediately what he was talking about.

"The dream in the tent," she said. "Outside of Blackridge Keep, the night after Elhrin destroyed the rift. You said it was nothing at the time. I assumed you had relived your fight and didn't pursue it. You saw something then, didn't you?"

"Yes."

"That explains the immediate talks with Goruth about starting the academy on the way home."

He nodded. "I told him there would come a time when a magical force would invade our nation. Up until recently I did not know when or if it would happen in my lifetime, and he and I wanted to make sure future generations would be prepared. I am afraid we are too late."

"How many others are in the program that I don't know about?" she asked.

"I have only one in mind at the moment, but he is not yet old enough. We have found no others that have the skills. Our other students hold only rudimentary powers."

"Who is the one?" she asked.

He glanced away. He did not want to answer her. She studied his profile, watching his face as he warred with the thoughts inside his head. She knew the answer, probably had known all along, but just refused to let the knowledge surface. It had to be inevitable.

"Marcus," she breathed.

He nodded.

"How long have you known?" she asked, knowing that magical energy developed late and did not show up until a child was around seven or eight and sometimes could even wait as late as the teen years. Marcus was only three.

"Since the day he was born," he shrugged.

"Why didn't you tell me?" she asked knowing why but certain he wouldn't say. He had a bad habit of keeping things to himself if he felt it would worry her. Raising a son destined to be a fighting magician like his father would do it, and he was right. The pit of her stomach churned when she thought about her baby in the hands of killers. *Marcus, my sweet baby, please be safe.*

"I was waiting for his energy source to develop before I said anything."

"Then I am assuming you know this from another dream."

"No," he said as laughter erupted from the rear of their caravan. "This came directly from Solisius."

"Will he be So'ladiun?"

"That has yet to be revealed to me," he replied.

With a heavy heart at the prospect of her son living the dangerous life of a So'ladiun, Marguerite looked over her shoulder to see what all the laughter was about. The unexpected sight made her laugh out loud. "Gryph, look at this."

They both turned their horses and halted. Bayle was escorting three very filthy young boys riding atop Doogan Phisk's homely, old bag-of-bones mountain pony. Marguerite was amazed the poor animal could hold all three youths on her back.

She glanced at Gryph. He was scowling fiercely, but she could see the façade did not reach his eyes. The boys had to be taught a lesson for disobedience and he could not laugh, no matter how hard he wanted to. She followed his lead and smoothed her grin away. The rest of their party halted around the nearby supply wagon, and Marguerite had to glance away from Landin, who had volunteered to drive the wagon and was perched atop the driver's bench. His ebony face held a huge, toothy grin, which was always infectious.

"Sir, I have your charges," Bayle said as he and the boys trotted up past the others. The comical bouncing of the three boys on the nag's back nearly broke her resolve not to laugh. That and the sick, I-think-I-might-wet-my-pants-for-getting-caught looks all three boys had on their faces.

"Thank you, Corporal," Gryph said, formally. He then looked the boys over in silence, not bothering to reprimand them or ask questions right away. A technique he used often, not only to school his own thoughts, but to see if the other party would speak first. He told her that people were uncomfortable with silence and it prompted them to speak, sometimes without thinking.

It worked.

"Sir, it was Jayce's idea," Zeike blurted out.

He was in front, and had to endure the full brunt of Gryph's stony stare. The other two were keeping their heads low behind the boy in front of them. Jayce punched Zeike in the back for telling on him.

"Ow!" Zeike yelled, a little too dramatically. The way Jayce was crammed between the two boys he couldn't have had much force in the blow. "He punched me."

Zeike retaliated by nailing Jayce in the chest with an elbow. Jayce yelped in pain and reared back to punch Zeike again. This time he was aiming for Zeike's head.

Without a word, Gryph raised his hand and jerked Zeike off the horse with his powers. Zeike yelled in surprise as Gryph dropped him on his rear in the dirt of the road.

"Oof," Zeike grunted when he hit the ground. He glared up at Gryph. "He punched me!"

"I know what he did," Gryph said quietly.

"Then why did you throw me off? He hit me first." He smacked the dirt with his hands.

"You were fighting. I simply took out the offender closest to me," Gryph said with a frown. "Does that sound familiar to you?"

"Yes, sir," Zeike squinted up at Gryph, he raised a hand to shield his eyes from the glare of the late afternoon sun. "But he punched first, and it was still his idea to come out here."

"Zeike, being the senior Eagle in your makeshift group, places all responsibility directly on your shoulders. It doesn't matter whose idea it was. What matters is the fact I told you boys to stay in Glimmerdale, yet you left despite my explicit orders. I highly doubt Jayce forced you to come on this adventure. Jayme might be another story." He glanced at the boys on the horse. "Jayme," Gryph called to the youngest boy.

A pair of shy eyes peered over his brother's shoulder, but Jayme remained silent. Marguerite felt sorry for the boy. He was a timid boy and, for some reason, was terrified of Gryph. He lowered his head again behind Jayce's back. All she could see was the wispy, unkempt locks of brown hair on the top of his head.

"Were you forced to leave Glimmerdale?" Gryph asked.

Jayme didn't answer.

"Don't make me repeat myself, Jayme," Gryph said, sternly.

Jayme's head shook from side to side.

"Are you sure?" Gryph asked.

The shock of hair bobbed in affirmation.

"Jayce," Gryph addressed the elder brother on the horse. Jayce flinched as if Gryph had slapped him. "I spoke with you directly about the reasons why you were to stay behind. Have you forgotten them?"

"No, sir," he whispered, staring hard at the mane on his horse's neck.

"I'm afraid I didn't hear your answer," Gryph said.

"No, sir," Jayce said a little louder.

"What were my reasons?" Gryph asked.

"We were too young," Jayce whispered, "and . . . ."

"I can't hear you," Gryph interrupted.

Jayce raised his voice. "We are too young, it is dangerous, and we need more training, and our parents would not want us to go. They would be worried about us."

"Has any of that changed since we last spoke?" Gryph asked.

"Yes, sir," Jayce's eyes flashed defiantly at Gryph, "I can do this." He raised both arms in front of him. In an instant, both boys on the horse disappeared. Marguerite was stunned as was everyone else in their party. Gryph was the only one she knew who had the ability to make himself physically disappear from view.

Gryph tilted his head back and looked down his nose at the empty space left on the old nag's back. He nodded to himself slightly as if answering a question only he heard. "Grey, did you know he had this ability?"

"No, sir," Grey answered, clearly impressed by Jayce's accomplishment.

"Can you see any part of the boys from your point of view?"

Grey sat on the other side of the Jayce's horse away from Gryph. He shook his head. "Nope."

"Jayce, I can see your left boot," Gryph said.

Jayce and Jayme reappeared on the back of the horse. "How?" he asked and leaned over to look at his boot.

"You make sure to cover yourself from above your head to the bottom of your feet, boy, or you will surely die if you ever use this technique to hide from an enemy." Gryph frowned. "This does not excuse your actions. All of my reasons are still valid, especially the one concerning the danger. Your parents will be extremely upset when they learn you are heading for a hostile area, and I do not have anyone to spare that can deliver a message to them or escort you home, so you will travel with me as far as Tuhnichi. From there, I will figure out what to do with you."

Jayce's face brightened at the prospect of being allowed to stay.

"However," Gryph growled, "while you are with us, you will be treated as any soldier would who is on campaign. You will be assigned tasks, and you will do as you are asked without question or complaint, day or night, even if you are beyond exhaustion. You want to be treated like men, trust me, you will be. Also, I am almost certain Doogan did not give you leave to borrow Hettie, did he?"

Jayce and Zeike both flushed a deep red. They immediately studied the ground as if it was the most fascinating thing they had ever seen, leaving no doubt as to who was responsible for removing Hettie from her paddock. Doogan was going to worry himself sick wondering what happened to her. He'd had the mare for over twenty years and treated her like a pet since he retired her from service as a cart-and-short-haul pony.

"Mm hmm, just what I thought. When you three return to Glimmerdale you will not only apologize to Mister Phisk for stealing his pony, but you will work for him during your free time for however long Doogan deems fit to make up for the cost of the use of his property. Do you boys understand me?"

"Yes, sir," they mumbled one after the other.

Gryph directed his gaze at Landin, who was leaned back comfortably in the driver's seat, his large coffee-colored eyes twinkling with amusement. "Landin, I place Zeike in your charge. Make sure he learns the ins and outs of making and breaking a camp well, and feel free to add anything else you find necessary for him to know. Maybe learning how to dig latrines would be in order."

"Yes, sir, how many will be required?" Landin asked, knowing full well they hadn't bothered with digging any before. They stayed on the move, so if anyone needed to relieve themselves they found a private spot away from camp.

"I think one or two for the ladies would be sufficient. It could avert another sticky situation like last night."

Landin flashed a knowing grin Marguerite's way. "Yes, sir."

Marguerite leveled her gaze on her husband, letting him know he had better keep his mouth shut on that topic. It had been black as pitch with cloud cover the night before, and when she had squatted to do her business in a stand of bushes, a holly branch hidden in the grove had stuck her on her exposed bottom. She hadn't meant to cry out as loud as she did and bring Bayle running, but those unexpected sharp pokes in her rear had hurt.

Gryph turned to his lead instructor. "Grey, Jayce is in your care. The boy needs to understand the meaning behind responsibility and being held accountable for one's actions. Do I make myself clear?"

"Yes, sir, clear as the bright blue sky over our heads," the slender middle-aged man said with a frown at the elder brother on the pony. While Grey wasn't a harsh individual, the students considered him to be a harsh instructor. Jayce looked miserable at the prospect of being forced into Grey's care.

"Marguerite, Jayme is in your care," he glanced at her, knowing the boy wouldn't be here if he hadn't been coerced, no matter that Jayme had denied it. Yet, he still had to be punished. "I will leave his punishment up to you."

"I'll think of something," she replied.

Gryph drew in a heavy breath. "Bayle, all three boys need to continue their weapons training. Since I had to leave Ivinne in charge back home, I want you to give them lessons when they are not involved with their superiors and have time on their hands. Do you remember Colonel Toome's regimen for new recruits?"

Bayle grinned wide. "That is something no one could ever forget, sir."

Colonel Toome had been a sword master and hand-to-hand combat trainer in the King's Army before he retired and had developed an intensive training routine that left new recruits begging for their beds at the end of each day. It was still used in every army garrison throughout Anderan.

"I would like for you to teach it to the boys," he said.

"Yes, sir," Bayle responded.

Marguerite smiled to herself. The three boys were going to find their grand adventure would lose its shine in a hurry. She had no doubt they would regret leaving Glimmerdale long before they reached Tuhnichi.

Gryph scanned the group around him. "Let's move out," he ordered.

When Marguerite fell in beside Gryph she noticed the huge grin on his face. "Jayce impressed you, didn't he?" she asked.

"I must say he did," he answered. "That boy will no doubt be a formidable leader one day, and it takes an impressive amount of concentration and talent to hide yourself and another completely from all sides."

A call rang out from one of the soldiers in the rear of the party. "Rider!"

Marguerite turned in her saddle. A single rider had appeared on the horizon and was galloping at top speed their way.

Gryph turned his mount and studied the rider. "Keep moving," he ordered the group. "He'll catch up to us."

"He's in a hurry," Marguerite commented.

"That he is," Gryph said.

When the rider caught up with the escort in the rear of their group, he drew back on his reins instead of passing them by.

"I'm looking for Minister Idwyr," he called out. He was a small, wiry man with a shock of blond hair draping low to the collar of his shirt. A floppy gray hat hung low over his eyes and was held tight to his head with a strap of leather. He was covered in a thick layer of grime from the dusty road and looked as if he hadn't slept in months. His horse, huffing hard from the exertion of a long run, was just as filthy as the rider and lathered in sweat.

Gryph reined Tyton to the side of the road. "You have found him," he said, gesturing for everyone else to continue moving. Marguerite reined in beside him.

The rider trotted up to them. "Minister, I am Gordy Bruister of Port V'Din. I have messages for you." He rummaged through a saddle bag behind him and pulled out a pack of letters which he handed over to Gryph.

Gryph reached into the interior of his coat and pulled out the spectacles the doctor had given him and put them on, then sorted through the letters to see who they were from. He glanced at her over his spectacles. "There is one from Elhrin."

Marguerite's heart slammed hard in her chest. She moved her horse close so she could read the letter with him.

Master Gryph and Marguerite,

It has been two days since our departure from Muryne in pursuit of Marcus and we are presently docked in Port V'Din for repairs as Captain Ostied's ship has been damaged. During our pursuit, we managed to gain sight of the ship I know in my heart is carrying Marcus while on the Wyndermir River. We thought we were lucky because the ship appeared to be in no hurry and we could easily catch them. It was not to be. The ship had waited on purpose to make sure we were the ones after them in order to set us up for ambush. An N'gethwyn and a host of Do'athrim attacked from the riverbanks in a portion of the river where our ship was sure to be close to shore. With the exception of a few unfortunate deaths of Captain Ostied's crew, we managed to prevail over the Do'athrim and the N'gethwyn who now resides permanently somewhere on the bottom of the river. It breaks my heart to have to tell you that the ship carrying Marcus escaped. We were so close. Marguerite, please forgive me for not being strong enough to get us through the fight quickly where we could overtake the ship.

Marguerite bit back a silent cry of anguish. Elhrin didn't need to apologize. She tried.

We are not giving up. As soon as the repairs are complete we will continue to pursue the ship in hopes that fate will favor us and we can overtake the faster vessel before Marmuht or wherever they may be heading. I will bring him home safely.

Master Gryph, I felt the presence of more than one N'gethwyn as we sailed from Muryne. I pray you are safe as well as the city of Muryne, and I hope King Goruth will understand that I could not turn around and come back to fight. Marcus is my brother in spirit if not in fact. I cannot sacrifice his life any more than I could Bayle's.

I love you both with my entire being,
Elhrin

Marguerite wiped tears from her eyes with a trembling hand. She glanced at Gryph, and saw that he was having a difficult time holding his own emotions in check. He was not going to forgive himself for abandoning their son. Without a word, he handed her Elhrin's letter and opened the next letter in his hand.

After quickly perusing its contents, he cleared his throat. "Goruth is on his way," he said gruffly. "There have been two more Do'athrim attacks reported on settlements in the east and one in the west. It seems Derrick and Obsudius have been sneaking Do'athrim into the country for awhile." He folded Goruth's letter with a sigh. "The amount of troops Goruth will be able to raise to fight against the invasion is not going to be much." He glanced at the final paper in his hand with a frown. "Son, if I am not mistaken, you have reached me in under two weeks." He glanced at the messenger. "Is that correct?"

"Yes, sir," the young man said. "The initial agreement was for Muryne. I was not expecting to travel beyond the city."

Gryph grunted. "Impressive, nonetheless, considering you stopped long enough in Muryne to gain the message from King Goruth."

"Yes, sir," the messenger said. "The king's steward informed me you had left the city, and said since I was already on my way to find you, he wanted me to deliver his message, as well."

"Very well, you will have the amount Miss Caddoch agreed upon." He turned his horse and gestured for the man to follow him. "I have found I could use a messenger if you care to earn more."

"Yes, sir," the man said eagerly as Marguerite tucked Elhrin's letter carefully away in her saddlebag.

Solisius, if you can hear me, please let Elhrin find my baby, Marguerite cried silently.

A sudden breeze washed gently by her. She lifted her face and breathed in the cool air, feeling slightly amazed that it seemed to help calm her battered nerves.

Late the next afternoon, Gryph called a halt for the day by a tiny rivulet that meandered off into a flat, grassy meadow before it disappeared into a dense forest on the other side. As the men set up their camp and the rebellious young boys began to learn life on the road wasn't such a glorious adventure, Marguerite and the girls worked together to prepare their supper for the entire party. Finally, when the first stars appeared in the fading light of the setting sun and the camp was set to Gryph's satisfaction, everyone was able to settle in for the evening.

Marguerite ladled a mixed vegetable stew laced with strips of salt-cured ham from her pot over the fire into a wooden bowl then straightened with a groan. She was exhausted, thinking maybe she was pushing herself too hard too soon after her ordeal in Muryne, but knew it couldn't be helped and she was more than willing to endure the toll the grueling ride was inflicting on her body. As a matter of fact, if it was up to her, she would be willing to leave everyone behind and ride day and night without stopping to reach Marmuht . . . she needed to know if her baby was there . . . but neither she nor Gryph could leave the others behind. The young students would be vital to winning a battle with Derrick's army if the invasion rumors ran true and they needed the days traveling to the city to be with Gryph and learn the roles they would play as part of Anderan's army during a full-scale battle . . . a battle that she knew would tear Gryph's soul in two no matter how much he claimed Derrick needed to be held accountable for his horrific actions and that it was his duty to rid the world of any N'gethwyn, even if it was his brother.

"Jayme, take this to Master Idwyr, please." She handed the steaming bowl to the boy. He stared at her as if she had just asked him to jump into a pit of venomous vipers. She wanted him to get over his fear of Gryph, and took every opportunity that presented itself to put him in Gryph's presence. She suppressed a tiny smile. That was part of Jayme's punishment, but he didn't know it. "Don't stand there, young man. Master Idwyr will not like it if his supper is cold."

She watched with amusement as Jayme crossed the short distance at a snail's pace to where Gryph sat leaning against the trunk of a long dead tree, "resting his eyes" as he put it. The boy came to a standstill a good distance away from Gryph. Marguerite thought she was going to have to go and shove him the rest of the way.

Gryph opened one eye and peered at Jayme. "You planning on throwing the bowl to me, boy?"

Jayme shook his head and reluctantly inched his way just close enough to give the bowl to Gryph. Marguerite had to stifle a laugh because the boy almost ended up throwing the bowl at him after all when he hardly gave Gryph time to grip the dish before he ran back to where she stood.

Gryph winked at her with a smile.

"Something smells good," Bayle said, appearing out of the darkness behind her. "Can I have some, Madam Idwyr?"

"Certainly, Corporal Caddoch." She gave him a bowl. "There is bread in the basket by the apple bag if you want it."

"This will do for now." He gave her a quick peck on the cheek and settled onto the ground near Gryph. "I gave Zeike and Jayce a good workout like you wanted. I don't know how easily they will be able to move tomorrow. Marguerite, if Jayce complains about his backside it's because I smacked him good with my sword."

Marguerite raised her eyebrows. "You did what?"

"I didn't hurt him—much," he grinned. "He got a little mouthy and was trying some kind of fancy move he thought would be superior to anything I was teaching. He made the mistake of wanting to turn around, and when he did, I nailed him on the rear with the flat of my blade. Fairly hard, I might add. He got mad and charged me. He wasn't expecting me to step out of his way and boot him in his ass. He did a complete flip in the grass. He won't make the mistake of turning his back on me again."

Gryph thought the story was funny and boomed with laughter. Marguerite hadn't heard him laugh that hard in a long, long time and it sounded so good.

Grey and Landin strode in from checking on the horses and accepted the bowls of stew she offered then joined Gryph and Bayle.

"What is so funny?" Landin asked. He had one of the deepest voices Marguerite had ever heard, and it made for an outstanding bass singing voice. Bayle, an excellent tenor, had paired up with Landin on several occasions the last few days to favor them with songs which helped to pass the time on their journey.

"I told him about bruising Jayce's backside," Bayle chuckled. He tipped his bowl to his lips and drained its contents then got up for her to fill it again. She dipped into the stew pot, thinking she had never been able to fill his stomach.

Landin laughed. "Those boys believe they are already grown and know all they ever need to know. Zeike called me an old fart that drifted in the wind and couldn't find a nose to smell it just because I couldn't find my hammer today."

Gryph covered his eyes. His whole body shook with laughter.

"You let the boy talk to you that way?" Grey laughed.

"No, sir," he drawled. "I wouldn't do that. He didn't know I heard him. He is still wondering why I had him move that last tent to three different spots." He winked at Gryph. "That boy can now put up and take down a tent in no time."

Gryph wiped his eyes and heaved a huge breath.

Marguerite smiled down at Jayme. "Are you hungry?"

"Yes, Madam Idwyr," he whispered.

No matter how hard she tried, she couldn't get him to speak up. She filled him a bowl and he started to sit down by the fire, but she made him go sit with the men. He ended up on the other side of Bayle as far away from Gryph as he could get.

She glanced around the camp to make sure everyone had been taken care of before she ate. The soldiers had designated their own camp area nearby and had set up a watch around the perimeter of the campsite. Gryph's students were settled around a separate fire.

They were so young. With the exception of Zeike, Jayce, Jayme, Phalen, and Leesha, who were teenagers, the rest were in their twenties. Ashlyn, her flawless dark skin reflecting the light of the fire, sat half asleep with her bowl resting on her crossed legs. Barron, with his bright orange waves of hair, was regaling them with some tale of an ancient monster from the sea as Kory and Tover shoveled their dinner into their mouths like Bayle was doing—as if it was the last meal any of them would ever get. Kull, the eldest of the group at the age of twenty-eight, sat watching Eowhyn from across the fire while he ate. She sighed, knowing she would have to keep an eye out on all the older boys. Eowhyn was a rare beauty with her pale features and sleek blond hair that draped close to her waist, making her an obvious focus of desire for the males in the young group and the just as obvious reason for the cloud of jealousy that resided around Leesha.

Marguerite watched Jayce and Zeike slowly wander in for their supper. Biting back a smile, she handed each of them a bowl.

"Rough day?" she asked.

"Yes, Madam," they murmured, not willing to look her in the eye.

"Well, eat then get some rest," she said, taking pity on them. "There is bread in the basket behind you."

"Thank you, Madam," they said, then joined the other students. Jayce decided to stand to eat.

Marguerite scanned the group one more time, looking for Phalen. He wasn't around the fire with the others which really didn't surprise her. He was a loner, and had been for quite some time before he found the academy in Glimmerdale, or more accurately, Gryph found him strolling into Glimmerdale one day, spring before last. Phalen was a young runaway, only sixteen-years-old, and she and Gryph had tried nonstop to find his family. Phalen refused to give them any information, including his surname, and they could not find any clues as to where he was from which was strange since Gryph had a large network of resources from all over Anderan and none of them could find anything to help. Marguerite glanced at her husband. It was ironic that the boy was a runaway at sixteen, and Gryph's own brother had left his home at the same age. It wasn't any wonder that Gryph had been so dedicated in his search for Phalen's family. He had failed at finding his own brother for his mother before she passed.

She ladled stew into a bowl for herself and joined the men, settling down beside Gryph.

"Do you know where Phalen is?" she asked.

"He's in the wagon," he responded.

She glanced at the wagon sitting just beyond the light of the fire and saw a shadow perched in its back. "Why does he go off by himself like that?" she asked then pursed her lips to blow on the hot stew in her bowl to cool it down.

"He's a thinker," he said, sitting his empty bowl on the ground, "and you can get more thinking accomplished when you are away from a crowd."

"Sounds like someone else I know," she commented, knowing he liked to find time alone to think, which usually involved holding a fishing pole next to a river when he was at home. She took a tentative sip of the broth in her stew, finding it still too warm to consume in a hurry. She wondered how the boys shoveled their food in without burning their tongues right out of their mouths. "I wonder what he thinks about."

"I know what I was thinking about when I was his age," he said lifting a corner of his mouth.

She narrowed her eyes at him. "You better stop right there before you get started."

He chuckled then rested his head back against the tree. "You mistake my meaning, dirty old woman. I was referring to magic. I had no teacher at his age, and if I wanted to know how something worked I had to figure it out on my own. Phalen has the advantage of having access to teachers, but he is a logical thinker and likes to work some things out for himself instead of having the answers handed to him. Makes him feel more in control, I suppose."

"Isn't that dangerous?"

"It can be," he said, "but on the other hand, Phalen is different than the others. He is capable of handling himself."

The faint cry of a lone wolf howled in the far distance, barely heard above the chatter of their group and the crackling from the fires.

Gryph cocked his head to one side, listening to see if the wolf would howl again.

"It's just a wolf, isn't it?" she asked quietly, knowing Do'athrim wolven would communicate in the same way as any ordinary wolf. She hoped it was the real animal traipsing through the woods. It would not be willing to attack the group.

"I don't know." He reached for his staff and hauled himself up to stand unsteadily in the grass. "Grey, Landin, come with me. Bayle, stay alert." He limped off towards the meadow on the other side of the wagon. "Phalen, get to the fire with the others," he ordered as he passed the boy and disappeared into the dark of the young night.

The youth jumped from the wagon and strode into the light of the fire as she and Bayle stood to watch.

Phalen swept a hand through the long bangs of his sun-streaked hair, pushing the stray strands out of his eyes. "What is going on?" he asked.

"I'm not sure," she answered, then walked to the wagon so that the fire was behind her and she could see the meadow more clearly. The sun had set completely and the sliver of the rising moon was just on the horizon behind her, barely giving enough light to reveal the meadow before it reached the black wall of the forest.

"Everyone, stand ready," Bayle called to the students. "You may be needed."

The group around the fire scrambled to their feet and joined Marguerite by the wagon.

Gryph, Landin, Grey, and half of their soldier escort strode a short way into the meadow but froze when a canine yip sounded from the trees in front of them. The cry was taken up by numerous canine voices. Howls and barks echoed over the meadow.

Marguerite went numb. "Oh no," she breathed. "Bayle, those are Do'athrim!"

The forest erupted. A host of black shadows separated from the trees and ran at the small group at top speed.

A wall of magical white light zipped across the meadow between Gryph and the rushing enemy. It exploded towards the forest with a deafening boom. The front line of the enemy host fell. The rest of the pack stopped in their tracks, momentarily stunned, but it didn't take them long to shake off their hesitation and resume their attack. Landin and Grey sent a series of fiery orbs of energy exploding within their ranks, killing several.

"Let's go," Barron yelled, running for the meadow. The students rushed after him as did most of the soldiers who had not followed Gryph and the others.

"Bayle, stop Jayce and Zeike!" Marguerite yelled.

Bayle caught up with Zeike and knocked him to the ground. "Get your ass back there and protect Madam Idwyr," he yelled without slowing down, chasing after Jayce.

The boy sat on the ground a moment then reluctantly ran back to stand with the two soldiers who had remained behind.

Marguerite felt a small hand grip hers. Jayme was trembling. She squeezed it reassuringly. "Climb up into the wagon and stay put. Everything will be fine." She pulled her blade from the scabbard on her side and joined the soldiers and Zeike on the other side of the wagon.

Another group of Do'athrim emerged from the trees and fired arrows at the small party exposed in the meadow, then rushed out into the field. A wall of bright blue rose high and wide in front of Gryph, expanding rapidly across the grass. Arrows popped into its blue mass, emitting brief flashes of light when they hit. Gryph pushed his wall towards the enemy host. The creatures halted once again in their tracks, unsure of the blue sizzling mass coming at them at a rapid pace. They made the mistake of not retreating in time. Gryph slammed the wall into the creatures. White, spidery strands of deadly light bloomed all across the surface of the wall and a strange loud crackling hum echoed over the land. The creatures caught up in the attack screamed and fell writhing on the ground as if they were on fire, but there were no flames. Gryph's magical wall detonated in a curtain of sparks.

Running across the field, the soldiers with bows loosed their arrows and Gryph's students launched their own attack. Numerous multicolored orbs of magical energy zoomed over the meadow in different directions. Thunderous explosion after explosion rocked the countryside. The Do'athrim had not anticipated such an intense fight from the small group and panicked. They scattered away from each other, no longer trying to attempt a concerted attack.

Landin and Grey spread out away from Gryph and gestured for the students to follow their lead. They did not hesitate. They understood the implications of allowing these creatures to roam free. It was not acceptable. This is what they had been trained to do. This is why they were in Gryph's Eagle program. Even Leesha, the least expected of them all to remain brave in the face of adversity, ferociously attacked a small pack of retreating Do'athrim wolven. The beasts had almost made it to the trees when she sent an amazing fiery ball of red and yellow resembling a miniature sun into their backs. Those who bore the brunt of her attack died, while those caught on the edges of the explosion were wounded and tried to limp or claw their way into the relative safety of the forest. One by one, she finished them off with cold deliberation.

Marguerite scanned the meadow, feeling that something was not right—the battle was changing—was becoming out of control. The students ran after the Do'athrim like cats after mice—so focused on their prey they were oblivious of anything else. They chased the Do'athrim in different directions to the woods. Fiery balls of energy screamed across the meadow haphazardly. No one was making sure their companions were out of harm's way before they launched their attacks. Barron dove and rolled across the grass to avoid injury from an explosion that killed a nearby Do'athrim he did not see. That particular attack had come from Kory. Kull fired tiny missiles of white among the trunks of the trees at Do'athrim brave enough to try and retaliate with bow and arrow just as Eowhyn ran along the edge of the forest after a Do'athrim. She barely managed to keep from being hit by the attacks. Series after series of near misses ensued throughout the battle and Gryph . . . Gryph had stopped his own attacks and had called off the soldiers, as well. He now stood leaning on his staff watching his students take over the fight as if he were a spectator at a tournament match in Muryne's Coliseum.

Fear for the students' safety burrowed deep into her bowels. It felt unreal that she no longer was concerned with the Do'athrim harming them, but that they would harm each other.

Bayle splashed through the little rivulet, hauling Jayce by the shirt. "Nothing like a practice run before the main event, huh?" he asked as explosions lit up the meadow behind him.

"Practice? This is no game, Bayle. Those creatures are very real, and the students are not coordinating their attacks, nor are they watching out for each other."

"Marguerite, I never said that this was a game. This is war. None of them have ever faced a true enemy where the possibility of being injured or killed existed, not even Landin or Grey, and all of us will be facing something far worse than this soon. As awful as it is, the fact remains they needed battle experience and the Do'athrim were stupid enough to provide it." He thrust Jayce ahead of him. The boy turned on him ready to fight. "You want to use your magic on me, boy?" Bayle growled.

The boy glared at him, then shook his head.

"Good, you wouldn't like what I would do to you if you did," Bayle warned. He glanced at the boys. "From now on, you three boys are designated as Madam Idwyr's personal guard."

"You can't order us around," Jayce spat.

"Yes, I can," Bayle said, and took a menacing step towards the boy. Jayce stumbled backwards. "You want to take it up with Master Idwyr?"

The boy scrambled away and ran to join Jayme in the wagon.

"They are gone," Marguerite said. "The Do'athrim are gone, yet the students are still fighting. Why doesn't he stop it?"

Landin and Grey now stood with Gryph and the soldiers, animatedly gesturing at the mayhem near the meadow's edge. They looked like men betting on who would be the top contender when the battle was through. It infuriated her. Why didn't he stop them? Three explosions rocked an area just inside the edge of the trees, and a natural fire blossomed among the forest floor. A missile of green shot across the meadow and bounced into the trees. A brief flash of light burst silently from deep within the woods as a blaze of red power seared off to the right and lit up the underbrush within the trees. A deep, agonizing howl of anguish echoed across the meadow followed by a quick, violent canine yelp of pain, then silence.

Gryph raised his hand high above his head and launched a comet of white straight up into the air. It exploded with a thunderous boom, sending rings of intense white light zooming outward across the starry sky like ripples created from a stone tossed into the still waters of a pond.

All fighting ceased. The meadow fell into stunned silence.

Gryph said something to Landin and Grey, then turned and limped through the line of soldiers back towards camp. He saw the look of disapproval on her face as he splashed through the rivulet of water.

"I know. We have work to do," he growled, clearly not happy with his students' performance.

The next morning, the students rode in a silent, subdued group surrounding Gryph. The night before, they had endured an unexpected tongue lashing from Landin and Grey concerning their dangerous lack of control during the fight. Now Gryph was dividing them into teams and they were going to practice working alongside each other while they traveled. He wasn't going to waste any time they had to spare. They couldn't afford to be in the heat of battle without organization. It would get them killed.

"Grey, you will take Eowhyn, Phalen, and Kory," Gryph said. "Barron, you are designated as a team leader." Barron flinched in surprise, not expecting to be chosen as a leader. "Your team will include Leesha and Kull. Landin, I want you and Bayle to switch places." Bayle eased his horse to the wagon and traded places with Landin, joining Jayce and Jayme on the driver's bench. "You will have Ashlyn, Tover, and Zeike."

Shocked, Zeike's eyes went round and he sat up straight in his saddle on Doogan's old nag. He had not expected to be included.

"Did I hear you right?" Marguerite asked, surprised as well. She was behind the group and had been immersed in her own thoughts until that moment. "I hope you are still planning to end his journey in Tuhnichi, Master Idwyr."

"Have you all noticed how my wife uses my title when she is not happy with me?" he addressed the young group surrounding him. Quiet chuckles rippled through the group. "Madam Idwyr," he winked at Ashlyn who rode beside him. "See, I can be formal, too." Ashlyn smiled wide. "Madam Idwyr," he repeated, "I have not changed my plans. I am merely providing him with the opportunity to work on expanding his skills. Does this meet with your approval?"

"For the moment, *Master* Idwyr," she said, emphasizing his title, letting him know his sarcasm was less than appreciated, "but be advised, I will certainly let you know immediately if my approval changes."

He chuckled. "I have no doubt you will."

"Sir, what about me?" Jayce complained loudly, sitting on the edge of the driver's seat in the wagon.

"You will be allowed to practice this evening," Gryph said.

"You treat me like a baby. I can fight, too." Jayce flung a ball of fire over the heads of the horses pulling the wagon, startling them. They jerked the wagon forward in a panic, but Bayle quickly reined the animals in before they were able to run. The fireball zoomed towards the unsuspecting soldiers escorting them. Gryph gestured quickly. The fireball slammed into something unseen and ricocheted harmlessly off to the side of the road, exploding in a spray of grass and dirt. The startled soldiers whipped around at the unexpected explosion behind them.

Gryph spurred his horse and drew alongside the wagon.

"Your reckless impulsiveness stops right now," Gryph growled, and reached for Jayce. Jayce instinctively backed away, squashing Jayme against Bayle, but Gryph grabbed him by the shirt and jerked him out of the wagon and flung him over the back of his horse.

"Gryph, what are you doing?" Marguerite yelled, spurring her own horse through the group of students. She had never seen him angry with any of his students and it scared her.

"He wants to fight. He is going to get a fight." Gryph jogged his large black steed into the grasslands beside the road. "Eagles, out here now!" he ordered. He pushed Jayce off into the deep waves of green and brown turf.

Frightened, Jayce scrambled across the grass on hands and knees away from Gryph's horse. Gryph dismounted and jerked his staff from his saddle. He turned to face Jayce. The boy had gone as far as he thought he could get away with and sat on his knees. Tears streamed down his face. He had not expected Gryph's angry reaction. It was new to all the students, and Marguerite was not totally sure why he was so angry, either. Yes, Jayce acted rashly and could have hurt those men if Gryph hadn't diverted his missile, but there was something more to Gryph's anger.

"All of you dismount," he growled, "and move out over there." He pointed to an open area away from their horses and the road. Several soldiers moved in to take their mounts and led them back to the road.

"Jayce, get up," Gryph barked at the boy as he limped further out into the field. "How many of you have faced a magical enemy in battle?" He glanced at his students as he moved across the grass. "Anyone?" They all remained silent. "I may be old, but I am far from deaf. I heard your comments, gentlemen. Last night was not a game or a bird hunt." Kull and Tover flushed a deep red and guiltily ducked their heads. "You were lucky that your first taste of battle did not include a magical force or more Do'athrim than there were because the outcome could have been decidedly different." He scanned the faces of all his students. "Up until last night you have only practiced in mock battles. Nothing real was ever thrown at you. What will you do when the attcks are deadly? What will you do when the unexpected is directed at you? Are you ready?"

The students nodded confidently and there were low murmurs of "yes, sir," and "of course, we are."

Gryph thrust a hand forward. An invisible force slammed into his students, knocking them all down.

"Gryph!" Marguerite shouted, afraid he was going to hurt them.

He pointed at her. "Don't," he breathed furiously, "interfere."

She clamped her lips shut. She knew that he was teaching them a lesson—that war was not a game, and they would die if they marched into battle thinking it was an adventure. She knew they needed this, but the mother instinct in her wanted him to calm down. He was too strong.

Coughing and groaning, his students sat up in the grass.

"I asked if you were ready. I see that you are not," he roared. "Get up and spread out."

Slowly, they did as they were told, warily eyeing him as they moved away from each other. Gryph turned his attention to the young boy standing between him and the older students.

"Landin, does Jayce know how to construct a shield properly?" Gryph called out.

"He does," Landin responded.

Marguerite groaned inwardly. She did not like this at all. Their training had been kept within the confines of the training yard where they had been monitored carefully. He had never allowed them to use deadly force on one another.

"Jayce, prepare yourself," he warned and sent a small sphere of blue light at the boy. Jayce stood frozen to the ground. Gryph flicked a hand. The orb thudded into the ground off to one side of Jayce and fizzled out. Gryph's face grew angrier. "Boy, what did I tell you? I won't divert the next one. Protect yourself."

Gryph shot another orb at Jayce. This time the boy managed a shield. The orb popped into it with a small spray of light.

Marguerite relaxed a little. Gryph wasn't throwing anything dangerous at Jayce.

Gryph flung a hand wide, a series of fiery balls of light shot across the field at the older students. They had not been expecting the attack. Phalen, Eowhyn, and Barron conjured protective shields while the others dove for cover out of the way. Explosions rocked the meadow. Dirt and grass flew into the air.

Marguerite felt the blood drain from her face. Those were not harmless.

"Look who is standing," Gryph shouted angrily. The ones on the ground rolled and sat up on their knees, breathing heavily. "You should all be standing. Get up! Never lie on the ground after being knocked down. Get up! No one will be willing to allow you to rest on the battlefield."

Gryph shot a missile of white at Jayce. He was ready and blocked it with a shield. The missile disintegrated. Gryph pounded Jayce with more missiles, increasing their strength with each round. The boy began backing away from the pressure. Gryph advanced. "Jayce, not all attacks are direct," he growled. He waved a hand. Jayce was slammed to the ground from behind. The boy cried out in pain and did not try to rise.

Marguerite slid from her horse, wanting to see if he was hurt, but a quick, menacing glare from Gryph stopped her in her tracks. As much as she hated it, she would stay out of his way.

The boy raised himself to his elbows and wiped the dirt and tears from his face. Stoically, he pushed himself to his feet and faced Gryph.

"You use everything you know in battle," Gryph said to Jayce, but spoke loud enough for everyone to hear. "If one thing doesn't work, try something else. Be observant and don't always rely on the obvious. You have to be smart. You have to think quickly and you have to move quickly."

Gryph launched another series of missiles at Jayce. Jayce blocked them all then dodged to the side. He used his magic to disappear. A corner of Gryph's mouth lifted. Gryph stepped back, scanning the meadow for Jayce. Gryph flicked his hand. A cry issued from above, not far from where Jayce had been standing. Jayce reappeared high off the ground, arms and legs flailing erratically as he flew through the air towards Marguerite. He hit the ground hard and somersaulted head over heels across the turf, coming to a rest on his back directly in front of her. She wanted to reach out to him and check to see if he was hurt, but she did not.

"How did you see me?" Jayce yelled to the sky.

"I have other senses, boy." Gryph growled. "Your invisibility does not hide your energy source from my awareness, nor does it cover the sound of your feet tromping through the grass. You better remember that when you use it next. Now get off the field."

Jayce picked himself up and moved to stand by Marguerite without argument.

"Are you hurt?" she asked quietly, knowing by his sullen demeanor he would not want to be mothered at the moment even if he was hurting.

He angrily shook his head without comment, pouting.

Gryph faced the older students. "Let me remind you, in case you have forgotten, that you will be facing a host of thousands. Within that host, will be a magical force who will outnumber you three to one at the very least. All of them want you dead."

He stabbed his staff into the ground and let go. It remained upright in the soft turf like an empty flag pole.

"Twice, I have attacked you," Gryph held up two fingers, "twice. Not one of you has retaliated." There was a murmur of confusion among the students. "This is not a game. Today, I am your enemy. Today, you will see what it is like to fight when it matters."

"No," Marguerite whispered. He was going to get someone killed.

Gryph raised both arms. One by one, Zeike, Kull, and Tover were slammed backwards to the ground. He was going to fight without mercy. He launched two forces of blue energy at Eowhyn and Barron. They barely managed to block the attack. Phalen shot a comet of flaming fire at Gryph. Gryph blocked it with a negligent flick of his hand while he knocked Leesha and Ashlyn flat with a flashing wall of white. He then shot a smoking plume of black and red power at Phalen. Phalen launched himself to the side, and rolled to his feet. He retaliated using the same attack against Gryph. Gryph deflected it. The plume slammed into the ground with a fiery explosion.

Leesha and Ashlyn struggled to their feet and fired sun-like orbs of flaming yellow across the meadow. Leesha had not aimed and Gryph just ignored her attack as it sped harmlessly across the meadow to explode into a lone tree, busting branches and bark, scattering splinters far and wide. Ashlyn's orb veered towards Marguerite. Marguerite saw it coming and instinctively grabbed Jayce, pulling him down as she ducked. Gryph immediately threw a shield in front her. The concussion from its detonation slammed into him, propelling him unsteadily backwards. His face contorted into a deep grimace of pain when he had to put his weight on his damaged leg.

He glared at her. "Marguerite, you two move back to the road," he ordered as Kull and Tover fired spheres of green energy at him. One exploded into the ground at Gryph's feet, while the other Gryph easily deflected, sending it far off into a stand of briars in the meadow. Gryph slammed Tover and Ashlyn back to the ground with an invisible force.

"Gryph, this is crazy," she yelled.

"Move back to the road," he shouted.

Zeike had scrambled over the grass farther out into the meadow. He shot a sparkling blue orb of energy at Gryph. Marguerite's stomach clenched. Gryph did not try to block it and allowed the orb to hit him. It disappeared harmlessly.

"Zeike, light will not do anything. You know better," Gryph roared. He flung a similar orb at Zeike only this one had a definite hum of power as it zoomed at the boy. Zeike hurled himself to the ground, narrowly avoiding being hit in the head by the orb. It hit the ground behind him with a boom, kicking up dirt and grass. Zeike pounded the turf with a fist in frustration.

Eowhyn and Leesha shot small comets of white sizzling energy at Gryph. Both attacks collided with each other well before they reached Gryph, resulting in a shower of sparks raining down over him. He covered himself with a shield for protection against the hot glowing sparks.

Kory raced across the grass towards Gryph, firing a series of hissing arrow-like missiles at the same time as Barron and Phalen launched huge orbs of red. All three attacks exploded against Gryph's shield. Red fire spiraled away from him in all directions. Gryph retaliated with a series of blue orbs he detonated amongst the students. Leesha screamed when one blew up close by and turf pelted her from behind.

Increasing uncertain whinnies and anxious huffs came from the wagon team and the students' personal mounts. Bayle and the soldiers were having a difficult time holding them in check, and if Gryph didn't stop soon they might lose control. They had only owned the mounts for a few months, and they were not fully battle trained like hers, Gryph's, and the soldiers'. They didn't like the loud concussions and flashing of bright light that would have been part of their training had they had more time with their trainer Allyn.

Marguerite shook her head at the madness, thinking her husband had completely lost his mind.

Kull and Tover sent comets of green across the meadow. Gryph deflected them both and they soared high up into the air, landing far off into the meadow with booms. The students were starting to coordinate their attacks and a twinge of worry for Gryph's safety shot through her.

Kory was now almost on top of Gryph, and Marguerite wondered what the boy was going to do and why Gryph was allowing Kory close. Her question was quickly answered when Kory pulled out his knife. Yelling, he raised the knife high over his head, intent on a physical attack. Gryph stepped back, jerked his staff out of the ground, and slammed Kory in the stomach with the carved eagle's head on its top end. The young man doubled over in pain and dropped to his knees like a rock, gasping for air.

"Good try, Kory, I'm glad someone listened to me when I said magic isn't always the answer to every fight," Gryph huffed. Marguerite hadn't noticed before now just how much this fight was costing him. "However, this was not the right time. Manual attacks are best used when you are in close quarters, or your energy is low, or if circumstances provide you with no other choice. Consider my blow a kill shot. You are now out of the fight. When you catch your breath, join Marguerite and Jayce."

"Yes, sir," Kory wheezed painfully and crawled slowly towards her out of Gryph's way.

Gryph dropped his staff and used both hands to fire large crackling orbs of intense energy at the remaining students, aiming them so they would land in the dirt well before they reached the kids. The resulting explosions were horrific. The concussions knocked everyone in the vicinity off their feet. Marguerite clapped her hands over her ears because the noise was so deafening. Frightened by the increase of intensity, the horses that the soldiers had been keeping in control, panicked. They reared and bolted, jerking the reins out of the soldier's hands and scattering in different directions across the other side of the road. The soldiers raced after them.

Gryph did not ease his attack. He slammed ground-shaking forces of explosive energy into the field all around his students.

"Gryph, stop!" she cried, but he did not heed her.

He was on a mission—a mission of hard truth, and he wanted them to have no doubts as to what the truth was. The students ducked, rolled, and covered their heads from flying grass, dirt, and stone. None thought to retaliate. They didn't have time. They were just trying to survive.

"I am one man," Gryph yelled loud enough for them to hear over his deafening attack. "Separate me into a hundred and you still will not come close to what you will face on that battlefield."

He changed the attack. A wall of flame burst from the ground and sped around the students in a complete circle. Tover cried out when he tried to roll out of harm's way only to be brushed slightly with the burning heat. They were all captured within the circle of fire. Barron and Kull ran as if they would jump the flames, but the flames roared high into the sky, stopping them from bursting through.

"Gryph," Marguerite screamed, he was going to burn them all. "Stop!"

Gryph was knocked to the ground by an unseen attack and landed hard on his back. The flames vanished immediately. The students stood unsteadily within the burned circle, surprised by the sight of their leader lying sprawled in the grass. They looked at each other questioningly, unsure of what to do next.

Gryph grinned at the sky and started to laugh.

"That confirms it," Marguerite shouted, angrily. "You have completely lost your mind, old man."

He laughed harder. He raised both hands into the air. A wall of white light spread in front of the students. Every one of them turned and started to run, but Gryph sent it slamming into their backs—they all sprawled face first into the grass. Slowly, Gryph sat up with a groan. "Never quit," he yelled, scowling at them. "Make damn sure your quarry is dead before you quit. Consider that last blow your final one on this earth. You are all dead."

"Damn it," Phalen muttered angrily at the proclamation. He glared at Gryph. "How is it we are proclaimed dead and you are not? You fell first."

Gryph rubbed his chest and had to haul in a huge breath. "Ashlyn," he called out and clapped his hands together instead of answering Phalen's question. Marguerite shook her head in disbelief. He was applauding, and she was trying to understand this new turn of events when Ashlyn appeared from behind her. Marguerite had been so focused on watching the battle she did not realize the girl had left the meadow.

"Yes, sir," the young girl answered with a touch of fear in her voice.

"I congratulate you," he breathed heavily. "You did well."

Holding his stomach, Kory pushed himself to his feet. "What did she do?" he asked.

"She moved to the one safe place on this entire field for cover," Gryph used his magic to retrieve his staff.

"Where was that?" Kory asked.

"Behind my wife," Gryph answered as he leaned heavily on his staff and pushed himself slowly, painfully to his feet. "If you can find a place of cover in battle where you can still work, then use it. Standing out in the open is extremely dangerous."

"But wasn't that a bit unfair?" Kory asked. "Here we were fighting and she was hiding."

"She wasn't hiding. I told you all to be smart. I believe I also told Jayce not all attacks are direct. If I'm not mistaken, Ashlyn was the only one who listened to me," he glanced at the girl. "Am I right?"

"Yes, sir," Ashlyn said, her dark skin flushed from embarrassment. "After you knocked me down, I thought about what you said. I saw facing you from the meadow wasn't going to work." She shrugged her shoulders. "I crawled to the road and snuck around the wagon to get behind Madam Idwyr. You were focused on the fight. I hoped you weren't tracking me, but if you were, I didn't think you would attack me here. You didn't seem to notice, so I used my shield to knock you down. Master, I couldn't bring myself to hit you with something deadly."

"There is your answer, Phalen. What Ashlyn did only stalled me. A shield hitting a body can kill someone if it is done right, however, her actions were not forceful enough to be deadly," he said as he limped heavily towards Marguerite.

"Did you not know she was here?" Marguerite asked with a frown.

"Yes, I knew she was there," he answered, reaching into the interior of his coat. "I wanted to see what she was going to do." He pulled his spectacles from his pocket. "She didn't take me out of the fight, but she did away with these quite nicely," he said holding up metal frames that no longer held glass.

Ashlyn's eyes widened in horror when she saw she had shattered his glasses. "I'm sorry, Master Idwyr," she apologized.

"Don't worry about it, Ashlyn. It's his own fault for starting all this madness," Marguerite said, taking the frames from him. "We'll get another pair for him in Tuhnichi. Master Idwyr, if you are through beating up your students, don't you think we should get started? You said you wanted to make it to the Midland Hostelry before nightfall?"

"You are right." He noticed the soldiers rounding up the horses. "Everyone help retrieve the horses," he called out. "Landin, Grey, they are to have an hour of rest. After that, I want the teams working on drills from horseback."

"Yes, sir," the two men answered.

"Jayce, you help too."

"Yes, sir," he said sullenly, still pouting from being thrown across the meadow. He raced after Ashlyn and the others.

"Why would you let her attack you? What if she had used something deadly?"

"I would hope I have enough skill to protect myself, but you never know," he said with a shrug of his shoulders.

"I do not like it when you take risks, Master Idwyr. What would you have done if you had hurt any of them?" Marguerite asked.

He wiped sweat from his face with his cloak. "None of them were in any danger, my love."

"I am going to have to beg to differ." She frowned. "All they had to do was make a simple mistake for them to get hurt."

"You don't trust me, do you? Appearances are not always what they seem." He winked at her.

She was confused. "Enlighten me please, sir."

He pointed at the ground. A tiny tuft of grass popped into the air, sending a small spray of dirt across the ground and leaving a tiny divot where the grass had been. "Add light, fire and sparks, sound, and a little invisible force to push them around for realism and you have one spectacular show, don't you think?" he chuckled.

She shook her head in astonishment. His attacks had been an illusion the entire time. "You amaze me."

"Now, if you would just repeat that tonight," he grinned mischievously. "We'll have a nice warm bed, you know?"

"You dirty old man." She smacked him affectionately on his arm. "Do you ever think of anything else?"

"Not where you are concerned, my love," he said, pulling her close.

"Good answer," she said, hugging him tight.

Chapter Fifteen

The large shadow of a ship emerged out of the mist. It was on a collision course with *Storm's Defiance*. The ship's crew erupted into action as Captain Ostied roared commands for evasive action. He and the helmsman both spun the wheel of the ship furiously to turn it out of the oncoming ship's path. Elhrin grasped the rail as the ship heeled over precariously to the right, but it was futile. The approaching ship was too close and moving in fast. There was no way out.

"Elhrin, move!" Tomas yelled. He grabbed her by the arm and hauled her with him off the sterncastle onto the main deck. Marissa, Clay, and Kyne landed with them.

The approaching ship crashed into the rear of *Storm's Defiance*. The ship heaved upwards and tilted violently to one side, sending everyone falling and rolling across the planks of the deck. A rain of shattered wood and rigging parts fell all around them. Huge explosions detonated underneath the ship. Ostied's Specialties had been set off. With an ear-piercing screech of wood grinding against wood and snapping timber, the ship rocked back towards the other side, and caught onto the crushed bow of the encroaching ship. Groaning against each other, both ships settled down into the water . . . and slowly started to sink.

Pushing shattered decking off her, Elhrin scrambled to her feet as did her companions, horrified at the sight before them. Captain Ostied and the helmsman lay dead in the tangled mass of debris that was once the stern. The other ship's bow was firmly entrenched within *Storm's Defiance's* hull. Crewmembers of the other ship scrambled to its bow. They were armed as if they were prepared to attack, but curiously they did not board, only waited silently for some unknown reason. Kyne and Tomas drew their swords, preparing for a fight. *Storm Defiance's* crew followed their lead and raced to arm themselves.

The crew of the other ship parted to either side of the ship, and the N'gethwyn's force of energy approached the bow.

"Marissa," Elhrin whispered. "Get ready."

Elhrin's breath caught in her throat when he stepped into view.

"Master Idwyr?" Marissa whispered in shock, thinking this was the man she had met in Muryne.

The man was almost an exact replica of Elhrin's mentor only his hair was much darker and was short-cropped with a receding hairline. He was also clean-shaven and somewhat shorter than Master Gryph, but the most obvious difference was the pure evil and hate emanating from his blue eyes. It felt bizarre to witness such arrogant malice on a face so closely resembling a man who was as compassionate and kind as Master Gryph.

"Do you feel his black and venomous energy source, Marissa?" Elhrin asked under her breath, taking in every detail of the man and noticing he held his right palm away from his waist in a strange position. It faced to the back of his ship. "This man is N'gethwyn, and he is extremely strong and dangerous. Be ready, he is not holding his right hand like that because he has nowhere to put it."

"Good morning, Miss Caddoch," the man smiled without humor, speaking as if he had just met an old friend while passing on the street. "I thought I would never have the opportunity to meet you personally—wouldn't have cared if I hadn't, but I guess fate has its own course of action with no consideration to my plans."

"Who are you?" she asked to buy them time. She needed a plan and quick.

"Really?" he grunted with feigned amusement. "You do not know who I am?" He shook his head. "I guess that shouldn't surprise me. Gryph was always good at keeping things to himself. I suppose revealing he had a rogue brother to the world would tarnish his high profile reputation. Well, no matter, allow me to introduce myself. I am Derrick Idwyr, Overlord of the First Order of N'gethwyn dedicated to the Lord of Darkness and brother of your esteemed teacher, who in all honesty, I had hoped would be aboard this ship instead of you."

"Why?" she asked.

"Because, my dear, he has a nasty habit of getting in the way of my plans, which he did once again by staying in the city instead of doing what any sane father would have done and run to the rescue of his son."

"If he gets in your way, then why have him leave, why not kill him?"

"Oh, in due time that will pass, but death relieves suffering. I couldn't let that happen just yet."

"Yet, you set up an ambush on the Wyndermir River." Out of the corner of her eye, she noticed Kyne easing his way closer to the enemy ship. "Was that not designed to kill him?"

"Why do you think we sent the female?" he scoffed. "You felt her energy. She was nowhere near a match for Gryph. It was just a delay tactic to keep him from reaching this ship until I was ready. While I did not want him dead at that point, the possibility of injury from a fight is always a good thing." Derrick shrugged. "But it was all a waste of my time in the end, you are here and he is not, and because my colleague did not have the chance to eliminate you in Muryne, I have been forced to come on this little side expedition to take care of you myself."

Elhrin swallowed hard. From the day she learned she was truly So'ladiun, she knew she would be a target, but still, hearing that she had been set up for assassination sent chills down her spine.

Storm's Defiance shifted abruptly and tilted sharply downward, pushing farther onto the enemy ship. Marissa and Clay slipped and fell onto the deck and Elhrin almost went down with them, but Tomas caught her about her waist and held her tight.

"I've got you, love," Tomas growled in her ear. His arm was clamped around the ship's rail to keep them steady as the ship ground to a halt leaning precariously to its side. "I won't let you go."

Kyne had used the shift to fall and roll all the way to the far rail nearer to the enemy. The enemy ship dipped downward unexpectedly and its crew fell forward. A few sailors were pushed overboard into the ocean by their mates colliding into them. Derrick Idwyr remained unbelievably upright and steady as if his feet were nailed to the deck. He did not appear to be concerned with the sinking of the two ships.

Kyne pushed himself to his feet, standing partly on the deck and partly on the wall of the ship's side. Marissa and Clay grasped desperately onto the mast to keep from sliding further across the deck. Sailors near the bow of the ship tried to drop a rowboat into the water, but couldn't get it untangled from its rigging.

"It seems our time is limited, So'ladiun," Derrick smirked, "and since you have been so diligent in your pursuit, I have decided to give you one last reward before you and your companions die." Derrick gestured to someone behind him with his free hand. The captain of his ship appeared holding a small crying child wrapped tightly in a blanket and gagged with a filthy strip of cloth.

"Marcus!" Elhrin screamed, and tried to move, but Tomas jerked her back. "Tomas, let me go!"

"Miss Caddoch, don't do anything stupid," Derrick barked a warning. A magical flow of energy flashed into view from the hand he had been holding out to his side. He held Marcus captive with his magic. "All it will take is a thought and Gryph's boy will fry like a little fish in a pan."

"He didn't do anything to you," Elhrin cried angrily as she frantically searched her mind for a way to free Marcus from his hold. "He is just a baby."

"Babies grow up, Miss Caddoch," Derrick snarled, "and this one, especially, will not be allowed to reach adulthood."

"You want to kill him? Marcus is your nephew. How could you do this to your own flesh and blood?"

"I have no family, So'ladiun," Derrick growled. "They have been dead to me for a long, long time. This boy is nothing but a future enemy."

"This doesn't make sense. If you were going to kill Marcus, why didn't you have your men do it back in Muryne?" she spat. The boat jerked under her feet. Tomas tightened his grip.

"I didn't want him dead then. The plan was to get my brother out of the city. If he found out his son was already dead he would not have left the city, and if he found out his son was dead while in pursuit, I didn't want to take the chance he would quit the chase. Besides, I wanted Gryph to witness his son's death on my field of glory. I wished to see his face as I killed his boy, but it did not work out the way I had originally planned. You came instead and fouled the plan. Still, I'm sure Gryph is beside himself with guilt and grief for his abnormal sense of dedication to his country and choosing to protect the city over saving his own son. I had hoped he wouldn't be in Muryne for the show I had planned for the city, but we will make up for the defeat in the end." He shrugged. "I do regret, just a tiny bit, the loss of my strongest fighters. I guess I will have to be satisfied with my small army of N'gethwyn to make up for their failure." He glanced at the boy in the captain's arms. "I no longer need his boy." He jerked Marcus from the captain with his magic and tossed the boy out into the ocean.

"No!" she screamed. She flung a wave of magic out over the water, desperately trying to catch Marcus, but she missed and he fell out of her sight.

At the same time, Kyne threw a blade, which embedded into Derrick Idwyr's shoulder. He then dove over the side of the ship before Derrick's retaliatory blast hit the wooden planks where he had stood leaving a jagged hole in the deck.

"Go," Derrick roared, jerking Kyne's blade out of his shoulder with a hiss of pain. The crew of Derrick's ship swarmed onto *Storm's Defiance*, slipping and sliding across the precarious decking in order to reach their enemy. *Storm's Defiance's* crew jumped into action and met the onslaught with a ferocious yell and the twangs of bow strings. Arrows flew into bodies, sailors screamed and fell, but their companions found their adversaries with a clash of steely swords.

White hot anger consumed Elhrin. She fired a deadly orb of energy at the foul N'gethwyn. He flicked it away as if it were a fly. It exploded far out in the ocean with a flash of light.

"Let me go," she growled at Tomas, jerking violently out of his grip. She immediately slid down the slope of the deck, intent on finding a way through the mass of fighting sailors so she could dive after Marcus on the other side.

Derrick had other plans for her. Before she reached the deck's midway point he grabbed her tight within his magical grasp and jerked her high into the air, hauling her out over the water—and far away from where he had thrown Marcus. He then sent a searing heat through his magic. She screamed. It felt like he had set her on fire. The pain was more than she could bear, and she knew she had to act fast or she would surely die. She sent the flow of her magic rushing through the pendant lying on her chest. Power surged into the gem, combining hers with that of Solisius' within its crystal. She pushed it outward and surrounded herself with a thin veil of magical skin, slipping it underneath Derrick's hold on her body and severing contact from his magical heat. The pain vanished, but he still held her tight and started to squeeze the life out of her. Her bones protested the force testing their strength as he pushed inward. She poured more power into the skin and pushed outward with all her strength. Derrick's grip on her shattered and she dropped like a heavy stone. Desperately, she shot a blast of energy in the direction of Derrick—then the cool waters of the southern ocean enveloped her. She plunged well into its depths, but immediately started to kick for the surface that seemed leagues above her. She had not filled her lungs before hitting the water and it wasn't long before she felt the urge to gulp for life-giving air.

Muted explosions boomed from above and she could feel concussion after concussion as Derrick methodically destroyed everything around him. A violent series of booms rocked through the water and a blast of bubbling fire blew through the underside of *Storm's Defiance*—his attacks had connected with the rest of the captain's supply of Ostied Specialties. The ship started to sink rapidly, ripping away from the *Shifting Winds* as it plummeted to the ocean floor.

She kicked away from the sinking ship and the heavy pull of the downward current it created, finally breaking the surface with a desperate gasp. She tread water trying to get her bearings, trying to find Derrick. He was going to pay. She made out the shadow of the *Shifting Winds* and after a few hard strokes to her left, she found him through the ghostly wafts of mist and smoke perched on the side of the ship's foremast like an evil vulture as the ship tilted dangerously over on its side. Ropes dangled from the mast into the water giving a few helpless sailors a moment of false hope as they tried to climb up out of the water to safety. But Derrick was a ruthless killer and he fired on them as if they were pesky rodents, killing them one by one, and from the amount of bodies floating around her in the water, it appeared that he had made sure to murder anyone living as he purposely sank the vessels. He had no concern for the men who had helped carry out his plans, and since he no longer needed them, he disposed of them without thought just as he had tossed Marcus in the water without thought.

She launched a crackling beam of white energy at the bastard, but the rolling of the waves moving the ship caused her aim to be off. Her attack blasted a hole in the planks of the decking, flinging deadly shards of wood all around him, but it appeared luck was on his side. Nothing touched him. He easily located her in the water and shot a plume of fire her way. She barely had time to protect herself with a decent shield. The force of his attack caused it to shatter, and she instinctively ducked under the water. Fire rolled over the surface above her. She kicked back up and found that he had managed to stand precariously on the mast that was now level with the water's surface as the ship slowly turned over.

"I'm ready," he shouted.

She launched another attack, but he deflected it easily as a line of red energy ripped into the air next to him and expanded into a small swirling maelstrom of power that was Obsudius' rift, coloring the surrounding fog an eerie shade of crimson. He fired one last attack at her. This time her shield held as his attack exploded against the barrier sending blazing sparks wide over the surface of the water. He then dove headfirst through Obsudius' fiery portal into the Realm of Darkness. The rift shrank back to a thin red line and winked out of existence with an echoing boom just as the *Shifting Winds* heaved further on its side and tilted upside down, dragging those who were trapped within its rigging under the water, cutting off their heartrending screams instantly.

"Marcus!" Elhrin screamed. Bodies and wreckage bobbed on the surface around her, but she could see no living forms. "Tomas!"

She swam furiously, searching through the debris. Horrible cries of pain echoed through the fog that surrounded her, but the sound was misleading . . . she would swim one way only to hear the next cry come from a different direction. The *Shifting Winds* finally slipped under the waves like a silent whale, and without its outline as a backdrop, the fog cloaked the water like an ethereal blanket. "Tomas! Marissa! Kyne!" she called their names desperately. "Clay!" *Marcus*, she screamed in her mind, knowing there was no need to call his name again. He couldn't swim. He was lost to her. "Please, someone answer!" she cried out.

"Elhrin," she heard a weak voice call.

Elhrin whipped around, treading water. "Marissa!"

"Over here," the girl answered.

It sounded as if the call came from her right.

"Marissa, talk to me so I can find you."

"Elhrin," Marissa sobbed. "I'm here."

Elhrin swam in what she hoped was the direction of the girl's voice. She skirted a large pile of wreckage, pushing chunks of wood out of her way. She found Marissa clinging to the side of a large crate on the other side.

"Are you hurt?" Elhrin asked, grasping a large plank for buoyancy. The girl was as pale as the ghostly mist surrounding them. A tiny river of blood drained from a large cut that slashed across her forehead.

"I hit my head, but I'm not hurt anywhere else," Marissa sobbed. "I tried to attack him, Elhrin, but the ship lurched. I lost my grip and fell overboard. I don't know where Clay is."

"What about Tomas?" Elhrin choked.

Marissa shook her head. She was trembling, even though the water was not that cold. "I don't know. He and Clay were still on board when I fell in. Elhrin, I saw the N'gethwyn jump into a red hole in the sky and disappear. How is that possible?"

"I know," Elhrin said. Marissa did not know about the rifts Obsudius could open between the living world and his spiritual realm. "Someday I will explain," she said, listening to the disembodied cries drifting over the water. None of the voices sounded familiar. "Marissa, hang on. I'm going to see who is out there."

"Elhrin, what will we do?" Marissa cried.

"We stay alive," Elhrin clasped Marissa's hand and squeezed. "The captain said this fog should be gone by the afternoon. We are not that far from shore, surely a ship will spot us. Just don't let go of that crate."

Elhrin pushed away and swam towards what seemed to be the closest cry for help. She checked every piece of large debris she passed as she swam, finding nothing. A low moan issued from her left, and she quickly made her way to a shadow in the thick mist. A sailor lay on a section of decking, half of his abdomen had been ripped away, but he lived. Elhrin bit back a wave of nausea. He wouldn't live long. Blood poured from the wound into the sea.

He rolled his head and saw her. "Help," he wheezed.

She swam up to him and grasped his arm. "Stay strong. Help is coming," she lied, knowing if it were true, it wouldn't matter. "I will be back." With tears in her eyes, she swam away, hating that she had no powers to save the injured.

She felt like she was swimming in circles. Each piece of debris looked like one she had already seen, and the cries always seemed to come from different directions, not giving her any guidance on which way to go. Listening, she tread water, grateful that this had not happened while they had been further north where the colder waters would have surely killed them without giving them a chance at rescue.

Solisius, I need your help, she sent her thoughts to the heavens.

The mists swirled around her. *I am here, my child*, Solisius whispered in her ear. *I will not leave you.*

Elhrin wept at the comforting sound of her god's voice. "What do I do?"

Swim, he said simply.

She swam hard, passing vast amounts of debris and bodies, but no one alive. Then she heard voices . . . healthy voices speaking to each other . . . not the voices or the cries of someone in distress.

"Hello," a voice rang out through the fog. "Is anyone there?"

"Over here," Elhrin yelled. She swam for the voice.

"I heard someone, captain," the voice shouted.

"Drop anchor now!" a different voice ordered, sounding familiar.

She heard a tremendous splash and swam harder for the noise. The huge shadow of a ship emerged from out of the veil of white.

Thank you, Solisius. Thank you, Solisius, she repeated over and over in her head.

Several splashes and the scrape of wood against wood sounded from the direction of the ship.

"Hello?" Elhrin called as she swam. She heard the rattling of oars.

"Over here," a voice rang out. "Someone is off the port bow."

"Row, man," the familiar voice ordered.

Elhrin saw the outline of several rowboats detach from beneath the ship's shadow. One headed in her direction. She swam for it. When she could distinguish the features of the boat's three occupants, she saw that one of them was Griffyn Masstersun.

"Elhrin, we're coming," he shouted, recognizing her. He pounded the back of the sailor rowing. "Put your back into it, sailor."

The rowboat shot forward and she had only managed a few strokes when Griffyn reached down and hauled her into the boat as if she weighed no more than a small child. She collapsed in the bottom of the boat with relief.

"Are you hurt?" he asked, his dark features lined with worry.

"No," she choked. "There are others. I found one of my companions. She is on a crate somewhere out there. I couldn't find anyone else in the mist."

"Don't worry," he gestured for the sailor to start rowing. "We'll find them."

They rowed in the direction where Elhrin had thought she had left Marissa.

"Marissa!" Elhrin shouted.

"Here," a weak voice sounded off, but it was not the girl.

Griffyn pointed to his left and the sailor came about and rowed hard. A figure clinging to a large clump of rope and wreckage emerged out of the mist.

Elhrin recognized him. "Clay!" she yelled.

"Here," he repeated. His head lay face down on the debris.

The sailor pulled the rowboat alongside the man. "Give me your hand, man," Griffyn said.

Clay looked up with a grimace. He weakly held up a hand and Griffyn and one of the sailors helped him into the boat. He shouted in pain as they hauled him over the side.

"Clay, where are you hurt?" she asked.

"My right leg," he gasped. "Something is in it."

She started to search his leg, but he grabbed her hand and held her fast. "Elhrin," his face was contorted in pain, but there was something else in his eyes that she couldn't read. "He didn't make it."

Cold fear swept through her body. "Who?" she asked, dreading any answer he could possibly give her.

"Tomas—he tried to go after the magician and was hit . . . ," Clay choked off the rest of what he was about to say. "It was quick, Elhrin. He died instantly. I'm so sorry."

Elhrin felt like her world had just been sucked into the dark vacuum of the Void. Mechanically, she nodded her head. "Okay," she whispered, "okay." She started to search for Clay's wound again and found a tear in his breeches on the side of his leg. She tried to widen the tear, but her hands shook so violently she couldn't manage to hold onto the fabric.

Clay grabbed her hand again. "This can wait," he whispered.

She sat heavily in the bottom of the boat and covered her face with her trembling hands. *This can't be real. Please, don't let it be real. I told him. I told him it was too dangerous to be near me. I told him. Oh, Solisius, why? Answer me! Why?* She screamed in her mind. *Why do you take people that I love out of my life?*

No, my child, I do not take them, and for once he responded to something she expected he would not give an answer to. *I have never taken anyone from you, and I did not take Tomas. Tomas' time in the living world was at an end.*

Elhrin moaned softly to herself. He confirmed Tomas was dead. There was no hope.

Elhrin, listen to me carefully. You must understand the course of fate for each individual has a path, and no matter how many diversions and turns the path takes during its lifetime, there comes a time when it has to end. This is true for every living entity, but be comforted, my child, the end is not final. The path begins anew when you reach my realm, and that path lasts forever. Tomas is here with me now, and will be here waiting patiently for you when your time comes to join him and begin your journey again in peace.

"There she is," Griffyn called out.

Elhrin lowered her hands from her eyes. She couldn't cry, and didn't understand why, since she wanted to desperately. She wanted to stand up in the boat and scream for all she was worth, but she couldn't. Numbly, she watched Griffyn and the sailor pull Marissa into the boat with them. Numbly, she watched as Marissa embraced Clay tightly and cry as if there would be no tomorrow.

No tomorrow.

That is just what it felt like for her, despite what Solisius had said about her being able to spend an eternity with Tomas in Ts'aura, the Realm of Light. Without Tomas here and now, there was no tomorrow. No lifetime together—nothing.

"Row us back, sailor," Griffyn growled. "Elhrin, we'll get you three aboard my ship so you can get dry and comfortable while we search for others."

Elhrin nodded mutely. She was going to get dry and comfortable while the bodies of her beloved and Marcus, and possibly Kyne were drifting somewhere out there in the currents. Her heart fell deeper into the black abyss at the thought. They were dead, and she may as well be drifting with them. Her light had been extinguished.

She stared blankly into the mist, not seeing anything, not feeling anything. Two hands clasped her arms and she turned her head to look into the tear-filled eyes of Marissa.

"Oh, Elhrin, I'm so sorry," Marissa cried, or at least that's what Elhrin thought she said. She couldn't seem to focus on the girl. She patted Marissa's hand absently and returned to watching the mist swirl around them, content to lose herself inside its nothingness. She felt Marissa's hands slip away from her arms and with them Elhrin slipped into the past, reliving the moment when Tomas first introduced her to his sweet mother, knowing the woman absolutely worshipped her firstborn son and would be devastated when she learned the news of his death.

The boat bumped against the side of the ship, jostling her back to the present. A strong hand gripped her shoulder. "Elhrin, can you climb?" Griffyn asked.

She nodded. There was a rope ladder slapping lightly against the side of the ship. She gripped it and pulled herself up the side of the ship, feeling extremely heavy as if she weighed more than a mountain. When she reached the top, the hands of strangers helped her over the rail and into the safety of the ship and she saw that Griffyn's other boats had been successful at finding a few survivors. Three men sat miserably propped against the side of the ship, unscathed, but there were others lying on the deck not so lucky. Two were horribly wounded and probably would not last into the afternoon.

One of the deck hands draped a blanket over her shoulders. "Find somewhere comfortable, Miss. Orrick'll be with you quick as he can to check on you."

Clutching the blanket to her, Elhrin started for the middle of the ship where she could get away from the injured, and out of the way of those coming onboard. Just as she was about to slide to the deck and prop herself against the main mast, the muted whimper of a child drifted out of the fog. Elhrin whirled around. She could just make out the top of a head sitting behind the helmsman's wheel in the stern of the ship. The cry of a child drifted over the ship again.

"Oh, dear god," she whispered. Hope bloomed in the pit of her soul. She threw the blanket from her shoulders and ran to the rear of the ship. She caught sight of Kyne sitting on a wooden box, holding Marcus in his arms, rocking him back and forth and trying to calm his fears.

"Marcus!" she cried.

Kyne's head jerked around at her cry. His face fell into an undisguised look of emotional relief, cracking his normal cynical hard features, almost as if he was on the verge of tears. "Elhrin, thank the light you are safe," he breathed, then held Marcus out for her. She scooped the little boy into a crushing embrace. He wrapped his tiny arms around her neck and buried his head under her chin, snuffling hard.

"Oh, sweet baby," she murmured as she kissed Marcus' wet hair, breathing in the pungent aroma of the salty sea. "Sweet, sweet, baby. I've got you now. You are safe. We are going home."

Elhrin lay in a coarse woven hammock, swaying gently in the empty crew's quarters one level below the main deck of Griffyn Masstersun's ship and watching a little black spider crawl across the thick wooden beam above her. Marcus was snuggled tightly to her side under the crook of her arm, sleeping peacefully for once in over a week since he had been tossed in the ocean like a piece of useless trash.

Like a piece of trash. The mere thought of Derrick's inhumane cruelty set her emotions on fire, which was surprising since she couldn't seem to generate any other emotion at all. She felt dead inside, and the days following the encounter with Derrick Idwyr had been like living suspended in one place where time had no meaning. She went through the motions of basic survival and the necessary actions required to see to Marcus' needs, but she had no desire to talk, to smile, to exist. Other than to despondently teach Marissa new forms of magic, she avoided the others as much as possible, especially Kyne. His sympathetic stares and random acts of kindness were foreign to his nature, and knowing how much he had disliked Tomas, his actions bothered her for some irrational reason. So she and Marcus stayed either in the crew's quarters where she tried to get him to sleep without nightmares or she would sit topside with him tucked in her lap, silently watching the coast of Anderan slide by as they continued the voyage to Marmuht. She had made the decision to continue to their original destination instead of turning around and heading back to Muryne, and Griffyn was more than willing to provide them with transportation. He was just as angry with Derrick, and if the invasion rumors were true and he was involved, then they were both going to do whatever they could to help stop him.

She heard the door to the upper deck creak open and the scuff of footsteps sound on the short stair that led to her level. She glanced in its direction just as Kyne stepped off the final step and paused to allow his eyes to adjust to the dim light of the lower deck.

"How are you faring?" he asked when he saw her watching him.

"I'm fine," she responded without emotion, her voice sounding flat to her own ears.

He skirted a table that still held the remnants from that morning's breakfast and made his way to where she lay. "You didn't eat," he said as he leaned against the post that held the foot of her hammock.

"I'm not hungry," she said. Marcus twitched under her arm and she looked at the small head propped on her chest. "At least, I was able to get him to eat. He has had a hard time keeping anything down."

"Is he sick?"

"In a way. His memories are raw and terrifying. He has nightmares just about every time he falls asleep—reliving the horror of it all," she said, softly brushing a stray ebony curl away from his eyes. "He wakes up crying and begs for me to save him from the bad men." She glanced up at Kyne. "Do you know how hard that is to take? How can you save a little boy from the monsters in his own mind?"

"I know it's hard, but you don't have the power to fix everything, Elhrin," he said with the tone of someone coddling a spoiled child.

"Kyne, I am well aware of just how limited my powers are," she snapped with a frown. She knew he was probably unaware of how he had spoken to her and was only trying to help, but she was not in the mood for his condescending demeanor even if it was not his intent. "Two ships now sit on the ocean floor and most of their crews with them and . . . and . . . ," she couldn't bring herself to voice acknowledgement of Tomas' death—not yet, "not to mention that Derrick was able to get away with only a wound in his shoulder. I failed, and that, my friend, shows you just how much I am aware of my limitations."

"Elhrin, it is not your fault, and Tomas . . . ."

"Don't, Kyne," she commanded, "I don't want to talk about this right now."

"You need to talk about it," he snapped back, his black eyes burned into hers, daring her to argue with him. "It is not good for you do this to yourself. You have avoided us as if we have the plague all week and we understand, but it is not healthy to keep something like this inside."

"This coming from a man who demanded that I quit asking him why he hates his mother," she said, letting the fire go out of her words. She didn't have the strength to argue.

"That's different. I'm a man. We are not supposed to share our inner feelings. It makes us feel vulnerable," he said lifting the corners of his mouth, trying to win a smile from her. It didn't work.

"Kyne, why are you here?" she sighed, ready for him to go away. She caressed Marcus' soft hair between her fingers.

He stared at her silently for a moment before answering. "I wanted to tell you we have entered the Bay of Marmuht. We will be in port within the hour." He pushed away from the post. "I just thought you might want to know." He turned and disappeared up the stair, quietly closing the door behind him and cutting off the brief flash of sunlight that had filled the stairway.

She sighed, staring back up at the exposed beams above her. She knew she had hurt his feelings and added that fact to the gargantuan load of overwhelming guilt sitting on her shoulders. It was her fault, and like she had told him, she had failed. She was So'ladiun. She was a defender, a protector. She should have never allowed Derrick the opportunity of the first strike. For that matter, she should have done something, anything to try and stop his ship from colliding into theirs in the first place. Instead, she ran out of the way. Now, she had the deaths of Captain Ostied and most of his crew on her shoulders . . . and Tomas'. Soon they would be in Marmuht, and she would have to leave the solace of the ship and face reality and the consequences of her failures once again, but this time she would not have the support and love of the one she needed the most.

Marcus whimpered in his sleep. His dreams were starting again.

"Marcus," she whispered and gently shook him. She did not want him going through the nightmares if she could help it.

He came awake with a start and the thumb he had in his mouth jerked out with a tiny wet pop.

"Hey, sweet boy," she stroked his hair, and he turned his beautiful blue eyes on her. "We are almost to the city. Do you want to go see?"

He nodded his head and ground a pudgy fist into one sleepy eye.

"Let's do it," she said and rolled out of the hammock with him in her arms.

When they stepped out on the upper deck, a stiff but comfortably warm southern breeze hit them, feeling nice after being below deck in the dark recesses of her own mind for most of the day. She breathed in a deep breath, allowing the thick, salty air to wash away her guilt, if only for a moment.

"Good afternoon, Elhrin and Marcus," Griffyn said. He turned the steering of the ship over to his helmsman and came to greet them. He held out his hands for Marcus, but Marcus shied away and held tight to Elhrin's neck. Unoffended, Griffyn smiled and ruffled Marcus' unruly curls. He had been trying to get Marcus to allow him to hold him, but the boy would not warm up to his half-brother. "Guess what, Marcus?"

Marcus stared at his brother warily, saying nothing.

"We will be in Marmuht soon, and do you know the people here make the best sweets in all of Anderan. My favorite is the taffy bites. Do you know what they are?"

Marcus shook his head no.

"I didn't think you would," Griffyn said with a grin. It made him look so much like his father Elhrin had to look away. She needed Master Gryph and Marguerite, and Bayle. She needed her family. "So you are in for a wonderful treat. It is a very chewy sweet, and they make it in many flavors. I like cherry. Do you like cherry?"

Marcus nodded.

"Then that shall be my first mission when we dock. I will get you an entire sack full and maybe a box of their finest chocolates which I find excellent, as well. Would you like that?"

"Yes," Marcus whispered.

Griffyn beamed. That had been the first word Marcus had spoken to him. "I'm making progress," he said to her, then his face turned serious. "Elhrin, we will be there soon. Do you know what your plans are, yet?"

It was ironic he asked that question because she had just been rolling all her options around in her head for the last hour. "I want to talk to someone who knows more about the invasion rumors, and I'll have to get Marcus back to his parents." She moved to the side of the ship. In the hazy distance she could see Marmuht situated on a steep incline that reached out into the bay.

Griffyn followed her and placed his hands on the rail. "If you need me to do anything, I'm available."

"Thank you, Griffyn. You have done so much, already. I don't know what would have happened if you hadn't followed the *Shifting Winds* into the fog."

"That was a fortunate piece of luck, I have to admit," he said as he perused the waters around them. Ships of all sizes were traveling in and out of the bay, including patrolling naval ships. "If my man hadn't noticed the Agadar colors before the ship slipped into the fog bank, we may not have gone in. As it is, I don't see how we managed to be close enough to see the flashes of light through the fog from the explosions that sank those ships."

"I think someone is looking out for us," she murmured, knowing Solisius wouldn't admit to manipulating events if she asked him.

Griffyn looked down at her. "Elhrin, here's an idea if you don't mind a suggestion."

"I don't mind," she said.

"Since I was able to send a message to my wife when we transferred the wounded aboard the *Sea Eagle*, I could escort Marcus home if it turns out you are needed here," he offered.

The ship he spoke of was one of two that had appeared to help look for survivors after the fog had cleared that fateful afternoon. Tomas' body was never found. She thrust that thought away quickly before her stomach rebelled.

Elhrin slowly shook her head. "Griffyn, please don't think I don't trust you because I do. It's just that Derrick Idwyr is so bent on revenge, I don't trust fate enough to think he won't find out Marcus and I have survived. I have no plans to leave Marcus' side until he is safely within his parent's care."

Griffyn smiled. "And for that, I admire you. Very well, but I may have to accompany you, anyway. For some reason, I have a strong desire to see my father at the moment."

She sighed, "Me, too."

He looked over her head to the front of the ship. "Excuse me. With this many ships moving around, I had better see to the helm. We won't be allowed to berth since we have no cargo to unload or pick up, so I will drop anchor as close to the docks as possible. We'll row in from there."

She nodded and moved to the bow where her companions watched the city near.

"There they are," Marissa said, smiling kindly at her and Marcus.

Another twinge of guilt flitted through her mind for being so distant to Marissa because she had been a tremendous help in taking care of Marcus. He wouldn't let the girl hold him for long, but he would sit by her and let her tell him stories whenever Elhrin had to take care of her own personal needs or just a moment to breathe.

"Good afternoon," Clay said with a smile. His wounds had turned out to be superficial, but painful. A large piece of decking had embedded in his thigh, but one of the men on the ship had been able to remove it, and the wound did not hinder his movements.

"Afternoon," she responded, taking note that Kyne moved closer to the prow to put distance between them. The move surprisingly hurt her, but she knew it was her own fault. She had shunned him at every turn and snapped at him whenever he tried to speak to her. She exhaled softly. She would have to apologize to him soon.

"Marcus, did you see the little fishing boats?" Marissa asked and pointed to several small single-sail boats close to the shores of the bay. Each sail was dyed a bright color which made for a pretty sight against the clear blue waters of the bay and the white sands of the beaches.

Marcus stuck his thumb in his mouth and shyly laid his head on Elhrin's shoulder, but Elhrin thought she caught a glimpse of a tiny smile when he looked at the boats. This was not the Marcus she was used to—a child who had been so full of energy and life. Derrick was going to be sorry for what he had done to him. She only regretted the three men who had abducted Marcus died without her assistance. Two were lost at sea, and the other died of serious wounds aboard Griffyn's ship shortly after he had been hauled on board. Kyne had told her the man was found with a wolf tattoo on his chest and they tossed his body overboard for the creatures of the sea to eat. She closed her eyes, fighting back the knot of nausea in her stomach. Tomas was to suffer the same fate. She had to quit thinking about these things or she would drive herself mad.

"Elhrin, are you ill?" Marissa asked.

Elhrin opened her eyes. "No," she said, "I'm fine, just tired."

"I know," Marissa rubbed Elhrin's shoulder, "it's been hard."

"Yes, it has," Elhrin sighed, then frowned when a force of energy brushed against her awareness. "Marissa, did you feel that?"

"Feel what?"

There it was again. "Someone . . . ," she drifted off, focusing on the faint power source. She couldn't distinguish the details of it yet, they were too far away.

"I don't feel anything," Marissa said. There was a touch of fear in her voice. "Do you think it is him?"

"No," Elhrin stared off into the distance without seeing, concentrating, "this is steady. If Derrick felt me, he would hide himself—I think."

She squinted against the sun and tuned everyone out. She wanted to know who it was as soon as possible. She was not going to be surprised ever again if she had anything to do with it.

The source was high above the coastline inside the city and was strong enough to be felt at such a distance . . . she concentrated on the nuances of its makeup as they drew closer. Each detail started to emerge like rays of sunlight streaming through breaks in a cloud, it was familiar, it was fierce, it was . . . lightning.

"Thank you, my Lord of Light," she breathed, barely keeping herself from collapsing on the deck. "He's safe."

"Elhrin, please tell me. What is it?" Marissa asked.

Elhrin glanced at the girl seeing the worry on her face. "Master Idwyr is in the city."

Marissa smiled wide. "Thank the light," she breathed with relief.

Clay beamed behind Marissa, and Kyne dropped his head to stare at the water directly below him. He wouldn't admit it, but she knew he was relieved by the news, as well.

"Marcus," Elhrin pulled him away from her shoulder so she could see his face, "your papa is here."

Marcus pulled his thumb from his mouth and looked around for his father. "Where?"

"He is in the city. See the city?" She pointed at the distant hillside covered in thousands of white boxlike structures with red, clay-tiled roofs. "And I am almost positive that he knows we are coming into port."

Marcus' lip quivered. "I want papa," he whispered.

"Soon, baby, it won't be long, okay?"

He stuck his thumb back in his mouth and laid his head on her shoulder.

Hugging him close, she leaned against the rail and willed the wind to hurry them into port. As they neared, she felt another concentration of combined magical energy near Master Gryph's source.

"He has the Eagles with him," she said.

Kyne finally looked her way. "Then I guess the invasion rumors are true, and Derrick Idwyr's army of N'gethwyn will be included." He turned back to watch the city approach. "You will need them," he said after a moment.

"Yes, we will," she replied with a sigh. She had forgotten Derrick's words before he threw her into the sea. If it was true, this invasion would be brutal and would stretch all of their abilities to their limits, including her own.

By the time they dropped anchor and put the rowboats in the water, she could feel Master Gryph's energy source moving into the lower city—he was coming to meet them—and when their rowboat finally thumped against the wooden piling of a small boat access, she could feel him come at her like a storm rolling in from the Northreach Mountains.

She climbed up a short ladder onto the wharf then reached down to get Marcus from Clay, thankful that for once the little boy let someone else hold him without crying, even if he did wriggle in Clay's hands like an unearthed bloodworm. She nestled him comfortably on one hip and turned to search the noisy crowd of dockworkers, sailors, and merchants for Master Gryph. It didn't take long for her to find him. He towered head and shoulders over everyone, holding tight to a tall wooden staff and walking with a more pronounced limp than when she saw him last, and when there was a brief break in the bustling crowd around him, she could see that Marguerite and Bayle were by his side.

He caught sight of Elhrin and smiled. He then saw who she held in her arms. With obvious relief, he tilted his head back and closed his eyes, giving thanks to Solisius, no doubt. At the same time, Marguerite spotted them too. Both of her hands flew to her mouth in shocked relief, and for the first time in all the years Elhrin had known Marguerite, she witnessed the stoic and always steadfast lady start to cry in public. She then broke into a run, leaving Master Gryph and Bayle behind.

"Marcus!" she wailed. "Marcus!"

He turned his head at the sound of his mother's voice. He started to squirm, wanting desperately to be with his mother, and it was all Elhrin could do to hold him so he wouldn't jump out of her arms before Marguerite reached them.

His mother finally pushed through the last of the crowd that stood in her way and wrapped them both in a tight hug. Marcus wriggled into his mother's arms, and she squeezed him hard, kissing his face and hair over and over. "Oh, my baby boy, you are safe. Thank the light you are safe." She turned to look for her husband as he limped up to her with open arms, tears freely running down his tanned cheeks and into his salt and pepper beard. "Oh, Gryph, look, he's home . . . he's . . . ." So overwrought with raw emotion, Marguerite couldn't speak any longer and fell into his embrace with Marcus. The reunited family stood wrapped in a tight circle, blissfully unaware of the stares of a growing crowd of curious onlookers.

Bayle enveloped Elhrin in a tight hug. "Thank god you all have made it here safely," he said, his voice gruff with emotion.

Elhrin stared past Bayle, watching Master Gryph and his family blissfully reunite. A surreal change took place within her state of mind. She became angry and couldn't understand why. These were the people she loved most in the world, and she needed them, yet, she was becoming furious.

Master Gryph looked up and smiled at her. He beckoned for her to join them. She pushed Bayle gently away and walked over to her mentor, but she did not accept the hug he offered.

"I met your brother," she said without emotion.

A flash of hurt or guilt crossed his face, but she wasn't sure which. He nodded slightly and dropped his arm to his side. "I'm sorry for not telling you. I . . . ."

She pointed a finger at him and interrupted whatever he had been meaning to say. "Don't you dare make excuses for something I should have known long ago," she fumed. "I'm tired of all your secrets that you don't want to reveal if it doesn't suit you. I'm tired of it, do you hear me? Tired of it!" She backed away from him. "He is an enemy of Anderan, and he is N'gethwyn. The fact that he exists should have never been kept from me . . . NEVER!" she spat. She turned on her heel and stalked into the crowd, leaving them all behind.

"Elhrin, wait!" Bayle called out. He caught up with her as she stepped onto a cobblestone road near the wharf, and grabbed her by the arm, but she jerked it away and strode up the road. "I don't understand what is going on. Elhrin, what are you doing?"

She rounded on him. "I don't know what I'm doing anymore, Bayle," she cried, running both hands through her hair and then threw them wide. "I haven't a clue what I'm doing."

"What's wrong?" He grabbed her by the arm again and held tight. He wasn't going to let her get away from him. "Please, tell me."

She covered her eyes with a trembling hand. She couldn't look at him. "Bayle, did you notice anyone missing? We didn't all make it here safely." She couldn't speak Tomas' name out loud. *Why can't I say his name?*

She felt Master Gryph's energy source surge her way again. She uncovered her eyes to scan the crowd behind Bayle. She wanted to run, but Bayle held her tight.

"Elhrin, I am sorry. I just assumed he was still on the ship," Bayle said, but she wasn't looking at him. Master Gryph had just stepped onto the road behind him, leaning heavily on his eagle carved staff, but he limped towards her with a gait that was stronger than she would have expected from any ordinary injured man. He was not concerned about pain or discomfort—he was clearly furious, and unlike usual, he did not bother to hide his emotions from anyone. The crowd practically pushed each other out of his way when they saw him coming. He was power, he was dangerous, and they knew it.

"Let me go, Bayle," she said, prying his fingers from her arm. She backed away from him, putting more distance between her and Master Gryph.

Master Gryph looked ready for a fight, and if that was what he wanted, she was ready. She stood rigid in the road—waiting. "You don't want to do this here," she called out.

"What?" Bayle asked uncertain of what was going on. He finally understood when Master Gryph slapped the eagle staff onto his chest and left it there.

"Oof!" Bayle blew out a surprised breath, grabbing the staff before it clattered to the ground.

"Yes, I do," Master Gryph growled, and advanced towards her, almost unable to walk without the support of his staff. He reached for her with both hands. Elhrin flinched back, thinking he might be angry enough to hit her, but instead he grasped her shoulders before she could back out of his reach and crushed her to his chest, holding her so tight she thought bones might break.

She tried to push away from him. "Let me go!" she seethed, but he gripped her tighter without saying a word. "Let me go!" She pounded at his arms. "Let me go!" she screamed, and the dam that had been holding all emotion in check, crumbled. All the grief she had kept locked safely away since losing Tomas, all the anger she had wanted to unleash but hadn't, came rolling down on her—suffocating her. Her knees buckled, but he held her firmly and would not let her sink to the stones below. She bunched the back of his coat tightly in both fists and pounded on his back with waning strength.

"Oh, dear god, he's gone," she sobbed into his shirt, thinking he couldn't understand. She had finally consented to spend the rest of her life with Tomas and now he was gone. "I promised . . . I promised."

"I'm so sorry, sweetheart," Master Gryph's deep voice rumbled with emotion. "Kyne told me what happened. No matter how much I wish I had the power to change the unchangeable the fact remains—I cannot. But I do promise you this—there will be retribution for Tomas' murder. I demand it." He lifted her chin and made her look at him. His face couldn't get any angrier. He gripped her hard. "I demand it."

Chapter Sixteen

"Marguerite, how did you do it?" Elhrin asked, finally breaking the long but comfortable silence between them. The two ladies sat alone on a covered terrace that ran along the central portion of Marmuht's mayoral mansion facing the bay. The hour was late, and the numerous lights of the city below seemed to be competing with the reflection of the half-moon on the bay to see which could sparkle brighter.

Marguerite sighed, shifting Marcus, who was sleeping peacefully in her arms, to a more comfortable position. She didn't have to ask what Elhrin was talking about—she already knew. "It wasn't easy, sweetheart. Losing someone you love is never easy. I just took one day at a time—and made it through. Having you and Bayle and my friends helped, but it never replaces that part of you that has been ripped away."

"I keep going back over it again and again, trying to see what I could have done differently," Elhrin whispered.

"Elhrin, don't do that to yourself. It won't change anything, and the needless guilt will consume you. Gryph is doing it, too, and you both need to stop."

Elhrin glanced at Marguerite, wondering how the woman remained so strong through the seemingly endless trials of her life. Many would have given in to depression and despair and gone through the rest of their life bitter and blaming the world. Not Marguerite. The woman had endured fight after fight, the many injuries and the death of her husband, the murder of a brother for whom Marcus was named, and the attempt on her own life and the abduction of her son. Elhrin decided right then and there, Marguerite was who she wanted to emulate. She would never get over the senseless death of Tomas, but she was not going to sit around and be useless because of it. He would not want her to.

"Marguerite, thank you," she said and smiled slightly. The act felt foreign to her face, and she realized that the last time she had smiled was at Tomas. Somehow, that gave her a small sense of comfort.

Marguerite smiled down at Marcus. "No, dear, I am the one who has to thank you."

"Not me, Marguerite. Kyne is the hero." *And thank the light for King Goruth insisting on him being in my life,* she admitted silently to herself. If it had not been for him Marcus would be dead, too.

"You all are heroes," Marguerite said softly as voices drifted out of the open doors behind them, coming from the mansion's westernmost common sitting room for several adjacent bedrooms, including the room she now shared with Bayle, and the one belonging to Master Gryph and Marguerite.

The men had returned. Master Gryph, Kyne, Landin, Grey, Griffyn, and Bayle, who was now designated as Master Gryph's personal assistant, had attended a dinner meeting to discuss preparations that were already underway to defend Anderan against the invasion. They had dined with Mayor Nambacus—who happened to be Kyne's uncle on his father's side—Prince Cahail, General Shifwood, Admiral Zoscalese, and other key members of the military and the city's council. She had been obligated to sit in on the meeting, as well, but had asked if she could forego the meal and stay behind to be with Marguerite and Marcus. She didn't feel up to conversation with anyone at the moment, and Master Gryph had understood and said he would fill her in on the details when he returned.

A few minutes later, Master Gryph limped out onto the terrace. "Good evening, ladies," he said as he placed a kiss on Marguerite's cheek, lightly touched the top of Marcus' sleeping head, and then kissed the top of Elhrin's head when he passed her chair. He settled tiredly in the chair next to her, propping his staff on the low terrace wall by his side. "How was your evening?"

"After checking in on the students it has been wonderfully peaceful," Marguerite answered. Because of lack of space in the mansion, Grey, Landin, and the rest of the students were given quarters in two prominent homes across the street from the mansion. Elhrin, Marguerite, and Marcus had ensured Marissa and Clay and everyone else was settled into their accommodations and all questions were answered before the three returned to dine alone in the sitting room behind them. The only interruptions came from the mayor's wife who had stopped by to make sure they were comfortable and the household servants delivering their meal and preparing their rooms for the night.

He grimaced. "I wish I could say the same."

"Why? What happened?" Marguerite asked.

"Arguments . . . many, many arguments. Prince Cahail and General Shifwood are butting heads like two angry goats," he said, then yawned loud enough for it to echo off the garden walls below the terrace.

"Gryph, be quiet, you'll wake Marcus," she reprimanded him.

"I apologize, my love. I will keep my yawning to a minimal roar." He smiled fondly at his son.

"Please do," she said. "I thought I heard others with you."

"You did, but they left. Bayle, Kyne, and our other young men have plans for the evening. They stopped by for money. I told them the night was on me."

"Did Griffyn go with them?"

"No, he needed to get back to his ship. He said he had a busy day tomorrow and will try to see us again tomorrow evening."

"So the boys are going out?" She narrowed her eyes at him. "Just what kind of plans do they have that you are willing to paying for?" she asked with a hint of suspicious disapproval.

"Plans that are none of our business," he responded with a twinkle in his eye. "They deserve the break."

"I know they do, but I hope their plans do not involve . . . ," she waved a hand, "trouble, because if that happens, then the trouble will be your responsibility. You know how Bayle can get out of hand, and I'm sure he has already had a few glasses of wine, hasn't he?"

"He may have. I don't monitor the boy, Marguerite."

"Where did you get the staff?" Elhrin asked, interrupting the conversation before Marguerite became angry. Even though Bayle was twenty-one, Marguerite didn't like it when he went out with the boys. He tended to drink too much too fast and get into trouble like she said, but Elhrin had to agree with Master Gryph, Kyne especially, deserved a night of relaxation.

"You like it?" he asked. "Landin carved it from a black walnut branch he found near the Green River."

"Can I see it?" she asked.

He picked it up, and handed it to her. The wood had a beautiful dark grain, and she could see that Landin had used the natural shape of the limb to find the inspiration for the eagle's head on top. The detail was impressive. "He found it near the Green River? I only know of one place that had walnut trees and those were destroyed."

She and Bayle knew the Green River well and had traveled its length for miles in either direction from Glimmerdale throughout their childhood. As young children, they collected the walnuts from the few trees that grew along the banks of the river where Master Gryph had died during the surprise Do'athrim attack, and those trees had been destroyed in his explosion when he succumbed to the poison that rendered him immobile. She knew of no others.

"Ironic, isn't it?" he smiled, confirming the location was the same spot.

"Fitting, is the word that comes to my mind," she said, handing the staff back to him. "I guess I can't put this off any longer. Am I in trouble for leaving Muryne?"

"Why would you think you were?" he asked. "I asked you to go."

"I know you did, but like you, I have a sworn duty to defend Anderan and its people."

"Yes, you do, but since you were doing something on my behalf, the responsibility for your absence is my burden to bear. We need to discuss this no further," he said, firmly.

"Yes, sir," she said, knowing she should drop the subject when he used that tone of voice. "Can you tell me what happened? You don't know how hard it was to leave you once again, knowing you were outnumbered."

He smoothed his beard and took a deep breath. "I survived this time," he said with a hint of a smile.

"Thank you for pointing out the obvious," she said with an impatient frown. "I know you survived, I know the city was damaged, and I know Derrick Idwyr lost some of his best N'gethwyn in the fight. What I don't know are the details."

He glanced at his wife instead of answering her. "Marguerite, she has become pushy, hasn't she?" he asked, and Elhrin knew he was just trying to lighten the mood after a long emotional day of joyous reunions and listening to the difficult details of their battles recounted by Kyne, Marissa, and Griffyn.

"No, she is just trying to get an old man to answer her with a straight answer for a change," Marguerite said as she shifted Marcus to her shoulder and stood up. "I think Marcus and I will retire so you two can talk. Good night, dear." Marguerite slipped a hand onto Elhrin's shoulder and squeezed it affectionately.

Elhrin clasped Marguerite's hand and squeezed back. "Good night."

"Don't you two stay up too late," she called over her shoulder as she disappeared into the mansion.

"Elhrin," Master Gryph said quietly, "the details of that fight do not matter. What matters is that Obsudius has been using Derrick and no telling who else to bring hundreds of Do'athrim and some N'gethwyn into this country and hiding them without our knowledge in the wildernesses. And the sad fact is, there is not one damn thing we can do to prevent it from happening. We just do not have the manpower to patrol every inch of the countryside and they know it. I am afraid that no matter the outcome of this invasion, they have set a precedent that will remain in Anderan from now on unless we can somehow take firm control of the situation."

"What do you mean?" she asked, slightly confused.

"Do not compare the Do'athrim we are hearing about and the ones we will face with those we fought years ago. These creatures are not coming through rifts out of Do'athra, the Realm of Darkness. They are from a living population that Obsudius has been raising for who knows how long, possibly hundreds of years."

"And you know this how?" she asked.

"Well, why don't you think about it for a moment, and see if you can come to a conclusion without me telling you."

"Why don't you save time and just tell me?" she asked, wishing he wouldn't do this right now. He was in the teaching mode he used on her occasionally, preparing her for the day when she would be the one who would have to answer questions for others. He wanted her to be able to think for herself.

He raised his eyebrows, saying nothing. He was not going to budge.

"Fine," she sighed, giving in. She sifted through what she knew. "Obsudius cannot open another large rift like the one at Blackridge Keep for possibly hundreds of years from now, so he is limited in his use of the portals. Which, by the way, I wish he couldn't use at all."

"I will agree with you there," he said.

"That means he has to choose wisely how he uses them. He will want to conserve energy." She thought for a moment. "Derrick jumped into a rift." Her voice caught in her throat at the reminder of the day she lost Tomas. "He is using them to get across the world, isn't he?"

"He is, but you are off subject. We will discuss him later." He stroked his mustache, waiting on her to continue.

"Okay, so Obsudius cannot open large rifts frequently, but he can open small ones. Over time, that would add up to a lot of Do'athrim in the world, but that would be energy draining, so it would stand to reason that natural reproduction would be more practical. He wouldn't have to do anything. Just wait. Now how do you know?" She stared out over the bay as she turned things over in her mind, discarding the useless information, and she wasn't coming up with anything except she couldn't get past the part concerning the rifts Obsudius opened. Something about the concept bothered her. "You told me to not compare these beasts with those from Blackridge." She glanced at him. "What happened to the Do'athrim in Muryne?"

"They were killed," he answered.

"I gathered that. I mean their bodies."

"They were buried in a mass grave far out in the countryside."

"So they did not disintegrate when they died like those from Blackridge which proves they were living beings."

She shook her head, thinking that even though she lived through the events surrounding the Do'athrim War, witnessed Obsudius' portals with her own eyes more than once, that it was a truly possible and very real concept. It was so confusing—living beings traveling through the realms of the dead, dead beings coming through portals giving life . . . taking life away.

"Master Gryph, how is it that Obsudius can overlook important details if he wants his plans to exterminate the human population to be successful?"

A corner of his mouth lifted beneath the hand he was using to stroke his mustache telling her she was heading in the direction he wanted her to go.

"What makes you think he cannot make errors?" he asked.

"He is a god, after all, and I just don't see how he has unfathomable power and can do amazing yet evil things, but be capable of forgetting important details like setting a condition within the magical makeup of his portal to keep his warriors alive after it closes?"

"I think I have explained before that Obsudius and Solisius are limited gods and that they are not perfect." He lowered his hand with a near silent sigh. "That being said, I am afraid I am going to have to beg for your forgiveness on this one. When I explained what happened that day outside of the keep, I told all of you that I was making a guess in my reasoning. I had no choice but to tell you at the time that I was guessing. I wasn't. I know the truth. He cannot set that kind of condition. Once a rift closes, all who had been dead before, die again and their bodies return to the earth."

She frowned at him, finding his words hard to grasp. "If that is so, then how is Grom's body still intact? You killed him long ago when I was a child and again on our way to Blackridge. He was one of the dead brought to life again by Obsudius' rift."

"I thought so, too, which is why I am surprised as much as you are by the fact his body is still on this earth." He unbuttoned his coat to get more comfortable.

"Have you spoken to Solisius about this?"

"Of course, and he is silent on the subject."

She nodded, thinking that sounded about right. This was one of those mysteries that they might never know the answer to unless they stumbled upon it themselves.

"You know from experience that a rift closing on a dead being will kill them again." She uncrossed her legs and leaned forward in her chair, propping her elbows on her knees. Here was something else he had been keeping from them. "Please explain this to me. Does this rule apply to a being from the Realm of Light, too?"

"It does."

"Then just how are you sitting here before me right now?" He had purposely told them a lie about the rift that day in his explanation and she wanted to know why.

"Because Solisius has not yet closed the rift I came through."

She felt the blood drain from her face. "How?" she whispered. "It has been nearly five years since your return. I thought a rift couldn't be maintained for a long time."

"A large one cannot, and opening and closing rifts on a continuous basis increases that fact even further because ripping through the two planes drains a vast amount of energy. But Solisius has never used his powers for such an energy-draining feat, so holding onto one small one after that initial drain will not hinder him for quite some time. Now, that's not to say he could hold it forever, but my lifespan is on the short end at this point, is it not?"

She was not about to answer that question. "Where is it?" she asked hoarsely.

"Well hidden. Only I know where it is, and it will remain that way. No one, including you and Marguerite, will ever know its location."

"It has to be somewhere in the Northreach Mountains. That was where we met you."

He crossed his arms over his chest. "One would think."

And that meant the portal into Ts'aura was not anywhere near there. A memory flashed through her mind from long ago. When he was dead—in Ts'aura, he had visited her in dreams—or something like dreams. The last visit before he returned through Solisius' rift, he had told her he would not be seeing her for awhile. That was because he was going to be traveling. She shook her head. The information was almost too much to bear.

"Does Marguerite know about the rift?"

He nodded.

"It's good to know you aren't keeping secrets from someone."

"I had my reasons for telling her."

She didn't like the sound of that. "Can you tell me?"

"I am a living dead man walking the earth, Elhrin—an anomaly that should not be, but I do only by the grace of my god. Marguerite has endured far more than any person should in one lifetime, and as much as I would like to keep one more worry from her mind, I could not let this remain a secret. She needed to understand what would happen if the rift closed for any reason."

A wave of fear rolled over her. He would turn to a pile of dust in an instant. "Why would Solisius need to close it?"

"If Obsudius knew there was an opening into Ts'aura what would you think he would do?"

"He would have his N'gethwyn hunt it down," she replied, horrified.

"Exactly," he responded, "which is why I will never reveal its location to anyone, even you."

"If you wanted this kept secret, why are you telling me now?"

He sighed. "Because of Tomas."

That answer was unexpected. Her stomach clenched in a knot from the grief that wanted to surface at the mere mention of his name.

"I did not want you to start thinking of the possibility that Solisius could do for Tomas what he did for me. I don't want you to waste your life looking down each road, hoping to see him one day. It will not happen."

Tears sprang into her eyes. She did not realize it, but subconsciously she must have been wishing for that very thing. She swallowed past the lump in her throat. "I know," she whispered.

"I'm sorry, sweetheart, I wish I could make it better for you." He reached over and clasped her hand. She squeezed it tightly, feeling the warmth from him—his solid realness. It seemed impossible that he was alive but dead at the same time.

She cleared her throat. "So, if one small rift can be maintained over a long period of time, why doesn't Obsudius do it? I'm sure it would take a bit longer to assemble a sizeable force like the one at Blackridge, but it could be done, right?"

"Yes, it could be done if he chose to do so." He squeezed her hand one last time then leaned back in his chair, breaking their contact. She wished he hadn't. The hurting little girl inside her wished he would hold her hand all night. She needed the comfort. "However, one small rift would not suit Obsudius. He wouldn't be able to move the portal if he wanted his subjects to stay alive."

"If he was concerned with them staying alive, why would he choose to openly engage in a war? Even if they win this initial onslaught, the rest of the country will fight to exterminate them. Their numbers would be depleted. Why risk it?"

"A good question and one I do not have a good answer to," he said with a hint of frustration.

She stared out over the water, trying to make sense of it all. "Where is Obsudius breeding his pets?"

"I am guessing Scathlamahn. It may not be the only place they are breeding, but it is a large remote island no human is interested in exploring much less settling which makes it perfect for his plans. The ships that will be carrying Derrick's invading force were spotted anchored off its coast."

She leaned back in her chair and crossed her legs. "How long do we have before the invasion?" she asked.

"Reports say it is to coincide with the full moon," he glanced up at the sky. "I'd say around a week."

"How can we be sure?"

"We can't, that's why Admiral Zoscalese has ships patrolling the coast and has his fastest ships scouting about two or three days out to sea to watch for any sign of the enemy fleet." Since he was facing to the side, something caught his eye inside the mansion behind her. She looked over her shoulder in time to see a servant move past one of the three open doors. "Mayor Nambacus informed us tonight that the Chyrzinians are also out to sea. They don't want to take the chance they are the target instead of us."

"Do you know where they are planning to land?" she asked, turning back to face him.

He kept watching the servant move about the room behind her and didn't answer her question. She heard the servant step out onto the terrace.

"Minister, would you and the lady care for refreshments?" the young man asked. Tall and lanky, he had on the livery of the male kitchen serving staff—a white starched shirt and vest, and gray trousers over polished black-buckled shoes.

"I do not. Elhrin, do you?"

"No."

"It appears we are fine for the evening, son," he answered. "If we need anything, we will let you know. Please inform the staff I am in a private meeting for the rest of the night and do not wish to be disturbed."

"Yes, sir." He bowed his head slightly in respect and disappeared back into the mansion.

Master Gryph studied his surroundings for a moment then picked up his staff. "Elhrin, come with me," he said without explanation.

She expected him to enter the sitting room, but he walked down the length of the terrace and entered one of the passageways that led into the interior of the mansion instead. The center structure of the mayoral mansion was built in a square around a central open-air courtyard. Two wide passageways on either side of the main structure ran from the terrace through the central courtyard and continued on to dual entrances in the front of the building. Wide double-doors at each entrance were kept open on warm, clear days to capture any breeze that drifted up from the bay.

"I don't think you have had the chance to see Mayor Nambacus' library, have you?" he asked as he turned down the central courtyard's covered walk. Potted palms and exotic plants with bright orange flowers surrounding the courtyard's decorative fish pond trembled as unseen air currents shifted their glossy leaves.

"No, not yet," she said, thinking the mansion was overly quiet even though the hour was late. She was accustomed to the nonstop activity of the palace in Muryne where people were up at all hours of the day. Here, there were very few people traveling the halls.

He smiled as he held open a door to an interior hall. "I think you might like it."

They entered a long, empty hallway lit by brass oil lamps. Their footsteps penetrated the wall of silence, sounding like drum beats as they trod over hard tiles of deep orange, almost brown in color that had been molded from the same clay as the bricks that were used in the construction of most of Marmuht's buildings. He then turned down a short side hall and led her to the set of double-doors at its end. He opened the one on the right, which swung into the room, and waited for her to enter first.

"Impressive," she commented, strolling into the shadowy, two-story room. Only two lamps were lit, one on a central table filled with several stacks of books and another somewhere on the second floor above her, casting its dim glow on the high ceiling.

With a wave of her hand she lit the rest of the room's lamps with her magic. Immediately, the library was filled with warm light. She turned in a slow circle to take it all in. The room held thousands of books in floor-to-ceiling bookcases and cabinets lining almost every wall. A staircase with wrought iron railings at the back of the room rose to a wide balcony where there were tables and chairs for reading along with more shelves filled to capacity with books of various colors and sizes. It didn't surprise her that he wanted to come here. Being in a room filled with books was paradise for him.

"It is second only to the library at the University in Gildas," he said as he limped over to a cabinet with glass doors that held hundreds of tightly rolled parchments inside. "Mayor Nambacus is passionate about books and education. He has added extensively to this library during his tenure as mayor. He collects books from all over the world, and he has his own reproduction company so that he can produce copies to share with others."

Elhrin crossed to one of the nearby bookcases. "Is he the one that sends you books on a regular basis?" His own library in Glimmerdale was impressive. When he had rebuilt his home he had added a room for his books, but because he collected so many, the room ended up being too small which meant the next project he intended to complete for the Glimmerdale Academy, after a dining hall and dormitories, was a library.

"He is one of many," he replied absently as he opened the doors to the cabinet and perused the parchments.

She heard something move on the second floor. Instantly on guard, she eased further into the room so she could see the balcony above her. A dark head quickly ducked low out of her sight, hiding.

"Hello?" she called out.

Caught, the deeply tanned face of a young girl rose into view and peered at her through the railing of the balcony.

"Um, hello," the girl said sheepishly. She pushed herself up from her belly and sat back on her knees.

"Hello," Elhrin said again with a smile.

Dressed in a night robe with her sleek ebony hair pulled up behind her head in a ponytail, the young girl appeared no older than thirteen or fourteen. "My father doesn't like for couples to use his library," she stated, obviously misunderstanding their reason for entering the library.

Elhrin burst into laughter at the notion.

The girl frowned at her. "I'm serious," she said.

"We are not here for that reason," Elhrin said, knowing the girl could not see Master Gryph who was noisily rustling through the scrolls in the cabinet, and not paying attention to their conversation.

"Oh," the girl said.

Picking up a book from the floor beside her, she stood up. She then tucked the book under her arm and hurried to the stairway. "Are you looking for anything in particular?" she asked as she jogged down the stairs. "Because I know where most everything is."

"I think he is." Elhrin pointed to Master Gryph.

The girl's eyes widened at the sight of him. "Minister Idwyr!" she squealed in delight and rushed over to him.

Master Gryph turned when he heard his name. "Hello there, young lady," he said, as the girl flung her arms around him as if she knew him well. Elhrin had witnessed this kind of scene thousands of times. Children flocked to him wherever he went, and once again the hurting girl inside her wished for something that could not be—the worry-free days of her childhood past in Glimmerdale when she could climb into his lap and have him tell her a story.

"Father said you were here, but you were busy and I couldn't bother you," she said.

"Tell your father I always have a minute to spare for you." He tugged playfully at her ponytail. "Aren't you supposed to be in bed?"

"I couldn't sleep and I wanted to get this," she said as she produced the book in her hand. "It's the works of Shelvar Missoulaigne."

"Excellent choice," he approved with a wink, "you will enjoy *Birdsong on the Water's Edge*. I think it is near the end."

"I will read it first," she smiled. "Do you need help finding something?"

"As a matter of fact, if you can help me find a map of the Veihl Coast I would be indebted to you."

"Oh, that's right here," she said. She pulled a map from its cubbyhole near the bottom corner of the cabinet and handed it to him.

"Now that is amazing," he chuckled. "I would have spent hours looking through all those maps. Well then, what do you require as payment?"

She grinned broadly. "You know."

"Aren't you getting a touch too old for this?" he asked.

"Never," she said excitedly. "Please, Minister."

"Elhrin, let me introduce you to Nambacus' daughter Marisel?" he chuckled. "She has a passion for flying." He picked the girl up with his magic. The girl giggled with delight as she soared high above the room. She spread her arms wide like a bird and soared over the room several times before he finally brought her down gently to the floor.

"That was wonderful, Minister Idwyr," she said breathlessly as if she had done all the flying herself. She gave him another hug. "Thank you."

"You are quite welcome," he said. "Now off to bed with you. Miss Elhrin and I have some work to do."

"Yes, sir." Marisel scampered to the door. "It was nice to meet you, Miss Elhrin."

"You, too," Elhrin said, as the young girl smiled then closed the door behind her.

Elhrin moved to the table in the center of the room and picked up a book with flowers and unusual letters embossed on its leather cover. Curious, she opened it to look inside. Delicate whorls, slashes, and dots made up the written language and there were colorful hand-painted, detailed diagrams of various plants throughout the book's pages.

"Are you interested in Goltivias horticulture?" Master Gryph asked as he moved the books on the table to the side and rolled out the map of the southern coast of Anderan.

"You can read this?" she asked, looking up from the book and noticing he had put on eyeglasses. "When did you get those?"

He peered at her over his glasses. "Which question would you like for me to answer first?"

"The eyeglasses, please." She snapped the book shut and set it down on the table.

"Doctor Dryke suggested I give them a try for reading before we left Muryne," he said as he placed books on the corners of the map to keep it from rolling back up.

"I wondered when you would finally start wearing a pair. You have been pushing everything so far away from you I thought you were going to have to hire another assistant just to stand across the room and hold things up for you to read."

"I wasn't that bad," he protested.

"Yes, you were. Marguerite said one day that you needed arms as long as your legs to read, but you refused to admit it," she grinned, thinking how good it felt to joke with him again. "So, you can read this?" She tapped the book's cover.

"I can," he said with a hint of a smile, "the glasses have special powers that give me the ability to read in any language."

"They do not," she laughed.

He chuckled. "No, they don't, but I do know several languages, and one of them is the Goltivias language."

"Is there anything you don't know?"

"Unfortunately, yes," he lost his smile, "and they are the things I need to know the most."

She understood his mind was back on their task ahead, but she was not ready to go in that direction just yet. Marguerite had filled her in on all the details since the day she had boarded Captain Ostied's ship and left Muryne, and she wanted to know more about the battle he had with his students.

"Marguerite told me about the intense training session you put the students through on your way here. Do you think you got your point across?" she asked.

"I think they finally understand the seriousness of what they face and no longer think it is a fun and exciting adventure," he said, placing both palms on the table and perusing the map of the Veihl Coast. "They have worked hard at coming together as a team since then."

"I wish I had been there to witness it," she said. "Marguerite said you created an illusion so real, she thought you were going to kill them."

"As you know, illusion can be very effective if you do it right," he said, knowing the both of them had the ability to conjure realistic looking images if they desired.

"Did she know that their attacks against you were not illusion?" she asked. Marguerite had said the students were forced to fight back. "They could have killed you if you had made a mistake."

"She did, and understood it had to be done. They needed the experience," he commented as he pointed to a spot on the map. He wasn't going to avoid why they came to the library any longer. "Here is the Bay of Marmuht and right here, outside of its mouth, is Brackenwood Cove. This is where I believe the landfall will be made."

She leaned over the map for a better look. The Southern Veihl Coast stretched hundreds of leagues from the Bay of Marmuht all the way to the village of Kit along the western shore.

"How can you be sure? There are hundreds of leagues of coast along southern and western Anderan, and why not Marmuht itself?"

"Marmuht is easily defended from the waterfront and is not a good landing site if you want thousands of troops on the ground before you launch an offensive assault. The beaches are not wide and would limit movement, even with a formidable N'gethwyn force. The better option would be to march overland and attack from the city's western side where it is the most vulnerable. And in order for that to happen, Derrick would need to get close to Marmuht but be far enough away for his fleet to disembark onto our shores without immediate conflict if possible. There are only two places large enough for a landing in the area, and I have ruled out the other site because of the time it would take to reach the city. I am sure Derrick would not want to give Marmuht enough time to fortify if they were discovered marching across the countryside." He tapped the map near the Bay of Marmuht. "No, I think I'm right about Brackenwood Cove. It is large enough and fairly sheltered by the cliffs on its sides which will reduce the size of the surf coming onto the beach and allow the boats closer to shore. The beach itself is wide and blends into a meadow leading up from the cove which makes it the perfect spot for a landing of this scale. You and I are going to take our team out tomorrow to look it over. Prince Cahail and General Shifwood may be joining us."

Elhrin frowned. She was not looking forward to being in Prince Cahail's presence. The man wasn't fond of persons with magical powers and had acted like he hated her the short time she was in Tuhnichi during the summer. "I know your instincts usually are right, but what if you are wrong this time? We will be unprepared."

"Elhrin, Councilor Shulftar told me that Derrick's men were to take Marcus to Brackenwood Manor on the coast of the Veihl Sea." He peered at her over his spectacles. "Brackenwood Manor does not exist. Never has. There are only small farms scattered about the area. I don't think it was by chance that Derrick specifically gave her the name Brackenwood Manor. I think he had a purpose for it."

"But wouldn't bringing a large fleet this close to a port city be risky? It would be spotted right away, wouldn't it?"

"It wouldn't matter at that point if we had not been forewarned. Their fleet would have outnumbered any naval defense we could have assembled, and all Marmuht could have hoped to do would be to shut down the walled part of the interior city and prepare for invasion. No one from neighboring cities would have been able to make it here in time to help."

"But the city is now preparing for invasion. What if Derrick knows we have been warned and changes his focus of attack or thinks of something else altogether?"

"Anything is possible, but he has his reasons for choosing this area, and I have no reason at this point to believe he will not follow through with his plans. However, if he does, then we will have to adapt quickly and do whatever we can to stop him."

She frowned at the map, not liking the odds that were against them—too many variables to consider and too much land to cover. "I find it bizarre that he is related to you." She glanced up at him, finding his bright blue eyes were fixed on her and waiting for her to continue. His eyes held no hate or malice whatsoever . . . so different. "He is nothing like you. His source is more polluted and evil than any N'gethwyn's that I've ever felt, including Cynder's."

His gaze dropped to the map, and he nodded in agreement, but said nothing.

"Did you know that he can hide his energy source?"

His gaze rose sharply to meet hers once again. "Are you finally ready to talk to me about that day?" he asked, knowing she had personally evaded reliving the events earlier to buy herself a little more time from thinking about Tomas.

"Yes," she swallowed hard, a picture of Tomas' passion-filled face when they were in the darkened passageway outside of the captain's cabin flashed through her mind. "The day Derrick rammed his ship into us I kept feeling a strong energy source that would come and go, and I thought at first I was mistaken because I had never considered before that day it was possible to hide a source of energy. Then right before the ships collided, his source flooded my awareness and it did not go away until he jumped into the rift."

He stood up straight and pulled his glasses from his face. "You are sure about this?"

"Yes, sir," she said.

He narrowed his eyes in thought, studying her face. "Did Ostied tell you that he suspected Derrick tried to kill me when we were young?" he asked after a moment.

"He did," she said, wondering how he could deduce that from what she just said.

"And from this story you came up with the idea that Derrick could hide his energy source?"

"Yes," she said with a shrug of her shoulders. "How else could he get close to you without you knowing he was there? Captain Ostied wouldn't lie, would he?"

"No, he wouldn't lie to you," he tilted his head back and stared at the balcony above them. Then with a heavy sigh, he picked up his staff leaning against the table beside him and limped to a nearby chair. He lowered himself into the hard seat and gave her a look that told her he already knew about Derrick's ability.

Once again, her anger towards his secretive ways started to bubble inside like a volcano preparing to erupt. She pressed her lips together, then huffed in exasperation, "You knew . . . why would you keep this from me?" She gritted her teeth against the desire to yell at him. "What reason could you possibly have? Did you ever consider I might run across him someday? Do you remotely trust me?"

"Explicitly," he said.

Giving in to her anger, she slapped a hand onto the Goltivias book. "Then why?" she implored.

"I will make no excuses," he stated. "Like so many things I have unwisely not done, this is one of them. Understand that I am a private person and have been trained most of my life to withhold secrets."

"But . . . ," she started to protest, but he held up a hand to still her.

"Like I said, I do not offer that as an excuse, Elhrin. I am only stating it as a fact of what is and who I am," he said. "I do not frivolously offer details of my life to anyone, even Marguerite, which you now understand has to happen sometimes in order to protect her and others I love. Yes, I should have told you from the start about Derrick and the fact he is an N'gethwyn, but I did not, and maybe I was not supposed to tell you before . . . I just don't know why. That is the bare simple truth. I can, and no doubt will many times before I leave this realm, make mistakes. Such is the way of being human."

She stared at him openmouthed, astounded. "But you left me," she pressed her hands to her temples, trying not to cry in frustration. "You left me unprepared. Tomas is dead and I could not . . . I was not prepared. He was the one, wasn't he? He was who you suspected in Muryne behind all those murders but wouldn't reveal to me when you said you ruled him out, wasn't he?"

"Yes."

"Then if you knew he could hide his source, why would you rule him out?"

"One, I did not know he could, and two, I had not considered that Obsudius was moving him around the world by using Do'athra as a stepping stone until I interviewed Idora. The pieces fell into place after you left Muryne."

He didn't know? How could he not know? Slowly, her anger evaporated. "You didn't know before I left?"

He smiled sadly. "I didn't know about Derrick having the ability to hide his source, which explains why I never was able to hunt him down easily after he ran away from home permanently, but I did know he was N'gethwyn and a potential suspect. Saying sorry to you for not confiding in you long ago when I admit I should have would not make up for the wrong I have done you. I will spend an eternity regretting having hurt you, but we have to move on from this and work on the conflict ahead of us."

"Yes, sir," she sighed, knowing he was right. Holding onto what should have been was not helping with what was, and she was not going to blame him for Tomas' death. Like Solisius said, it was Tomas' time to go, and that fact would not have changed even if she had known every last detail about Derrick and his abilities. "Do you know how a source can be hidden?"

"No, I do not. I've tried, but the technique eludes me. I'm afraid it may be another unique ability that is specific to an individual and cannot be learned. However, if you ever find that is not the case, let me know."

"I can't imagine not being able to have contact with my energy source. I would think it would be like cutting off an arm."

"It is very much like that," he said.

She moved around the table and leaned back against its hard edge, knowing he referred to the time he was poisoned with Uihrian Serum. It had paralyzed him and snuffed out his energy source causing him to lose control of his magic before he succumbed to death.

"If I asked you about your relationship with Derrick, would you tell me?"

He looked away without answering. The library was deafeningly silent with the exception of a clock ticking somewhere behind her. She was about to give up on him and ask another question when he finally spoke.

"We were close as children," he said quietly, unable to keep the hurt out of his voice, "inseparable." His lips twitched, almost smiling as he remembered his past. "Leaving the house well before dawn many times to get out of chores, and coming home to an angry father who spoke fire but never laid a hand on us and a forgiving mother who adored her boys, especially Derrick, her baby." He sighed. "But our relationship started to change after we came into our powers and grew into our teenage years."

"Why?"

He shifted in his seat to a more comfortable position and leaned his staff back, resting its length against his shoulder. "Everything turned into a competition with Derrick, no matter what I did, he wanted to do better. Whoever I had as friends, he wanted them for himself. And when I broke the news I was leaving for Muryne to study with Odrun Jorme, he stormed out of the house and took my father's fishing boat out into the marshes. We hunted for him for days with no luck, but he eventually came back home on his own much to my mother's relief."

"He hid his powers from you then?"

"I suppose he could have. Back in those days I didn't know how to recognize and follow an energy source, but even still, I always seemed to know when Derrick was nearby. That was why I dismissed Ostied's claims that Derrick was in the woods the day the fort collapsed."

"What happened after he came back home?"

"He hated me and that hate never left." He swiped a hand across his mouth and chin, smoothing his mustache and beard down. "He accused me of taking his place as Odrun's apprentice—that the minister had come to our home for him, and I had somehow swayed the man to accept me instead. The fact was Odrun knew I was So'ladiun and had come to Pago Duhn specifically for me. When he met Derrick, he knew he was N'gethwyn or soon would be, and he refused to train him. I never told Derrick I had tried to sway Odrun to allow him to come, too. I even threatened that I would not go if he didn't let Derrick come, but Odrun was adamant and said it was my choice not to come, but he would not train Derrick."

"And then there was the girl," she said.

He nodded slowly. "And then there was Lynh," he sighed. "I failed to see, or maybe just failed to let myself see, how he felt about her. I have to admit I was a typical teenage boy caught up in his own affairs. Marguerite thinks Bayle is feisty." He hiked one eyebrow up high. "It is a good thing she did not know me then."

"Then Derrick did catch you being, uh, intimate with the woman he loved," she said, slightly embarrassed to bring up something so personal.

"According to Ostied he did, but I never saw him there," he said eyeing her. "That was the first of only two times she and I were intimate. Both of which were mistakes and the result of emotions going too far."

She smiled slightly. "Do you consider Griffyn a mistake?"

He shook his head. "No, I suppose I do not."

"You know, I never asked you about the time when Odrun Jorme first told you were So'ladiun. How did you take it?"

He lifted a corner of his mouth. "Well . . . ," he drawled the word out.

"Oh ho, not well, did you, Master Idwyr?"

"No, it was not a pleasant day for me," he agreed. "I admit I took the news far less graciously than you."

"At least, he wasn't a ghost when he told you," she pointed out.

"Again, who said I was a ghost at the time?"

"Me, for lack of a better word."

He chuckled.

"Did he tell you that Derrick would be N'gethwyn or did you figure it out later?"

His smiled faded. "He told me. That was a hard day, as well. He predicted the day would come when I would be forced to kill Derrick or be killed by him."

"How old were you?"

"Mm, nineteen or so," he said, staring at the tip of his staff resting on his boot.

Elhrin's heart wept for him. She could not fathom being told such news concerning Bayle and wondered how he managed to live with the knowledge that Odrun's prediction may come to pass soon.

"You said he ran away from home. You never saw him again?"

"Only once, years later—when I retrieved the crystal for your pendant."

She touched the bulge of the gem under her shirt. "What happened?"

He pursed his lips in thought. "I have never told this story to anyone except

Marguerite," he said, hesitantly. He closed his eyes briefly at the memory, and she could tell he warred with his emotions.

"I was just outside of Bram's Well, on my way back home to Glimmerdale," he said, finally, "when I felt the foul black energy source of an N'gethwyn. When he stepped in the middle of the road to face me . . . I was shocked to find it was Derrick. To this day I do not know how he knew I would be alone on that particular road at that particular time, but he did. He didn't waste any time attacking me. He wanted to show me how powerful he had become and that he was no longer the little brother who hid in my shadow. We fought a long time. He is indeed powerful, but I was stronger and I tried everything I could to keep from hurting him. He was still my brother, and I had made a promise to my mother to . . . ," he blew out a long pensive breath, not finishing his thought. "But he was relentless and had every intention of killing me that day."

"What did you do?"

"I stabbed him. He was not expecting a non-magical attack. It was enough to put him down but ended up not being enough to kill him. He wanted me to finish the fight and I should have, but I didn't—I couldn't. I walked away, and now we are faced with this."

Unexpectedly, the door to the library flew open and banged hard against a bookshelf. A couple entangled in each other's arms fell to the floor with drunken laughter. The woman, who had landed on top of the man, pushed herself to her knees revealing two bulbous ivory breasts draped on the outside of her bodice.

Shocked, Elhrin's face flamed in embarrassment, not because she was seeing the woman's nudity, but because she was in Master Gryph's presence and they were both seeing it at the same time.

The woman pushed a handful of tangled blonde hair off to one side of her face where it had spilled from her hairpins. "I've got you where I want you now," she slurred as she leaned over to offer her lover one of her exposed breasts.

Wide-eyed, Elhrin glanced at Master Gryph. He appeared unfazed by the scene.

"I beg your pardon, Madam, should we leave?" he asked without concern, as if he and Elhrin were the ones who had walked in on a private affair.

The woman shrieked in surprise at the unexpected voice and scrambled off of the man. "Minister! Oh, my god!" she cried in shock when she recognized him, having the decency to cover her bosoms with one arm while trying to drag her bodice back into position. She failed miserably and finally gave up, covering her breasts with both arms and crumpling over to shield herself from his stare.

Her lover tilted his head back to see who was in the room with them.

"Bayle!" Elhrin hissed and should have known it was her foolish brother hidden underneath a silly green hat squashed on his head.

Bayle grinned drunkenly as he stared at her upside down. "Hello, sishter," he slurred. "Hello, Mashter Gryph."

Master Gryph grasped his eagle staff and planted it on the hard tiles of the floor with enough force to echo the sharp contact throughout the room, belying his outward calm demeanor. Bayle was in trouble. "Come along, Elhrin. We have a busy day tomorrow," he said then pushed up out of the chair and limped towards the door. He stopped beside Bayle and gave him a hard look of impatience. "Young man, a word of advice. Do not go anywhere near Marguerite in the morning unless you can hide the magnificent hangover you are sure to have. Also, I told you I would be leaving right after dawn for Brackenwood Cove, and you were expected to go with me. Be on your horse before I make it to the courtyard." He started to leave, but hesitated. "Oh, and one other thing. If this woman's husband finds you are dallying with his wife, do not expect me to save you." He poked Bayle sharply in the stomach with the end of his staff, then limped out the door.

"Oof," Bayle grunted. Massaging his stomach, he glanced at the woman cowering in shame beside him. "You are married?" he asked, fearfully.

The woman whimpered miserably confirming that she was.

"Bayle, you are an idiot," Elhrin fumed, following Master Gryph out the door. "I won't save you, either. You're on your own this time," she added as she stepped out in the hall. She then used her magic to slam the door shut with a resounding bang.

Chapter Seventeen

"I don't care what you think, General. I said last night that there is no way of knowing for certain that the landing will be in this particular cove, no matter what the minister says. The men we questioned could not confirm anything beyond the fact that Marmuht is the intended target," Prince Cahail said angrily. He was in a black mood and had finally turned his complaining and anger on Master Gryph. "The beaches around White Cliffs are a possibility and we cannot rule out a direct attack on Marmuht from the bay."

"Admiral Zoscalese said that there would be a blockade in place at the mouth of the bay by tomorrow night at the latest to slow down any invasion from that direction, and I agree with him when he says only a fool would attack from the bay. There just isn't enough room to support ground troops. White Cliffs is a possibility, but a landing force would have to split into two groups in order to come ashore. No, I believe Minister Idwyr is right about Brackenwood Cove being the landing point. As we discussed before, it is close to the city and has a wide beach that would be the perfect location for getting large numbers of troops on the ground. If we had not been forewarned, Marmuht could have been easily attacked from this direction before the city had substantial time to prepare." General Shifwood kept his voice level, but Elhrin, who was riding directly behind the leaders with Kyne and Bayle, could tell the man was trying to keep his anger in check. Prince Cahail's consistent tirade was pushing everyone's patience to a breaking point. "I'm positive King Goruth would say the same if he were here."

"He is not here and won't be until tomorrow at the earliest, so that leaves it up to me to make a decision because we are running out of time," Prince Cahail said as he raked a hand across his forehead, swiping long strands of auburn hair that had fallen into his eyes aside and tucking them behind one ear. "How can we trust you?" He turned in his saddle to address Master Gryph riding on his left. "This is your brother we are talking about, after all. How can I believe you will not protect him if you face him on the battlefield? If I understand correctly, you failed to kill him once in battle. Why should I believe you will not let him go this time?"

Master Gryph's back stiffened and he cocked his head to one side. "I am sorry, my prince, but can you elaborate as to what you are referring?"

"Did you or did you not have an altercation with your brother where you had the opportunity to apprehend or kill him, but you chose to let him go?"

Elhrin frowned, wondering how the prince knew about that battle if Master Gryph never told anyone but Marguerite, and she knew Marguerite would die before she betrayed his confidence.

Master Gryph leveled his gaze on the prince. "I did," he said without hesitation.

The Prince grinned smugly. "And why would you do such a thing if you knew he was a dangerous enemy? It is your duty to protect the interests of our country, is it not?"

"It is."

Prince Cahail stared at him, waiting for him to continue, but Master Gryph offered nothing further on the subject. "Is that it?" Prince Cahail asked with a short laugh of contempt. "Are you not going to explain yourself?"

"There is nothing to explain. I made a mistake. I accept all responsibility for that mistake."

"As you should, and after all this is over, I will make sure you do," he said with heat. "You might offer no explanation to me, but I'm sure the High Court would be interested in an explanation."

Elhrin stared at Prince Cahail's back in shock. He was going to accuse Master Gryph of being a traitor? How could he do that?

"My Prince, surely you are not going to bring charges against him?" General Shifwood sputtered in surprise.

"General, our country has been compromised by what this man calls a mistake. How are we to know if he tells the truth? I think an investigation is the least we should do," Prince Cahail said.

Kyne growled low in his throat. "Cahail, you are a fool," he said in disgust.

Prince Cahail jerked his horse around to confront Kyne. His face was blood red in fury. "How dare you call me a fool, cousin? Do I have to remind you who you are speaking to?"

"Please do," Kyne retorted, "because for the last five minutes, I have been wondering where the heir to the throne of Anderan has gone. Look around you, *cousin*," he sneered the word. "We are not out here on a stag hunt. We are riding to face an enemy that could kill us all, and you pick a fight with the one man who is the only hope we have of surviving this battle. Only a fool would place himself in that position."

Prince Cahail spurred his horse so that he was face to face with Kyne. "For the sake of our mothers only, do I not kill you now, Kyne," he snarled low and even. "You will keep your mouth shut from now on or I will not hesitate to run you through, cousin or no."

Kyne leaned closer to the Prince. "Cahail, I can guarantee that no blade of yours will ever draw my blood," he said with deadly intent.

Prince Cahail reached for his blade.

"Enough," Master Gryph barked the order with enough force to still Prince Cahail's hand. "My Prince, do what you think best concerning me when this affair is over, but might I suggest we move along. The day is slipping away from us and we have more pressing affairs to attend to. Captain Pittwold, you have a duty to His Highness. Please remember that."

Kyne visibly relaxed his stance. He smoothed the anger off his face and nodded his head respectfully. "As you wish, Minister."

Cahail clamped his lips in a thin line, displeased with the respect Kyne had just shown the older man. He jerked on his reins, violently turning his horse back around. Without a word, he spurred his horse and left them behind.

Master Gryph glanced at Kyne and discreetly raised a hand, silently warning Kyne to back off and let him handle the situation. He nudged his horse to catch up with Prince Cahail.

Kyne spat a stream of saliva off to one side. "Fool," he muttered under his breath.

Elhrin edged her horse closer and touched Kyne on his arm. He cut his eyes at her and shook his head in disgust. He then kicked his horse and sped up the road.

"That was tense," Bayle said.

"And unnecessary," she said, sparing a quick glance at the huddle of their students behind her. They looked at her questioningly. "Everything is fine," she assured them. "Let's move out." She nudged her horse forward. "I can't believe he is planning to bring charges against Master Gryph," she said to Bayle.

"I don't think King Goruth would let him, do you?"

"I don't know," she sighed. "I would hope not. This accusation is out of line. Master Gryph didn't want to kill a brother he loved. Any person with a conscience would do the same."

"*Conscience* being the key word here," Bayle said, then lowered his voice as they neared the leaders. "Not sure if that applies to Prince Cahail."

When they reined in behind Master Gryph, they found that Prince Cahail was not finished with attacking him.

"You never answered my question, Minister," Cahail said, nearly shouting. "How can I trust you?"

"Trust is like respect, Your Highness. It is something that is earned, not given," Master Gryph said.

Prince Cahail shot him a glance as if he was crazy. "What does that have to do with anything? Just answer my damn question."

"The answer is that you cannot trust me," Master Gryph said simply.

Elhrin was stunned. Why was he giving Cahail the answer he wanted?

"Really? I knew you weren't to be trusted, Minister. I just never thought you would admit it."

"My Prince, I think you have misunderstood me," Master Gryph turned his gaze on the younger man. "I said you could not trust me because you have chosen not to, not because I could not be trusted." Master Gryph pointed at General Shifwood. "He can trust me," Master Gryph jerked a thumb over his shoulder, "and they can trust me. I give my absolute word to all here that I will do whatever it takes to ensure the safety of this country and its people. Yes, I failed at killing a brother I once loved, but understand me, Your Highness, the boy that was my brother is long gone." He paused for a moment.

"Who remains is a man that will be held accountable for his actions."

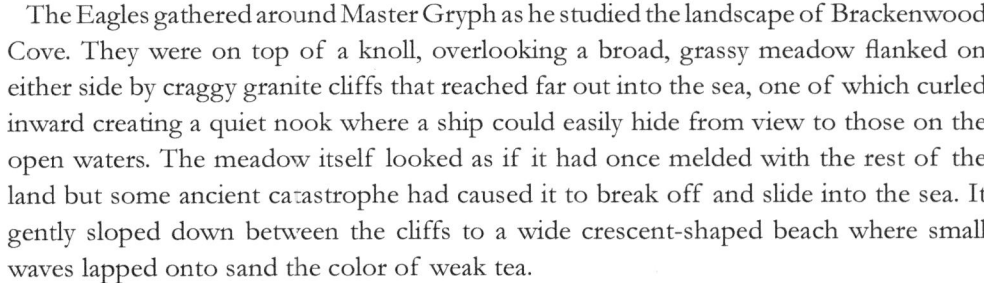

The Eagles gathered around Master Gryph as he studied the landscape of Brackenwood Cove. They were on top of a knoll, overlooking a broad, grassy meadow flanked on either side by craggy granite cliffs that reached far out into the sea, one of which curled inward creating a quiet nook where a ship could easily hide from view to those on the open waters. The meadow itself looked as if it had once melded with the rest of the land but some ancient catastrophe had caused it to break off and slide into the sea. It gently sloped down between the cliffs to a wide crescent-shaped beach where small waves lapped onto sand the color of weak tea.

Prince Cahail and General Shifwood had moved off with their two regiments and were consulting with their army engineers on where to set up defensive fortifications. Prince Cahail had reluctantly agreed that Brackenwood Cove was the logical landing spot when one of his scouts had returned and reported the other possible site had suffered a landslide from a cliff on one side of the beach and was not a viable location for a large scale landing. Elhrin had to wonder if Solisius was in any way responsible or if it was just happenstance.

She shielded her eyes from the bright midday sun and scanned the horizon. Three ships were on the water, but they were too far away to determine their origin.

"They won't be able to bring all the ships in at once," Grey said.

"Most likely, they will get in as close as they can and drop rowboats to ferry their men in," Kyne responded.

"That would take a fair amount of time to get the army onshore," Landin said. "If we are ready, we could reduce their numbers before they reach land."

Master Gryph turned to look over Elhrin's head at something across the meadow. She followed his gaze. The only thing behind them was the wide expanse of rolling grassy fields dotted with several large groves of trees. Far in the distance on top of a hill was a small farmhouse and barn.

"The cliffs could be useful," Grey pointed to the land's end overlooking the cove below near where Prince Cahail and General Shifwood stood, "but anyone up there would be exposed."

Elhrin studied the cliffs. They were accessible from the top of the meadow. Rocky outcrops from where chunks of land had peeled away and fallen were scattered along the bottom of the cliffs all the way down to the water's edge.

"There is not much cover out here, that is for certain," Barron spoke up. He sat astride his horse behind Elhrin.

"And we all have learned you get your asses handed to you when you have no cover," Tover snorted, earning chuckles from the rest of the students.

"I think you learned to make your own cover if you need it," Grey said.

"Or you provide cover for someone else," Elhrin responded. "Haven't you been working in teams?"

"We have," Ashlyn answered.

"They are going to stay in teams, aren't they?" she asked Master Gryph.

"Do you think they should?" he asked, and once again looked over her head across the meadow to study something behind them.

"I do," she said, wishing she knew what he was looking at. "What are the teams?"

"I have Ashlyn and Tover," Landin spoke up.

"Hey, I'm on your team, too," Zeike added.

"Is he staying?" Elhrin asked, thinking he was too young at fourteen even though Master Gryph had said he had enough experience and could handle himself. Zeike, Jayce, and Jayme had all been allowed to continue to travel with Master Gryph to Marmuht. Jayce and Jayme had been designated as Marguerite and Marcus' bodyguards. At least, that is what Master Gryph had told them. They were to follow the orders of Corporal Bayle Caddoch who had assigned them the task.

"Of course, I'm staying—right, Master Idwyr?"

"Zeike, are you ready to die?" Master Gryph asked.

"Now that wasn't a blunt question at all," Kyne murmured.

"Yes, sir," Zeike responded enthusiastically.

Kyne snorted at his enthusiasm.

Master Gryph nudged his horse around to face everyone. "Is anyone else ready to die?" he asked with a frown.

They all remained silent.

"No one should ever be ready to die, Zeike. You don't fight to die. You fight to live. You fight so that others may live. Never go into battle presuming you will die because you will if that is your mindset. Why do you think I battled you the other day?"

"Because we needed to learn a lesson?" Phalen phrased his answer into a question, unsure of himself.

"Yes, you needed to learn a lesson, a lesson where you are to do everything within your power to stay alive. Do I make myself clear?" He scowled at them then cocked his head to one side when they remained silent.

"He asked you a question," Elhrin said sternly, not liking their lack of response.

Master Gryph nailed her with his blue eyes as the students around her responded with a loud, "Yes, sir."

"Zeike, for now you will stay with Landin," Master Gryph said. "I have not yet made a decision to let you fight."

"Yes, sir," Zeike said. He could not contain a smile.

"Listen to me, son, and understand that if I say no, you are to stay where you are told. I will not have anyone here responsible for you."

"Yes, sir," Zeike said, his smile slowly fading under the pressure of Master Gryph's stony stare.

Master Gryph's gaze flicked to Elhrin. "You asked about the teams," he said. "Barron is a team leader and he has Leesha and Kull. Grey will have Kory and Eowhyn."

"Marissa will be with me," she said, glancing at the fiery red-head on the other side of Kyne.

"Marissa, are you ready for this?" Master Gryph asked.

Elhrin had told him that the girl had come a long way in her abilities while they were on the ocean. She knew how to defend herself and she knew some attack maneuvers. Elhrin just hoped that the girl's unusual strength and ability to adapt would see her through a full-scale battle.

"Should I say, yes sir, and lie to you?" Marissa asked. "Or should I tell the truth and say, no sir, I don't have the training the others do, and I am scared from head to toe, but I am not going to run from this fight. I have seen what your . . . the N'gethwyn can do. He is heartless and he has to be stopped, and from what I have heard, you need all the help you can get."

He slowly smiled at her. "I prefer to be told the truth." He glanced at Clay. "You will stay by her side. Elhrin tells me you are good with a bow."

"Yes, sir," Clay answered, "and I have no intentions of leaving her side, ever."

"Good, now . . . ," Master Gryph said.

"Master Idwyr," Phalen interrupted, "am I still with Mister Leahr?"

"No, you are going to be with Prince Cahail," Elhrin answered instead, and honestly didn't know where the idea had come from. She and Master Gryph had not discussed Phalen being positioned with the Prince, but it felt right. That was where he was supposed to be. She glanced at Master Gryph to see if he disagreed with her, but he remained silent, allowing her to take the initiative.

"No," Phalen protested loudly. He glanced from her to Master Gryph, hoping he would contradict her. "I'm not going to do it."

"Yes, you are," Elhrin said, frowning at the boy. "And you should be honored to be chosen as the one to protect the heir to Anderan's throne."

"Some honor," Kyne muttered under his breath.

Elhrin turned to glare at Kyne. "Did you say something, Captain?"

Kyne raised his eyebrows at her. "Nope," he replied, innocently.

"Master Idwyr, please," Phalen pleaded. "I don't want to be with the prince. She can't order me to."

"Phalen, I think you have forgotten that Elhrin is also in command here and you will do as you are told. He will need one of us by his side, and you have been chosen. You will do whatever he asks as long as it involves staying by his side. You are to never leave him at any moment, and if he orders you to leave him without reasonable cause, you are to refuse. This is the one time I give you leave to refuse a direct order from a superior. Do you understand me?" Master Gryph asked.

"Yes, sir," Phalen growled, sullenly.

"Phalen, this is extremely important." Elhrin tried to appeal to his sense of honor.

"You are protecting the future of our country."

Phalen shot a fierce glare at her, then quickly glanced away as if he couldn't bear to look at her. "You do it," he grumbled.

Elhrin looked to Master Gryph for help. Phalen was going to have to understand his position soon. Understanding her look, Master Gryph shook his head slightly, wanting her to drop the subject for now. He turned his horse around to gaze over the cove again.

"I want all of you to be aware that you have to be adaptable to whatever situation arises out here. A battle changes constantly, and you will have to change with it." He watched as a messenger broke from the prince's group below and raced up the hill. "Listen to your leaders. Be aware of the army around you because you have to ensure their safety, as well. Whatever you do don't mistakenly kill our own men."

The messenger thundered by their group and headed towards Marmuht.

"Leaders, take your groups over the entire field from cliffside to cliffside and down to the water. I want you to become familiar with the terrain. Phalen, from this point forward you are to stay with Prince Cahail. I am sure he will try to get rid of you, but stand your ground until I join you."

The boy shot Elhrin one last furious glance and spurred his horse, unleashing his anger by running his horse at a full gallop down the slope.

"He is not happy with me," Elhrin commented.

"He will get over it," Master Gryph responded as the groups left them to inspect the field. When they were out of earshot he glanced at her with a smile. "Your instincts are good."

"I spend too much time with you," she said with a snort. "I don't know where that idea came from."

"Yes, you do," he said, as they watched the students move across the meadow. "It was self-preservation."

Elhrin flashed him a grin. "You know me so well." She had to admit being near Prince Cahail was the last place she wanted to be as she watched Phalen rein in by his entourage. The prince did not appear to be pleased by his arrival.

"I know you well enough, I suppose," he said, looking over her head across the meadow again, "but you do understand you will not be able to get out of your duty."

She sighed. "I know, but I could hope, couldn't I?" She followed his gaze and still only saw the countryside. "What are you looking at?"

"The trees," he said, "there are too many trees."

"They will cut some of them down for fortifications," Kyne said.

"But why does it matter?" Clay asked. "The attack will come from the water."

"Unless there are more Do'athrim lurking in the woods like the ones we encountered on our way here," Bayle mused aloud.

"Exactly what I was thinking, son. I wouldn't put it past Derrick to already have some of his forces standing ready nearby," Master Gryph said, nudging his horse into motion. "Let's go take a look."

They traversed the tree lines of several copses until Master Gryph decided to take a look at the interior of one large stand of woods. Elhrin allowed her horse to pick the best path behind Master Gryph. The canopy overhead was not dense, so sunlight filtered brightly from above, which made it easy to see, but the open foliage had made it possible for the thick undergrowth to grow and fill in the gaps between the trunks of the trees. Branches and vines snagged at her clothing and the tack on her horse.

"A good place to hide, but not a good place to get through if you are in a hurry," Kyne commented. "Ow, whoa!" he grumbled at his horse as a vine with thorns snagged his leg, and he had to back up to free himself.

"They will not be on horseback, Kyne," Bayle said. He swiped at group of vines with his sword and cut them down. "Dogs know how work their way through tight spaces."

"Do you truly think they would come through something like this, horseback or no, if they are nearby?" Elhrin asked, not sure if he would hear her over all the noise they were making.

Master Gryph turned his head to speak to her. "Anything is a possibility. The element of surprise is an advantageous tactic for any offensive plan." He reined in his large horse and scanned the trees. "However, they are not here now nor are there any signs that they have been here at all."

"Are we going to search every stand of trees?" Bayle asked.

Master Gryph shook his head. "We don't have the time. I will have Shifwood send someone to make sure the trees are clear of enemy." He turned his horse around. "Let's go back out."

When they cleared the tree line Prince Cahail, Phalen, and some of the prince's men were riding towards them.

"Who do you think you are, Minister?" Prince Cahail roared. He reined in his horse so hard the animal slid in the grass, kicking up turf under its hooves.

"Ignorance does not become you, my prince," Kyne sneered. "I would think it quite clear who he is."

"Shut up, Kyne," the prince barked, "or I'll have you arrested."

"On what charge?" Kyne laughed. "Stating the obvious? I don't think it is an offense."

"Kyne, enough," Master Gryph frowned at the wiry man. He turned his gaze back to Prince Cahail when he was sure Kyne would remain silent. "Your Highness, I am afraid you will have to enlighten me as to what is bothering you."

"You have no authority to order a bodyguard for me," Prince Cahail snapped. "Take your boy back into your little group. I will not have him or any of your kind anywhere near me."

"My kind?" Master Gryph slowly grinned at the obvious attempt to label them as something less than a normal human, but he was not amused. "Prince Cahail, Phalen is your last defense should you be attacked magically. I thought you were concerned with someone who could kill with a wave of their hand. Isn't that what you told Mayor Nambacus at dinner last night?"

Prince Cahail's face flushed red with fury. He did not like having his words thrown back at him. "None of those vermin will reach the beach if I have anything to say about it. My men will see to it. I do not need your boy," he yelled vehemently.

"Phalen," Master Gryph addressed the angry youth behind the prince, "your orders stand."

The prince's face deepened in color. "How dare you? You do not outrank me, Minister."

"No, I do not, Your Highness," Master Gryph growled. "However, I do have the authority to order a bodyguard for you. I must remind you it is the duty of my office to see that the royal line is well guarded, and I take this responsibility quite seriously. And because my office reports to the monarch only, my orders supersede any you may have concerning your welfare. When King Goruth arrives you may take the issue up with him. If he deems me out of line then I will gladly obey his orders. Until that time, Phalen stays with you."

"Minister, when I rise to the throne your office will be a thing of the past," Prince Cahail hissed.

"That is your right as a ruling monarch, My Prince," Master Gryph said. "I look forward to retirement."

Kyne snorted in amusement.

"You have no respect for the monarchy or royal line, Minister. You never have," Prince Cahail snarled, not liking that Master Gryph had taken his threat in stride and was not bothered by it in the least.

"Oh, but I do, yet I do think you will do well to heed the words I spoke to you earlier today."

"What words?" the prince snapped.

"Trust and respect are to be earned and not demanded because it will never be truly given that way." Master Gryph nudged his horse closer to the prince. He was an intimidating figure, towering high over the stocky heir to the throne. "You have demonstrated nothing to me or my *boy* that would earn trust or respect, and you need both. You may not think so now, but trust me in this, Cahail," he leaned closer to the prince's face as he dropped the prince's title on purpose. "While I personally may not be a factor, there will come a time when you will need both from Miss Caddoch and my *boy*." He nodded his head to emphasize his point. "Yes, indeed, there will be a day when you will need them both." He nudged his horse away. "Phalen, you have your orders. Miss Caddoch, come along, we have work to do."

Without a backward glance he beckoned for them to follow, then spurred his horse to a gallop. They left an astonished and infuriated heir to the throne behind.

They spent the rest of the afternoon having the teams practice mock battles in various locations across the battlefield, and Master Gryph sent Kyne and Bayle to join a troop of General Shifwood's men to search the closest stretches of wooded areas for signs of

Do'athrim while they worked.

The rest of Prince Cahail and General Shifwood's men worked on preparations of the battlefield. Wooden stakes and earthen pits were being strategically placed along the beach and lower meadow to slow down the landing. Timber was being cut for catapults, usually a weapon better used for sieges, but Cahail's engineers had decided, since the boats would have no choice but be closely packed together coming in, Anderan's army could make use of the plentiful rock in the area to bombard the invaders with a deadly rain of stone, hopefully taking out enemy forces and boats before they reached shore.

The messenger that had left early in the day had been sent for the rest of Prince Cahail's troops camped outside of Marmuht. They arrived by late afternoon, followed an hour or so later by the first train of supply wagons because Prince Cahail had decided to stay and oversee the preparations himself instead of traveling back and forth from Marmuht.

"Marissa learns quickly, doesn't she?" Master Gryph commented as they watched the teams practice near the edge of one of the cliffs.

Marissa had spent the night before getting to know the students and she and Eowhyn had immediately formed a friendship. Eowhyn was showing Marissa an attack technique that she favored. A fiery sun-like orb shot out over the cove and landed with a sizzling thud into the surf. Marissa sent a duplicate out over the water. It exploded with a deafening boom before it hit the water.

"She does," Elhrin said, "and she can create techniques on her own. Did you see the ice shards?" She wasn't sure he had witnessed Marissa firing the deadly shards across the field because he had been talking with General Shifwood at the time.

"I did," he acknowledged, transferring his staff to his right hand and leaning on it to get the weight off of his left side. "I'm impressed with her line of thinking. It is important that they all use their unique abilities to the fullest potential." He heaved in a huge breath and let it out slowly. "Elhrin, I have come to a decision that will be reprehensible."

She glanced up at him. "What decision?"

"I am going to allow all three young boys to join us in battle," he said.

Her mouth dropped open in shock. "No," she stammered, "absolutely, not!" He couldn't. Zeike maybe, but Jayce and Jayme were definitely too young. "They are just children."

"I know," he pounded the ended of his staff into the ground with frustration, "damn it, I know, and as much as I hate it, we will need them."

"No," she repeated, "we will manage without them. You cannot do this. Marguerite won't allow you to do it, anyway."

"Marguerite will not have a say in the matter," he stated.

"What is wrong with you?" she asked. "You know they are not skilled enough. Why are you considering this?" She couldn't believe how serious he was about the matter.

"Elhrin, I saw this battle long before I knew those boys. That was why I made sure we began the academy right away and insisted we fill it with students well before the academy was ready for them," he snapped. "And when those boys answered the call for enrollment that we sent throughout the country, I knew the time was at hand and Anderan would be facing a dire situation before we were ready." He was angry, but she knew it was not with her. He was doing something that went against his nature, and it was killing him inside. "We will be outnumbered, and it will take everything we have to stand any chance of surviving this battle."

Elhrin felt numb. "Marguerite won't allow you to do this," she repeated quietly, knowing he faced a hard fight ahead if he was to get his way.

"I've already said it is not Marguerite's decision," he frowned down at her.

"I know what you said." She turned to face him. "I can't be . . . I don't want you to do this."

"I," he pointed at his chest, "don't want to do this, but it has to be this way."

"Then what are you going to do?" She threw her hands up in frustration. "If you had planned for this all along, then why aren't they out here with us right now? They are not ready."

"They are more ready than you think." He glanced over her head. The students had heard them arguing and were openly watching them. "Why have you all stopped?" he snapped. "We will have to leave shortly, and you need this time for practice. Do it!"

The students turned back to the water.

Elhrin crossed her arms over her chest. "What happens if they die? How will you explain your actions to their parents?" she asked.

"You sound just like Marguerite," he growled.

"I take that as a compliment," she responded.

He sighed. "Despite the dream, I have tried to keep them out of it. Fate keeps stepping in and making sure they are where they need to be, no matter what I do. Up until this morning, I had planned for them to stay with Marguerite."

"Really, then what happened to make you change your mind?"

"Jayme," he said.

She raised her eyebrows in surprise. Jayme was the one she was concerned about the most because of his shy and timid nature. He wouldn't be able to stand up to the pressure or the horror of battle, and she was still unsure why Master Gryph had even allowed him to participate in the Eagle Program.

"How did he manage that?" she asked.

"Do you know he avoids me?" he asked.

"He is afraid of you, so what?"

"Yes, he is so afraid of me, he will do anything to not be in my presence alone," he transferred his staff back to his left hand, "so much so, that he has found he is capable of hiding his energy source."

"What?" She dropped her arms to her sides. "When were you planning to tell me this?"

"I haven't had the chance before now. I didn't know he had the ability until this morning," he said. "After you and the others left for the courtyard, he was alone on the terrace. I went out to talk to him about what I needed for him to do while we were away and he jumped off the wall and hid in the hedges below. I then felt his energy source disappear."

She furrowed her brow. "I must have been busy answering questions at the time. I did not feel it go," she said, not liking that she had not been aware of the loss of his source.

He grunted. "It would not be hard to miss, being surrounded by so many power sources and as busy as our minds are," he said. "I'm just as guilty of not recognizing the loss when he has done it before this morning."

"Is that so?" she asked, more than a little disturbed that they both could let something so important slip past them. "We really need to pay attention more to our students, don't we?"

He chuckled. "I think we should."

"How long has he been able to do this?"

"Not long. He discovered he could do it by accident in Tuhnichi."

"He spoke to you?"

"If you call nods and shakes of a head talking, then yes, we talked. I was able to find out this ability is new to him, and Jayce was the one who told me about Tuhnichi before I left the mansion."

"That explains why you were late to the courtyard. Prince Cahail nearly burst a main artery having to wait on you." She then realized the similarity in the boy's story and his own. "Is this not familiar to you?"

"Yes, they do parallel my own story, but this time will be different. Jayme is not destined to be N'gethwyn."

"How can you tell what his destiny will be? None of us know for sure." She looked away, blinking back tears that threatened to form. Somehow, despite the determination to keep her mind busy after a sleepless, thought-filled night, the reality of Tomas not being a part of her future crept into her mind.

"No, our destinies are not set in stone, but I have plans for Jayme if I survive this battle," he said.

"Excuse me, sir," she said, "are *you* ready to die . . . again?"

He raised an eyebrow at her. "It's not nice to throw my own words back in my face."

"It's not nice to scare me, either," she said, frowning with unease at his statement. He had never been one to talk about his own mortality—an unwanted chill crept up her spine. "What are your plans for Jayme?"

"I think he will make an excellent teacher one day."

"The boy can hardly talk to anyone but Marguerite and Jayce. How did you come up with this idea?"

"He'll grow out of his shyness. Wait and see."

"You are assuming he will get to grow up. I don't see how his ability to hide his powers validates your cause to let him and Jayce fight."

"Elhrin, do you trust me?"

"I do," she said without hesitation. She was not Cahail.

"Then trust me in this."

And with that, the discussion was over. He had used the one thing that would stop any argument from her. All of her life, she had put her complete and total trust in him even if she sometimes had doubts. She wasn't going to change now. He had never failed her.

Thinking of Cahail reminded her of something the prince had said to him. "How did Cahail know about your fight with Derrick? I thought you didn't tell anyone about that battle."

His brow drew together in a deep frown. "I would like to know the answer to that question myself. I did not share that information with anyone but you and Marguerite."

Elhrin looked out across the meadow below the cliffs. She could not find Prince Cahail among the crowd of men working below or the ones at the top of the meadow setting up the prince's encampment. "Do you think he had someone listening to us last night?"

"It is possible," he responded with an aggravated sigh.

"If someone heard us talking, what if they . . . ," she lowered her voice, "what if they heard what else you only told me and Marguerite?"

"That would be unfortunate, wouldn't it?" he asked.

"I'd say it would. Aren't you worried about it?"

"The possibility that we were spied on does concern me, but I am not going to pursue the issue at the moment," he said then nodded at the line of students at the cliff's edge. "My concern for now is ensuring they are as ready as they can be for this battle."

She frowned, not happy with allowing a person with vital information to roam free. "Do you mind if Kyne and I discreetly look into the matter?"

A corner of his mouth lifted. "Do what you think is best," he said.

She narrowed her eyes at him, knowingly. "If you wanted me to do this in the first place why not just tell me?"

"My dear, I won't always be around to issue orders. You need to make decisions on your own."

Leesha laughed heartily, drawing their attention. "Look, everyone," she said, pointing at something in the water below.

Marissa turned around, smiling. "Elhrin, come look at this."

Elhrin shot a quick glance at Master Gryph. "We'll continue this later," she said as they walked to join the others.

He agreed with a nod of his head.

When she peered over the cliff's edge, there was a pod of skulowhal, a sea creature that closely resembled a dolphin but had the unusual feature of a hard bone-like substance on their heads, congregating in the water below chattering excitedly as they tossed their heads back and forth.

"What are they doing?" she asked.

"They are saying hello," Kory answered, shielding his eyes from the setting afternoon sun.

"You can hear them?" Elhrin asked, remembering he claimed to be able to communicate with certain animals of the sea.

"I can," he grinned, revealing a row of healthy teeth that gleamed white against his honey-colored Chyrzinian skin. "They were nearby so I called to them. I knew you all didn't believe me. I wanted to show you I could talk to them."

"Amazing," Master Gryph said.

The skulowhal slung their heads back and forth one last time then disappeared under the surf. Occasionally, they would return to the surface for air, blowing sprays of water from the air holes behind the bony structures on their heads as they headed back out to sea.

"They are leaving to hunt," Kory said.

"We must leave, too, youngsters," Master Gryph said and turned to go. "Tomorrow, we will pack up our gear and move out here to prepare for battle."

Chapter Eighteen

Elhrin dropped her new travel pack in the chair across from Kyne. He had evidently been waiting on her for some time because he had an empty breakfast plate on the table beside him and now sat comfortably with his ankles crossed as he sipped on a cup of tea.

"Have you been waiting long?" she asked as a very unladylike expletive drifted out of the open doorway of Master Gryph and Marguerite's room.

"Long enough to know that if I were Minister Idwyr, I would choose to face the entire enemy host alone than go back into that room and face her." He gestured at the open door with his cup.

She winced. "I guess he told her about the boys. Where is he?" she asked as she sent her senses out in search for him and found his energy source somewhere in the central interior of the mansion.

"King Goruth arrived before dawn. They are having a quick meeting, and he said if he is not through by the time we are ready to leave, to go on ahead. He will catch up later."

"Are you ready?" she asked.

"As ready as I'll ever be."

"Let me say goodbye to Marguerite and Marcus," she said. "I'll be right back."

"Good luck," he said.

She walked through the door just as Marguerite slammed an article of clothing into Master Gryph's travel pack on the bed. Marcus sat cross-legged in the middle of the bed curiously watching his mother while he sucked on his thumb. He waved at Elhrin with the free fingers of his hand without taking his thumb out of his mouth. She grinned at him and waved back, and put a finger to her mouth so he wouldn't let Marguerite know she was there.

"I swear, Marcus, your father can make me angrier than a thousand hornets," she fumed as she slammed a shirt into the bag. "What madness is crawling through that brilliant mind to allow children on a battlefield? I'll not have it."

Elhrin wrapped her arms around the woman and squeezed her tight. "I love you, Marguerite."

Marguerite yelped in surprise and almost jumped out of Elhrin's arms. "Elhrin, don't ever sneak up on me like that." She narrowed her eyes at Marcus. He was grinning behind his thumb. "You saw her coming and didn't warn me. Some help you are." He grinned wider.

"Do you know what he plans to do?" Marguerite asked.

Elhrin nodded. "I do, and I tried to talk him out of it, but he says to trust him." She shrugged her shoulders. "I have to trust him."

"Oh, good heavens," Marguerite said and slumped onto the bed. Marcus scrambled across the mattress to nestle under his mother's arm. She hugged him close. "Trust is one thing. Madness is another. I don't know if I can take this."

Elhrin didn't see how Marguerite was going to do it, either. She was staying behind in Marmuht. Close enough to hear any news that arose, but she would have to wait for it, and it was the waiting that was hard. Elhrin never wanted to be the one who had to wait.

"The boys won't fight initially. They are to stay back out of harm's way." Elhrin sat on the bed beside her. "We won't allow them anywhere near the battle unless there is no other choice. We will keep them as safe as possible."

"I know you will." Marguerite patted Elhrin's knee. "Who will keep you safe?"

"I will," Elhrin said with a smile. "I'm good at it, too."

"You better be," Marguerite smiled sadly. "I expect every one of you to come back here safely."

"We will," she said, hoping her words would be true. "Thank you for my new clothes, and especially the hairbrush." Elhrin had returned to the mansion to find Marguerite had spent the day while they were gone to shop for her and the others who had left Muryne without any belongings and had purchased several changes of clothing and necessities Elhrin needed. It felt good to have something fresh on again. She had thrown her old clothes in a heap on the floor and left a note for the maids to burn them. It was the last physical reminder she had of her journey to Marmuht and she wanted them gone.

"You are quite welcome." Marguerite stood up and crossed the room to remove another shirt from a tall wardrobe with exotic plants painted on its doors. "You were looking a little ragged."

"It felt that way, too." Elhrin narrowed her eyes at Marcus and held up her hands like claws. He giggled and backed across the bed. "Where do you think you are going?" she asked, and launched herself across the bed to pin him down and tickle his stomach. He squealed and tried to wriggle free. She pulled up his shirt and placed her lips on his soft stomach to blow loud, wet noises on his belly. He roared with laughter.

"Enough?" she asked. He shook his head. She blew more wet noises until his tiny hands tried to push her head away. She kissed him on his cheek. "I love you, Marcus."

"I wuv you, Elhwin," he said.

She picked him up and squeezed him tight. "You take care of your mother, okay?"

He nodded. She kissed his cheek again and sat him back on the bed.

When she looked at Marguerite, there were tears streaming down the lady's face. Marguerite swiped them away and smiled. Elhrin slid off the bed and hugged her fiercely.

"We are coming back," she whispered. "I promise."

"Then it will be true," Marguerite whispered back. "You always keep your promises. I love you, Elhrin."

"I love you, too." Elhrin stepped out her embrace. "Don't be too hard on Master Gryph. We will need him whole on the battlefield."

Marguerite laughed, "I might bruise him a little, but I won't break anything."

"Good, then I'll see you two later," she said and looked over her shoulder one last time before going out the door. Marguerite stared blankly at the bag on the bed, and Marcus waved once before popping his thumb back into his mouth. She winked at him.

"Is everything okay?" Kyne asked when she came out. He slung his pack over his shoulder.

"Yes," she replied and picked up her bag. "Have you seen Bayle?"

"He went to round up the others across the street," Kyne said as they entered the busy hallway and headed for the front courtyard.

Elhrin and Kyne had to push their way through throngs of mansion visitors and staff rushing about their tasks. King Goruth's arrival and the preparations that were underway for the impending invasion had everyone in a hurry.

"Okay," she said, sending out her senses to determine where everyone was and immediately ran across Master Gryph's located in the open air courtyard in the center of the mansion. "The meeting must have ended," she commented as they entered the courtyard. Master Gryph was next to the fish pond talking with his son Griffyn.

"They remind me of a before and after illustration I once saw in a book on aging," Kyne commented as they stepped down into the central courtyard area that was unusually windy.

"You can read?" Elhrin asked in feigned surprise as she glanced up at the sky. Dark clouds raced across the opening. "Oh wait, you just said you only looked at the illustrations."

"Ha, ha," Kyne responded without smiling.

"And just why were you looking at a book on aging?" she laughed. "Are you afraid of getting old?"

He shook his head. "No, I have no fear of that as long as I am around you."

"Ouch!" she winced. "That was a mean thing to say."

"I have never claimed to be nice," he smirked as they joined her mentor and his son.

"Elhrin, Kyne, nice to see you again," Griffyn said and held out his hand.

Elhrin placed her hand in his rough calloused grip. "Where have you been?" she asked. "Marcus loved the basket of sweets you sent him." She nodded her head at Master Gryph. "So did he."

Griffyn laughed. "I stopped by to see him and Marguerite earlier. She said the same thing."

"I only had one piece," Master Gryph replied innocently.

"He had five," she mouthed silently, holding up five fingers.

Griffyn grinned wide. "Well, I'm glad my gift was well received. Marcus still won't talk to me, though."

"He will one day," she said. "Are you leaving?"

"As soon as my ship is finished being outfitted with ballistae this morning," he said. "Then I will be out on the coast not far from where you will be."

"I didn't know you were staying to fight," she glanced at Master Gryph questioningly, wondering what he thought, but his face did not reveal his thoughts on the matter and he remained silent.

"I was just telling my father about Ostied's Specialties," Griffyn lifted a corner of his mouth. "I was lucky enough to have been one of the few he entrusted on how to make them. My crew and I were able to find the components from the suppliers Ostied used here and worked through last night putting them together. Hopefully, we will be an asset to Anderan's naval force."

"You will be facing ships loaded with N'gethwyn," Elhrin said.

"I know," he nodded at his father, "he has already run down the long list of things I am to do and not do."

"You approved this with Admiral Zoscalese, I presume," Master Gryph spoke up.

"I have, and I forgot to tell you he requested some of the bolts for himself," Griffyn said. "He wants me to run alongside his ship so we can coordinate on the water. We are going out as soon as we can to test the ballistae and see if we need to make any modifications."

"Very well, watch your back." Master Gryph glanced at Elhrin and Kyne. "I see you two are ready to go."

"We were on our way out," she said.

"Good, I am just going to say goodbye to Marguerite and Marcus." He clasped his son by the shoulder. "I will see you back here when this is over."

"Yes, sir," Griffyn put his arms around his father and pounded him on the back then turned to Elhrin. "I'll walk out with you two."

"I'll be out shortly," Master Gryph said as he limped across the courtyard. "Elhrin," he called over his shoulder, "Goruth is taking his army ahead, as well. Tell the others to wait in the courtyard. He wants to meet them before we go."

The front courtyard was in chaos and she wondered how it was possible to have so many people, horses, and wagons in such a small space.

"Nothing like a good organized and orderly departure for a war, is there?" Kyne smirked.

"You call this orderly?"

"Of course, you don't?" he asked.

"No," she said.

"I had better be on my way," Griffyn said, and placed a hand on her shoulder. "Elhrin, after this is all over I think I am going to bring my family to Glimmerdale. I want my daughter to get to know her extraordinary family."

Elhrin smiled at him. "That would be wonderful. I bet Master Gryph is ecstatic at the prospect."

"He doesn't know yet," he said with a small sigh. "I just made the decision." He glanced back to the doorway of the mansion. "Seeing him . . . I realized time was slipping away and I haven't had the chance to really get to know him. I hope it will not be too late."

"It's not," Elhrin said, understanding how he felt. "Just make sure you stay safe, and we'll do the same."

"I'll hold you to that," he smiled. He patted her shoulder and pushed his way through the crowd of the courtyard.

"Elhrin?" a deep voice called out from behind her.

She turned to see an older man with shaggy silver hair walk out of the mansion's doorway.

"Master Toome!" she cried with delight. "You're here."

"That, I am." He held out his arms and she gave him a huge hug. Master Toome was a retired colonel of the King's Army and had been living out his retirement years in Glimmerdale as the village's master blacksmith. He was also a lifelong friend of Master Gryph's, and had at one time been his partner, serving as his bodyguard just as Kyne was currently doing for her.

"I didn't know you were coming," she laughed.

"King Goruth has conned me once again to help him win a war," he chuckled. "He can't do it without me."

"I have to agree," she said. Master Toome was known for his expertise in field tactics. He had been the one to devise a strategy in the last war that kept Cynder and the enemy forces from overrunning the King's Army in the Northreach Mountains.

Master Toome held out his hand to Kyne. "Captain, it is good to see you."

"The same here, sir," Kyne said, shaking the older man's hand.

"You keep my girl here safe out there," Master Toome said.

"I intend to, sir," Kyne responded.

"Good, good," Master Toome looked over the crowd. "Well, Elhrin, I must be off. The army is stationed outside the city waiting on us. I have to inform them we will be moving on."

"We will be right behind you," she said. She gave him one last hug and watched him step down off the mansion's front patio and make his way through the crowd.

"Where are our horses?" she asked Kyne, scanning the courtyard.

"Follow me, my lady."

He elbowed his way through the crowd to a spot near the main entrance where a line of horses were tied to a row of posts. Nearby, a stable boy was doing all he could to try and control Master Gryph's large black stallion who had picked up on the energy of the crowd and was being more unruly than usual. More than once the boy dodged being bitten by the agitated steed.

"Here they are." Kyne pointed out the obvious and slapped his mount on her hindquarters.

"Thank you so much. I would have never have found them." She rolled her eyes.

"Now, where is our team?"

He pointed behind her. "Here comes Marissa and Clay, but I didn't have to tell you that, Miss-I-Can-Sense-The-Magical-Aura, did I?"

"It's too early to be obnoxious, Kyne." She threw her pack behind the saddle and started tying it down.

Marissa wedged in between their horses. "There are a lot of people out here, and what's up with this weather? It looks like it's going to rain. I thought it rarely rained around here," Marissa said as she put her own pack on the back of her mount. Marmuht was known for its arid climate, but the ugly sky belied the fact.

"It's late fall," Kyne answered. "Rain occurs more often in the fall and winter months down here."

"Marissa, where is everyone else?" Elhrin asked.

"They are coming," Marissa said. "Leesha was still in bed when Bayle knocked on her door and the others were finishing breakfast."

"Kyne, could you go over and help Bayle hurry them out here?" Elhrin asked as she checked her girth.

"Do I look like your errand boy?" he asked, finishing his own check of his horse's gear.

"Why, yes, today you look exactly like my errand boy." She smiled sweetly at him. "Would it help if I said, please?"

He frowned at her then threw his hands up in the air and stalked off without a word.

"Saying please usually works," Clay said, grinning wide.

"Yes, it does. I suppose I should try to use it more often on him," she laughed.

A few moments later, a rider barreled into the gate of the courtyard heedless of the crowd.

"Move!" he yelled.

"What in the name of the light is wrong with him? No one can move quickly in this crowd," Marissa commented.

Elhrin didn't like what she was seeing. Something was definitely wrong.

"Move out of the way, now," he ordered a stable boy who was trying to escort a horse across the courtyard.

"I'll be right back," Elhrin said to Marissa and pushed her way to the soldier's side. She grabbed his leg. "Private, what is it?"

He saw the new officer's pin on her collar that Master Gryph had replaced the night before and decided he could speak to her. "Major, they are here. The enemy is already here."

The blood ran out of her head. "Where?"

"They were still out to sea when I left Brackenwood Cove, but Prince Cahail has no doubt they are heading his way."

"Good god, they are here too soon. We are not ready. The king is inside. Get to him quickly," she ordered the man. She ran back to her horse and clambered on. "Marissa,

I can't wait. Get there as fast as you can."

"What are you talking about? I'm coming with you now," Marissa said as she and Clay pulled themselves up into their saddles and the three of them clattered out of the city at a full gallop.

———————⟫———⟩

Elhrin galloped past a line of soldiers still making their way across the rolling grass covered countryside, and dismounted by the supply wagons sitting at the top of the cove's meadow. She was shocked by the number of enemy forces that had already landed on shore and were engaged with Cahail's men. It seemed as if Obsudius had opened another rift, allowing an endless supply of soldiers and Do'athrim to swarm from the sandy beach and up onto the sweeping emerald green hillside. It appeared that the battle had been engaged for some time. Already, hundreds of bodies littered the ground.

Darting a brief glance out onto the Veihl Sea, ships of all shapes and sizes dotted the water as far out as the eye could see, and hundreds of rowboats, and transport vessels choked the shoreline. She wondered what had happened to the naval ships who were supposed to have warned them of their coming, but guessed it would not have mattered in the end. Obsudius and Derrick had planned well. Those boats were loaded down with warriors and N'gethwyn to ensure victory. Sweeping as far out as she could manage with her magical senses, she couldn't count how many N'gethwyn were in the fleet because their magical energies blended with each other, but she knew there were far more of them than their force of sixteen. They would be lucky to survive.

"Solisius, be with us," she murmured.

"*I am always with you, my child*," she heard the voice of her god whisper on the gale force wind that ripped by her ears. It seemed even the weather had arrived for war. A storm was escorting the enemy fleet of ships to the coast. The sky was the color of dark clay, and flashes of jagged lightning stabbed the ocean along the distant horizon. Rumbles of thunder rolled inland constantly, like the beating of war drums.

Marissa and Clay jumped from their mounts and joined her. "There are so many. What do you need us to do?" Marissa asked, clearly frightened.

"Stay with me unless I say otherwise."

A burst of light and a thunderous boom, followed by screams of agony, indicated that Grey was on the battlefield. He had stayed overnight with Phalen so the boy did not have to be alone with Prince Cahail the night before. Across the expanse of the descending meadow, Grey stood among a company of shielded pike men who were forming a line on the western flank of the prince's troops. He directed another sizzling ball of energy downhill, but it met against an invisible barrier and exploded in a shower of fiery sparks, causing no harm to any of the enemy. Elhrin quickly searched the area where it exploded, and found what she was looking for . . . an N'gethwyn. Elhrin wondered how many Grey and Phalen had to face before she had arrived, since there was only one on shore at the moment, but figured there had to be a few because of the number of dead along the waterline and the Prince's forces had been pushed back from the beach into the meadows. They would need reinforcements, and soon. Another explosion from Grey blasted into the enemy ranks.

The N'gethwyn, a woman pale as morning mist and dressed in dark leather armor, smiled maniacally at Grey then clapped her hands together as if she were applauding his efforts. A low rumble crept up the hill, and the ground started to tremble. Suddenly, the ground beneath Grey's feet shifted, and then shot upward. Grey was launched into the air and soared up the hillside. He landed with a crash among the soldiers descending the incline. Elhrin lost sight of him, but could still feel his magical energy, so she knew he still lived.

Elhrin gathered her powers and created a forceful downdraft of wind over the N'gethwyn. The bitch was slammed to the ground, and those close by were flung in all directions. Do'athrim and enemy soldiers swarmed over the area, filling in the gap, so Elhrin could not see if her wind burst had caused permanent damage.

Elhrin sent a blast of fiery energy into the midst of the enemy, creating massive holes in their ranks but their companions still swarming in from the water quickly filled in the gaps. Then Elhrin saw the N'gethwyn rise to her feet, sweeping her golden hair out of her face. The woman searched the hillside until she found Elhrin. Their eyes met, and the woman slowly grinned. She started to applaud.

"Everyone move, now!" Elhrin shouted to those around her, just as a low rumble emitted from the ground below her feet. Elhrin sprinted with Marissa and Clay down the meadow, trying to remain upright as the earth shifted. Behind her, rock and soil erupted upward like a volcano. Wagons exploded. Horses screamed and scattered. Bodies landed heavily on the soft turf with sickening thuds. Elhrin was thrown to the ground, but managed to roll and regain her feet. She flung a blazing ball of fire in the direction of the N'gethwyn. It exploded into a mass of bodies, briefly clearing a path amongst the enemy. Seeing the opening, a captain from one of the prince's regiments directed his men into the area, creating a wedge into the enemy's front line.

A rumble behind Elhrin swept down the hillside. As she fired another assault into the enemy line around the N'gethwyn, a cavalry regiment thundered by her and crashed full force into the open left flank of the enemy.

The N'gethwyn retaliated with a wall of fire along the front line of fighters, not caring who she killed by the blaze. Men from both sides, Do'athrim, and horses alike were set on fire. Some ran crazily throughout the fray like living torches only to be cut down by an enemy. Weirdly, a low gray mist formed over the line of the fire, and turned into a downpour of water. The flames struggled against the downpour then died. The N'gethwyn screamed in anger.

Elhrin spared a quick grin for Marissa. "She didn't like you putting out her fire," she said.

Marissa scrambled to her feet. "I don't think she is going to like much of anything that is going to happen to her today," she huffed.

"I like your way of thinking," Elhrin said as a small regiment of archers ran into position alongside them.

Loading their bows, they fired at will high into the air. Elhrin groaned. Strong wind gusts funneled up the meadow from the sea and caused the arrows to fly erratically onto those below, wounding and killing some of their own soldiers. An officer ran across the knoll screaming for the archers to hold fire.

"Marissa, see what you can do with the N'gethwyn, I'll be right back," Elhrin said and ran after the officer. "Sergeant," she called out to the man.

"What is it?" he huffed in anger turning to look at her.

"I'm no expert, but wouldn't you have a better vantage point from up there?" she asked pointing to a spit of land rising alongside one of the cliffs that would be just large enough to hold his men.

He surveyed the layout. Boulders riddled the area which would also allow the archers a small amount of cover. "The wind would still play a factor, Major, but the height would give us an advantage. Men, follow me," he shouted waving his men into action.

"Elhrin, damn it!" a voice rang out. "Don't ever leave without me again!"

Elhrin glanced over her shoulder as Kyne flung himself from his horse.

"I couldn't wait," she retorted as he drew his sword and planted himself defensively beside her. "There was no time to wait for you. Is the King and Master Gryph not with you?" She couldn't feel his magical energy.

"No," he surveyed the battle, "They are behind me somewhere. King Goruth was yelling for everyone to move when I left the courtyard. He is furious."

"I am sure he is. We aren't prepared for this."

"Damn, look at all those ships," Kyne said.

"Stand back," she yelled, just as a ball of fire zoomed at them then exploded against her invisible shield of protective energy.

"Son of a . . . ," Kyne yelled, instinctively ducking from the blast while covering his head. "Can't you find a better place to fight than standing out in the middle of the field?"

"No time," she growled as she raised her hands high over her head and clapped them together then pushed outward. A sizzling white ball of energy shot from her hands, growing in size as it sped over the heads of the army. It exploded into enemy forces near the N'gethwyn. The pale lady had conjured a protective shield, but the force of Elhrin's attack sent her sprawling along with the masses of dead and injured.

"Damn, she's a tough one," Elhrin spat out, feeling the N'gethwyn's energy still vibrating strong among the bodies of soldiers. Elhrin wanted to use her god-given powers and blast them all off the field, but she had to conserve her energy. If she drained herself too quickly she would be useless for the rest of the battle, and from the looks of the amount of ships choking the cove, the battle was going to be long and hard.

She spared a quick glance up the hillside to make sure Phalen was with Prince Cahail.

Neither of the two knew that their futures were already entwined, despite what the prince wanted. Phalen was working hard against any enemy slipping through the lines and charging towards their position while the prince shouted commands to his officers and pointed at a catapult. The prince's men had evidently worked overnight and had been able to complete two working catapults that they had positioned along the ridge not far from Prince Cahail. A loud crack resounded over the confusion of battle. Chunks of rock soared high overhead, raining heavily into the enemy ranks near the beach.

The pale N'gethwyn appeared again. Elhrin gathered her energy to attack, but Marissa beat her to it. A pike was jerked out of the hands of an astonished soldier, and flew as if it had a mind of its own at the N'gethwyn. Concentrating on her next attack, the N'gethwyn did not see it coming. The pike went straight through her neck, and impaled her to the back of a nearby Do'athrim. Both fell. This time Elhrin knew the N'gethwyn was dead. Her magical energy evaporated from Elhrin's awareness, which was good. What was not good was the fact that other N'gethwyn were now on the beach.

"What kind of ship is that?" Kyne pointed to a boxy looking transport vessel being tossed in the waves just off shore.

As they watched it struggle in the angry surf, a large hatch opened from the side of the ship and banged against its hull. She wondered why they would take such a risk. With the waves rolling it around the ship was sure to take on water in its hold. Then she saw why . . . huge beasts resembling overgrown hairy porcupines with long snouts and a long, spiked tail, began to leap out of the hatch and swim to shore, and to her amazement, Do'athrim wolven were riding them like horses.

"What are those?" Kyne asked.

"Those have to be the bynduwhin," she groaned, "and, from what Master Gryph has said about them, we are in big trouble."

"Like we weren't already?" Kyne commented.

She darted a brief glance his way. "Come on." Elhrin sprinted across the hill to where Marissa stood firing hard-as-steel ice missiles into the enemy.

"Marissa," she yelled, "save your energy for the N'gethwyn. We may have to fight the bynduwhin, too."

"What are bynduwhin?" Marissa yelled back.

"The creatures that are swimming to shore," Elhrin pointed to the beasts nearing the beach. "They have deadly poison in spines they can fire from their tails. Just those few could wipe out our army. Kyne, I don't think Prince Cahail knows about them. I need you to go tell him."

"I'm not leaving you."

"Yes, you will," Elhrin commanded. "We don't have time for you to argue with me. Go!"

"Damn it, Elhrin, don't you dare leave here until I get back," he ordered then sprinted up the hillside.

Another cavalry regiment thundered across the meadow passing Kyne, and several riders cut away from them and raced towards her. To her relief, reinforcements were finally filtering in from Marmuht and the rest of the Eagles had arrived, but Master Gryph was not among them.

"Elhrin," Barron yelled, bringing his mount to a skidding halt.

"Barron, take your team to the other side of the field. We . . . ."

"Elhrin," he repeated forcefully, and jumped from his horse. She didn't like the look on his face as he approached her. Something was wrong. "We were ambushed on the way here. King Goruth and Master Idwyr are down. Colonel Toome is dead."

Elhrin felt like her heart stopped. "What happened?" she asked through a sudden wave of nausea.

"We were coming through the last stretch of forest on the road. It was so sudden. Our horses spooked and went out of control. An N'gethwyn's force of energy suddenly flared to life, and Master Idwyr was immediately hit and went down. Then Do'athrim appeared from the trees and fired on us from both sides of our line. Arrows cut down many around us before we had time to put up our shields, including the king." Barron shook his head helplessly. "The king tried to rise, but was hit several more times. Colonel Toome put his horse directly in front of the king to protect him, but he too was cut down. Elhrin, the N'gethwyn disappeared from our awareness as soon as the king fell, and the Do'athrim that could get away drifted back into the woods and disappeared as if they had never been. General Shifwood ordered everyone into a defensive position so that the King Goruth's personal physician and his staff could help those that had fallen. They wouldn't let us near, but we saw Colonel Toome. He . . . it wasn't . . . ," Barron's voice broke and he couldn't finish what he was about to say.

"We will talk about this later," Elhrin croaked. "Is Master Idwyr dead?"

"He wasn't when they took him away to the medical wagons," Landin said. "I could still feel his source. General Shifwood left a protective regiment with them, and I think they were to go back to Marmuht. Zeike fell from his horse and broke his arm so I sent him back with them. The rest of us were ordered to hurry here."

"What about Bayle?" she asked, but both of them shook their heads.

"I don't know. There was a lot of confusion. Bayle had been riding close to Master Idwyr, but I honestly don't know what became of him," Landin said.

Elhrin felt like stone. "Barron," she said, "take your team to the other side of the field. Concentrate on the N'gethwyn and the bynduwhin beasts. One of you tell Prince Cahail and Phalen to be alert for a rear attack. The N'gethwyn and the Do'athrim are still out there. If the prince needs you for anything, do it."

"Yes, ma'am," he said and mounted his horse. Waving for his team to follow, he shot off across the meadow.

"Elhrin," Marissa whispered, her freckles were vivid against the pallor of her frightened face, "what will we do?"

"We will do what we have to do. We already know what our jobs are, let's get to it." She turned to Jayce and Jayme. She exhaled grimly, hating the anxious looks on their young faces. Boys their age should be enjoying a carefree life, not facing a life-threatening situation. "Jayce, you and Jayme are to stay back out of harm's way for right now." She held up a hand when Jayce started to protest. "No, listen to me. I am not keeping you out of the battle. Do you feel all the N'gethwyn out on the water?"

He nodded.

"There are more behind them that are out of your range, so you two are our reserves. When we become tired, we will need you to back us up. Do you understand?"

"But, Elhrin, can't we help now?" he frowned, looking out at the approaching ships. "There are so many."

"I know, but we will need you in a little while. Just stay back away from the enemy and be ready. Okay?" She could tell he didn't like it, but reluctantly, he nodded. "Good, go wait near the wagons until I call you."

Explosions rocked the hillside. Elhrin scanned the battlefield. There were more N'gethwyn on shore than she thought. Three were halfway up the hillside hurling lethal attacks into the army, and four were along the beach. More were closing in on the shore. She had to wonder where so many had come from.

Barron's company launched an attack on the advancing enemy as they hurtled across the field, sending a barrage of exploding orbs of energy including Kull's signature attack of tiny white arrow-like missiles that burned painful holes into flesh.

Elhrin turned back to the rest of the team.

"Landin, I think Grey is out of the fight. He was attacked and I haven't seen him back up yet, so Kory will join your group and Eowhyn will stay with me. We need to somehow try to take out as many N'gethwyn on the water before they reach shore as possible. If you and your team can reach the cliff top east of us, it should be close enough for you to work, but you will be exposed. Ashlyn, it is your job to protect them. Tover, the distance may stretch your limits, but do what you can. Kory, do you think your friends in the sea could help us in any way?"

"Yes," he answered. "The skulowhal have been known to capsize fishermen's boats who hunted them. Those dinghies wouldn't stand a chance against their strength."

"Are there any out there?"

"I don't know." He closed his eyes tightly to concentrate on finding the sea creatures. He blew out a breath of frustration. "I am too far away. I can't hear anything."

"Try again when you reach the cliff."

He nodded, and Landin's team spurred their horses back up the hill. They had to go back through the wagons and the Prince's camp to reach the flatlands above that would take them to the cliff's edge overlooking the cove.

Enemy explosions tore into the group surrounding Prince Cahail, sending bodies flying in all directions. When the smoke cleared, Phalen stood like a sentinel, with hands extended in front of him. He had managed a shield large enough to protect Prince Cahail, Kyne, and the surrounding officers. The ones in front of his shield had not been so lucky. A frightening mass of gore lay below the boy, but he did not falter. Solisius had chosen well. This boy was going to be strong, indeed. Prince Cahail screamed for another wave of men to charge.

The archers had finally reached the outcrop of land and positioned themselves among the rock. Their arrows flew across the meadow, still shifting wildly in the wind, but they managed to reach the enemy successfully. Enemy archers retaliated. Their arrows rode along the current of wind and carried easily uphill. Some aimed for those among the rocks, others just allowed theirs to find anyone rushing down the meadow. Men all over the field fell in midstride. Along the shore, the bynduwhin and their Do'athrim riders were pushing their way to the front.

"Girls, let's go," Elhrin yelled, wanting to get closer to the fight. "Clay, we are counting on you to be our eyes while we are occupied."

"I won't fail you," he growled.

Her small group veered parallel to the fighting, skirting along the base of the cliff and trying to get a better fighting point with some cover from flying arrows and N'gethwyn attacks. Elhrin found a ledge of rock jutting outward, and the four of them climbed to the top.

"Eowhyn, see what you can do about the bynduwhin on this side. Marissa, go after any of the N'gethwyn."

The N'gethwyn seemed to be concentrating their attacks on the bulk of Anderan's army and not paying attention to their location. Elhrin decided to do something that would leave her vulnerable, and hoped she would have time before they decided to attack her. Raising her hands wide, she directed her energy over the shoreline where the enemy was swarming out of the boats. Several N'gethwyn were in the area. She could feel a strong pocket of energy. She blocked out the chaos of battle, and focused on what she wanted to do. Painfully slow, an orb of intense energy appeared and grew above the heads of the enemy on the beach. She poured energy into the orb, creating a contained sphere of deadly power. Elhrin faintly heard Marissa suck in a surprised breath.

"Look out," Clay yelled.

A crushing force slammed Elhrin flat on her back, knocking the breath out of her and making her lose control of her magic. Distantly, a great boom rocked the beach. Elhrin sucked in a painful breath of air. Coughing, she rolled to her side. Eowhyn's sightless eyes stared back at her.

"No," she breathed, clawing her way to Eowhyn's side. "No!" She grabbed Eowhyn's tunic and shook her, but the girl was lifeless.

"Elhrin," Marissa cried, crawling on her hands and knees across the ledge. Blood trailed down the side of her face. "Dear god!" Marissa sobbed, reaching out a shaky hand to smooth Eowhyn's bright hair from her pale face. "Oh, Eowhyn, you tried." Marissa looked at Elhrin. "I saw the attack coming out of the corner of my eye. She moved to protect us. It must have hit her before she was fully ready. Clay," Marissa breathed, looking wildly around the ledge. "Clay!" she screamed.

"I'm here," they heard a faint voice cry. Scrambling across the ledge of rock, they peered over the side and found Clay lying below. "I'm okay." He grasped at the rough rock and pulled himself up. With a groan, he started to climb back up to where they were.

Elhrin looked where her orb had detonated along the beach. It had not reached the size she had hoped for, but the damage had been substantial, anyway. A small crater in the sand was being filled by the tide. Sea water mingled with blood and body parts of those who had been caught up in the blast. N'gethwyn energy in the area was depleted indicating she had managed to kill some of them.

A strange popping sound came from over the water, and fist-sized chunks of stone rained down on the boats close to shore. Most of the stone fell harmlessly into the water, but those that made contact were damaging. Exposed heads were crushed, bones were broken, and a few lucky shots punctured holes in the bottoms of boats. An N'gethwyn nearing shore stood in his rowboat and fired a succession of sizzling blasts of energy at Landin's team on the cliff top. Suddenly, the rear of his boat shot upward and flipped. The N'gethwyn and the rest of the boat's occupants were hurled into the water. Those weighted down by armor and weapons did not resurface, but the N'gethwyn, who was not encumbered by overly heavy clothing, reappeared.

A dorsal fin briefly appeared behind his back then went under. Shortly after, the N'gethwyn was jerked underwater. His energy force disappeared as another mass of stone rained down on the surf. Elhrin exhaled heavily, thankful for the additional help. Kory had been able to locate at least one skulowhal. She scanned the cliff above. Tover was using his magic to hurl large rocks out over the water then causing them to explode in mid-air, resulting in the damaging rain of stone.

"Oh, no!" Marissa shouted. A bynduwhin was charging in their direction. She bombarded the beast with a hailstorm of ice shards. The beast did an amazing sideways flip and avoided Marissa's attack.

"How did the damn wolf stay on his back?" Clay asked, amazed at the feat. He raised his bow and fired a series of arrows at the beast. The ones that connected bounced harmlessly off its thick hide. The Do'athrim wolven on the bynduwhin's back barked a command. The beast slowed, raised his tail and fired his poisoned spikes at them, then charged. Elhrin and Marissa created protective shields. The spikes burst against the barriers, sending a spray of liquid into the wind. Elhrin pushed her shield downward and used it as a battering ram, slamming it into the charging beast. The force against her shield was tremendous and she had to let it go.

Momentarily stunned, the beast shook his head back and forth, and backed up a few steps. Clay fired, having a clear shot at the Do'athrim. Despite the strong wind, his arrow hit its mark and pierced the beast's chest. The Do'athrim slumped forward, but did not fall.

"He has to be strapped on the thing," Clay muttered.

The bynduwhin bellowed, baring rows of sharp teeth. He scrambled over the rocks littering the slope, intent on reaching them, not caring that his rider was dead.

Elhrin slammed another shield into the beast as Clay reloaded his bow, then turned his head to look at something up slope.

"What the . . . ?" he asked as a horse and rider raced at full speed across the meadow for the bynduwhin.

Kyne, bent low over the horse's neck, held a long pike out front. The bynduwhin hesitated long enough to send another volley of spikes at Elhrin and Marissa, and did not see him coming.

"Son of a bitch," Elhrin said angrily, not liking the risk Kyne was taking. She conjured another shield against the spikes just as Kyne slammed into the bynduwhin. Beast, horse, and rider flipped down the slope. The dead Do'athrim flopped lifelessly onto the ground.

"Kyne," Elhrin screamed, and scrambled down the ledge.

"Elhrin," Marissa yelled. "It's not dead."

The beast rolled to its feet, roaring in rage. The broken shaft of Kyne's pike stuck in its side, having snapped when they rolled. The beast attacked Kyne's horse that was struggling to get up. It swiped the animal with its sharp claws, rending a huge gash in the horse's side. The horse stilled without a sound. The bynduwhin then turned his attention to Kyne. Limping, Kyne was trying to circle behind the beast. He drew his sword. The beast charged. Elhrin and Marissa both sent flaming orbs of energy at the beast. Marissa's missed, but Elhrin's attack caught him in the side. It blew a hole into the beast's hide, exposing muscle and rib bones, but the beast did not fall as expected. Instead, it stood as if confused which way to turn, towards her or the closer prey that was Kyne.

"Obsudius had to create this bastard," Elhrin growled to herself, thinking the god had given the beast a body strong as steel. "Damn it!" she yelled in frustration when the beast once again lumbered after Kyne. She launched one assault after another. The forces of energy ripped into the beast in succession taking out small chunks of flesh. The bynduwhin staggered from the onslaught but did not give up on attacking Kyne. The beast swiped at Kyne with its deadly claws. Kyne jumped backwards, trying to stay out of reach. The Bynduwhin whipped its spiked tail around, intent on impaling him. Kyne leapt to the side, tripped over rocks, and fell. The spikes barely missed him, zooming mere inches over his body.

Elhrin tried another tactic. Hurtling over knee high rocks, she screamed at the beast and flung a bolt of white sizzling energy at him. The beast bellowed from the shocking blow, and turned its huge head to look at her. Kyne took advantage of the diversion to scramble to his feet and back away from the beast. Seeing its prey move, the beast lunged at him. Elhrin put all she had into a force shield, not caring about depleting her energy and allowing her god-given power reserves surge through her hands. She slammed it into the beast's side. She heard the sound of bones snapping as the beast flipped through the air and crashed to the rocky ground. Kyne ran at the beast flailing on its back trying to turn its huge body over.

"Kyne, no!" she screamed.

Kyne did not heed her. He leapt past the beast's elongated claws waving wildly in the air and plunged his sword to the hilt in the exposed soft underbelly of the bynduwhin. It roared once, then was still. Kyne staggered backwards and fell to his backside.

Elhrin raced across the rocky turf, falling to her knees when she reached his side. His face was covered in blood from scratches across his cheek and forehead.

He gave her a crazy smile. "Wasn't that fun?" he choked out, then turned to spit a stream of blood on the ground.

"No, it wasn't, you lunatic." She wanted to punch him, and found she was shaking. He had scared her more than she realized. "I could kill you myself for attempting such a thing. What were you thinking charging him like that?"

"Sometimes, it's just better to not think," he replied, wiping his face with his sleeve. "I told you to stay out of harm's way until I returned. I should have known you wouldn't listen."

"Come on," she offered him a trembling hand to help him stand. "We need to get out of here."

Retrieving his sword from the beast, they scrambled back towards the rock ledge. Boulders soared overhead from the catapults creating pockets of dead within enemy ranks. The enemy didn't break stride, filling in the pockets as they pushed forward. The other bynduwhin beasts had made it to the front line, and were massacring men with ease. Barron's team was dividing their attention between the closest beast and the N'gethwyn that were advancing on their side of the field.

"That was the bravest, but stupidest thing I have ever seen anyone do," Clay said when they reached the top of the ledge.

"Whatever," Kyne replied, noticing Eowhyn's lifeless form. His face turned to stone. "Elhrin, we need to make our way further up the hill." Kyne's voice matched the stoniness of his face. He did not take his eyes off of Eowhyn. "The enemy is pushing our forces slowly back. Cahail is going to fortify the line along a rise. He wants the Eagles to attack the front line so his men can retreat. "

Elhrin glanced uphill. Soldiers who weren't already engaged in battle were forming ranks along either side of Cahail's position.

"Clay, run tell Jayce and Jayme to get ready. It is time for them to help. Tell them to attack only when I begin and they are to stay behind our line." Following Clay, Elhrin started down from the ledge. Kyne bent over to scoop Eowhyn in his arms. "Kyne," Elhrin said, "we can't take her."

Kyne had formed a tentative relationship with Eowhyn over the last year whenever they had visited Glimmerdale. Because of his inclination for keeping his personal life to himself, she didn't realize just how much he had cared for the girl until now.

He ignored her and began to pick Eowhyn up.

"Kyne . . . ."

"I will not leave her," Kyne yelled, daring her to contradict him with an icy stare.

"You will have to," Marissa said, placing a hand on his arm. "Look."

The enemy was close to their position and advancing fast. An N'gethwyn within their ranks launched an attack at them. Elhrin launched a counter-attack. The two spheres of energy met in midair and exploded, showering the enemy below with painful sparks of fire.

"Kyne, come on!" Elhrin yelled, scrambling off the ledge. Marissa was right behind her. Kyne reluctantly lowered Eowhyn, and whispered something low under his breath. He slid down behind the girls.

Flinging attacks at the advancing enemy, they ran up the meadow and through a new line of archers who were positioned along a rise in the meadow. An explosion kicked up mounds of dirt and rock behind them, but Elhrin didn't stop to retaliate because there was a dark-headed boy running down the hill towards them.

No, she thought, *he will be too close.* She scanned the hillside as she ran. Where was Jayme?

"Clay, stop him," Elhrin screamed at the man's back just as another explosion boomed right behind her. The force from the concussion knocked her face first to the ground. She rolled to her back, wiping dirt out of her eyes. Kyne grabbed her by the arm and jerked her to her feet. Marissa was on her other side and aimed an attack at the N'gethwyn. Elhrin sent one of her own. The two forces of energy zoomed over the line of archers and found their mark. The N'gethwyn's body was torn in two by the consecutive blasts.

Elhrin felt a black force of power enter the battlefield on top of the ridge behind her. Her blood ran cold.

"No!" she whispered, whipping around.

Behind Prince Cahail's position was a mass of Do'athrim rushing from an opening between two stands of nearby trees. A tall man bearing the same features as Master Gryph rode at their head on a white horse. Elhrin's world seemed to slow down, and it felt as if she watched events unfold from outside her own body. Prince Cahail slowly turned as if he was slogging through a pit of quicksand to face the new threat just as an unseen force ripped into him and those around him.

"Phalen!" she screamed. The world sped up.

Bodies flew in all directions. Derrick reined in his horse and allowed the Do'athrim forces to swell around him. They slammed into the ranks of soldiers on top of the ridge.

The N'gethwyn on the field below intensified their attack and launched a series of long-range attacks into the ranks on top of the hill. Soldiers tried to avoid the attack, but some were not successful and were blown apart.

Elhrin growled, hurtled a quick succession of attacks at the nearest N'gethwyn on the field, not bothering to aim, and took off at a dead run for the top of the hill. Phalen lived, but she did not know in what condition.

Anderan's soldiers rallied around the fallen prince, as troops that were filtering in from

Marmuht rushed into the fray with a roar. Derrick fired a succession of lethal blasts of energy into their midst, then turned his head in her direction—and found her. Before Elhrin had a chance to attack or defend herself, she was swept off her feet into the air and then slammed back to the earth. Her world went black.

"Elhrin," a voice said distantly. "Elhrin, can you hear me?"

She heard someone groan.

"I think she is coming around, Marissa. Elhrin?"

She became aware of an intense pain lancing through her back. "Ohhh," she groaned, and opened her eyes. Clay hovered over her. "What?" she coughed, as she tried to sit up. Pain seared through her back. She hunched to the side, propping herself on one elbow. A nearby explosion caused her to flinch. She saw that Jayce was stoically holding a magical shield against a powerful attack, protecting them. At the next attack, Jayce was knocked to his knees, but he remained in control of his magic. She was amazed that the boy was able to withstand Derrick's attack when her own shield had ripped apart. Then she saw why. Derrick was not directing the full brunt of his powers at Jayce, but was dividing them between the boy and blowing a line of charging pike men to pieces.

She looked back at her companions around her. Marissa lay in the grass beside her, holding a hand to her head. Kyne was sprawled face down in front of her. Her heart dropped, but then he moved his leg, and she breathed a sigh of relief. Clay had positioned himself between her and Marissa, firing arrows downfield at the enemy.

"Clay, I've got to get to the top," she said hoarsely. If Derrick hadn't known she had survived the shipwreck before, he did now. It was going to be up to her to kill him. Master Gryph had asked her to allow him to face Derrick alone if possible because that particular fight was his responsibility, but then a familiar magical force that had been steadily growing stronger broke through the turmoil of her battered mind, finally making her pay attention to its presence. She clawed at the mounds of grass, turning herself around to see the top of the ridge behind her.

A beam of bright white energy shot across the meadow at Derrick who had to break off his attack against Jayce and the others in order to block the beam. It exploded in a thunderous spray of power out away from Derrick, blowing those within its path apart and creating a pocket of calm around the N'gethwyn. He sat alone on his white horse as the battle surged away from him, waiting on the newcomer.

Dozens of riders thundered into view, hurtling at full speed across the broad expanse along the top of the meadow. Master Gryph was in the lead. Riding low over his mount's back, he launched another beam of energy at his brother. There was no doubt he had every intent to kill the man. Elhrin saw with relief that Bayle was right behind him as a roar of rallying voices rose over the din of battle. The fighting soldiers saw Master Gryph and his reinforcements and renewed their efforts to obliterate the Do'athrim around the fallen prince.

"Clay, look," she breathed.

He grinned.

Kyne groaned then rose up onto his forearms.

"You okay?" she asked. He looked at her through one eye.

"Is my head still on?" he asked, lowering his face into his hands.

"For now," she replied, pushing herself to her knees. "Kyne, he's here."

"Well, I can't fight him. Can you ask him to come back later?" he asked, raising his head and looking out over the battlefield below.

"No, Master Gryph is here."

"So is the enemy," Kyne responded matter-of-factly as if announcing the arrival of a dear friend.

A line of enemy soldiers and Do'athrim were bearing down on them. They had overrun the army's line on their side of the meadow. There was nothing standing in the enemy's path to the top except Elhrin and her team.

Lightning zipped out of the sky above, hitting something nearby. An earth-shattering boom of thunder broke over the battlefield, and the black clouds overhead could no longer contain the weight of water. It began to pour. The storm had arrived.

Chapter Nineteen

—◦◦❖◦◦—

Gryph rode low over his horse's neck, ignoring the throbbing pain in the back of his head where it had connected with the rocky ground when he had fallen. He was furious at himself for not being on guard—for being taken down so easily. The fall had knocked him out long enough to cost him dearly. He had lost one of his best friends and Goruth was seriously wounded and might not live.

Gryph hurled a beam of white fire at Derrick. His brother saw it coming and blocked it. Gryph launched another. Again, Derrick blocked it, and smiled. He did not retaliate. Gryph knew he wouldn't. Not yet, anyway. He wanted Gryph close.

Not taking his eyes off Gryph, Derrick raised his arms over his head. Smiling maliciously, he fired two bolts of deep green energy downhill. With amazing accuracy, they exploded into Jayce's shield. The force shattered the shield and flung the boy into Elhrin and the others on the ground.

Gryph's rage seared white hot. He spurred his mount, willing him to go faster, knowing the steed was already running at top speed. Behind him, his troop fanned out into a wedge, and drew their weapons.

Enjoying Gryph's obvious anger, Derrick's smile widened. He directed his next attack at the soldiers following Gryph. Bolts of green energy sped across the field. Gryph dropped Tyton's reins and flung his arms wide. He fired a force out of both hands. The bolts took a direct hit, and ricocheted into the turf exploding out of harm's way. Derrick clapped his hands together softly, impressed with Gryph's accomplishment.

Ignoring the pain in his left leg, Gryph rose in the stirrups, smacked his hands together over his head, and pushed an invisible force outward. It slammed into his brother before he had time to defend himself. Derrick was flung from his horse as both he and the animal hit the ground hard and rolled away from the mass of fighting men and Do'athrim.

Derrick's horse clambered back to its feet and bolted away. Derrick lay still as stone in the high grass, but Gryph was skeptical that his brother was dead. He couldn't feel Derrick's energy, but knowing how his brother worked, he had cut himself off to bring Gryph in closer.

With a wave of his hand, Gryph directed Bayle and the men with him to the fight around the catapults where Phalen was desperately working alongside Prince Cahail's men who were outnumbered by Derrick's Do'athrim. He then used his magic to retrieve the reins that were whipping wildly from his horse's bridle and veered his mount to where Derrick lay. Gryph brought his horse to a skidding halt and slid to the ground. He jerked his staff from his saddle and approached his brother warily.

For the first time in years, blue eyes like his own stared back at him. Derrick grinned without humor. "Hello, brother," he said, and slammed Gryph with his magic. Gryph landed on his back and flipped, coming to a rest face down in the cool grass.

Growling in anger at himself for being so foolish as to not be ready for an attack, he pushed himself up to one knee, and glared at his brother. Derrick was already on his feet, waiting patiently. Gryph snatched his staff with his magic and struggled to stand up.

"Gryph, I expected you to be a little more prepared. Twice now I have been able to take you down. How is the mighty King of Anderan, by the way?"

"He lives," Gryph snapped. He fired on his brother.

Derrick dodged sideways to the ground, rolling easily back to his feet as Gryph's attack exploded behind him. He retaliated, shooting bolts of green at Gryph. Gryph expected the attack and easily deflected them with a wave of his hand just as a tremendous force slammed him from behind. He crashed hard into the ground. Pain seared throughout his skull. For a moment, he was disoriented.

"You see, dear brother of mine, I'm no longer the stupid, weak boy that was forever standing in your shadow," Derrick snarled.

Gryph shot a strand of energy towards Derrick and wrapped it around his body. He jerked forward at the same time as he pushed himself to his knees, ignoring the pain the movement caused his damaged leg. Derrick landed on his hands and knees in the turf a few yards away from him. Gryph scrambled across the ground and tackled his brother. They rolled across the uneven lumps of dense grass and Gryph ended up straddled on Derrick's chest. He punched Derrick in the face.

"You broke our mother's heart, you bastard," Gryph growled as he punched Derrick again, releasing years of frustration in the blow. He hated that their mother had never recovered from Derrick's loss and that she went to her grave loving a boy that had died in spirit long before she had in the flesh.

Derrick deflected Gryph's next blow then grabbed him by the neck. A blazing heat seared through his skin as his brother tried to burn and crush his throat at the same time. Gryph forcefully jerked back out of Derrick's grasp. Derrick heaved him off his body as a strong clap of thunder boomed overhead and a heavy downpour of rain swept over the field.

Gryph rolled away from Derrick firing bolts of energy, putting distance between them. His brother knocked them aside and fired back, landing them short of Gryph. Grass and dirt covered him as he magically wrapped Derrick in a cocoon of sizzling energy. Derrick roared in pain and anger. Gryph pushed power into the enclosure before Derrick could break through. His brother disappeared from view as the enclosure turned into a crackling cone of blinding white light.

Derrick pushed against the cell, testing for weaknesses. Holding onto his magic,

Gryph struggled to his feet without the aid of his staff. He limped painfully towards his brother until he was just a few paces away. He increased the pressure of energy and compressed it into Derrick's body, knowing that whatever magical protection Derrick used against his deadly force would soon fail.

An unwanted memory of a small boy staring in wonder at him as he juggled multi-colored balls of light flashed through his mind. *Mother, please forgive me*, he begged silently. He forced the walls of his enclosure into Derrick's body. Derrick screamed then pushed against Gryph with surprising strength. Gryph's cocoon exploded. He staggered backwards, nearly falling again in the slippery grass.

Derrick lurched to the side then regained his balance. "You will not take me that easily, So'ladiun," Derrick breathed furiously. "I am a child of the high god, Obsudius, and I am his favored son."

Two forces of energy slammed Gryph on either side. He whipped around as if caught in the draft of a tornado. It was a miracle he managed to remain on his feet, but then Derrick's next blow struck his injured leg. A blinding pain seared throughout his body and he dropped like a stone to his hands and knees, breathless. He struggled against the massive pain rendering him momentarily useless, wondering why his brother did not finish his attack and kill him. He raised his head to glare at his brother, blinking away the rivers of rain that wanted to fill his eyes.

"Oh, I apologize," Derrick mocked. "I forgot you have a serious injury to that leg." He stepped closer, swiping rain and blood from his face. "Did you think I haven't kept up with you all these years, *brother*?" Derrick sneered. "I know all about you. As a matter of fact, there was a time that I was you. Now, that was fun."

Gryph realized that Derrick was playing with him and had something to say before he killed him.

"What are you talking about?" Gryph gasped through his pain. He had to recover quickly if he hoped to survive. Derrick was far stronger than when they last met and Gryph had to admit that the injuries to his body, both new and old, had put him at a serious disadvantage.

"Do you remember Lynh?"

Gryph's body went cold at the mention of his son's mother.

Derrick smiled wickedly. "I see you do. How could anyone ever forget her, right? She was so pretty, so innocent and trusting."

"What about her?" Summoning all the will he could muster, Gryph forced himself to stand.

Derrick raised a hand and magically wrapped Gryph in a binding hold. Gryph fought to break free. Derrick tightened his grip and Gryph was forced to quit in order to breathe.

"Ah, ah, ahhh, my brother, stay still like a good boy or you won't get to hear the rest of the story." Derrick barked a humorless laugh. "And I might add, it is not what I did to her . . . it is more like what you did to her. How could you call me a heartless bastard when you are just as cold? You broke Lynh's heart twice and never looked back." Derrick dropped his smile. He stepped forward and leaned in close. "In the years we were growing up, did you ever see that I had feelings for Lynh? That I loved her? She knew me first, yet after I introduced you, she only had eyes for you. Did you love her?"

"Of course I did," Gryph growled. "If you had feelings for her why did you not tell me? I cannot read your mind."

"What was I supposed to say? You were the perfect one. The perfect son, the perfect friend, and you were the perfect match for her, even her father said he hoped one day you two would marry. Did you know that?"

"No, I didn't," Gryph said.

"Of course not," Derrick hissed, "you were too busy with your head up your own ass to see anything, so intent on getting to Muryne and not caring about what you left behind."

"My destiny was not in Pago Duhn, Derrick. I think you would understand that now that you know who I am."

"Understanding now does not make up for what happened at the time. Do you know what life was like after you left?" Derrick spat out. "Lynh wouldn't have anything to do with me, and our dear father constantly compared me to you. Of course, I always fell short of his expectations. Did you know he beat me every time I fell short?"

"I don't believe you." Gryph knew what he said had to be a lie. His father may have had a hard time understanding Derrick, but he would never beat a child.

"Believe what you like. I honestly don't care. But in the end, I returned to Pago Duhn and made sure he knew just how I felt about him as my father. You see, he didn't die in that storm like everyone believed . . . I killed him slow and with great care."

Gryph went numb. Their father had left home right after breakfast one morning to check his crab traps and cast his fishing nets, but that day an unexpected storm had blown across the coast, and it was assumed he had drowned. Neither his body nor his boat had ever been found.

"You bastard," Gryph hissed. He pushed hard against Derrick's bindings.

"I have one other thing to ask you, Gryph." Derrick gritted his teeth against Gryph's struggles. "Do you truly believe you are Griffyn's father?"

Shocked to the core of his being, Gryph stopped struggling and stared wide-eyed at his brother.

Derrick laughed. "I thought that would get your attention. I told you before I had a fantastic time being you. Do you remember the last time you were with Lynh?"

"Yes," Gryph growled. He had been in Pago Duhn to visit his mother's grave after he learned of her death. It was also the last time he saw Lynh alive. He had not returned to Pago Duhn until years later.

"I visited Pago Duhn not long after you left that summer and was surprised when everyone thought I was you, even Lynh. She was overjoyed you had come back. I made her think you had returned because you couldn't get enough of her." Derrick swiped rainwater from his face. "On our first night, she commented on how much she liked me, uh, you without the beard. I honestly don't know how you could have walked away from her. She was so beautiful . . . so soft and eager, but you just walked away from her. I do have to give you credit, my brother. The women you choose are nice." He narrowed his eyes at Gryph as a malicious idea formed in his mind. "As a matter of fact, they are so nice I have just decided to take back what I said in my letter about destroying your family. It would be a shame to quench such a fiery spirit as Marguerite, don't you think? After I have done away with you, I know she would need someone to comfort her. I look enough like you that I think she will come to love me, eventually."

Gryph lost all coherent thought. He forced his energy through Solisius' pendant, gathered its strength and combined it with his own. He obliterated Derrick's bindings. He slammed both fists into his brother's face. Derrick's head whipped back with an audible snap. He staggered backwards. Blood spewed from his broken nose.

Gryph advanced on his brother, no longer feeling the pain in his body. Sometimes, it felt good to use physical force. He wanted to rip Derrick in half with his bare hands.

Derrick spat blood out of his mouth, understanding the look in Gryph's eyes. He readied his fists, content to forgo magic for hand-to-hand combat. "Why are you so angry, brother? Don't you want your wife to be happy when you are gone?"

Gryph swung his right fist. Derrick side-stepped and punched him hard in his exposed lower back. Gryph grunted from the pain and swung backhanded. His fist connected with Derrick's jaw. He faced his brother.

Derrick grinned as he wiggled his jaw from Gryph's blow. "What is bothering you more? The possibility that I could be Griffyn's father, or bedding your wife and she finds she married the wrong brother the first time?" he asked enjoying Gryph's rage.

"You will not live to see that day," Gryph snarled and swung again. Derrick blocked it and counter-punched Gryph in the face. White lights shot through Gryph's eyes, momentarily blinding him. Derrick punched him in the stomach. Gryph doubled over, and was immediately knocked to the wet ground from a blow to his back. Derrick kicked him in the side and rolled him over. Pain shot through his side. Gryph couldn't breathe again, damning Obsudius and his realm for destroying the health of his lungs.

"What happened to the strong, perfect brother of mine?" Derrick asked angrily, and kicked him in the side again. "You are weaker than I expected."

Pain ripped through Gryph's side. This time he thought something may have cracked. He ignored it, and fired a bolt of energy at Derrick. Derrick leaned back, barely blocking the attack. He staggered backwards when the force hit his shield. Gryph struck again. This time his attack caused Derrick to hit the ground, grunting in pain.

Gryph rolled to his knees and summoned his staff with his magic. It flew across the field and hit his palm with a wet smack. He used it to haul himself to his feet as Derrick pushed himself to his feet, as well, wiping away blood draining from his nose with the back of his hand.

Gryph was through listening to Derrick's taunts. Through with whatever game Derrick was playing by keeping him out of the battle below. Gryph unleashed his fury. A blast of sizzling energy shot from his hand. Derrick blocked it and it exploded with a huge spray of sparks. The force caused Derrick to stumble back. Gryph repeated the attack. Again, Derrick was forced to retreat under the explosion of sparks, but he then dropped his shield and retaliated.

He shot a plume of red fire at Gryph. Gryph launched a blue orb and the two spheres of energy met between the men, exploding in a stunning show of fire and trails of white smoke.

Derrick released a series of attacks, blasting Gryph with bolts of green energy. One by one, Gryph deflected them all then used an invisible strand of his magic to grasp Derrick by the neck and jerk him face down to the ground. He then fired at Derrick's form on the ground. Derrick sensed the danger and rolled quickly across the grass, barely deflecting Gryph's blistering attack.

Derrick rose to his knees firing on Gryph. Ear splitting concussion after concussion drowned out the sound of pouring rain and the massive battle below as his spheres of energy slammed into Gryph's protective shield.

When Derrick hesitated, Gryph rammed his shield into Derrick's body, sending him sprawling backwards. He landed flat on his back in the grass. This time, he was the one heaving for air.

Gryph limped towards him. Derrick saw him coming and whipped a hand across his body. Gryph was slammed in the side by Derrick's magical force. His staff was ripped out of his hand and sailed high in the air. He hit the ground hard.

Derrick scrambled to his hands and knees and launched his body on top of Gryph, purposely slamming a knee into Gryph's injured leg. Gryph yelled in pain. Derrick then straddled him and started to strangle him. Again, he used magic to sear skin as he squeezed the breath out of Gryph. The combination was effective at disorienting Gryph. He could not grasp his energy source.

"Brother, you will suffer as I suffered," Derrick hissed. His face flamed red as he pressed against Gryph's neck. "You will never know what it was like after I left home. Near starvation, I was forced to live on rotting scraps from the trash piles, but then I got smart and found out it was much more profitable to kill the ignorant rich. Yes, that life suited me better until you and your cohorts started pursuing me." Rain dripped off Derrick's head into Gryph's eyes as he tried to pry Derrick's hands from his neck. "Sending your little minions to track me down until I finally had to stow away on a ship out of Marmuht and leave Anderan. I had plans, damn it, and you ruined them."

Derrick intensified the heat against Gryph's neck and pressed harder. Gryph choked against the overwhelming pain unable to scream—unable to focus. Years of sustaining countless injuries had caught up with him, and old internal scars from innumerable wounds and broken bones all seemed to be mimicking the fire burning into his neck. He was losing the fight. His lungs burned with the need to breathe.

Send him to me, the voice of Solisius jolted into his frantic mind.

I will not! He is N'gethwyn, Gryph shot the thought to the heavens. An N'gethwyn in the Realm of Light was too dangerous.

Send him to me! Solisius demanded.

Trying not to fall into the darkness threatening to overwhelm him, he let go of Derrick's arm. His hand dropped to his chest, lifeless. He struggled to concentrate—to will his hand to move. Slowly, his fingers clawed at his shirt and dragged his collar to the side. Desperately, he fumbled for his chain but then realized it was trapped under Derrick's hands and the pendant had fallen to one side out of his reach. Derrick pushed harder into Gryph's neck. The desperate need to breathe and the pain was more than his body could take. Against his will, both hands flopped to his sides in the grass and his vision blurred and faded into gray.

Do not yield, Solisius' voice forcefully ripped through his fading awareness. The image of Marguerite holding Marcus before he left Marmuht flashed through his mind, jolting him back to his senses.

Suddenly, Derrick cried out in pain and the pressure on his neck loosened as one of Derrick's hands let go of him. Gryph sucked in desperate breaths of cool, rain-soaked air.

Enraged, Derrick twisted to reach for something behind him. Gryph took advantage of the diversion and slapped a hand on his brother's chest, felt his magic respond to his summons, and sent a blast of energy into his brother's body. The force shot Derrick backwards off him and his body crashed heavily into the turf at Gryph's feet.

Gryph stared at the ominous, lightning streaked sky above him. He no longer felt his brother's energy force, but knew this time Derrick wasn't responsible for hiding it. He had just killed his own brother. Blinking rainwater out of his eyes, he rolled his head to look at the frightened boy standing nearby, drenched to the skin.

"Thank you, Jayme. You did well," he said hoarsely. He reached a weary hand to his collar and pulled it away from the burns on his neck. The cool rain streaming over his skin soothed the pain. "I owe you my life."

He wearily waved Jayme closer as he rolled over and managed to rise far enough to prop on an elbow. Reluctantly, the boy moved to his side and sank to his knees, bringing him eye-level with Gryph.

Gryph tried to smile but was sure it looked more like a grimace. "You were brave to do what you did," he said, glancing at Derrick's twisted body. Blood oozed out of a massive wound in his chest. A small dirk, the kind that Gryph gave his male students at the end of their first year in the academy, was embedded in Derrick's back near his neck. Gryph suspected Jayme had hidden his magical source of energy in order to sneak up on the fighting men without them being aware of his presence, and opted to stab Derrick instead of using a magical attack which would have revealed his presence right away. "I am proud of you. You aren't hurt, are you?"

Jayme shook his head, wordlessly blinking away tears that mixed with the rain pouring down his face.

"Good," Gryph said, wishing he could stop the boy's tears. Elhrin had been right. Jayme had not been ready, but there wasn't anything he could do about it now. "Will you retrieve my staff for me, son?"

Without a word, Jayme scrambled to his feet and hurried to where Gryph's staff lay half hidden in the mounds of thick meadow grasses. Gryph closed his eyes, listening to the unending booms echoing over the land, some coming from the battle, some from the storm raging above his head. He knew killing Derrick had been necessary, but still, he couldn't help the overwhelming sense of loss that settled over him. He didn't mourn the man at his feet. He mourned the loss of a boy he once knew and loved and a soul that could never be redeemed.

"Here, sir," a weak voice said, breaking into his thoughts.

He lifted a corner of his mouth. That was the first time Jayme had voluntarily spoken to him first. He ran a weary hand across his face to wipe away the rain and opened his eyes. "Thank you, son," he said and reached for the staff Jayme offered. He forced himself to his feet, and had to lean heavily on the staff to allow a sudden spell of dizziness to pass. "Jayme," he said after the dizziness faded away.

"Yes, sir?" the boy responded so quietly Gryph barely heard him.

"I have to go help the others," he said and reached out to clasp the boy's shoulder, feeling him trembling uncontrollably. "You have a choice to either stay with me or find a place safely away from the battle. What do you wish to do?"

Jayme glanced towards the violent struggle taking place around the catapults. Sporadic pops of deadly explosions flashed among the mob where Phalen stood his ground. "I will go with you," he said through trembling lips and ragged huffs of breath, trying not to sob.

Gryph furrowed his brow, hating that the boy had chosen to fight. He knew he could order Jayme off the field, but he would not. "You do not have to fight, Jayme. No one will think less of you," he said, giving the child one final chance to run to safety.

"I will go with you," the boy whispered.

"So be it," Gryph said, squeezing Jayme's shoulder reassuringly. He then used his magic to retrieve Jayme's dirk. The knife jerked easily out of Derrick's body and the hilt hit his palm, cold and wet. He wiped the blade on his pants staining them with streaks of his brother's blood. "Stay close, understand?" he said as he handed the blade over to the boy.

Jayme nodded, nervously eyeing the blade in his hand as they started across the field.

Chapter Twenty

———✦———

Plumes of fire sizzled over Elhrin and Jayce and burst into the advancing enemy line. The line collapsed then reformed without slowing down.

"Get up," Elhrin said, pushing the boy off her, thankful that the bulk of Derrick's energy had been diffused away from Jayce when his shield shattered.

He held out a hand to help her up. "Look, it's Grey," he said pointing with his free hand.

Grey was racing towards them astride a warhorse—barely. His feet were not in the stirrups. Both legs were bandaged and braced, and they banged uselessly against his horse's sides. His face was a mask of agony as he hung desperately onto his mount. She could tell he rode by sheer force of will. He hauled in the reins, and the horse skidded in the slippery wet grasses a few paces away from them. He sent another plume of fire pounding into the enemy line. Marissa followed his lead and sent her own attack. Missiles of ice tore into the faces of the attackers. The line stalled from the onslaught.

"Elhrin, fall back," Grey yelled as Jayce flung a series of attacks at the enemy. The boy did not take the time to aim, so some of his deadly missiles fell short and kicked up small divots in the earth in front of the enemy.

A monstrous, unearthly bellow roared over the din of the battle and the downpour of rain. A bynduwhin was charging through the ranks of the enemy, not caring who or what it ran over. Screams of agony erupted from the Do'athrim and enemy soldiers that could not get out of its way in time. The front line split wide and the bynduwhin raced toward them.

"Here we go again," Kyne growled and braced for the attack.

"Jayce, run!" Elhrin yelled. She flung a powerful force of energy at the bynduwhin. The creature's head snapped back and it reared violently, roaring in pain. Claws blindly ripped through the air as it tried to regain its balance.

Elhrin hit it again. A portion of the beast's side was ripped away and it landed on its back. The Do'athrim rider yelped as the crushing weight pinned him to the ground. Before she could attack again, the bynduwhin flipped over with amazing speed and scrambled back to its feet, leaving a dead Do'athrim planted in the grass. The beast roared in fury and raised its tail, firing a barrage of its poisonous spines at them as he charged.

Elhrin and Marissa were hard pressed to get their shields up in time. Most of the spines shattered against their barriers in a spray of deadly black liquid, but the rest flew over their heads. A horse screamed. Grey yelled in heart-wrenching pain, but Elhrin couldn't spare him the barest of glances to see how he fared. The Bynduwhin was almost on top of them.

"Marissa hit him with your shield," Elhrin yelled as she pushed her shield in the beast's path. The animal hit the shield as if it had run into a stone wall and reared back from the unexpected blow. Marissa's shield hit him in the underbelly. The beast was slammed to its back. A bolt of flame zipped across the meadow to bore a hole into the soft flesh of the beast's stomach. The animal screamed and tried to roll to its feet. Clay, who had been firing arrows into the enemy lines, turned to fire at the beast. His arrows sank into its underside as another round of flames blasted holes into the creature. The beast roared once then went still.

"Jayce, I told you to run," Elhrin yelled at the boy standing beside her, breathing heavily from the exertion of throwing his flaming bolts of energy. "Go! Now!"

He nodded without a word and ran up the hill. Elhrin flung a series of explosive attacks into the enemy line. Out of the corner of her eye, she could see Barron's team fighting furiously on the other end of the meadow. The N'gethwyn were spreading throughout the field. Some aimed for the top of the hill and the catapults and connected with one of them. It exploded in a horrific spray of shards and splinters.

Elhrin and Marissa retaliated, pounding the area around the nearest N'gethwyn and the line rushing towards them.

She then grabbed Marissa by the arm. "Let's go," she yelled, turning to follow Jayce up to the top of the hill, and saw that Grey's horse was down. A bynduwhin spike was embedded in its side. "Oh, no!"

Kyne and Clay reached Grey first and tried to pick him up. He screamed in agony. One of his legs was pinned underneath the horse.

"Leave me," he shouted.

"No!" Elhrin said, and used her magic to create a wedge of energy underneath the animal, but the dead weight of the large warhorse was too much for her. "Help!" she cried, trying to push more energy underneath to lift the animal off Grey's leg. Kyne and Clay reached underneath the horse to help. Marissa fired into enemy lines, trying to buy them more time.

Jayce stopped running when he saw the others were not following. He ran back, attacking the line with a barrage of fiery missiles as he ran. Archers within the enemy ranks stopped long enough to retaliate. A wave of arrows rose over the enemy line and soared up the hill.

"Look out!" Jayce screamed.

Marissa backed up and created a luminescent half-dome over her companions. Arrows thudded into the ground all around them and pinged off the glowing dome to fall harmlessly away. Marissa screamed.

"Marissa!" Clay yelled and jumped over the body of the horse. Marissa sat on the ground hard and grabbed her leg. An arrow had penetrated her boot and lodged in her foot.

"Clay, get her to the top!" Elhrin yelled. She swept a line of fiery missiles all across the front line of the enemy. Do'athrim dropped like rocks.

"No," Marissa protested in agony, pushing Clay away. "You need us." Marissa shot a sun-like orb into their midst, creating a huge gap in the line, but it filled in immediately. Clay dropped to one knee beside her and began firing the last of his arrows.

"Kyne, let's do this!" Elhrin shouted.

Elhrin pushed hard on her magical wedge as she and Kyne tried to lift the dead weight of the horse. It shifted. Grey tried to pull himself out but was still stuck. Elhrin pushed harder. Even with her god-given powers, her magic was limited by her size and physical strength when she used it to move or pick up objects larger than herself. The strain on her was agony, but she refused to give up on him. The enemy was nearing at a rapid pace despite Marissa, Clay, and Jayce's efforts to keep them at bay.

"Get out of here," Grey ordered angrily. He shot a burst of sizzling energy over Elhrin's head. It exploded somewhere within the enemy ranks just as lightning from the storm flashed directly overhead, followed by deafening thunder that shook the earth. Jayce and Marissa flung several attacks at the enemy, blasting holes within their ranks. Another wave of arrows zoomed towards them. Elhrin had to let go of her wedge under the horse in order to place a shield in their way. More of the enemy coming in from the water jumped out of their boats and surged up the meadow behind their companions.

"Go, I say," Grey hissed through clenched teeth. "I will cover you."

Do not yield, she heard Solisius' voice roar directly overhead, riding along the waves of a deafening thunderclap, stunning her with the ferocity in his voice. She had never heard him speak so forcefully, and even though she knew only a So'ladiun could hear his voice, she darted a quick glance at her companions just to be sure, but they were intent on surviving the fight. Elhrin raised her gaze to the sky. Dangerous spidery veins of raw energy flashed within the black clouds . . . raw energy.

Elhrin created a blazing wall of fire directly in the path of the closest enemy. Unable to stop, those in front ran into flames, screaming as the unnatural heat seared their bodies. She then raised both hands to the sky and directed her energy upward. She did not pause to think about how or what she was doing. She just used her instincts, feeling the amazing force of energy contained within the storm clouds. She tapped into its power and combined it with hers, then forced it to the ground. Strands of white energy shot out of the clouds and boomed into the enemy ranks with devastating effects. The ground shook with every connection as ranks of their enemy were blasted by its magnificent force. Screams of agony surged to a fevered pitch across the battlefield.

Elhrin saw the remaining bynduwhin break off an attack on Anderan's soldiers and hurtle towards the other side of the field heading for Barron's team. She aimed her next attack at the beast. A flash of light ripped from the sky. The beast's body exploded.

An N'gethwyn focused on her. A blazing plume of fire shot up the meadow just as a luminescent globe of energy roared by her head. The two forces of energy met head on with a thunderous explosion.

Flaming orbs slammed into the Do'athrim still trying to reach them. Jayce was relentless. His and Marissa's attacks were slowing those still trying to reach them as Grey tried to reach the N'gethwyn from his position on the ground.

Elhrin picked out the N'gethwyn energy forces closest to them. Three were standing together. Lightning shot out of the black clouds and slammed into their midst. They died instantly.

She methodically went after the others. Some tried to hide behind their shields, but they could not endure the power being unleashed on them. Shields shattered under her onslaught and, one by one, the energies of the N'gethwyn began to wink out. Chaos erupted among the enemy army as they realized their leaders were being destroyed.

Elhrin had felt amazing power, but never like what she was experiencing. This was the power of nature, and its force was tremendous. She spread her arms wide and directed the energies further into the ranks of the enemy. They didn't know where to go, where to run. Bolts of lightning lanced out of the sky. The deadly strands slashed relentlessly into the enemy. Flesh, blood, dirt, and rock spewed across the battlefield.

"Son of a bitch," Kyne gasped. He had been standing by her side protectively, making sure she was not caught off guard as her attention was diverted elsewhere.

She could barely hear him from the roar of power pulsing through her system and the tremendous noise from her attacks hitting the ground. She saw him move out of the corner of her eye. The sound of steel clashed directly in front of her, and somewhere behind her, an explosion shook the top of the hill. She wavered. She had forgotten about the enemy behind them and started to send an attack in that direction.

"Elhrin, don't stop. Phalen is holding steady on the hill. Our men below need you more," Grey choked through his pain as a flash of light zoomed by her. "The Do'athrim have figured out you are the one they need to kill the most, but Jayce has confused them momentarily by hiding you with his powers. The rest of us are trying to keep them from reaching our position."

Elhrin sent strands of lightning crawling across the front line to relieve their efforts, careful to stay as far away as possible from their own soldiers who had moved into the area. Her attack, combined with the forces of Anderan standing strong against them, started to break the enemy's resolve. Many broke away from the battle and raced for the shore, hoping to make it back to the safety of their ships.

Anderan's army sensed a change developing. Voices yelling the battle cry of Anderan started to drift over the fight, and weary soldiers heartened by the cries, caught up the call until the entire army was roaring Anderan's name. The sound demoralized the enemy even further causing a massive retreat. Anderan's army surged after the enemy, not willing to let them get back into their boats and head for the safety of the sea.

Elhrin continued her attack until she felt the last of her energy supply waning. Not wanting to push herself to unconsciousness she let the energy go, and when it left her, so did her strength to stand. She collapsed to her rear on the wet turf, breathing heavily as if she had run the distance from Muryne to Marmuht in a single day. Her lungs burned as if they were on fire and, to her amazement, she was sweating in the downpour of cool rain.

She tilted her face to the sky and closed her eyes. "Thank you, my lord," she whispered. Solisius said nothing, but she knew he was there.

Jayce flung his arms around her.

"Oof!" she grunted, smiling at his young face. She was proud of the way he had stood his ground against the enemy. Master Gryph had been right. She still thought he was too young for battle, but he had been needed. He was a fierce fighter.

"Elhrin, that was amazing. I didn't know you could call down lightning," he cried, excitedly.

"Honestly, I didn't know I could, either. Thanks for your help, mister," she said, and his smile widened even further from her praise. She hugged him briefly and looked back towards the battlefield.

Kyne was on one knee not far from them, leaning heavily onto the pommel of his sword. He was safe—and surrounded by several bodies of Do'athrim and enemy soldiers. She scanned the battlefield below him. Hundreds of craters and mangled masses of bodies were scattered all over the meadow. The line of fighting had moved closer to the shore. Barron's group had followed, and they were engaging the remaining N'gethwyn. Elhrin frowned because she wasn't feeling all of their energy sources. Kull's was missing. She directed her attention to Landin's team. Tover was gone, too. She let out a weary sigh. So far, they had lost three. She needed to ensure they lost no more.

"Kyne, are you okay?" she called out.

He glanced her way, blinking rivers of rainwater out of his eyes. "I've been better." He pushed himself to his feet and trudged wearily back uphill.

"Marissa, how about you?" she asked. Clay slung his bow over one shoulder and helped the injured girl up off the soggy ground.

"I'm alive," she smiled slightly, then winced when she tried to put weight on her foot. "Remind me never to make you mad. I wish you had used that technique a bit sooner."

Elhrin smiled. "You and me, both." She patted Jayce's back. "Help me up, Jayce. We are not done." She turned to look at Grey. He was deathly white and was shivering violently. She was afraid he may have pushed himself too far. "Grey, hang on. We will get you out."

He nodded.

"Jayce, stand on the other side of him. We will need to build a wedge of energy underneath the horse and try to lift it up enough so Kyne and Clay can help him out."

Jayce positioned himself, and with the combined energy of the two of them, they managed to raise the horse a mere handspan off the ground, but it was enough. Kyne and Clay pulled hard on Grey. The man yelled in heart-wrenching agony as his leg slowly scraped free.

"Would you look at that?" Jayce whispered in awe, gazing at the battle still raging below.

Elhrin looked up just in time to witness the largest orb of magical energy she had ever seen explode at the shoreline. She clapped her hands to her ears and closed her eyes from the resulting blinding flash of light. The magnitude of the detonation was tremendous.

"My god," Marissa breathed as the last echoes from the blast faded.

Elhrin opened her eyes. A crater covering most of the beach was the only thing left on shore. Nothing but churned up earth could be seen along the beach until partway up the slope where hundreds of injured enemy lay writhing among a carpet of their dead companions. Those who managed to survive the blast now faced Anderan's army, far outnumbered.

Out on the water, bodies and unmanned boats drifted in the waves and farther out to sea, the boats that had been making their way to shore were now rowing back to the relative safety of their ships. Elhrin could see fresh sails on the water. Anderan's naval force had arrived.

Behind her, Grey started to chuckle. She darted a questioning glance his way, seeing that he needed medical attention desperately.

"I'm glad he is on our side," Grey chattered, trying to smile through his pain.

"Me too," she had to agree, and turned to look to the top of the hill. Master Gryph stood alone with Jayme along the ridge. The battle had moved away from the catapults as Phalen and their men pushed the enemy towards the western cliffs.

"Me too," she murmured again, as she watched her hero turn his head in her direction, briefly taking note of her position, he then limped away with Jayme by his side to help Phalen.

Elhrin and Jayce left Marissa and Grey in the care of Clay and a field surgeon and wandered through the crowd of soldiers who searched the bodies that littered the ground for the living. She stopped long enough to glance once more over the battlefield. Jayce stood silently by her side.

The storm had calmed to a steady rain, and now a fog started to settle over the waters of the cove. She could barely see the outline of ships out to sea. The main battle was now up to the navy, and Elhrin could hear distant booms rolling in over the water. She hoped they were coming from the Ostied Specialties Griffyn and Admiral Zoscalese had onboard and not from the N'gethwyn.

The battle on the field below was winding down, and Landin's team was returning from the cliffs. The only magical attacks now were the occasional bursts of fire from Barron and Leesha. All N'gethwyn on shore were gone. There was no doubt that victory on the ground would be Anderan's, but it came with a heavy price. Two-thirds of their army had been destroyed and then there was the loss of three of their students.

She searched for Kyne on the eastern side of the field and found that he was on his way back with Eowhyn's lifeless body in his arms. She shoved her grief to the side. It would have to wait.

She continued on her way until she started to pass a wagon that had been draped with a banner of the Royal House of Muryne and one from the Tuhnichi garrison. Prince Cahail's body was lying in state in the back. Guards were posted on all corners of the wagon, but they did not stop Elhrin and Jayce from approaching, and she gazed upon the man who she thought she would be working with in the future.

"Is that the prince?" Jayce asked, having never met the heir to the throne.

"Yes," Elhrin said sadly. No matter how much she had disliked his person, she never would have wished him dead. She looked at his face. Cahail's rock hard features had been smoothed away by death, and she wondered what kind of king he would have been had he lived. A strong one, she had to give him that. He had guided Tuhnichi's forces with a steel hand, and despite his hatred of her kind, as he put it, she wondered if he would have been a good king like his father. She sighed. They would never know.

"Come," she said, and pushed away from the wagon.

Her destination was the catapult where the remaining leaders of the army had congregated to observe the fight on the beach. Master Gryph leaned against one of the catapult's supports. Bayle stood by his side and Jayme and Phalen sat in the wet grass at his feet. She had to stop and stare at them, moved by the sight. She imprinted the image into her mind, and decided she would sketch the scene as soon as she had the chance. She knew of the perfect portrait artist, and would have a painting commissioned when she returned to Muryne.

Jayce ran ahead and dropped to the ground to hug his brother. He might give the younger boy a hard time, but he loved him fiercely.

Master Gryph glanced down at the boy then turned his head to look at her questioningly, probably wondering why she had stopped to stare at them. His fight had not left him unscathed. His left eye was swollen, and he had bruises and cuts all over his face, and when she got close enough, she stared in horror at his neck. Hand prints were burned into either side.

He saw her look of horror. "Is something wrong?" he asked raising an eyebrow.

"You look horrible."

"So people keep telling me," he responded with a grunt.

"Are you okay?"

"I'm fine," he raised a corner of his mouth. He was lying.

"Master Idwyr?" Jayme said, surprising her. Not only was the boy sitting as close to Master Gryph as he could without sitting on the man's feet, but he had also overcome his fear of speaking to him.

"Yes, son," Master Gryph replied.

"When can we go home?" he asked, looking miserable sitting in the rain.

Master Gryph studied the battlefield. "Soon, we will go home soon."

Chapter Twenty-One

———❦✻❧———

Elhrin was tired to the bone, even though she had been able to catch a few hours sleep. She and the uninjured students had spent the afternoon after the battle helping to retrieve the wounded while they waited for word from the sea. Finally, close to dusk, a ship from the navy appeared in the cove and dropped anchor. A dinghy was lowered and rowed to shore where General Shifwood met with the naval officers.

The news was better than expected. Anderan's navy had been successful at sinking or disabling much of the enemy fleet that had not reached the coast. The rest had turned around and headed back out to sea with Admiral Zoscalese, and what was left of Anderan's naval force in pursuit. The navy had sustained substantial losses, as well, and there was no news of Griffyn's fate. They would have to wait.

Seeing that their presence was not necessary any longer, Master Gryph had decided they could return to the city with the group escorting the injured and Prince Cahail's body back to Marmuht. The rest of the army stayed behind to bury the dead.

The trip back had been slow, and they did not reach the city until well into the night. Master Gryph went immediately to King Goruth's side and Elhrin sought out Marguerite. Surprisingly, she found the woman awake and sitting in the common room with several ladies Elhrin did not recognize. Marguerite had jumped up from her chair looking hopeful and relieved when Elhrin entered the room, but the news of the deaths of Eowhyn, Tover, and Kull, had quickly turned her hope into anguish. But being the stoic lady that she was, her instincts as a caregiver took over and she asked one of the ladies to watch over a sleeping Marcus so she could help Elhrin settle Marissa, Grey, and the rest of their group comfortably in the houses across from the mansion.

This time, Elhrin and Bayle were to stay in the same house with Marissa instead of the mayor's mansion. King Goruth had been placed in the mayor's personal rooms and all other available rooms had been given to his entourage. The mansion was filled over capacity.

While Marguerite checked on Marissa and Grey's wounds, they filled her in on the details of the battle. Elhrin knew Marguerite was especially worried about Master Gryph's health after Elhrin had explained his injuries to her. Occasionally, Marguerite would look out a window or glance at the door and then ask Elhrin where he was, knowing she could locate him. He remained with King Goruth until right before dawn, and Marguerite had left the house immediately to go back to the mansion in search of him.

Now it was well after midday, and since she couldn't seem to sleep any longer, Elhrin had decided to go to the mansion to find out news about King Goruth's welfare or if any word had been received about the rest of the naval force and Griffyn's whereabouts, praying that he was safe. She walked through the front doors of the mansion, immediately sensing the somber atmosphere. There were people everywhere, but they spoke in hushed tones, and some were openly crying. Elhrin feared the worst. She headed for the rear of the mansion where she felt Master Gryph's energy and found the doors leading outside were closed. This surprised her since the weather had cleared and it was warm—the type of day that would normally have the doors open to catch the breeze from the bay. She opened the door and walked out onto the covered terrace. It and the gardens below were empty. No one was outside except Master Gryph.

A servant appeared out of the doorway of the sitting room and saw her. He held up a hand for her to stop and hurried her way. "I'm sorry, miss, but Mayor Nambacus has ordered that the rear of the house is off limits to everyone for now. Minister Idwyr has requested the use of the terrace and is resting. He is not to be disturbed," the young man said softly.

Elhrin looked past him to Master Gryph. He was fast asleep on a chaise lounge that had been brought out for him. She glanced back at the servant. "Where is Madam Idwyr?" she asked quietly.

"She and the little one are resting in her room," the young man replied.

Elhrin nodded. "Do you know how the king fares?"

He shook his head. "The last report said he was in serious condition. That was this morning. I haven't heard anything new."

"Thank you, kind sir. Could you do a favor for me?" she asked.

"I can try," he said.

"Could you find me a pen and sheets of paper and bring them to me?" She pushed past the servant. "I won't disturb the minister. I promise." She smiled at him when he started to protest and held a finger to her lips for him to be quiet, then sat down next to Master Gryph. The servant frowned his displeasure, but then retreated back inside the building without a word.

She glanced at her mentor. He had bathed and changed into a soft white shirt with an open collar. Someone had wrapped a bandage around his neck, covering the burns. He was breathing deeply, and she could hear the faint rasp that was associated with his injuries from Obsudius years ago. He didn't look comfortable. His head was tilted back against a pillow and his hands were clasped together across his chest. His injured leg was propped on top of the chaise, but his right leg sprawled off the chair onto the bricks of the terrace. She didn't see how he could sleep upright like he was—he needed to be in bed.

She looked out across the bay. Sunlight sparkled off the clear blue water and ships were sailing in and out of the bay's mouth. Life still moved on no matter that hundreds had lost their lives on the battlefield the day before—no matter if King Goruth lived or died. Life moved on, and she was going to have to move on with it . . . without Tomas.

Minutes later, the servant returned to her side, breaking her out of her dark thoughts and the images she had been reliving of the battle. "Will this do, miss?" he whispered, offering her a sheave of papers and a writing kit in a wooden box.

"Yes, thank you," she whispered, taking them from him. He nodded his head politely and left her to go back inside.

She opened the box quietly, and found that it turned into a miniature lap desk where she could put her papers to draw. Recalling the image from the day before, she began to sketch, and lost herself in her work. She let her mind drift aimlessly as she scratched her pen across the paper. Her thoughts returned to the ride home, remembering how it had been somber and relatively silent. Everyone in the long train of riders and wagons had low spirits even though they had pushed the enemy off shore. None of the students riding with her and Master Gryph mentioned the loss of their companions. She was sure the shock of their experience would wear off and the day would be a hard one, indeed.

Master Gryph groaned softly, and she glanced at him. He was frowning in pain. She wondered if she should awaken Marguerite, but then his face smoothed over and he relaxed. His breathing deepened once again back into the steady rhythm of sleep.

She glanced back down at her drawing. She had sketched the basic outline of her scene and now wanted to catch a few details while she had the chance. It was rare to find him still. Glancing at his face, she decided to do him a favor and leave out the swollen eye.

She lost track of time as she worked. The servant interrupted her once when he sat a pitcher of juice on the table beside her and asked her to let him know if she needed anything else. He had also asked her to tell Master Gryph that the mayor had requested a meeting with him when he awakened. Elhrin sat back to study her work. She had completed Master Gryph and Bayle's figures, now she needed to finish the boys sitting in the grass.

"Elhrin," Master Gryph said and had to clear his throat to continue. Eyes closed, he frowned in pain. "Could you get me something to drink?"

"I have some juice right here," she said as she sat her things on the table. "Will that do?"

"Yes." He opened his eyes to look at her. They were extremely bloodshot. "How long have you been here?"

She poured him a glass from the white ceramic pitcher. "A little while. Are you hurting?"

He pushed himself upright with a groan. "I'm a little sore," he admitted as she handed him the glass.

"Why are you out here?" she asked. "You should be in bed."

"It's cooler out here, and I find it easier to breathe sitting up." He drained the glass and placed it on the ground beside his chair.

"You broke a rib didn't you?" she asked, knowing he had slept upright for an entire week the last time he had broken ribs.

"I don't think so," he said as he rubbed a hand over his side which told her he was probably lying again, but she let it go.

"How does King Goruth fare?"

He heaved a heavy sigh. "Not good. They removed the arrows and he lost a considerable amount of blood. Dryke says he should have already died, but Goruth is a tough fighter. He may surprise us all and pull through."

"Does he know about Prince Cahail?"

"No, he is unconscious and no one is going to tell him if he awakens unless he asks," he frowned. "Where is Marguerite and Marcus?"

"The servant said they were sleeping." She looked over her shoulder into the sitting room, but saw that it was empty. "Do you want me to get her?"

"No, she has been up all night, too." He shifted in his seat.

"What do we need to do now?" The bodies of their students had been taken with Cahail's underneath the city to holding crypts where they kept the dead out of the heat if burial arrangements had to wait. Master Toome's body was already there.

"I'm afraid the end of the battle does not end our trials. The ships still out there won't give up on trying to find a place to land if our navy can't take care of them, and there are Do'athrim, possibly N'gethwyn, out in the countryside that will need to be hunted down. But right now, I have to write some very tough letters to the families of Eowhyn, Kull, and Tover, since I can't talk to them in person, and we will have to prepare their bodies for travel so they can go home." He drifted off, staring out over the city below in silence.

The loss of the students had been hard on the both of them. When they had observed the bodies lying in the back of the transport wagon for the first time, Master Gryph had stormed away, and Bayle had supported her while she emptied her stomach. She had witnessed horrific violence to human bodies, had been the cause of the violence on most of those occasions, but it was different when the horror was inflicted on someone she had known and cared for. Kull had been decapitated and Tover was missing part of his left side exposing what was left of his internal organs. Only Eowhyn looked like she was at peace. Her injuries had been internal.

"Elhrin, do you want me to write to Tomas' family or do you want to do it?" he asked, breaking the silence.

Her heart stopped at the mention of Tomas' name. "I think it would be best if I do it," she said. She had become close to Tomas' family during her years in Muryne and loved them dearly. Writing to them about his death was going to be next to impossible, but she had to do it . . . it was her responsibility.

"Let me know if you change your mind."

"What about Derrick?" she asked. He had ordered for his brother's body and the bodies of the other N'gethwyn to be loaded onto wagons and transported back to

Marmuht.

"He and the rest of the N'gethwyn will be buried in a manner so that they will take a long time to rot."

Elhrin checked around her to make sure they were alone. She leaned closer to him and lowered her voice. "How can we prevent Obsudius from taking his body like Solisius did you?"

"A tomb in the underground catacombs is being prepared for them. We will use the crystal seals to prevent anyone from accessing the tomb. I don't know if it will be effective against Obsudius personally, but it will be effective against anyone else."

"I hope no one innocent tries to open it and gets themselves killed."

"The tomb will be hidden behind a solid rock wall. There will be no entrance." He looked at her. The blue of the irises in his eyes were a sharp contrast against the deep, unnatural red surrounding them. "If someone should try, however, their fate will be unfortunate, but I will not let that weigh on my conscience. It is too vital that those bodies remain on this earth as long as possible."

"Could Obsudius draw the bodies into his realm without someone retrieving them for him? Isn't that what happened to you?" Thinking back, she realized he never explained how Solisius took his body from the open grave outside of Glimmerdale.

He shook his head slowly. "Solisius did not draw my body into his realm. He destroyed it completely."

She stared at him in utter shock. The amount of violence Solisius had to enact in order to achieve that task would have been tremendous. And it was a surreal concept that was difficult to wrap her mind around with him sitting before her intact and relatively healthy.

Seeing the look on her face, the corner of his mouth lifted slightly in amusement. "I will ask you to keep that information to yourself," he said.

"Of course," she answered with a slow shake of her head. "That would explain the destruction of your casket."

"No doubt."

"Then Obsudius should be able to do this, too."

"It is possible, I suppose, but we have no other options available to us. We will have to hope that either he cannot or will not try."

"I don't like those odds."

"Neither do I."

The mere thought that either of them would have to face Derrick again made her nauseous. She sighed heavily at the notion.

"Elhrin," he said, reaching out to touch her hand, "don't worry about this right now, dear. If it comes to pass, we will face it then, understand?"

"Yes, sir." She clasped his hand and squeezed it, comforted by the fact that he did not withdraw his touch, but left his hand in hers. "It doesn't end, does it? The constant struggle—the conflict."

"Such is the way of life for everyone. We all must travel down a hard road at one time or another, but in between those times of struggle is peace and love and happiness. Those are the times we need to remember the most, right?" Giving her a small smile, he squeezed her hand. "Take Toome, for instance," he said, and she was glad to see a hint of humor in his eyes. "Do you know what one of the last things he said to me was before he left the manor yesterday morning?"

"No."

"He said, 'Gryph, you stay so vigilant about everything you never really relax. I bet your asshole is so tight you couldn't drive a nail into it, could you?'"

Elhrin laughed. "What did you say?"

"I told him he was probably right." He leaned his head back with a sigh and a small smile, scanning the harbor below. "That was Toome. He always knew when to take me down a notch," he said. "He should not have been here, but I understand why he wanted to come."

"I thought King Goruth asked him to come out of retirement like he did for the Do'athrim War."

"No, this time Toome volunteered his services against Maye's vehement wishes that he stay home." He paused for a moment to take in an audible breath. "Elhrin, I am going to tell you something that needs to remain between the two of us." His bloodshot gaze shifted back to her. "Toome was dying and he did not want anyone to know. Not even Maye."

"He was dying?" she asked, puzzled. Master Toome appeared fine to her when she saw him the day before, except now that she thought back on it, he did look like he had lost weight. "What was wrong?"

"He had the wasting illness."

"Oh, no," she breathed. The disease was dreadful. It was known to slowly destroy the internal organs and there was nothing anyone could do to stop it. She understood why Master Toome did not want anyone to know. He had always been a tough, robust man, and the disease would have painfully reduced him to a weak shell of a person before he succumbed to the peace that death offered.

"But why didn't he want to tell Maye?" she asked. Maye was Master Toome's wife, and she didn't think he should have kept his illness from her.

"He knew what he was going to face—what Maye would have to do when the disease advanced to the point he could no longer take care of himself. He didn't want her to spend senseless time worrying about something they couldn't change." He slowly shook his head. "He had no intentions of going back home to Glimmerdale alive."

She nodded in understanding. He wanted to go out as the warrior that he had always been and had sacrificed himself when he stood between the enemy and his king. She smiled sadly at Master Gryph. "He died a hero."

"Yes, he did," Master Gryph agreed.

"Maye is going to be devastated," she sighed, thinking how the elderly lady who handed out sweets to any child that passed by her shop's door was going to have to weather Master Toome's passing alone. The couple did not have any children of their own. Their only child had tragically died at the age of four, long before Elhrin's time, when she had jerked out of her mother's arms and ran into the path of a team of fast-moving horses pulling a transport coach.

"I know. I really do wish I could tell her personally and not send a cold letter letting her know Toome is gone," he said, finally letting go of her hand to scrub at his tired eyes. "I think I will ask Marguerite to write a letter of her own to go with mine. I think it will be of some comfort to Maye to hear from her."

"I do too," Elhrin agreed, knowing the two women were close friends.

Elhrin heard the scuff of footsteps as someone walked out onto the terrace. She turned to see the servant who had retrieved her paper and pens was coming back to check on them. A look of annoyance crossed his face when he saw Master Gryph was awake, and he eyed her accusingly as if she had awakened the injured man on purpose.

"Minister Idwyr, Mayor Nambacus has requested a meeting with you at your earliest convenience," he said, when he reached their chairs.

"Tell the mayor I am currently occupied with my assistant, but I will be happy to meet with him as soon as I am free," he replied.

"Yes, sir," the servant said, nodding his head respectfully. "Is there anything I can get for either of you?"

"Not at the moment."

"Very well, sir," he replied again with a slight bow and turned on his heel to retreat back into the common room to speak with two young maids who were now inside cleaning the furniture and laying out refreshments on a sideboard.

"Master Gryph, something has been on my mind that I just can't figure out," she said when she was sure the servants could not hear her.

"What is that?" he asked.

"You know when I had the dream about Marcus?" she asked. "The one back in Muryne that you said you had, as well. Do you remember?"

"I do," he said.

"I can't figure it out. What did the darkness mean? Why couldn't we see what was happening?"

"I think the dark represented the fact that it was not going to be up to us to save him. That is why we couldn't see him. He was out of our reach. We knew he was in danger. We knew he was scared and needed us, but in the end it was Kyne who rescued him."

She slowly nodded in agreement. "That makes sense."

Heated male voices drifted through the open doorway of the sitting room. Major Fellen, one of Prince Cahail's men, had stepped into the room deep in an argument with another officer in his regiment.

"Fine, Major," the officer she did not know spat loud enough for them to hear and threw up his hands in mock surrender. He turned his back on Major Fellen and stalked out of the sitting room into the residential hall. A moment later, a resounding bang echoed out onto the terrace.

Master Gryph, not being able to see into the room, raised his eyebrow questioningly at her. She shrugged her shoulders and shook her head, not knowing what their argument concerned.

She looked back inside to see that Major Fellen had noticed her and Master Gryph out on the terrace and was weaving his way through the assortment of tables, chairs, and settees to come outside.

The manservant saw where he was headed and cut him off at the door. "Sir, I'm afraid the terrace is off limits for the moment," he said.

"You will let me pass," he said, angrily.

Grunting with the effort it took to move his sore body, Master Gryph decided to see what was happening behind him.

"I'm sorry, sir, but Minister Idwyr asked for privacy," the servant said.

The major looked past the man and saw he had Master Gryph's attention. "Minister, might I have a brief word with you?" he called out.

Master Gryph signaled him forward with a quick jerk of two fingers. The major shoved past the servant, knocking him to one side without apology.

Elhrin bit back a groan, knowing that he was about to start trouble. He marched out onto the terrace ready to fight.

Without preamble or introduction of himself, he got right to the point of his mission. "Sir, are you aware of the murder of two of my men before dawn?" he asked, coming to an abrupt standstill in front of Master Gryph. He stood rigid as a stone wall, blocking out the sun and casting a long shadow over Master Gryph's chair.

"I am not, Major," Master Gryph responded with a frown.

"Then I presume you are also not aware that my men were killed because they happened to be needlessly guarding the bodies you specifically ordered to be transported from the battlefield to here," the major hissed.

Elhrin's heart sunk. "What?" she asked in disbelief.

The man flicked an annoyed look her way, but did not bother to respond.

Master Gryph breathed in displeasure. "I am not aware of that either, Major. What happened?"

"Those bodies were brought in as you requested, Minister," he said with heat. "And while my men dumped enemies of the state in a tomb underneath the city, the two men left behind to watch the wagons were murdered. Strangely, the body identified as your brother and two others were taken. Can you tell me why someone would want the bodies of three dead men so desperately as to murder for them?"

Elhrin stared wide-eyed at Master Gryph. Surely he would not tell the man that the most likely explanation was that the God of Darkness had someone retrieve the N'gethwyn. What were they going to do? It was bizarre that they had just discussed this possibility and it had already come to pass without them knowing it.

"I would guess that there is someone sympathetic with our enemy and thought it necessary to have their bodies out of our possession," Master Gryph said evenly. "Was the area searched?"

"Of course it was," the major responded, barely keeping himself from shouting. "The whole city, inside and out, is being searched. Minister, I had my doubts as to Prince Cahail's suspicions of you, but in light of the events of the last two days, I am led to believe he may have been right. Rest assured there will be a full-scale investigation into the events surrounding Prince Cahail's death, the ambush on King Goruth, and your involvement concerning both of their downfalls. Maybe you are the one who is sympathetic with our enemy."

"This is insane," Elhrin sputtered. "How dare you accuse Minister Idwyr of treason, Major? If King Goruth were able, he would tell you himself that the minister is the last person who would ever betray him or this country." She pointed at Master Gryph. "You would not believe what he has sacrificed for all of us. He killed his own brother to protect us. He was instrumental in ending the Do'athrim War years ago and forcing that very same enemy off our shores yesterday. Why would you think he is sympathetic with those monsters?"

"Who knows what a person will do for power, Miss Caddoch," he growled. He glared down at Master Gryph. "I will be heading an investigation, Minister."

"I expect no less from you, Major," Master Gryph said calmly. "Do what you must."

"How can you let him do this?" Elhrin asked in shock.

"Elhrin, be still," he ordered, abruptly. "Major Fellen, if there is nothing else, our interview is at an end."

"But the subject is not," Major Fellen said and dipped his head sharply in farewell, then stalked across the terrace for the hall door.

Elhrin held her peace until the man disappeared inside the manor. "I don't understand," she hissed. "How can you let him walk out of here knowing he is about to raise false accusations against you?"

"There is nothing I can do or say to change his mind right now. To continue to argue with him while he is clearly angry and full of emotion over the loss of two good men is pointless."

"But it is wrong—he is wrong," she cried, frustrated. "You have to stop him."

"I'm afraid there is no stopping this turn of events, my dear. I will just have to work through it like any other obstacle thrown in my path, right?" he said with a small smile.

"I don't see how you can be so calm about this," she muttered, then a horrific thought crossed her mind. "What happens if King Goruth dies? They will use that against you, too."

"That will be the least of our troubles, I'm afraid."

"Why?"

"Because Movlin will rise to the throne, and that will start a firestorm of its own."

"Why would Movlin be king? I thought Princess Destiel was next in line."

"And that will be part of the firestorm," he said with a heavy sigh. "Goruth petitioned the council a few months ago to instate Movlin as heir to the throne should Cahail die without issue. The council approved the request, and as far as I know, neither Destiel nor Lexisa are aware of the decree, as of yet. Destiel is a power hungry lady. She will not be pleased when she learns her father has taken her out of the line."

"Which means she will fight to gain control," Elhrin said.

"Correct, and I'm not sure Movlin is strong enough to withstand her should she do so. That is, if he cares to fight her at all."

"Why wouldn't he?"

"He has never had any ambition to be in a position of power. His passion has always been the arts and architecture. I'm not so sure he will be happy if he is forced into ascending the throne instead of being allowed to continue his studies at the university and follow his own interests."

"If it comes down to it, would Destiel not be a good queen?"

He cut his eyes at her. "Goruth had a reason for skipping his daughters, and it had nothing to do with their abilities of handling the pressures of the monarchy. He took into consideration not only their individual personalities, which according to him left much to be desired even though he loved them dearly, but also whom they married and the type of people they kept in their close circle. As much as I hate to say it, I'm afraid if either princess rose to the throne it would not be in the best interest for Anderan's welfare, especially now. Goruth understood this, and I hope those who revere him and his wishes will too. Movlin will need supporters should it come to that point."

Master Gryph eased his injured leg off of the chair and reached for his staff lying next to him. "I better go see what Nambacus wants and check on Goruth." He grimaced as he pushed himself out of the chair holding his side. He couldn't convince her he hadn't broken a rib or at least damaged one.

"Would you please assure me you will talk to the mayor and General Shifwood about Major Fellen's accusations?" she pleaded. "You will need supporters, too."

"I'm almost positive they already know," he said, then smiled slightly when he saw her obvious look of worry. "Elhrin, the truth will come out. All will be well." He leaned over and planted a kiss on top of her head. "Are you staying out here?"

"Yes, I will wait for Marguerite and Marcus to awaken, and Kyne said he would come here when he returns from running an errand in the city," she said.

"Very well, tell Marguerite where I have gone. When I return, you and I will go to the catacombs and take a look around. We need to set the crystal seals for the rest of the N'gethwyn."

"Yes, sir," she said.

His gaze fell on her sketch lying on the table. "What are you drawing? Can I see it?"

She picked it up and handed it to him. His smile faded and she feared he hated the picture.

"You are talented," his voice broke with emotion as he studied her work. "When you get a chance, would you do one for me?"

"Of course, what would you like?" she asked.

"I want one of my children together, you, Bayle, Griffyn, and Marcus."

"I would be honored." She held back the tears that wanted to form. She loved this man who had enfolded her and Bayle into his family without hesitation, hating with all of her being that there was anyone who could possibly think someone so kind and gentle could be a traitor. "Speaking of Griffyn, has there been word?"

"No," he shook his head and glanced out to the bay. "None of the ships have returned yet." He handed her drawing back to her. "Elhrin, one other thing before I go. Phalen told me he heard Solisius' command on the battlefield. He thinks something is wrong with him and is hearing voices. It is time to tell him."

"You didn't explain it to him?" she asked.

"I told him you would talk with him when there was time," he said.

"Why would you tell him that?" she asked.

"Phalen is your protégé, dear, not mine. You are mine. He falls under you."

Her mouth fell open. She had never thought about it that way. Each So'ladiun had been trained by their successors if they were able. Some had died before meeting their charges thanks to Obsudius, but this was different. Before, there was no magical academy for training, now there was, and Phalen had been trained under his watch while she had been running all over the country the past year.

"So, aside from revealing to him who he is and who we are, is he to come with me when I return to Muryne?"

"You tell me," he said. "It will be up to you to decide."

"I think he needs to get to know Movlin," she said, not knowing how that thought popped into her head.

He winked at her. "So be it." He limped for the door. "I will see you when I return."

She exhaled a long breath. She was not sure she was ready for the responsibilities that were heading her way at a rapid pace. Bit by bit, he was turning control over to her, and she knew change was inevitable whether she liked it or not. No longer was she his apprentice. Soon it would be up to her to make the decisions she was used to him making, and she wasn't so sure she was ready for that responsibility, yet.

She picked up her things and moved to the chaise, sighing with fatigue as her tired and sore body sank into its softness. She had planned to continue working on her drawing, but she couldn't concentrate. Her mind churned over one topic after another—Major Fellen's accusations and what she could do to help thwart his plans. The letter she had to write to Tomas' parents—what was she going to say? And then there was the major problem of Derrick's missing body which meant it was more than likely gone from the physical realm by now, and he would be allowed to reenter the land of the living for a short time if Obsudius chose to let him through a rift.

She was so tired of thinking—of worrying. She closed her eyes against the bright sun and tried to quiet her mind and relax for just a moment before Marguerite and Marcus awoke. The sunlight was warm on her face, but a soft breeze drifting up from the harbor made the terrace comfortable and pleasant. Employing the technique she used to help her focus, she let go of all disturbing thoughts and just concentrated on the sounds around her—the wind rustling palm tree fronds nearby, the dim sounds of the voices of those outside the garden walls, and the rattling of carriages on the road that ran next to the manor, the sporadic clinking of whatnots being moved by the maids inside, and the distant bark of a dog. She let the sounds of normal everyday life soothe away the dark thoughts and allowed herself to drift in the comfort of its wake.

Elhrin walked through the front door and into the marble tiled entryway of one of the most beautiful homes she had ever seen. She had no idea where she was and no idea why she was in the home. Puzzled, she wondered where she was supposed to go from here.

A grand staircase curved up the left side of the foyer to a balcony on the second floor. To her right were two doorways and she could see one opened into a formal sitting room filled with beige and gold trimmed furniture and glass-topped tables. The other appeared to be a hallway.

She was trying to decide which way to go when she heard the laughing voices of children drift from a separate hallway nestled behind the stairway. Curious, she followed the voices.

The hallway was painted white and was brightly lit from sunlight spilling through the large picture window at the end where the hallway intersected with another stairway. The children's voices came from an open door near the end of the hall.

She headed for the door, but then came to an abrupt halt when she glanced at a painting on the wall. She stared at it in shock. It was a painting of the sketch of Master Gryph, Bayle, and the young boys on the battlefield she had been working on while Master Gryph slept on the terrace, and it was amazingly accurate. She glanced at the signature to see who painted it. Her knees went weak. The artist was not who she expected—she had fully expected to see the name of the artist from Muryne who she had planned to commission to paint it, but instead, by her own hand, was her name. She was confused? She didn't know how to paint. At least, she had never tried.

She turned her head as the children erupted in laughter again. Weakly, she continued down the hall and peered into the open doorway. The room was a children's playroom. Toys were scattered everywhere and in the midst of them were three girls, ranging in age from somewhere between three or four to about nine or so. The eldest had wild unkempt brown hair and was dressed in trousers and a blue tunic. She had a book in her lap, but it was forgotten as she laughed at the wild antics of the youngest girl who was making faces at a very unhappy auburn-haired girl with her hands on her hips.

"I am going to tell mother if you don't stop, Kaye!" she fumed.

Elhrin started at the name. That had been her mother's maiden name.

The youngest child mimicked the middle child by tossing her head back and forth, making her black curls bounce across her head. She stuck her tongue out. The act pushed the older girl over the edge and she lunged. The little girl jumped out of the way and ran for the door. Immediately, the two girls saw Elhrin in the doorway and the older child skidded to a halt.

"Mother!" Kaye yelled, running to Elhrin. She wrapped her arms tight around Elhrin's leg. "Gracy

is trying to hurt me."

Mother?

Elhrin needed to sit down. This was too much. She picked up the child, stepped into the room, and almost dropped the girl. Tomas stood by a cold fireplace on the other side of the room. Her heart felt like it was going to burst from her chest.

"Tomas," she whispered as tears bloomed in her eyes.

"Who's Tomas?" Kaye asked. She put her tiny hands on either side of Elhrin's face and made Elhrin look at her. The girl had green eyes like her own. "Mother, are you okay?"

"No, I mean, yes," she choked and looked back at the fireplace. Tomas smiled that lopsided grin she loved so dearly. He raised a hand to his lips and blew her a kiss. He mouthed the words, I love you, and then faded away as if he had never been.

"Tomas, no," she cried. "Don't go."

"Elhrin, look what I found," a male voice called.

She whirled around at the familiar sound.

Kyne stood smiling in the doorway holding up a silver bracelet with a tiny hummingbird charm dangling from its loop. "It had fallen behind your dressing table." His smile dropped when he saw her. "What's wrong?" he asked.

She could not find her voice. He had aged. His jet black hair was sprinkled with gray and the natural lines around his eyes and mouth had deepened. He actually looked . . . distinguished?

"Papa," the middle child cried with joy and rushed to wrap her arms around him.

Elhrin jolted awake. "Papa?" she cried, sitting straight up and planting her feet on either side of the chaise. Blinking against the bright sunshine, she realized she had been dreaming and was still out on the terrace of the mayor's mansion.

"Is something wrong?" a cynical voice asked.

She glanced sharply at Kyne who was standing a few paces away with one foot propped on the short terrace wall, staring at her as if she had lost her mind. She stared back at him in shock, speechless, afraid that she had indeed lost her mind.

"What is wrong with you?" he asked again when she didn't answer. He had a smirk on his face that was true Kyne. "Nevermind," he said, reaching into a pocket, "look what I found in a rustic little shop not far from here." He pulled out a silver bracelet with a tiny hummingbird charm dangling from its loop. "I remembered you saying how you liked hummingbirds, so I thought you might like it."

"No," she breathed in disbelief, staring round-eyed at the bracelet.

"No what? No, you don't like the bracelet, or no, you don't like hummingbirds?" he asked with a frown.

"Neither, I mean, I like both," she stammered. "Oh, dear god."

"Then what is wrong with you?" he demanded frowning in aggravation.

She could see her reaction was far from what he expected. "I'm sorry. It's nothing, really. The bracelet is lovely. Thank you," she said, reaching for his gift.

He snorted in contempt, not believing her, but he dropped the bracelet in her hand, anyway.

She stared at the delicate circle of silver and hand-crafted charm nestled in her palm. The bird had a small green crystal for an eye and it glinted in the sun as if mocking her confused state of mind. She could not believe what was happening to her. She had no romantic feelings towards Kyne, whatsoever—she barely tolerated him and his obnoxious ways, for that matter, or did she?

She slowly shook her head in denial. Her dream was only a dream, and for once, the bracelet was only a coincidence—it was not one of the dreams that visited her as a So'ladiun predicting a possible event in her future. She breathed in a steadying breath to calm her nerves. And just as she had firmly convinced herself of that fact, a live hummingbird zoomed across the terrace to hover in front of her face, pointedly staring at her before it turned and buzzed out over the city, and as it flew away she heard a soft laugh drift around her on the gentle breeze.

She didn't bother to ask Kyne if he had seen the bird or heard the laugh because she knew he wouldn't have—only she knew that her god had sent the bird to make his point, and only a So'ladiun could hear that soft but glorious laugh. Her god might not direct the steps she must take in order for her to have a successful or peaceful future, but he was not above giving her something else—hope.

Acknowledgements

I can't begin to express how grateful I am to all of you who have supported me in this crazy-wonderful mountain of a dream I am daring to climb. It's a tough journey but all of you make it so much easier to travel.

To my editor, Elaine Leslie, you are an absolute blessing. Thank you for your hard work and encouraging words. I couldn't have done this without you.

Alexis and Cheryl, you girls rock! When I need an honest opinion, I certainly know where to turn. Y'all hold nothing back and I love the two of you all the more for it.

To my husband and my son, you boys always make me smile, and in a world that seems full of negativity and discouragement, those smiles mean a lot. I love you both so very much.

To my parents, Ray and Rachel Youngblood, I don't know if I can find the right words to express how much you mean to me. Just know that this old girl realizes that the Good Lord Above graced her with two of the most beautiful souls a child could ever wish for in a parent.

And most importantly, to God. Thank you for the many blessings both seen and unseen you have bestowed upon me and my loved ones. Thank you for the gift of creativity for without it my world would be bleak indeed. And thank you for guiding my steps each and every day. I pray my path through this life always honors You.

About The Author

Laurie Y. Elrod, an artist of varying talents, wallows in creativity every chance she gets. While she does possess a Bachelors Degree in Business, and has held a myriad of jobs throughout the years, she is a true believer that one is never too old to start anew and follow a dream. So, stepping out on that ever swaying but sturdy branch of faith, she dove head first into the waters of the writing world and is swimming hard, come what may. A South Carolina native, Laurie is surrounded by her loving family and an assortment of much-loved pets.